Patrick O'Brian is the author of the acclaimed Aubrey-Maturin tales and the biographer of Joseph Banks and Picasso. He translated many works from French into English, among them the novels and memoirs of Simone de Beauvoir and the first volume of Jean Lacouture's biography of Charles de Gaulle. In 1995 he was the first recipient of the Heywood Hill Prize for a lifetime's contribution to literature. In the same year he was awarded the CBE. In 1997 he was awarded an honorary doctorate of letters by Trinity College, Dublin. He died on 2 January 2000 at the age of 85.

PATRICK O'BRIAN

The Mauritius
Command

HARPER PERENNIAL
London, New York, Toronto and Sydney

Harper Perennial
An imprint of HarperCollins*Publishers*
77–85 Fulham Palace Road
Hammersmith
London w6 8jb

www.harperperennial.co.uk

This edition published by Harper Perennial 2007
1

Previously published in paperback by HarperCollins 2002
(reprinted seventeen times),
1996 (reprinted three times), 1994 (reprinted twice)
and by Fontana 1976 (reprinted ten times)

First published in Great Britain by
William Collins Sons & Co. Ltd 1977

A catalogue record for this book
is available from the British Library

ISBN-13 978-0-00-725586-3
ISBN-10 0-00-725586-1

Set in Imprint by
Rowland Phototypesetting Ltd, Bury St Edmunds, Suffolk

Printed and bound in Great Britain by
Clays Ltd, St Ives plc

CONTENTS

To Mary Renault

γλαῦκ᾽ εἰς ᾽Αθήναζ

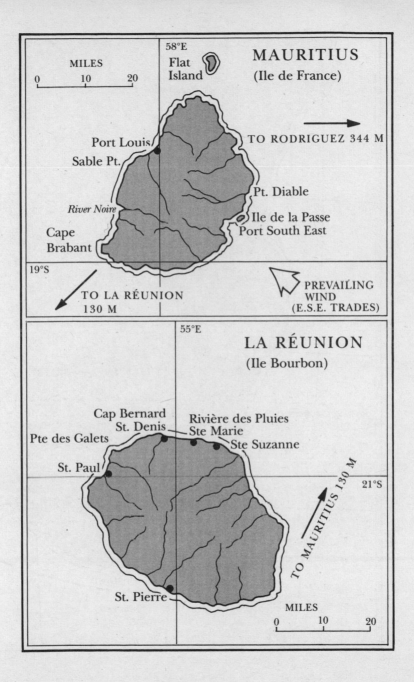

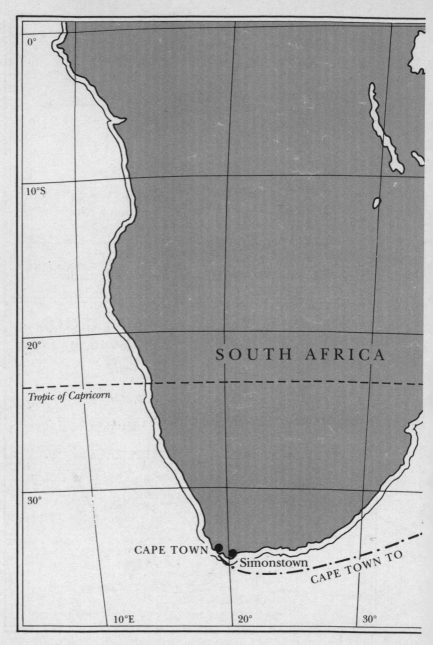

0°

10°S

20°

Tropic of Capricorn

30°

SOUTH AFRICA

CAPE TOWN

Simonstown

CAPE TOWN TO

10°E

20°

30°

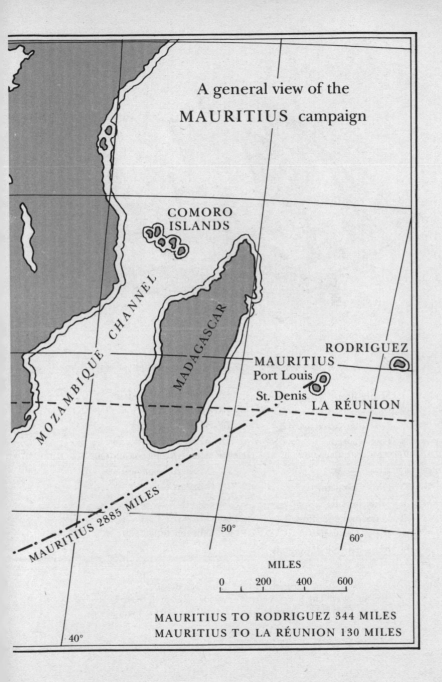

A general view of the
MAURITIUS campaign

COMORO
ISLANDS

MOZAMBIQUE CHANNEL

MADAGASCAR

RODRIGUEZ

MAURITIUS
Port Louis
St. Denis
LA RÉUNION

MAURITIUS 2885 MILES

50°

60°

40°

MILES

0   200   400   600

MAURITIUS TO RODRIGUEZ 344 MILES
MAURITIUS TO LA RÉUNION 130 MILES

The sails of a square-rigged ship, hung out to dry in a calm.

1 Flying jib
2 Jib
3 Fore topmast staysail
4 Fore staysail
5 Foresail, or course
6 Fore topsail
7 Fore topgallant
8 Mainstaysail
9 Main topmast staysail
10 Middle staysail
11 Main topgallant staysail
12 Mainsail, or course
13 Maintopsail
14 Main topgallant
15 Mizzen staysail
16 Mizzen topmast staysail
17 Mizzen topgallant staysail
18 Mizzen sail
19 Spanker
20 Mizzen topsail
21 Mizzen topgallant

AUTHOR'S NOTE

Sometimes the reader of a novel, particularly a novel set in another age, likes to know whether the events have any existence outside the author's mind, or whether, like the characters, they are quite imaginary.

There is no doubt a great deal to be said for complete freedom within a context of historical accuracy, but in this case the groundwork of the tale, a little-known campaign in the Indian Ocean, is factual; and as far as the geography, the manoeuvres, the ships taken, burnt, sunk or destroyed, the battles, triumphs and disasters are concerned, the writer has kept close to contemporary accounts, to the log-books and despatches of the officers who fought the actions, and to the Admiralty records. Apart from the necessary fictions at the beginning and the very end, he has not done anything to neaten history except for the omission of a few confusing, unimportant ships whose fleeting presence was neither here nor there; nor has he thought fit to gild the lily by adding in any way to the Royal Navy's pugnacious resourcefulness in time of adversity.

P.O'B.

Chapter One

Captain Aubrey of the Royal Navy lived in a part of Hampshire well supplied with sea-officers, some of whom had reached flag-rank in Rodney's day while others were still waiting for their first command. The more fortunate had large, comfortable houses overlooking Portsmouth, Spithead, St Helens, the Isle of Wight, and the constant procession of men-of-war; and Captain Aubrey might have been among them, since as a commander and as a young post-captain he had done so well in prize-money that he was known in the service as Lucky Jack Aubrey. But want of a ship, the failure of his agent, his ignorance of business, and the sharp practice of an attorney had reduced him to half-pay and no more; and in fact his cottage lay on the northern slope of the Downs, not far from Chilton Admiral, and the rising hill shut out all the sea, together with most of the sun.

This cottage, though picturesque among its ash trees and even romantic, ideally suited for two in the early days of his marriage, was neither large nor comfortable; it had always been low-ceilinged, pokey and inconvenient, but now that it also contained two babies, a niece, a ruined mother-in-law, some large pieces of furniture from Mapes Court, Mrs Williams's former home, and a couple of servants, it was something like the Black Hole of Calcutta, except that whereas the Hole was hot, dry and airless, Ashgrove Cottage let in draughts from all sides, while the damp rising from the floor joined the leaks in the roof to form pools in many of the rooms. These people Captain Aubrey maintained on nine shillings a day, paid half-yearly and often long after the anxiously-awaited date; and although in his mother-in-law he had a remarkable economist to help him, the effort of doing so had imprinted an expression of abiding worry on a face that nature had meant to look cheerful – an expression that sometimes had a touch of frustration in it as well, for Captain Aubrey, a scientific as well as a natural-born sailor, devoted to hydrography and navigation, was deeply concerned with a plan for finding the longitude at sea by the moons of Jupiter, and although he ground the mirrors and lenses for his telescope himself he would dearly have loved to be able to spend a guinea or two on brass-work from time to time.

At some distance below Ashgrove Cottage a deep lane led up through the fungus-smelling woods. The heavy autumnal rains had turned the clayey bottom into a quagmire, and through this quagmire, sitting sideways upon his horse with his feet so withdrawn from the mud that he appeared to be crouching on its back, like an ape, rode Dr Maturin, Captain Aubrey's closest friend, the surgeon in many of the ships he had commanded, a small, indefinably odd and even ill-looking man with pale eyes and a paler face, topped by the full-bottomed wig that marked him as a physician, if a somewhat old-fashioned one. He was, for him, unusually well dressed in a snuff-coloured coat with silver buttons and buckskin breeches; but the effect was spoilt by the long black sash that he wore wound three times round his waist, which gave him an outlandish air in the English countryside. On his saddle-bow lay a net, filled with a variety of mushrooms – bolets of all kinds, blewits, chanterelles, Jew's ears – and now, seeing a fine flush of St Bruno's collops, he sprang from his horse, seized a bush, and scrambled up the bank. As he did so an uncommonly large black and white bird lifted from among the trees, its vast wings labouring in the calm. Maturin's hand darted into the folds of his sash, whipped out a little spy-glass and presented it well before the bird, now harried by a pair of crows, crossed the valley and vanished over the hill that divided Ashgrove Cottage from the sea. With great satisfaction he stared after it for a while and then lowered his glass to the cottage itself. To his surprise he noticed that the little home-made observatory had been moved a considerable distance to the right, a good furlong, indeed, to a point where the ridge dropped fifty feet. And there, standing by its characteristic dome and over-topping it as Captain Gulliver might have overtopped a temple in Lilliput, stood Captain Aubrey, resting an ordinary naval glass upon the dome and peering steadfastly at some object far remote. The light was full on him; his face was sharp and clear in Maturin's telescope, and with a shock the Doctor saw not only that look of anxiety but also the marks of age and unhappiness. Stephen Maturin had thought of Aubrey as powerful resilient cheerful youth itself for so long that this change and the slow, weary motion as the distant figure closed the instrument and stood up, his hand pressed to an old wound in his back, were unusually distressing. Maturin closed his glass, picked the mushrooms and whistled his horse, a little Arab that came like a dog, looking affectionately into his face as he made his awkward journey down the bank with his hatful of collops.

Ten minutes later he stood at the door of the observatory. Captain Aubrey's bottom now protruded from it, entirely filling the gap. 'He must have his telescope as nearly horizontal as it will go, and he bending double over it,' reflected Dr Maturin. 'There is no weight lost in these posteriors, however: would still tip the beam at fifteen stone.' Aloud he said, 'Hola, Jack.'

'Stephen!' cried Jack, shooting out backwards with sur-prising nimbleness in so large a man and seizing his friend by both hands. His pink face was scarlet with pleasure, and a slight answering flush appeared in Maturin's. 'How very happy I am to see you, old Stephen! How are you? Where have you been? Where have you been all this time?' But recollecting that Dr Maturin, as well as being a medical man, was also an intelligence agent – that his movements were necessarily obscure – that his appearance might well be connected with the recent Spanish declaration of war upon France – he hurried on, 'Looking after your affairs, no doubt. Splendid, splendid. You are staying with us, of course. Have you seen Sophie?'

'I have not. I paused at the kitchen door, asked the young woman was the Captain at home, and hearing domestic sounds within – the massacre of the innocents came to my mind – I merely left my offering and my horse and came along. You have moved the observatory.'

'Yes. It was no great task, however: the whole contraption don't weigh three hundredweight. Killick and I just unshipped the dome – it is copper from the old *Diomed* that the Dockyard let me have – and then we clapped on a couple of purchases and rolled it up in a forenoon.'

'How is Killick?' asked Stephen. Killick had been Jack's servant these many years; the three had been shipmates in several commissions, and Stephen valued him.

'Very well, I believe. I had news of him from Collard of *Ajax*; he sent a shark's backbone walking-stick for the twins. I had to turn him away, you know.'

Stephen nodded and said, 'Did the observatory not answer by the house, so?'

'Yes, it did,' said Jack hesitantly. 'But I tell you what it is, Stephen: from here you can see the Wight and the Solent, the tip of Gosport and Spithead. Quick, come and have a look – she will not have moved yet.'

Stephen lowered his face to the eyepiece, shading it with his hands; and there, inverted on a pale luminous background, hung a misty three-decker, almost filling the disc. As he shifted the focus she sprang sharp and clear into view. Brilliantly clear: her sails, topgallants down to courses, limp in the flat calm: the cable out of her hawsehole as her boats ahead carried out the warps to bring her to her mooring. Whilst he gazed he heard Jack's explanations – this was his new six-inch speculum – three months' grinding and buffing – finished off with the finest Pomeranian sludge – Miss Herschel's help invaluable – he had taken off a shade too much on the rim and had very nearly given up heart when she put him in the way of recovering it – admirable woman.

'Why, it is not the *Victory*,' cried Stephen as the ship began to move. 'It is the *Caledonia*. I can see the Scotch arms. Jack, I can positively see the Scotch arms! At this

4

distance! You are the speculum-maker of the world, so you are.'

Jack laughed with pleasure. 'Well do you see, it is the purest day for viewing,' he said modestly. 'Never a shimmer even by the water's edge. How I hope it will hold out until tonight. I will show you such a double star in Andromeda, less than a second of arc apart. Think of that, Stephen. Less than a second apart! With my three-inch glass I could never resolve anything much better than two. Should you not like to see a double less than a second apart?'

'Sure, it must be prodigious. But for my part I should as soon watch the shipping. Such life, such activity, and we Olympian above it all. Do you not spend hours and hours up here?'

'I do, Stephen, I do indeed. But I beg you will not mention it at the house. Sophie don't mind my stargazing, however late – and we shall have to sit up until three this morning before I can show you Jupiter – but staring at the Solent ain't astronomy. She don't say anything, but it makes her low in her spirits to think I am pining for the sea.'

'Do you pine much, Jack?' asked Stephen, but before Captain Aubrey could answer their attention was distracted by a clamour from the cottage, by Mrs Williams's hoarse martial voice and the shrill, defiant replies of the servant she was rebuking. Sometimes the motionless air carried the words up the hill with perfect clarity, and they heard the cry 'a foreign gentleman left them in my kitchen' several times repeated, but generally the passionate voices overlaid one another, and they were further confused by the echo from the hanging wood on the other side of the valley, by the wail of children, and by the repeated slamming of a door.

Jack shrugged his shoulders: yet after a pause he looked benevolently down at his friend, surveying him. 'You have not really told me how you are, Stephen,' he said. 'How do you do in fact?'

'Amazingly well, I thank you, Jack. I took the waters at Caldas de Bohi not long ago, and derived great benefit from them.' Jack nodded: he knew the place, a village in the

Pyrenees not far from Dr Maturin's high sheepwalk; for Stephen, though an Irishman, had property in those parts, coming down to him from his Catalan grandmother. 'And as well as growing as supple as a fawn,' continued Dr Maturin, 'I was able to make a number of valuable observations on the cretins of Bohi. Bohi is largely inhabited by idiots, my dear.'

'Bohi is not the only place, not by a long chalk. Look at the Admiralty, and what do you see? A general as First Lord, that is what you see. Would you believe it, Stephen? And the first thing this infernal redcoat does, is to take away one of the captain's eighths – he reduces our prize-money by a third, which is stark, raving lunacy. And then, quite apart from the idiots in Whitehall, this village has half a dozen; they squeak and gibber in the market-place. And in sober earnest, Stephen, I am sometimes cruelly worried by the twins. They do not look over bright to me, and I should take it very kind, was you to survey them privately. But I dare say you would like to look at the garden first?'

'I should like it of all things. And the bees.'

'Why, as to the bees, they seem to have piped down these last few weeks. That is to say, I have not been very close since I tried to take their honey, but I have not noticed them about. It must be more than a month since I was stung. But if you would like to see them, let us take the upper path.'

The hives stood in a trim row on white painted stools, but never a bee was to be seen. Stephen peered into the entrances, saw the tell-tale cobweb, shook his head and observed, 'It is the fell wax-moth.' He prised a skep from its stool and held it out, inverted, showing the dirty wreck of combs, with the vile grubs spinning their cocoons.

'The wax-moth!' cried Jack. 'Is there something I should have done?'

'No,' said Stephen. 'Not that I know of.'

'I would not have had it happen for the world. I am so concerned. Sophie and I valued them extremely, as your present.'

6

'Never mind,' said Stephen. 'I shall bring you some more, of a bolder stock. Pray let us view the garden.'

In the Indian Ocean Captain Aubrey had dreamt of a cottage, with a little land to it: rows of turnips, carrots, onions, cabbages and beans; now his dream was realized. But it had taken no account of the blackfly, the wireworm, the turnip-beetle, the leather-jacket, the green-fly and the black, the cabbage white. The rows were there, half an acre of them, dug as straight as a ruler in the poor, shallow, spewy, earth, and in them stood some dwarfish plants. 'Of course,' said Jack, 'there is nothing to be seen at this time of the year; but I mean to get three to four loads of dung on to the land this winter, and that will make a marvellous difference. I have already put some to my Brunswick cabbages, beyond Sophie's rose-garden. This way.' As they skirted the meagre potatoes he pointed over the hedge and said, 'That is the cow.'

'I thought it must be a cow: for milk, I make no doubt?'

'Just so. Vast great quantities of milk, butter, cream, veal: that is to say, we look forward to them presently. At the moment she happens to be dry.'

'Yet she does not look gravid. Rather the reverse, indeed: lean, Pharaonic, cadaverous.'

'Well, the fact of the matter, Stephen,' said Jack, staring at the cow, 'the fact of the matter is that she refuses the bull. He is game enough, oh Lord, yes; but she will have nothing to say to him. Then he flies into a hellfire passion, bellowing and tearing up the ground; and we go without milk.'

'From a philosophical point of view, her behaviour is logical enough. Reflect upon the continual, wearisome pregnancies, the price of a momentary and I may say aleatory pleasure. Reflect upon the physical discomfort of a full udder, to say nothing of the necessary parturition, with its attendant perils. I do not mention the uneasiness of seeing one's offspring turned into a blanquette de veau; for this is peculiar to the cow. Were I a female of any kind, I should beg to decline these general cares; and were I, in this particular case, a heifer, I should certainly choose to remain dry. Yet it must be confessed that from a domestical point of view celibacy in a cow takes on a different aspect entirely: here the general good calls out for teeming loins.'

'Yes,' said Jack. 'It does. Now here is Sophie's garden. It will be full of roses, come next June. Do you think they look a trifle spindly, Stephen? Do you think I should cut them back very hard, this winter?'

'Nothing do I know about gardening,' said Maturin. 'Nothing at all. But perhaps they may be a little, shall I say, rachitic?'

'I don't know how it is,' said Jack, 'I don't seem to have much luck with ornamental plants: that was supposed to be a lavender hedge, do you see? The roots came from Mapes. However, come and look at my cabbages. I am quite proud of them.' They passed through a wicket-gate and came to a plot at the back of the cottage: a sea of greenery, with a noble steaming dunghill beyond it. 'There,' cried Jack, 'have you ever seen the like?'

'I have not,' said Stephen.

'You may think them rather close, but I reasoned this way: for slinging hammocks we allow fourteen inches a man; now a man will eat a cabbage, and the part cannot be greater than the whole; so I set them by that reckoning, and it has answered amazingly.' He laughed with satisfaction. 'Do you remember the old Roman that could not bear to cut 'em?'

'Diocletian, I believe.'

'Just so. How I understand him. And yet, you know, whenever I do bring myself to spoil a rank, precious little encouragement do I get. Always this silly cry of caterpillars. Lord, if they had ate a tenth part of what we have ate in the way of weevils and bargemen in our biscuit, month in month out, on blockade, they would thank Heaven fasting for an honest green caterpillar.'

They stood a while, contemplating the cabbage-patch, and in the stillness Stephen could actually hear the innumerable jaws at work. His eyes wandered from the mass of green to the dunghill: on top of it he noticed the bolets, chanterelles, blewits and collops that he had picked a little while before. The crash of a slamming door above interrupted their meditations; this was followed by the sound of heavy steps within, and the back-door opened, to display a square, red-faced woman, the spit of Mrs Williams but for a cast in her left eye and, when she spoke, a shrill Welsh voice. She had her box on her shoulder.

'Why, Bessie,' cried Jack. 'Where are you going? What are you about?'

Passion so choked the woman that for a moment her lips moved with never a sound; then all at once the words came darting out, accompanied by so venomous a look that Stephen crossed himself. 'A character, a character, that's all I want. Near with the sugar, nearer with the tea. A character I want, is all.' With this she vanished round the corner of the cottage.

Jack looked after her, and observed in a low voice, 'That makes the fourth this year. It is the damnedest thing, Stephen: I managed a ship's company of three hundred odd as easy as kiss your hand, but I cannot get the least notion of discipline into this establishment.' He paused, brooding, and added, 'You know very well I was no friend to the cat at sea; but rot me, I can see it has its uses.' Another reflective pause in which his face took on the stern, implacable expression of one who orders a dozen lashes to be laid on; then this look was replaced by one of concern and he cried, 'Oh Stephen, what a wretched host I am. You must be clemmed. Come in, come in, and we'll have a glass of grog. This way: you will not mind walking through the scullery – no ceremony, eh? Sophie must be somewhere in front.'

As he spoke a minute window opened above their heads and Sophie's head emerged. Her distracted look instantly changed to open delight, the sweetest smile. 'Oh Stephen,' she cried, 'how very happy I am to see you. Come in. I shall be down directly.' Stephen plucked off his hat, bowed and kissed his hand, though indeed he could perfectly well have reached hers from where he stood.

'Step in,' said Jack, 'and mind your head on the beam.'

The only thing in the scullery apart from a vast copper and its smell of boiling baby-clothes was a young woman on a chair with her apron over her head, rocking mutely to and fro. Three paces carried them through it however, into a narrow passage and so to the parlour, a pleasant little room with a bow window, made more spacious by a number of sea-going devices such as lockers under the windows and compact brass-bound ship's furniture, yet somewhat marred by incongruous great objects never designed for a cottage, such as a high-backed caned seat for five or six people and a long-case clock whose hood would not fit under the ceiling and which therefore stood bareheaded in a corner, shedding desolation. Jack had scarcely time to ask Dr Maturin whether the bow did not remind him of the stern-window of the brig in which they had first sailed together when there was the sound of steps on the stairs and Sophie ran in. She kissed Stephen with sisterly affection and holding him by both hands scrutinized him for his health, his happiness and his general welfare with a tenderness that went straight to his heart, talking all the time with extreme rapidity – 'she was amazed, delighted – where had he been? – had he been quite well? – he could not imagine how pleased she was – had he been here long? – why had not Jack called her? – she had missed a quarter of an hour of him – she was sure the twins would remember him – they would be so excited – and little Cecilia too of course – he was hungry, was he not? – he would take a piece of seed-cake – how *was* he?'

'I am very well, I thank you. And you too, my dear, you are blooming, blooming.' She was indeed. She had caught up most of the wisps of hair he had seen streaming from the window, but one had escaped and its disorder enchanted him; yet for all the complacency with which he gazed upon her he could not conceal from his private mind that the tendency to plumpness he had once warned her of was quite gone, that were the present flush of pleasure not on her face she might look worn and even haggard, and that her hands, once so elegant, were now coarse and reddened.

Mrs Williams walked in. Stephen rose to bow, to ask after her health and that of her other daughters, and to answer her questions. He was about to sit down again after a tolerably detailed account of Mrs Williams's providential recovery when she cried, 'Not on the settle, Dr Maturin, if you please. It is bad for the cane. You will be more comfortable in Captain Aubrey's chair.'

A thump and a dismal howling above-stairs called Sophie from the room, and presently Jack went after her. Mrs Williams, feeling that she had been a little abrupt in the matter of his sitting, gave Stephen a history of the settle since its manufacture in Dutch William's time: she had brought it with her from dear Mapes, where no doubt he remembered it in the summer drawing-room; she liked Captain A's cottage to have something of the air of a gentleman's house, and in any case she could not bear leaving so valuable, so historical a piece to her tenant, a worthy sort of man no doubt, but something in the commercial line, and people in that walk of life would not scruple to sit on it. The clock also came from Mapes, the most accurate clock in the county.

'A handsome clock it is too,' said Stephen. 'A regulator, I believe. Could it not be set a-going?'

'Oh, no, sir,' said Mrs Williams with a pitying look. 'Was it to be set a-going, the works would instantly start to wear.' From this she carried on to wear in general and the prohibitive cost of repairs, with an aside about Captain A's being handy in the house.

Captain Aubrey's voice, though well calculated to carry from one end of a ship to another in a gale, was less suited to the confidential domestic whisper, and at intervals in Mrs Williams's stream of words his deep rumble could be heard, not perhaps quite as good-humoured as once it was, expostulating about a fair-sized piece of ham that could be dressed, a sea-pie that could be knocked up in a moment. Stephen turned his attention to Mrs Williams, and shading his eyes with his hand he studied her carefully. It appeared to him that her misfortune had had remarkably little effect on her: her restless, aggressive urge to dominate seemed if anything to have increased; she looked well, and as happy as it was in her nature to be. Her frequent references to her former grandeur might have been references to a myth in which she did not herself believe, a dream from which she had wakened to her present reality. Perhaps she had been born to play the part of a contriving manager with two hundred a year, so that at last she was fulfilling her real purpose. Was it a remarkable display of courage, or was it stark insensibility? For some time now she had been on the subject of servants, producing the usual threadbare observations with great conviction and volubility. In her young days they had been perfect; now they were difficult to find, impossible to keep, idle, false, dishonest, and often downright evil. 'Only this morning, only this very morning,' she said, 'I caught the cook fingering a heap of toadstools. Can you imagine such wickedness, Dr Maturin? To finger toadstools and then to touch my grandchildren's food with her nasty hands! There's a Welshwoman for you!'

'Did you attend to her explanation, ma'am?'

'Of course not. Lies, all lies, you know, in the kitchen. I flung them out of the door and gave her a piece of my mind. Character, forsooth! Don't she wish she may get it.'

After a short pause Stephen said, 'I saw an osprey this morning in that noble hanger over the way.'

'Did you, sir, indeed? Well, I declare. In that little wood we see from the window? It is quite well, for Hampshire. But when you know the neighbourhood as well as I know it, you will find that it is nothing in comparison of the woods at Mapes. They stretched into the next county, sir, and they were full of ospreys. Mr Williams used to shoot any number of 'em. I dare say this osprey of yours was a stray from Mapes.'

For some time Stephen had been aware of a snuffling behind the door. Now it opened and a little girl with yellow hair and a heavy cold came bursting in. She stared at him with an arch look, then buried her head in her grandmother's lap; to Stephen's relief all Mrs Williams's entreaties that she should stand up, that she should shake the gentleman's hand

and give him a kiss, were in vain, and there she reclined, while her grandmother gently stroked her hair.

Mrs Williams had never, to Stephen's knowledge, shown the least kindness to her daughters; her face, voice and manner were unfitted for the expression of kindness; yet here it was, glowing in her whole squat person as she explained that this was little Cecilia, the child of her middle daughter, who was following her husband's regiment and who therefore could not look after her, poor thing.

'I should have known her anywhere,' said Stephen. 'A fine child.'

Sophie returned and the child at once began to shout, 'Aunt, Aunt, Cook tried to poison me with toadstools.' She kept up this unvaried cry for some time, and over it Stephen said to Sophie, 'I am strangely remiss: you must forgive me. I am come to beg you all to dine with me, and I have not yet delivered my invitation.'

'You are very good,' said Mrs Williams at once, 'but I am afraid that would be quite impossible, because –' she looked about for some reason why it should be quite impossible, but was obliged to take refuge in hushing the child. Stephen went on, 'I am staying at the Crown in Petersfield, and have bespoke a variety of dishes.'

Sophie asked how he could be so monstrous; he was staying at the cottage, and dining there too. Again the door opened, and both women eagerly turned to Jack. 'How they do talk,' reflected Stephen: this was the first time he had ever seen the slightest possible evidence of a relationship between Sophie and her improbable mother.

'Uncle Aubrey,' cried Cecilia, 'Cook tried to poison me and the twins with toadstools.'

'What stuff,' said Jack. 'Stephen, you dine and sleep with us. The galley is all ahoo today, but there will be a capital sea-pie.'

'Jack,' said Stephen, 'I have bespoke dinner at the Crown. These dishes will be on the table at the appointed hour, and if we are not there, they will go to waste entirely.'

This remark, he noticed, had a striking effect upon the

women. Although they still protested that he should not go, the conviction and the volume of their arguments declined. Stephen said nothing: at times he looked out of the window, at others he watched Sophie and her mother, and their kinship became more apparent. Where did it lie? Certainly not in tone of voice, nor in any particular feature or physical movement. Conceivably it arose from a certain not childish but rather un-adult expression common to both, an expression that a French colleague of his, a physiognomist and a follower of Lavater, had called 'the English look', attributing it to frigidity, a well-known characteristic of Englishwomen, and thus to an ignorance of the warming, ripening delights of physical love. 'If Dupuytren was right, and if this is indeed the case,' he reflected, 'then Jack, with his ardent temperament, must be strangely put about.' The flood of talk continued. 'How well he bears it,' thought Stephen, remembering Jack's short way with cackle on the quarterdeck. 'I honour his forbearance.' Compromises made their appearance: some should go, some should stay. Eventually, after a very long typical family discussion that often began again where it had started, it was agreed that Jack should go, that Stephen should return the next morning for breakfast, and that Mrs Williams, for some reason, should content herself with a little bread and cheese.

'Nonsense, ma'am,' cried Jack, goaded beyond civility at last, 'there is a perfectly good piece of ham in the larder, and the makings of a monstrous fine great sea-pie.'

'But at least, Stephen, you will have time to see the twins before you leave,' said Sophie quickly. 'For the moment they are quite presentable. Pray show them, my dear. I will be with you in a moment.'

Jack led him up the stairs into a little sloping room, upon whose floor sat two bald babies, dressed in fresh frocks. They had pale, globular faces, and in the middle of each face a surprisingly long and pointed nose called the turnip to an impartial observer's mind. They looked at Stephen steadily: they had not yet reached the age of any social contact whatsoever and there was not the least doubt that they found him uninteresting, dull, even repellent; their eyes wandered elsewhere, dismissing him, both pairs at exactly the same moment. They might have been infinitely old, or members of another genus.

'Very fine children,' said Stephen. 'I should have known them anywhere.'

'I cannot tell one from t'other,' said Jack. 'You would not credit the din they can kick up if things are not quite to their liking. The one on the right is probably Charlotte.' He stared at them; they stared at him, unwinking. 'What do you think of them, Stephen?' he asked, tapping his forehead significantly.

Stephen resumed his professional role. He had delivered some scores of babies at the Rotunda in his student days, but since then his practice had lain among adults, particularly among seafaring adults, and few men of his professional standing could have been worse qualified for this task; however, he picked them up, listened to their hearts and lungs, opened their mouths and peered within, bent their limbs, and made motions before their eyes.

'How old are they?' he asked.

'Why, they must be quite old by now,' said Jack. 'They seem to have been here for ever. Sophie will know exactly.'

Sophie came in, and to his pleasure Stephen saw both the little creatures lose their eternal, ancient look; they smiled, wriggled and jerked themselves convulsively with joy, mere human larvae.

'You need not be afraid for them,' he said, as he and Jack walked over the fields towards their dinner. 'They will do very well; they may even turn out a pair of phoenixes, in time. But I do beg you will not countenance that thoughtless way people have of flinging them up into the air. It is liable to do great harm, to confuse their intellects; and a girl, when grown into a woman, has greater need of her intellect than a man. It is a grievous error to fling them to the ceiling.'

'God's my life!' cried Jack, pausing in his stride. 'You don't tell me so? I thought they liked being tossed up – they laugh and crow and so on, almost human. But I shall never do it again, although they are only girls, poor little swabs.'

'It is curious, the way you dwell upon their sex. They are your own children, for all love, your very flesh; and yet I could almost suppose, and not only from your referring to them as *swabs*, a disobliging term, that you were disappointed in them, merely for being girls. It is, to be sure, a misfortune for *them* – the orthodox Jew daily thanks his Maker for not having been born a woman, and we might well echo his gratitude – but I cannot for the life of me see how it affects *you*, your aim being, as I take it, posterity, a vicarious immortality: and for that a girl is if anything a better assurance than a boy.'

'Perhaps it is a foolish prejudice,' said Jack, 'but to tell you the truth, Stephen, I had longed for a boy. And to have not one girl but two – well, I would not have Sophie know it for the world, but it is a disappointment, reason how I may. My heart was set on a boy: I had it all worked out in my mind. I should have taken him to sea at seven or eight, with a good schoolmaster aboard to give him a thorough grounding in mathematics and even perhaps a parson for the frills, Latin and morality and so on. He should have spoken French and Spanish as well as you do, Stephen; and I could have taught him a deal of seamanship. Even if I could get no ship for years and years, I knew just what admirals and captains to place him with; he would not have lacked for friends in the service; and if he had not been knocked on the head first, I should have seen him made post by twenty-one or -two. Maybe I should have seen him hoist his flag at last. I could help a boy along, at sea; and the sea is the only thing I know. What use can I possibly be to a parcel of girls? I cannot even give them portions.'

'By the law of averages the next is very likely to be a boy,' said Stephen, 'and then you will carry out your benevolent scheme.'

'There is no likelihood of another. None at all,' said Jack. 'You have not been married, Stephen – but I cannot explain – should never have mentioned it. This is the stile to the turnpike: you can see the Crown from here.'

They said nothing as they walked along the road. Stephen reflected upon Sophie's confinement: he had not been present, but he understood from his colleagues that it had been unusually difficult and prolonged – a bad presentation – yet there had been no essential lesion. He also reflected upon Jack's life at Ashgrove Cottage; and standing before the fire in the Crown, a fine great, posting-inn on the main Portsmouth road, he said, 'Were we to speak generally, we might say that upon the whole sailors, after many years of their unnatural, cloistered life, tend to regard the land as Fiddler's Green, a perpetual holiday; and that their expectations cannot be attempted to be fulfilled. What the ordinary landsman accepts as the common lot, the daily round of domestic ills, children, responsibilities, the ordinary seaman is apt to look upon as a disappointment of his hopes, an altogether exceptional trial, and an invasion of his liberty.'

'I catch your drift, old Stephen,' said Jack with a smile, 'and there is a great deal in what you say. But not every ordinary seaman has Mrs Williams to live with him. I am not complaining, mark you. She is not a bad sort of a woman at all; she does her best according to her own lights, and she is truly devoted to the children. The trouble is that I had somehow got the wrong notion of marriage. I had thought there was more friendship and confidence and unreserve in it than the case allows. I am not criticizing Sophie in the least degree, you understand –'

'Certainly not.'

'– but in the nature of things . . . The fault is entirely on my side, I am sure. When you are in command, you get so sick of the loneliness, of playing the great man and so on, that you long to break out of it; but in the nature of things it don't seem possible.' He relapsed into silence.

After a while Stephen said, 'So if you were ordered to sea, brother, I collect you would not rage and curse, as being snatched away from domestic felicity – the felicity, I mean, of a parent guiding his daughters' first interesting steps?'

'I should kiss the messenger,' said Jack.

'This I had supposed for some time now,' murmured Stephen.

'For one thing, I should be on full pay,' continued Jack, 'and for another, there would be a chance of prize-money, and I might be able to give them portions.' At the word prize-money the old piratical look gleamed in his bright blue eyes and he straightened to his full height. 'And indeed I have some hopes of a ship. I pepper the Admiralty with letters, of course, and some days ago I wrote to Bromley: there is a frigate fitting out in the Dockyard, the old *Diane*, doubled and braced with Snodgrass's diagonals. I even pester Old Jarvie from time to time, though he don't love me. Oh, I have half a dozen irons in the fire – I suppose you have not been up to anything, Stephen? Not another *Surprise*, with an envoy for the East Indies?'

'How come you to ask such a simple question, Jack? Hush: do not gape, but look privily towards the stair. There is a most strikingly handsome woman.'

Jack glanced round, and there in fact was a most strikingly handsome woman, young, spry, a lady very much alive, wearing a green riding-habit; she was aware of being looked at, and she moved with even more grace than nature had provided.

He turned heavily back to the fire. 'I have no use for your women,' he said. 'Handsome or otherwise.'

'I never expected you to utter so weak a remark,' said Stephen. 'To lump all women together in one undiscriminated heap is as unphilosophical as to say . . .'

'Gentlemen,' said the host of the Crown, 'your dinner is on the table, if you please to walk in.'

It was a good dinner, but even the soused hog's face did not restore Captain Aubrey's philosophy, nor give his expression the old degree of cheerfulness that Stephen had known outlast privation, defeat, imprisonment and even the loss of his ship.

After the first remove, which had been entirely taken up with memories of earlier commissions and former shipmates, they spoke of Mrs Williams's affairs. That lady, having lost her man of business by death, had been unfortunate in her choice of a new one, a gentleman with a scheme of investment that must infallibly yield seventeen and a half per cent. Her capital had been engulfed and with it her estate, though up until the present she still retained the house whose rent paid the interest on the mortgage. 'I cannot blame her,' said Jack. 'I dare say I should have done the same myself: even ten per cent would have been wonderfully tempting. But I wish she had not lost Sophie's dowry too. She did not choose to transfer it until the Michaelmas dividends were due, and in decency we could hardly press her, so it all went, being in her name. I mind the money, of course, but even more than that I mind its making Sophie unhappy. She feels she is a burden, which is the greatest nonsense. But what can I say? I might as well talk to the cathead.'

'Allow me to pour you another glass of this port,' said Stephen. 'It is an innocent wine, neither sophisticated nor muddy, which is rare in these parts. Tell me, who is the Miss Herschel of whom you spoke with such warm approbation?'

'Ah, now, that is another case altogether: there is a woman who bears out all you say about heaps,' cried Jack. 'There is a woman you can talk to as one rational being to another. Ask her the measure of an arc whose cosine is nought, and instantly she replies pi upon two: it is all there, in her head. She is sister to the great Mr Herschel.'

'The astronomer?'

'Just so. He honoured me with some most judicious remarks on refraction when I addressed the Royal Society, and that is how I came to know her. She had already read my paper on the Jovian moons, was more than civil about it, and suggested a quicker way of working my heliocentric longitudes. I go to see her every time she comes down to Newman's observatory, which is pretty often, and we sit there either sweeping for comets all night or talking about instruments. She and her brother must have made some hundreds in their time. She understands telescopes from clew to earring, and it was she who showed me how to figure a speculum, and where to get my superfine Pomeranian sludge. And it is not mere theory: I have seen her walking round and round a post in Newman's stable-yard for a good three hours without a break, putting the last touches to a six-inch mirror – it will never do to take your hand from the surface at that stage, you know – taking snuff from a saucer every hundred paces. An admirable woman; you would love her, Stephen. And she sings, too – hits the note plumb in the middle, as pure as the Carlotta.'

'If she is Mr Herschel's sister, I presume she is a lady of a certain age?'

'Oh, yes, she must be sixty or so: she could never have come by such a knowledge of double stars in less. Sixty at least. Yet it is all one. Whenever I come home from a night with Miss Herschel there are wry looks, a tolerably frigid welcome.'

'Since it has physical effects, the sorrow and woe that is in marriage no doubt belongs to the province of the physician,' said Stephen. 'But I am as little acquainted with it as I am with gardening, or domestic economy.'

He was brought nearer acquainted the next morning, when he walked up to breakfast at the cottage. He was far too early, and the first sight that met his eye was the twins flinging their pap about and shrieking as they did so, while their grandmother, protected by a coarse canvas bib and apron, endeavoured to feed them with a spoon and little Cecilia wallowed in the bowl itself; he recoiled into the arms of the servant-girl carrying a basket of malodorous cloths, and worse might have happened if Sophie, suddenly appearing from above, had not whipped him away into the garden.

After a little general conversation from which it appeared that Jack had enjoyed his dinner, had come home singing, and was now grinding the coffee himself, she said, 'Oh, Stephen, how I wish you could help him to a ship. He is so unhappy here. He spends hours up on the hill, looking at the sea through his telescope, and it breaks my heart. Even if it were only for a short cruise – the winter is coming on, and the damp is so bad for his wound – any sort of ship at all, even if it were only a transport, like dear Mr Pullings.'

'How I wish I could, my dear; but what is the voice of a ship's surgeon in the councils of the great?' said Stephen, with a veiled though piercing glance to see whether any of her husband's knowledge of his double character had been sacrificed to marital confidence. Her next words and her totally unconscious air reassured him: she said, 'We saw in the paper that you were called in when the Duke of Clarence was ill, and I thought that perhaps a word from you . . .'

He said, 'Honey, the duke knows Jack very well, by reputation – we spoke of his action with the *Cacafuego* – but he also knows that recommending Jack for a command would be the worst service he could do him. His Highness is in bad odour with the Admiralty.'

'But surely they could not refuse the King's own son?'

'They are terrible men at the Admiralty, my dear.'

Before she could reply the church clock of Chilton Admiral told the hour, and on the third stroke Jack's hail of 'Coffee's up' followed by his manly form and some remarks about the wind having backed two points in the night – heavy rain for sure – broke up their conference.

Breakfast was spread in the parlour, and they walked into a fine smell of coffee, toast and wood-smoke: the ham stood on the table, flanked by Jack's own radishes, each the size of a moderate pippin, and a solitary egg. 'There is the great advantage of living in the country,' he said. 'You get your vegetables really fresh. And that is our own egg, Stephen! Do help yourself. Sophie's crab-apple jelly is by your side. Damn that chimney; it will not draw when the air is anything south of west. Stephen, let me pass you an egg.'

Mrs Williams brought Cecilia in, so starched that she held her arms from her sides, like an imperfectly-articulated doll. She came and stood by Stephen's chair, and while the others were busily wondering why there was no news from the rectory, where the birth of a child had been hourly expected these many days past, she told him loud and clear that they never had coffee except on birthdays and when there had been a victory, and that her uncle Aubrey usually drank small beer, whereas her aunt and grandmama drank milk:

if he liked, she would butter his toast for him. She had buttered a good deal of his coat too before Mrs Williams, with a delighted shriek, plucked her away, remarking that there never was such a forward child for her years; Cecilia, her mother, could never have buttered a piece of toast so prettily at that age.

Jack's attention was elsewhere; his ear was cocked; his cup was poised; several times he looked at his watch. 'The post!' exclaimed Mrs Williams at the thundering double knock on the door, and Jack made a visible effort to sit still in his chair until the servant appeared, saying 'A letter and a book, sir, if you please, and a shilling to pay.'

Jack felt in his pocket, frowned, and called across the table, 'Have you a shilling in change, Stephen? Here's nothing small.'

Stephen too plunged his hand into his breeches and came up with a mixed bag of currency, English, French and Spanish. 'The gentleman has three gold pieces,' said Cecilia, 'and a large quantity of silver.' But Stephen was deaf: he picked out twelve pence and handed them over, saying, 'Never mind me, I beg.'

'Well, if you will all forgive me . . .' said Jack, breaking the seal. Mrs Williams craned her neck to make out all she could from her indifferent point of vantage, but before she could move to a better, her curiosity was satisfied. 'Oh,' said Jack, throwing the letter down, 'it is only that fellow Bromley. I always knew he was a rake; now I know he is a scrub into the bargain. However, here is the *Naval Chronicle*. That is always worth reading. My dear, Stephen's cup is empty.' He turned first to the appointments and promotions. 'Goate is made post at last; I am heartily glad of it.' Considerations upon the merits and demerits of Captain Goate and other acquaintances, also made post. Then, after a calculating pause, Jack said, 'You know, Stephen, our losses last year were not as heavy as I made out last night. Listen: *Jupiter*, 50, wrecked in Vigo Bay; *Leda*, 38, wrecked off Milford Haven; *Crescent*, 36, wrecked off Jutland; *Flora*, 32, wrecked off Holland; *Meleager*, 36, wrecked on Barebush

Cay; *Astraea*, 32, wrecked off Anagado. Only five frigates, you see. And as for the post-ships, only *Banterer*, 22, wrecked in the St Lawrence; *Laurel*, 22, taken by the *Canonnière*, 50 – you remember the *Canonnière*, Stephen? I pointed her out to you once, when we were looking into Brest. An ancient old ship, built somewhere about 1710, but an amazing fine sailer; she can still give most of our heavy frigates topgallants on a bowline. Stephen, what's amiss?'

Stephen was gazing through the acrid smoke at Cecilia, who, bored with the conversation, had opened the clock's door with her greasy hands to get at the pendulum, a heavy jar of quicksilver.

'Oh, let the poor little treasure be,' said Mrs Williams, looking at her granddaughter with the fondest admiration.

'Madam,' said Stephen, his heart in pain for the exquisite mechanism, 'she will do herself a mischief. That quicksilver is most delicately poised; furthermore it is poison.'

'Cecilia,' said Jack, 'cut along now. Run away and play.'

Contention, tears, Mrs Williams's nimble protective tongue, and Sophie led her niece from the room. Mrs Williams was not at all pleased, but in the silence the sound of the passing-bell came clear from the church; it instantly diverted her mind, and she cried, 'That must be for poor Mrs Thwaites. She was due last week, and they sent for the man-midwife last night. There, Captain Aubrey.' These last words were delivered with an inimical jerk of her head, a retaliation, as it were, for his list of male wreckage and death, an assertion of women's sacrifice.

Sophie returned with the news that a horseman was approaching the cottage. 'It is news of poor Mrs Thwaites, no doubt,' said Mrs Williams, looking hard at Jack again. But she was mistaken. It was a boy from the Crown, with a letter for Jack: he was to wait for an answer.

' "Lady Clonfert presents her compliments to Captain and Mrs Aubrey, and would be most grateful for a passage to the Cape. She promises to take up no room and to give no trouble whatsoever; and flatters herself that Mrs Aubrey will, as a fellow-sailor's wife, understand and support this sadly informal and hurried application. She also proposes, if perfectly convenient to Mrs Aubrey, to do herself the honour of waiting upon her in the forenoon,"' read Captain Aubrey aloud, with a very high degree of astonishment, adding, 'Certainly she may have a lift to the Cape, whenever I happen to be going there, ha, ha.'

'Jack,' said Stephen, 'a word with you, if you please.'

They walked out into the garden, pursued by Mrs Williams's angry voice – 'A most improper application – no compliments to me – and disgracefully ill-wrote; she has spelt promises with one m – I have no patience with these attempts at thrusting oneself into a strange house.'

At the end of the wan row of carrots Stephen said, 'I must beg your pardon for having evaded your question last night. I have in fact *been up to something*, as you put it. But first I must speak very briefly of the position in the Indian Ocean. Some months ago four new French frigates slipped out of the Channel ports, ostensibly for Martinique – that was the general rumour on shore, and that was the destination stated in the orders delivered to their respective captains: but no doubt these captains also carried sealed orders, to be opened somewhere south of Finisterre. At all events the frigates never reached the Antilles. Nothing was heard of them until they reached Mauritius, where they upset the balance of power in those waters entirely. The news of their presence reached England a very short while ago. They have already taken two Indiamen, and clearly they threaten to take many more. Government is extremely concerned.'

'I am sure of it,' cried Jack. Mauritius and La Réunion lay right in the path of the eastern trade, and although the Company's ships were usually well enough armed to deal with the privateers and pirates that swarmed in those seas, while the Royal Navy, by stretching its resources to the utmost, could just contain the French men-of-war, the sudden arrival of four frigates would be catastrophic: furthermore, the Frenchmen had excellent deep-water harbours in Port-Louis and Port South-East and St Paul's, sheltered from the frequent hurricanes and full of marine stores, whereas the Navy's nearest base was the Cape, more than two thousand miles to the south.

Stephen was silent for a moment. 'Do you know the *Boadicea*?' he asked abruptly.

'*Boadicea*, 38? Yes, of course. A weatherly ship, though slow: fitting foreign for the Leeward Islands station. Charles Loveless has her.'

'Well, listen now: this vessel, this frigate, is to be diverted to the Cape. And Captain Loveless, as you say, was to take her there to form part of a squadron made up of what the Admiral could spare: a force intended not only to counteract the French frigates but to take their bases away from them. In short, to capture La Réunion and Mauritius, to install a governor, and to possess them as colonies, valuable not only in themselves but as posts along this most interesting route.'

'A capital notion,' said Jack. 'It has always seemed absurd to me, that those islands should not be English – unnatural.' He spoke a little at haphazard, because he had noted – oh, with what keen attention – Stephen's 'Captain Loveless *was* to take her.' Might this possibly be an acting command?

Stephen frowned. 'I was to accompany this force, together with the proposed governor,' he went on. 'And I was in a position to offer a certain amount of advice; that is to say, I was consulted on various points. It did not appear to me that Captain Loveless was fitted for the political side of the task, either mentally or physically; but he has great interest at the Admiralty. However, his malady increased upon him, and in spite of my colleague's efforts and of my own he is now on shore with an obstinate tenesmus that will keep him there. In London I caused it to be suggested that Captain Aubrey would be admirably suited for the vacant command –' Jack gripped his elbow with a force that made him catch his breath, but he continued '– that it was probable he would accept it in spite of his domestic situation and of the very short notice, and that I should be seeing him myself directly. Alternative names were advanced; some very frivolous objections to do with seniority and the flying of some kind of flag, some trumpery mark of distinction, were raised, for it seemed desirable that the person, or the ship, in question should be so ornamented . . .' With a prodigious effort Jack swallowed the words 'A broad pennant, a commodore's broad pennant, for God's sake!' and Stephen continued, 'and most unhappily several people had to be consulted.' He bent to pick a stalk of grass and put it into his mouth; for some time he shook his head, and the farther end of the grass magnified its motion, showing anger, disapprobation, or a most decided negative. Jack's heart, raised by the mere mention of a broad pennant, the sailor's sweetest dream short of the admiral's flag itself, sank into the dark, everyday world of half-pay. 'Most unhappily, I say,' went on Stephen, 'for although I carried my point, it is evident that at least one of those consulted has been talking. The rumour has already spread about the town. Lady Clonfert's appearance is clear proof of that; her husband is on the Cape station, captain of the *Otter*. Oh, oh, it is always the same thing – gabble, gabble, gabble, blab, blab, blab, like a parcel of geese on a common, or a pack of old women . . .' his voice soared shrill in indignation, and Jack was aware that he was giving instances of loose talk, of intelligence conveyed to the enemy by spreading gossip; but Jack's glowing mind was filled with a picture of the *Boadicea*, her simpering figurehead with its vast bosom spreading over the frigate's fine seaworthy bows – a trifle slow, perhaps, and he had seen her miss stays; but a careful stowing of her hold to bring her by the stern might make a world of difference, and cross-cat-harpins; Charles Loveless had no notion of cross-cat-harpins, still less of Bentinck shrouds. He found Stephen's eye fixed angrily upon him, bent his head with an expression of the gravest attention, and heard the words, 'As though the French were deaf, dumb, blind, incompetent! That is why I am most unwillingly obliged to give you this short summary. In any other event I should infinitely have preferred the news to reach you through the proper channels, without the least explanation – your provisional orders are at the port-admiral's office this minute – for not only does this require speaking openly of what should not be mentioned at all, but I am extremely averse to appearing in the role of fairy godmother, a purely fortuitous fairy godmother in this case. It can inflict an apparent, though fallacious, burden of obligation, and cause great damage to a relationship.'

'Not to ours, brother,' said Jack, 'not to ours. And I will not thank you, since you don't like it; but Lord, Stephen, I am a different man.' He was indeed. Taller, younger, pinker, his eyes blazing with life. His stoop had gone, and a great boyish grin kept ruining his attempted gravity.

'You will not mention this to Sophie, nor to any other person,' said Stephen, with a cold, penetrating glare.

'Must I not even start looking to my sea-chest?'

'What a fellow you are, Jack!' cried Stephen, in great disgust. 'Of course you must not, not until the port-admiral's messenger is come. Cannot you see the obvious cause and effect? I should have thought it plain even to the meanest intelligence.'

'A ship!' cried Jack, springing heavily into the air. There were tears in his eyes, and Stephen saw that he might wish to shake hands at any minute. He disliked all effusion, privately thinking the English far too much given to weeping and the flow of soul; he pursed his lips with a sour expression, and put his hands behind his back. He said, 'Plain to the meanest intelligence: I appear – you have a ship. What must Sophie conclude? Where is my character?'

'How long do you think the port-admiral's messenger will be, Stephen?' asked Jack, with nothing but a loving smile at these harsh words.

'Let us hope he outpaces Lady Clonfert by a few minutes at least, if only to prove that casual gossip does not necessarily have to run faster than official orders every single time. How we shall ever win this war I cannot tell. In Whitehall they know perfectly well that success in the Mauritius enterprise is of capital importance, and yet some fool must be prating. I cannot express my abhorrence of their levity. We reinforce the Cape, and tell them so: they instantly reinforce the Ile de France, that is to say, Mauritius. And so it runs, all, all of a piece throughout: Mr Congreve invents a military rocket with vast potentialities – we instantly inform the world, like a hen that has laid an egg, thus throwing away all the effect of surprise. The worthy Mr Snodgrass finds out a way of rendering old ships serviceable in a short time and at little expense: without a moment's pause we publish his method in all the papers, together with drawings, lest some particular should escape our enemy's comprehension.'

Jack looked as solemn as he could, and shook his head; but very soon he turned a beaming face to Stephen and asked, 'Do you imagine this will be one of your stand-off-and-on capers? Ordered to sea at a moment's notice, recalled, turned on shore for a month, all your hands drafted elsewhere, and then sent to the Baltic at last in your hot-weather clothes?'

'I do not. Quite apart from the absolute importance of the operation, there are many members of the Board and of the ministry that have their money in East India stock: ruin the Company and you ruin them. No, no: there is likely to be a wonderful degree of celerity in this case, I believe.'

Jack laughed aloud with pleasure, and then observed that they must be getting back to the house – the boy from the Crown was waiting for an answer. 'I shall have to give that wretched woman a lift,' he added. 'You cannot refuse a brother-officer's wife, the wife of a man you know; but Lord, how I wish I could get out of it. Come, let us walk in.'

'I cannot advise it,' said Stephen. 'Sophie would detect you instantly. You are as transparent as a bride. Stay here till I desire Sophie to make your joint reply to Lady Clonfert: you cannot be seen until you have your orders.'

'I shall go to the observatory,' said Jack.

It was here that Stephen found him some minutes later, with his telescope trained on the Portsmouth road. 'Sophie has answered,' said Stephen, 'and every woman in the house is now scrubbing the parlour and changing the lace window-curtains; they turned me out with very little ceremony, I can tell you.'

The promised rain began to fall, drumming briskly on the copper dome: there was just room for them both, and there they crouched in silence for a while. Beneath the bubbling current of his pure joy, Jack longed to ask whether Stephen had in some way arranged Captain Loveless's tenesmus; but although he had known Stephen intimately these many, many years, there was something about him that forbade questioning.

Presently, his mind sobering, he reflected on the Indian Ocean, on the fine blue-water sailing with the south-east trade-wind, the perilous inshore navigation among the coral reefs surrounding La Réunion and Mauritius; on the typical Admiralty decision to send one frigate to counterbalance four; on the immense difficulty of maintaining even a blockade, above all in the hurricane months, let alone that of landing upon those islands, with their few harbours (and those fortified), their broad reefs, the perpetual heavy surf on their inhospitable shores; on the question of water, and on the nature of the force likely to oppose him. To oppose him, that is to say, if ever he reached the station. Furtively stretching out to touch a piece of wood, he said, 'This hypothetical squadron, Stephen, have you any idea of its strength, and what it might have to deal with?'

'I wish I had, my dear,' said Stephen. 'The *Néréide* and the *Sirius* were mentioned, to be sure, together with the *Otter* and the possibility of another sloop; but beyond that everything is nebulous. Vessels that Admiral Bertie had at the time of his latest despatches, dated more than three months ago, may very well be off Java by the time the squadron is actually formed. Nor can I speak to what Decaen may have had in Mauritius before this reinforcement, apart from the *Canonnière* and possibly the *Sémillante* – they range so wide. On the other hand I can tell you the names of their new frigates. They are the *Vénus*, *Manche*, *Bellone* and *Caroline*.'

'*Vénus*, *Manche*, *Bellone*, *Caroline*,' said Jack, frowning. 'I have never heard of a single one of 'em.'

'No. As I said, they are new, quite new: they carry forty guns apiece. Twenty-four-pounders, at least in the case of the *Bellone* and the *Manche*: perhaps in the others too.'

'Oh, indeed?' said Jack, his eye still to his telescope. The rosy glow in his mind had strange lurid edges to it now. Those were in fact the French navy's most recent, very heavy frigates, the envy of the British dockyards. Buonaparte had all the forests of Europe at his command, splendid Dalmatian oak, tall northern spars, best Riga hemp; and although the man himself was the merest soldier, his shipbuilders turned out the finest vessels afloat and he had some very capable officers to command them. Forty guns apiece. The *Néréide* had thirty-six, but only twelve-pounders: *Boadicea* and *Sirius*, with their eighteen-pounders, might be a match for the Frenchmen, particularly if the French crews were as new as their ships; but even so, that was a hundred and sixty guns to a hundred and ten to say nothing of the broadside weight of metal. Everything would depend on how those guns were handled. The other forces at the Cape hardly entered into the line of count. The flagship, the ancient *Raisonable*, sixty-four, could no more be considered a fighting unit than the antique French *Canonnière*: he could not offhand recall the smaller vessels on the station, apart from the *Otter*, a pretty eighteen-gun ship-sloop: but in any case, if it came to a general action, the frigates alone must bear the brunt. The *Néréide* he knew of, the crack frigate of the West Indies station, and in Corbett she had a fighting captain; Pym he knew by reputation; but Clonfert of the *Otter* was the only captain he had ever sailed with . . . Across the round of his objective-glass travelled a purposeful Marine, mounted on a horse. 'O blessed form,' murmured Jack, following him behind a haystack with his telescope, 'he will be here in twenty minutes. I shall give him a guinea.' All at once the Indian Ocean, the Mauritius command, took on a new, infinitely more concrete reality: the characters of Admiral Bertie, Captain Pym, Captain Corbett and even Lord Clonfert assumed a great practical importance: so did the immediate problems of a new command. Although his intimacy with Stephen Maturin did not allow him to ask questions that might be judged impertinent, it was of such a rare kind that he could ask for money without the least hesitation. 'Have you any money, Stephen?' he said, the Marine having vanished in the trees. 'How I hope you have. I shall have to borrow the Marine's guinea from you, and a great deal more besides, if his message is what I dearly trust. My half-pay is not due until the month after next, and we are living on credit.'

'Money, is it?' said Stephen, who had been thinking about lemurs. There were lemurs in Madagascar: might there not be lemurs on Réunion? Lemurs concealed among the forests and the mountains of the interior? 'Money? Oh, yes, I have money galore.' He felt in his pockets. 'The question is, where is it?' He felt again, patted his bosom, and brought out a couple of greasy two-pound notes on a country bank. 'That is not it,' he muttered, going through his pockets again. 'Yet I was sure – was it in my other coat? – did I perhaps leave it in London? – you are growing old, Maturin – ah, you dog, there you are!' he cried triumphantly, returning to the first pocket and drawing forth a neat roll, tied with tape. 'There. I had confused it with my lancet-case. It was Mrs Broad of the Grapes that did it up, finding it in a Bank of England wrapper that I had – that I had neglected. A most ingenious way of carrying money, calculated to deceive the pick-pocket. I hope it will suffice.'

'How much is it?' asked Jack.

'Sixty or seventy pound, I dare say.'

'But, Stephen, the top note is a fifty, and so is the next. I do not believe you ever counted them.'

'Well, never mind, never mind,' said Stephen testily. 'I meant a hundred and sixty. Indeed, I said as much, only you did not attend.'

They both straightened, cocking their ears. Through the beating of the rain came Sophie's voice calling, 'Jack! Jack!' and rising to a squeak as she darted into the observatory, breathless and wet. 'There is a Marine from the port-admiral,' she said between her gasps, 'and he will not give his message except into your own hands. Oh, Jack, might it be a ship?'

A ship it was. Captain Aubrey was required and directed to repair aboard HMS *Boadicea* and to take upon himself the command of the said vessel, for which the enclosed order was to be the warrant: he was to touch at Plymouth, there to receive on board R.T. Farquhar, Esquire, at the Commissioner's office, and any further orders that might be transmitted to him at that place. These stately, somewhat inimical documents (as usual, Captain Aubrey was to fail not, at his peril), were accompanied by a friendly note from the Admiral, asking Jack to dine with him the next day, before going aboard.

Now that direct action was legitimate, it burst forth with such force that Ashgrove Cottage was turned upside-down in a moment. At first Mrs Williams clung tenaciously to her scheme for changing the parlour curtains, clamouring that it must be done – what would Lady Clonfert think? – and protesting that she should not be overborne; but her strength was as nothing compared with that of a newly-appointed frigate-captain burning to join his ship before the evening gun, and in a few minutes she joined her daughter and the distracted maid in brushing uniforms, madly darning stockings and ironing neck-cloths, while Jack trundled his sea-chest in the attic and roared down to know where was his neat's-foot oil, and who had been at his pistols? adjuring them 'to bear a hand', 'to look alive', 'to lose not a minute below there', 'to light along the sextant-case'.

Lady Clonfert's arrival, so much in the forefront of Mrs Williams's mind not an hour before, passed almost unnoticed in the turmoil, a turmoil increased by the howling of neglected children, which reached its paroxysm as her coachman thundered on the door. A full two minutes of strenuous battering passed by before the door was opened and she was able to walk into the naked parlour, whose curtains lay on one end of the settle and the new on the other.

Poor lady, she had but a sad time of it. She had dressed with particular care in garments designed not to offend Mrs Aubrey by being too fashionable or becoming yet at the same time to beguile Captain Aubrey, and she had prepared an artless speech about sailors' wives, Clonfert's respect and affection for his old shipmate, and her perfect familiarity with life aboard a man-of-war, together with some slight hints as to her acquaintance with General Mulgrave, the First Lord, and with Mrs Bertie, the wife of the Admiral at the Cape. This she delivered to Stephen, wedged into a dim corner by the clock under a drip, with some charming asides to Sophie; and she was obliged to repeat it when Jack appeared, trailing cobwebs from the attic and bearing his chest. It is difficult to sound artless twice in quick succession, but she did her best, for she was sincerely devoted to the prospect of escaping an English winter, and the idea of seeing her husband again filled her with a pleasurable excitement. Her confusion caused her bosom to rise and fall, a blush to overspread her pretty face, and from his corner Stephen observed that she was doing quite well against heavy odds – that Jack, at least, was not unmoved by her distress. Yet he also noticed, with regret, a certain stiffening in Sophie's attitude, a constraint in her civil smile, and something near acerbity in her reply to Lady Clonfert's suggestion that she too might darn the Captain's stockings and make herself useful during the voyage. Mrs Williams's stony reserve, her repeated sniff, her ostentatious busyness, he took for granted; but although he had long known that jealousy formed part of Sophie's character – perhaps the only part that he could have wished otherwise – he was grieved to see it thus displayed. Jack had caught the signals as quickly as his friend – Stephen saw his anxious glance – and his cordiality towards Lady Clonfert, never very great, sensibly diminished; although he did repeat what he had said at the beginning – that he should be happy to carry her ladyship to the Cape. What had preceded that glance, to make it so anxious? Dr Maturin lapsed into a meditation upon the marriage state: monogamy, an aberration? How widely spread in time and place? How strictly observed? From this train of thought he was aroused by Jack's strong voice stating that her ladyship was certainly aware of the

33

tediousness of tiding down the Channel, that he strongly recommended her posting to Plymouth, that he begged stores and baggage might be kept to a minimum, and that once again he must urge the most exact punctuality however short the notice: 'for his part he should gladly lose a tide to be of use, but on the King's service he must not lose a minute.'

Now everybody was standing up: soon Jack had led Lady Clonfert, under an umbrella, to her carriage, had firmly closed the door upon her, and was back in the house, his face radiating universal goodwill, as though she were utterly dismissed.

Mrs Williams was abusing Lady Clonfert's tippet, complexion and morals with a volubility that Stephen could not but admire, yet Jack's statement that a couple of hours would see his dunnage corded up, that Stephen would oblige him infinitely by riding straight to Gosport in order to bring back John Parley in Newman's dogcart to pack the telescope, and that he was determined to go aboard before the evening gun and to get the *Boadicea* to sea on the ebb, struck her dumb. It had no such effect on her daughter, however, who instantly produced a number of reasons why Jack could certainly not join tonight: the state of his linen would bring discredit on the service; it would be shockingly rude to dear, kind Admiral Wells not to dine with him, most impolitic if not direct insubordination; and Jack had always been such a friend to discipline. Besides, it was raining. It was clear to Stephen that she was not only horrified at losing Jack so soon but that she was also sorry for her recent – shrewishness was far too strong a word – for she now ran straight on into praise of their visitor. Lady Clonfert was a most elegant, well-bred woman, with remarkably fine eyes; her wish to join her husband was in every way meritorious and understandable; her presence aboard would certainly please the gun-room, indeed the whole ship's company.

Sophie then returned to arguments against Jack's leaving quite so soon: tomorrow morning would be far, far better in every way; they could not possibly have his clothes ready before then. In spite of her nimble wit, logical arguments soon began to run short, and Stephen, feeling that at any moment she might resort to others, even to tears, or appeal to him for support, slipped quietly out of the room. He communed with his horse in its outhouse for a while, and when he came back he found Jack at the door, staring up at the scudding clouds, with Sophie, looking exceptionally beautiful in her anxiety and emotion, beside him. 'The glass is rising,' said Jack thoughtfully, 'but the wind is still due south . . . and when you consider where she lays, right up the harbour, there is not a hope of getting her out on this tide. No, my dear; perhaps you are right. Perhaps I should not go aboard until tomorrow. But tomorrow, sweetheart,' he said, looking fondly down, 'tomorrow at the crack of dawn you lose your husband to his natural element.'

Chapter Two

Upon that damp element, always unstable, often treacherous, but for the moment both warm and kind, Captain Aubrey dictated an official letter to his happy clerk:

> *Boadicea*, at sea
>
> Sir,
>
> I have the honour to acquaint you, that at dawn on the seventeenth instant, the Dry Salvages bearing SSE two leagues, His Majesty's ship under my command had the good fortune to fall in with a French national ship of war with a prize in company. On the *Boadicea*'s approach she bore up, abandoning her prize, a snow, whose topmasts were struck down on deck. Every exertion was made in this ship to come up with the enemy, who endeavoured to lead us among the shoals of the Dry Salvages; but missing stays in consequence of the loss of her mizzen topmast, she struck upon a reef. Shortly afterwards, the wind having fallen to a flat calm, and the rocks sheltering her from the *Boadicea*'s guns, she was boarded and carried by the boats, when she proved to be the *Hébé*, formerly His Majesty's twenty-eight-gun frigate *Hyaena* but now mounting twenty-two twenty-four-pounders, carronades, and two long nines, with a complement of 214 men, commanded by Mons. Bretonnière, lieutenant de vaisseau, her captain having been killed in the action with the prize. She was thirty-eight days out of Bordeaux, on a cruise, and had taken the English vessels named in the margin.

My first lieutenant, Mr Lemuel Akers, an old and deserving officer, commanded the *Boadicea*'s boats and led the attack in the most gallant manner; while Lieutenant Seymour and Mr Johnson, master's mate, displayed great activity. Indeed I am happy to say, that the conduct of the *Boadicea*'s people gave me great satisfaction, and I have no greater loss to deplore than two men slightly wounded.

The snow was secured without delay: she is the *Intrepid Fox* of Bristol, A. Snape master, from the Guinea Coast, laden with elephants' teeth, gold-dust, grains of Paradise, hides, and skins. In view of the value of her cargo, I have thought proper to send her into Gibraltar, escorted by the *Hyaena* under the command of Lieutenant Akers.

I have the honour to be, etc.'

Captain Aubrey watched his clerk's flying pen with great benevolence. The letter was true in essence, but like most official letters it contained a certain number of lies. Jack did not think Lemuel Akers a deserving officer, and the lieutenant's gallantry had in fact been confined to roaring at the *Hébé* from the stern-sheets of the launch, to which his wooden leg confined him, while the conduct of several of the *Boadicea*'s people had filled their new captain with impatience, and the snow had not been secured without delay.

'Do not forget the wounded at the bottom of the page, Mr Hill,' he said. 'James Arklow, ordinary, and William Bates, Marine. Now be so good as to let Mr Akers know that I shall have a couple of private letters for him to take to Gibraltar.'

Left alone in the great cabin he glanced out of the stern-window at the calm, crowded, sunlit sea, with his prizes lying upon it and boats plying to and fro, the *Hébé*'s or rather the *Hyaena*'s rigging full of men putting the last touches to her repairs, the shrouds of her new mizzen rattled down already: he had a first-rate bosun in John Fellowes. Then

37

he reached out for a sheet of paper and began: 'Sweetheart – a hasty line to bring you my dear love and tell you all is well. We had an amazing prosperous voyage down as far as 35°30', with a fine double-reefed topsail quartering breeze – *Boadicea*'s best point of sailing in her present trim – all the way from the moment we sank Rame Head right across the Bay and almost to Madeira. We put into Plymouth at the height of flood on Monday night – black, with squalls of sleet and blowing hard – and since we had made our number to Stoke Point, Mr Farquhar was ready waiting, bag and baggage, at the Commissioner's office. I sent to Lady Clonfert's inn, desiring her to be at the quay by twenty minutes past the hour; but through some mistake she did not appear, and I was obliged to proceed to sea without her.

'However, to cut things short, this pretty wind carried us across the Bay, where the *Boadicea* proved she was a dry, wholesome ship, and at one time I thought we should raise the Island in just over a week. But then it backed into the south-east and I was obliged to stretch away for Tenerife, cursing my luck: and at four bells in the morning watch I happened to be on deck to make sure the master, an ignorant old man, did not run us on the Dry Salvages as he had nearly run us on Penlee Point, when there, right under our lee at the dawn of day, was a Frenchman, lying to with her prize. She had scarcely a chance, for the prize, a well-armed Guineaman, had mauled her briskly before she was taken; her rigging was all ahoo, she was bending a new foretopsail, and many of her people were in the Guineaman, setting her to rights: and of course she was not half our size. And since we had the weather-gage we could afford to yaw and let fly with our bow guns: not that it did her much harm, apart from flustering her people. However, she did her best, peppering us with her stern-chaser and trying to lead us into the four-fathom water of the Dog-Leg Passage. But I sounded that channel when I was a midshipman in the *Circe*, and since we draw twenty-three foot, I did not choose to follow her, although there was no swell worth speaking of.

Had she got through, we might have lost her, *Boadicea* being a trifle sluggish (though you will not repeat that anywhere, my dear); but we knocked away her mizzen topmast – she missed stays in the turn of the passage – ran on to the reef, and there being no wind could not beat across. So we lowered the boats and took her without much trouble, though I am sorry to say her commanding officer was wounded – Stephen is patching him up at this moment, poor fellow.

'There was no glory in it, sweetheart, not the least hint of danger; but the charming thing is, that she can just be called a frigate. She was our old *Hyaena*, a jackass twenty-eight as ancient as the Ark, that the French took when I was a boy: she was overgunned, of course, and they reduced her to what they rate a corvette, with twenty-four-pounder carronades and a couple of long nines – I scarcely recognized her at first, she was so changed. But she is still a frigate for us, and of course she will be bought into the service (she is a fine sailer too, particularly on the wind, and we hauled her clear with no damage at all, bar a fathom or two of her copper being scraped off). And then there is head-money, and above all this Guineaman. She is no prize to us, being English, but she is salvage, and she does represent a certain amount of cash, which, the kitchen copper being in the state it is, will not be unwelcome. Unfortunately the Admiral shares. Although mine were Admiralty orders, the cunning old dog added some nonsense of his own, to make sure of one of my eighths if I took anything; and this he did in the most barefaced way, after dinner, laughing cheerfully, ha, ha. All admirals are tarred with the same brush, I fear, and I dare say we shall find the same thing at the Cape.' He had scarcely written the last word before Stephen's grave warnings about close counsel came to his mind: he carefully changed it to 'our destination', and then returned to the Guineaman. 'Ordinarily she would have been crammed with blacks for the West Indies, which would have added much to her value; but perhaps it was just as well that there were none. Stephen grows so outrageous the minute slavery is mentioned, that I dare say I should have been obliged to set them ashore to prevent his being hanged for mutiny. Only the last time I dined in the gun-room, Akers, the first lieutenant, got on to the subject, and Stephen handled him so severely, I was obliged to intervene. Mr Farquhar is of the same opinion with Stephen, and I am sure they are right – it is a very ugly thing to see, indeed – yet sometimes I cannot help feeling that a couple of biddable, able-bodied young blacks that attended to their duty and could give no month's warning might come in uncommon handy at Ashgrove Cottage. And now I am on the cottage, I have written to Ommaney to send you all he will advance on the *Hyaena* directly, with which I beg you will instantly buy yourself a pelisse and tippet against its infernal draughts, and . . .' There followed a list of domestic improvements to be made: the copper, of course; the parlour chimney to be rebuilt; Goadby to be set to work on the roof; a newly-calved Jersey cow to be bought with Mr Hicks' advice. 'My dear, time is flying,' he went on. 'They are hoisting in *Hyaena*'s boats, and the snow has won her anchor. We may touch at St Helena, but otherwise I must take my leave until we reach our port. God bless and keep you, sweetheart, and the children.' He sighed, smiled, and was about to seal when Stephen walked in, looking mean and pinched. 'Stephen,' he said, 'I have just written to Sophie. Have you any message?'

'Love, of course. And compliments to Mrs Williams.'

'Lord,' cried Jack, writing fast, 'thank you for reminding me. I have explained about Lady Clonfert,' he observed, as he closed the letter up.

'Then I trust you kept your explanation short,' said Stephen. 'Circumstantial details destroy a tale entirely. The longer, the less credible.'

'I merely stated that she did not appear at the rendezvous, and passed on.'

'Nothing about three o'clock in the morning, the hocus-pocus at the inn, signals disregarded, the boat being made to row as though we were escaping from the Day of Judgment, and the lady ditched?' asked Stephen, with the unpleasant creaking noise that was his nearest approach to a laugh.

'What a rattle you are, to be sure,' said Jack. 'Come now, Stephen, how is your patient?'

'Why, he has lost a great deal of blood, it cannot be denied; but then on the other hand I have rarely seen a man with so much blood to lose. He should do very well, with the blessing. He has the late captain's cook with him, a famous artist, and desires he may be kept aboard, if agreeable to the gallant victor.'

'Capital, capital. A famous artist in the galley will set the crown on a very pretty morning's work. Was it not a very pretty morning's work, Stephen?'

'Well,' said Stephen, 'I wish you joy of your capture with all my heart; but if by "pretty" we are to understand an elegant economy of means, I cannot congratulate you. All this banging of great guns for so pitiful a result as the mizzen topmast of a little small slip of a thing, and it embarrassed among the rocks, the creature – Armageddon come before its time. And the infamous backing and filling before the Guineaman is even approached, in spite of her captain's ardent pleas; and all this interminable while no one is allowed to set foot upon these rocks, on the grounds that not a minute is to be lost. Not a minute, forsooth: and forty-seven are wantonly thrown away – forty-seven minutes of invaluable observation that will never be made up.'

'What I know, Stephen, and what you don't know,' began Jack, but a messenger interrupted him: with the Captain's leave, Mr Akers was ready to go aboard. On deck Jack found the south-west breeze setting in steadily, just as if it had been ordered, a perfect breeze to waft the *Hyaena* and her charge to Gibraltar. He gave his letters to the first lieutenant, again recommended the utmost vigilance, and urged him towards the side. Mr Akers displayed a tendency to linger, to express his extreme gratitude for his command (and indeed the recovered *Hyaena* meant his promotion) and to assure Captain Aubrey that if a single prisoner showed his nose above the hatchway it should instantly be blown off with his own grapeshot, but presently he was gone; and leaning over the rail Jack watched the *Boadicea*'s boats carrying him and his companions away. Some went to the man-of-war, to work the ship and guard the prisoners; some to the *Intrepid Fox*, to strengthen her sickly and diminished crew: a surprising number of men in both cases.

Few captains, far from a press-gang, a receiving-ship or any other source of hands, could have smiled at the sight of so many of them pulling awkwardly away to other vessels, never, in all probability, to be seen again, but Jack beamed like the rising sun. Captain Loveless had had excellent connections, and the *Boadicea* a plethoric crew: a good average crew, upon the whole, with no more than a fair share of landsmen and with a gratifying proportion of hands who deserved their rating of able seaman; yet with a number of hard cases too, not worth the food they ate nor the space they occupied, while the last draft had been made up entirely of quota-men from Bedfordshire, odd misfits, petty criminals and vagrants, not one of whom had ever used the sea. The *Hébé*'s English prisoners, right sailormen taken out of the British ships for the most part, together with a couple of prime hands pressed from the *Intrepid Fox*, far more than compensated for their loss; and now, with real satisfaction, Jack watched eight sodomites, three notorious thieves, four men whose wits were quite astray, and a parcel of inveterate skulkers and sea-lawyers go off for good. He was also happy to be rid of a great lout of a midshipman who made the youngsters' lives a burden to them: but above all he was delighted to be seeing the last of his first lieutenant. Mr Akers was a harsh, greying, saturnine man with one leg; the pain from his wound often made him savagely ill-tempered; and he did not see eye to eye with Jack on a number of matters, including flogging. Yet far more important, honourable wound or not, Akers was no seaman: when Jack had first stepped aboard the frigate he found her lying with two round turns and an elbow in her cables, a very disgusting sight; they had lost an hour and twenty minutes clearing their hawse, with *Boadicea*'s signal to proceed to sea flying all the time, reinforced by guns at frequent intervals: and this impression of busy, angry inefficiency had grown stronger day by day.

So there it was: he had made two charming captures; at the same time he had freed himself of men whose presence would have gone far towards preventing the frigate's becoming a fully efficient instrument for distressing the enemy, let alone a happy ship, and he had done so in a way that would confer the utmost benefit on Mr Akers. That was where the prettiness lay. He was now in command of a crew whose collective seamanship was already tolerably good in spite of the remaining fifty or sixty raw hands, and whose gunnery, though of the lowest standard, as it so often was under officers whose one idea of action was a yardarm-to-yardarm engagement where no shot could miss, was certainly capable of improvement. 'Vast capabilities, ma'am, vast capabilities,' he murmured; and then his smile changed to an inward chuckle as he recollected that for once his low cunning had over-reached Stephen Maturin: for what Jack knew, and what Stephen did not, was that those forty-seven minutes had made all the difference between salvage and no salvage, between the *Boadicea*'s right to an eighth of the Guineaman's value and a mere letter of thanks from her owners. The *Intrepid Fox* had been taken at forty-six minutes past ten on Tuesday, and if he had accepted the surrender of the French prize-master one moment before twenty-four hours had passed, by sea-law the Guineaman would not have been salvage at all. And as for Stephen's passing three-quarters of an hour on the Dry Salvages, searching for problematical bugs, Jack had set him down on remote oceanic rocks before now, and had been obliged to have him removed by armed force, long, long after the appointed time: but, however, he would make it up to him – there were coral reefs in plenty on the far side of the Cape.

'Frigate signalling, sir, if you please,' said the signal midshipman. '*Permission to part company*.'

'Say *carry on*,' replied Jack. 'And add *happy return*.'

The *Hyaena* dropped her topsails neatly, sheeted them

home and gathered way, followed by the Guineaman a cable's length to leeward; and having watched them for a while, true on their course for Gibraltar, Jack gave orders that would carry the *Boadicea* slanting away towards the tropic line, close-hauled on the freshening breeze, and walked into his great cabin. The bulkheads, knocked down when the frigate cleared for action, were already back in place, and the two massive eighteen-pounders were housed again, fore and aft; but the starboard gun was still warm, and the smell of powder and slow-match hung about the air, the most exhilarating scent by land or sea. The beautiful room was all his own, with its noble space and its gleaming curve of stern-windows, in spite of his distinguished passenger; for although Mr Farquhar was to be a governor, his status was still highly theoretical, since it depended on the defeat of a powerful French squadron and on the conquest of the islands he was to govern; and for the moment he had to be content with what would otherwise have been the captain's dining-cabin. Jack threw one last loving glance at his captures, dwindling northwards over the sparkling light-blue sea, and called out, 'Pass the word for Mr Seymour, Mr Trollope and Mr Johnson.'

Seymour, the second lieutenant, and Trollope, the third, followed by Johnson, a master's mate, hurried in, looking pleased but somewhat apprehensive: they knew very well that the *Boadicea*, though successful, had not distinguished herself, particularly in the operation of hauling the *Hyaena* off her innocuous ledge of rock and towing her clear of the channel, and they were by no means sure what their new captain would have to say. Seymour and Johnson might almost have been brothers, short, pink, chubby men with round heads and fresh open faces upon which their expression of respectful sobriety seemed less natural than cheerfulness: they were the kind of men Jack had seen a hundred times in his career, and he was happy to have them aboard. He had seen other Trollopes too; Trollope was a big man, black-haired, with a dark, unhumorous, determined face and a strong jaw; he might be a right hard-horse lieutenant under the wrong kind of commander, or a devil of a captain himself, if ever he reached post rank. But for the moment he was young; he was not yet set. They were all young, though Johnson might be nearing thirty – old for his station.

Jack knew very well what was in their minds; as a lieutenant he had often been summoned to bear the blame for others' shortcomings. But what he did not know was that the deferential expression on the faces of these capable, enterprising, seasoned young men was the outcome not merely of respect for his rank but of something resembling awe of his reputation in the service: in his fourteen-gun brig the *Sophie* he had taken the thirty-two-gun Spanish *Cacafuego*; he was one of the few frigate-captains who had ever attacked a French ship of the line, a seventy-four; as acting-captain of the *Lively* he had compelled the *Clara* and the *Fama*, Spaniards of equal force, to strike to him in the memorable frigate-action off Cadiz; and in cutting-out operations and in generally harassing the enemy he had few equals among those of his standing in the Navy list. Jack neither knew it nor suspected it, partly because he still felt very much their contemporary, and partly because he sincerely regarded his more outstanding actions as the effect of luck: he had happened to be on the spot, and in his place any other sea-officer would have done the same. This was not false modesty: he had known officers by the score, good officers, excellent seamen, their courage beyond question, who had served throughout the wars without any chance of distinguishing themselves; men on convoy-duty, in transports, or even in the ships of the line perpetually blockading Brest and Toulon, who very often encountered danger, but from the violence of the sea rather than that of the enemy, and who therefore remained obscure, often unpromoted and always poor: had they been in the right place at the right time, they would have done as well or better: it was a question of luck.

'Well, gentlemen,' he said, 'this is quite a pleasant beginning to a voyage. But we have lost Mr Akers. Mr Seymour, you will be so good as to take his place.'

'Thank you, sir,' said Seymour.

'And Mr Johnson, you have passed for lieutenant, I believe?'

'Oh, yes, sir. On the first Wednesday in August, 1802,' said Johnson, blushing and then turning remarkably pale. He had passed, but as it happened for so many other midshipmen with no influence, the longed-for commission had never come. All these years he had been a master's mate, a senior midshipman, no more, the likelihood of promotion fading with every birthday; it had almost vanished now, and he seemed fated to end his career as a master at the best, a mere warrant-officer until he was thrown on the beach, with never a command of his own. And in the *Boadicea* there were midshipmen with claims far higher than his own: Captain Loveless had shipped the godson of one admiral, the nephew of another, and the heir of the member for Old Sarum; whereas Johnson's father was only a retired lieutenant.

'Then,' said Jack, 'I shall give you an order as acting-lieutenant, and let us hope the Admiral at the Cape will confirm it.'

Johnson, flushed scarlet now, brought out his acknowledgments, and Jack hurried on, 'For I will not disguise from you, gentlemen, that the Cape is our destination. And what you may not know, is that there are four French forty-gun frigates waiting for us round the other side of it. Now today's little brush was very well in its way. It pleased the raw hands – entered 'em, as you might say – and it clapped a stopper over the *Hébé*'s capers; she had been playing Old Harry with our trade these past few weeks. So I believe we may drink a glass of wine to it. Probyn!' he called, Probyn being his steward. 'Rouse out a bottle of Madeira and then jump forward and see that the French captain's cook is comfortably stowed: use him civil. Here's to the *Hyaena*, ex-*Hébé*, then; and a safe landfall to her.' They drank gravely, certain that this was by no means all the Captain had to say. 'Very well in its way,' he continued, 'but I scarcely suppose that any one of you would have called it pretty.'

'Not quite in your Minorca style, sir,' said Trollope.

46

Jack looked hard at the lieutenant. Had they ever been shipmates? He could not recall his face.

'I was a midshipman in *Amelia*, sir, when you brought the *Cacafuego* into Mahon. Lord, how we cheered the *Sophie*!'

'Was you, though?' said Jack, somewhat embarrassed. 'Well, I am glad it was not the *Cacafuego* we came upon today, let alone one of those Frenchmen round the Cape; because although the Boadiceas seem a willing, decent set upon the whole – no sign of shyness that I could see – their gunnery is pitiful beyond all description. And as for pulling, never, never have I seen so many creatures in human shape incapable of handling an oar: in the red cutter there was not one single man apart from old Adams and a Marine that knew how to pull. But it is the gunnery that is my chief concern: pitiful, pitiful . . . Broadside after broadside at five hundred yards and even less; and where did they go? Not aboard the Frenchman, gentlemen. The only shot that told was the one fired from the bow-chaser, and that was pointed by Jack of the bread-room, who had no business to be on deck at all. Now do but imagine that we had run into a well worked-up French frigate, hulling us with her twenty-four-pounders at the best part of a mile: for their practice is devilish accurate, as I dare say you know.' In the solemn pause that followed he refilled their glasses and went on, 'But thank God this happened early: it could not have fallen better. The raw hands are over their seasickness; they are all pleased with themselves, poor honest lubbers; and every foremast Jack is richer by a year's pay, all won in a sunny morning. They must be made to understand that by teaching them their duty we are putting them in the way of getting more. They will attend now, with a good heart; no need for rattans and the rope's end. By the time we reach the Cape, gentlemen, I trust that every man and boy on the ship's books will at least be able to pull an oar, hand and reef a sail, load, point and fire a musket and a gun: and if they can learn no more than that, and to be obedient to command, why, we shall be in a fair way to meet any French frigate on the far side of it.'

With the lieutenants gone, Jack considered for a while. He had no doubt that they were entirely with him; they were the sort of men he knew and liked; but there was still a great deal to be done. With their help he might make the *Boadicea* into a most lethal floating battery of tremendous power; but still she had to be brought to the scene of action, brought as rapidly as the elements would allow. He sent for the master and the bosun, and to them he stated that he was not satisfied with the frigate's sailing, either in the article of speed or in that of lying close to the wind.

There followed a highly technical conference in which he encountered steady resistance from Buchan, the master, an elderly man set in his ways, who would not admit that any restowing of the hold, any attempt to bring her by the head, would have the least favourable effect. Slow she had always been and slow she always would be: he had always stowed the hold in exactly the same way, ever since he had been in her. The bosun, on the other hand, a young man for his important office, a seaman through and through, brought up in the North Sea colliers, was as eager as his captain to get the best out of the *Boadicea*, even if it meant trying something new. He spoke feelingly on the good effect of cat-harpins, well-sniftered in; he entirely agreed with the plan for raking the foremast; Jack's heart warmed to him.

At least a part of Mr Buchan's sullenness arose from hunger. The gun-room dined at one o'clock, an hour now long past; and although today dinner would have been indifferent in any case, its absence rendered the master positively morose. The bosun had dined at noon together with the carpenter and the gunner, and Buchan, smelling both food and grog upon him, hated his cheerful face; even more his steady flow of talk.

Jack too was somewhat given to worshipping his belly, and when he had dismissed them he walked into the coach: here he found Stephen and Mr Farquhar, eating cake. 'Do I interrupt you?' he asked: not at all, they said, clearing a space for him among the books, documents, maps, proclamations and broadsheets that they were trying to reassemble after the abrupt disappearance and reappearance of their quarters. 'I hope I see you well, sir?' he said to Mr Farquhar, who had suffered more than most in the Bay of Biscay and who had spent much of the time since rising from his cot in conference with Dr Maturin, the two of them deep in papers, talking foreign to the intense vexation of their servants, two ship's boys told off to look after them, who liked to indulge their natural curiosity – a curiosity much stimulated by their shipmates before the mast, eager to know what was afoot. Farquhar had lost a stone, and his lean, intelligent, hook-nosed face still had a greenish tinge, but he replied that he had never felt better in his life, that the tremendous din of battle, the more than Jovian thunder of the guns, had completed the work – with a civil bow to Stephen – of Dr Maturin's preternatural physic, so that he felt like a boy again; he had a boy's appetite, a restless eagerness to be at table. 'But,' he went on, 'you must first allow me to congratulate you most heartily upon your splendid victory. Such instant decision, such a determined onslaught, and such a happy issue!'

'You are too kind, sir, too kind by half. But as for the happy issue that you are so obliging as to mention, it has one aspect that cannot but rejoice us all. We have the French captain's cook aboard, and I am come' – turning towards Stephen – 'to ask whether you think he might be persuaded . . . ?'

'I have already attended to him,' said Stephen. 'A sucking pig, one of a large surviving farrow, was one of the few casualties aboard the *Hébé*, and I understand that it is to provide a first example of his powers. I have also seen to it that Monsieur Bretonnière's wine and comforts have been transferred: to these I thought fit to add his late captain's stores; foie gras in jars, truffles in goose-grease, pieces of goose in goose-grease, a large variety of dried sausages, Bayonne hams, potted anchovies; and among the rest of the wine, twenty-one dozens of Margaux of '88, with the long cork, together with an almost equal quantity of Château Lafite. Sure, I cannot tell how we shall ever get through them all; yet it would be the world's shame to let such noble wine go back, and in these conditions another year must see it the mere ghost of itself.'

The claret never saw another year, however, nor did that splendid vintage go to waste: with steady application and with some help from Bretonnière and other guests from the gun-room Jack and Stephen drank almost every drop as the days went by. And there were days enough in all conscience, since the kind winds of their departure deserted them well north of the line, and sometimes they would lie on the oily, heaving sea, drifting slowly towards America on the equatorial current, with the *Boadicea's* figurehead simpering all round the compass and the frigate nearly rolling her masts by the board. Ten days on end when she wallowed with flaccid sails on the stagnant water, clean in herself but so surrounded by the filth of three hundred men – by Admiral Brown as the old hands called it – and by her own empty beef-casks, peelings and general rubbish that Jack was obliged to take the jolly-boat a quarter of a mile away for his morning's swim, while at the same time he caused the crew to tow their ship, thus rendering the view more agreeable and training them in the art of managing an oar, so beating two birds with one bush, as he put it, or even three, since after they had pulled her for an hour or two it was the *Boadicea's* custom to lower a sail into the pure, tepid water, buoying its outer corners and thereby making a shallow pool in which those who could not swim – the great majority – might splash about and enjoy themselves, perhaps learning how to stay afloat in the process.

But they crossed the line itself in style, with studdingsails aloft and alow, and with more than the usual merriment, for when they reduced sail to let Neptune come aboard, accompanied by an outrageously lewd Amphitrite and Badger-Bag, he found no less than a hundred and twenty-three souls who had to be made free of the equator by being lathered with rancid grease – tar was forbidden, being in short supply – and shaved with a piece of barrel-hoop before being ducked.

Southward still, with Canopus and Achernar high over-head, and Jack showed his attentive midshipmen the new constellations, Musca, Pavo, Chamaeleon and many more, all glowing in the warm, pellucid air.

Strange, unpredictable weather, for even when the *Boadicea* found the trades in 4°S they proved apathetic and fitful. It was clear that this was not to be a rapid passage, but although Jack often whistled for a breeze, a stronger breeze, he was not deeply worried by the length of their voyage: his ship was well-found, several storms of rain had filled her water, and her men were remarkably healthy; and as the weeks turned into months it came to him that this was a happy period, a time set apart, lying between the anxieties of home on the one hand and those that would surely be waiting for him in the Indian Ocean, where his real work would begin. And then although he longed for the 'real thing' to start, he knew that no power on earth could bring him to it any earlier: he and Fellowes had done all they could to increase the frigate's rate of sailing, and they had accomplished much; but they could not command the wind. So with a tranquil conscience and that fatalism which sailors must acquire if they are not to perish of frustration, he rejoiced in this opportunity for making the *Boadicea* into something like his notion of a crack frigate, a fighting-machine manned entirely by able seamen, men-of-war's men, every one of them an expert gun-layer and a devil with the boarding-axe and cutlass.

Insensibly the lubberly part of the *Boadicea's* crew began to resemble sailormen as the unchanging naval routine came to be their only real way of life, a life in which it was natural and inevitable that all hands should be piped just before eight bells in the middle watch and that the sleepers should start from their hammocks to the muster and then to the scrubbing of the decks in the first light of dawn; that all hands should be piped to dinner at eight bells in the forenoon watch, that this dinner should consist of cheese and duff on Monday, two pounds of salt beef on Tuesday, dried peas and duff on Wednesday, one pound of salt pork on

Thursday, dried peas and cheese on Friday, two more pounds of salt beef on Saturday, a pound of salt pork and some such treat as figgy-dowdy on Sunday, always accompanied by a daily pound of biscuit; that at one bell dinner should be followed by a pint of grog, that after supper (with another pint of grog) all hands should repair to their action-stations at the beat of the drum, and that eventually hammocks should be piped down so that the watch below might have four hours of sleep before being roused again at midnight for another spell on deck. This and the perpetual living movement of the deck underfoot, and the sight of nothing but the Atlantic Ocean clear round the horizon, nothing but endless sea and sky, cut them off from the land so completely that it seemed another world, with no immediacy at all, and they adopted the values of the sea.

They also came to resemble sailormen in appearance, since one hour and forty minutes after the *Boadicea* had passed under the tropic of Cancer the carpenter's mate banged two brass nails into the deck, exactly twelve yards apart: twelve yards of duck, needles and thread were served out to each man, together with sennet, and they were desired to make themselves hot-weather frocks, trousers and broad-brimmed hats. This they did, helped by their handier colleagues, to such effect that at next Sunday's divisions the landsmen dressed in a mixture of rag-fair clothes and purser's slops, old leather breeches, greasy waistcoats and battered hats, had vanished, and their captain paced along lines of men as clean and white in their way as the Marines, drawn up on the quarterdeck, were clean and red in theirs.

There were still some fools belonging to the afterguard who were only good for heaving on a given rope; there were a dozen or so in either watch whose heads could not stand the swingeing ration of grog and who were continually punished for drunkenness; and there were some remaining hard cases; but on the whole he was pleased with them: a very decent set of men. He was pleased with his officers too, apart from Buchan and the purser, a very tall yellow-faced man with knock-knees and huge splay feet, upon whose books

Jack kept a very sharp eye indeed: all three lieutenants seconded him with admirable zeal, and the older midshipmen were of real value.

Not the least part of that wonderfully lucky stroke off the Dry Salvages was the *Boadicea*'s acquisition of a large quantity of ammunition. Regulations confined Jack to a hundred round-shot for each of his long eighteen-pounders, and he had to hoard them with jealous care, for there was no certainty of any more at the Cape – a wretched situation in which he knew that if he did not train his gun-crews by firing live they would not know how to do it when the moment came, and that if he did then at the same critical juncture they might have nothing left to fire – but from that blessed day onwards the *Boadicea*'s daily exercise with the great guns had not been the usual dumbshow. Certainly the crews rattled their eighteen-pounders in and out, going through all the motions of firing them, from casting loose to housing; but since the *Hébé*'s twenty-four-pound balls fitted the *Boadicea*'s carronades and her nine-pound the two chase-guns, every evening heard their savage roar: every man was accustomed to the deadly leap of the recoiling gun, to the flash and the din and to seizing his tackle, rammer or wad with automatic speed in the dense swirling powder-smoke. And on high days, as when they saluted the tropic of Capricorn with a double broadside, it was a pleasure to see their spirit: they demolished a raft of empty beef-barrels at something over five hundred yards and ran their guns up again, cheering madly, to blast the scattered remains in a trifle less than two minutes. It was nothing like the mortal rate of fire that Jack so valued; it was not even the three broadsides in five minutes that was coming to be thought normal by those captains who cared for gunnery, far less the three in two minutes that Jack had achieved in other commissions; but it was accurate, and a good deal faster than some ships he knew.

This 'time out', this happy interval with a straightforward and agreeable task in hand, sailing through warm seas with winds that, though often languid, were rarely downright

53

contrary, sailing southwards in a comfortable ship with an excellent cook, ample stores and good company, had its less delightful sides, however.

His telescope was a disappointment. It was not that he could not see Jupiter: the planet gleamed in his eyepiece like a banded gold pea. But because of the ship's motion he could not keep it there long enough or steadily enough to fix the local time of its moons' eclipses and thus find his longitude. Neither the theory (which was by no means new) nor the telescope was at fault: it was the cleverly weighted cradle slung from the main topgallant mast stay that he had designed to compensate for the pitch and roll that did not answer, in spite of all his alterations; and night after night he swung there cursing and swearing, surrounded by midshipmen armed with clean swabs, whose duty it was to enhance the compensation by thrusting him gently at the word of command.

The young gentlemen: he led them a hard life, insisting upon a very high degree of promptitude and activity; but apart from these sessions with the telescope, which they loathed entirely, and from their navigation classes, they thoroughly approved of their captain and of the splendid breakfasts and dinners to which he often invited them, although on due occasion he beat them with frightful strength on the bare breech in his cabin, usually for such crimes as stealing the gun-room's food or repeatedly walking about with their hands in their pockets. For his part he found them an engaging set of young fellows, though given to lying long in their hammocks, to consulting their ease, and to greed; and in one of them, Mr Richardson, generally known as Spotted Dick, because of his pimples, he detected a mathematician of uncommon promise. Jack taught them navigation himself, the *Boadicea*'s schoolmaster being incapable of maintaining discipline, and it soon became apparent to him that he should have to keep his wits as sharp as his razor not to be outstripped by his pupil in the finer points of spherical trigonometry, to say nothing of the stars.

Then there was Mr Farquhar. Jack esteemed him as an

intelligent, capable, gentlemanlike man with remarkable powers of conversation, excellent company for the space of a dinner, although he drank no wine, or even for a week; but Mr Farquhar had been bred to the law, and perhaps because of this a little too much of his conversation took the form of questioning, so that Jack sometimes felt that he was being examined at his own table. Furthermore, Mr Farquhar often used Latin expressions that made Jack uneasy, and referred to authors Jack had never read: Stephen had always done the same (indeed, it would have been difficult to refer to any author with whom Jack was acquainted apart from those who wrote on foxhunting, naval tactics, or astronomy), but with Stephen it was entirely different. Jack loved him, and had not the least objection to granting him all the erudition in the world, while remaining inwardly convinced that in all practical matters other than physic and surgery Stephen should never be allowed out alone. Mr Farquhar, however, seemed to assume that a deep knowledge of the law and of public business embraced the whole field of useful human endeavour.

Yet Mr Farquhar's vastly superior knowledge of politics and even his far more galling superiority at chess would have been as nothing if he had had some ear for music: he had none. It was their love of music that had brought Jack and Stephen together in the first place: the one played the fiddle and the other the 'cello, neither brilliantly, yet both well enough to take deep pleasure in their evening concerts after retreat; they had played throughout every voyage they had made together, never interrupted by anything but the requirements of the service, the utmost extremity of foul weather, or by the enemy. But now Mr Farquhar was sharing the great cabin, and he was as indifferent to Haydn as he was to Mozart; as he observed, he would not give a farthing candle for either of them, or for Handel. The rustling of his book as they played, the way he tapped his snuffbox and blew his nose, took away from their pleasure; and in any case, Jack, brought up in the tradition of naval hospitality, felt bound to do all he could to make his guest comfortable, even to the extent of giving up his fiddle in favour of whist, which he did not care for, and of calling in the senior Marine lieutenant as the fourth, a man he did not much care for either.

Their guest was not always with them, however, for during the frequent calms Jack often took the jolly-boat and rowed away to swim, to inspect the frigate's trim from a distance, and to talk with Stephen in private. 'You cannot possibly dislike him,' he said, skimming over the swell towards a patch of drifting weed where Stephen thought it possible they might find a southern variety of sea-horse or a pelagic crab related to those he had discovered under the line, 'but I shall not be altogether sorry to set him down on shore.'

'I can and do dislike him intensely when he pins my king and a rook with his lurking knight,' said Stephen. 'At most other times I find him a valuable companion, an eager, searching, perspicacious intelligence. To be sure, he has no ear at all, but he is not without a tincture of poetry: he has an interesting theory on the mystic role of kings, founded upon his study of tenures in petty serjeanty.'

Jack's concern with petty serjeanty was so slight that he carried straight on, 'I dare say I have been in command too long. When I was a lieutenant, messing with the rest, I used to put up with people far, far more trying than Farquhar. There was a surgeon in the *Agamemnon* that used to play "Greensleeves" on his flute every evening, and every evening he broke down at exactly the same place. Harry Turnbull, our premier – he was killed at the Nile – used to turn pale as he came nearer and nearer to it. That was in the West Indies, and tempers were uncommon short but no one said anything except Clonfert. It don't sound much, "Greensleeves", but it was a pretty good example of that give and take there has to be, when you are all crammed up together for a long commission: for if you start falling out, why, there's an end to all comfort, as you know very well, Stephen. I wish I may not have lost the way of it, what with age and the luxury of being post – the luxury of solitude.'

'So you are acquainted with Lord Clonfert, I find? What kind of a man is he, tell?'

'Ours was a very slight acquaintance,' said Jack evasively. 'He only came into the ship just before we were ordered home, and then he exchanged into the *Mars*.'

'An able, dashing man, I believe?'

'Oh,' said Jack, gazing beyond Stephen's head at the *Boadicea*, a lovely sight on the lonely sea, 'the *Agamemnon's* wardroom was crowded, she wearing a flag; so I hardly knew him. But he has made quite a reputation for himself since those days.'

Stephen sniffed. He was perfectly aware of Jack's dislike for saying anything unpleasant about a former shipmate, and although he honoured the principle in theory, in practice he found it somewhat irritating.

Jack's acquaintance with Lord Clonfert had in fact been brief, but it had left its mark. They had been ordered away with the boats to take, burn or destroy a privateer lying far up a broad, shallow creek, out of range of the *Agamemnon's* guns, an estuary lined with mangroves, whose unbuoyed channels through the mudbanks presented many interesting problems of navigation, particularly as the boats had to advance against the fire of the privateer and of some guns planted on the shore.

Clonfert's boats took the north channel, Jack's the southern; and by the time of the final dash across the open water where the privateer was moored, Clonfert's were grouped behind a spit of land somewhat nearer to the ship than Jack's. Jack emerged from the narrow channel, waved his hat, gave a cheer, urged his men 'to stretch out now, like good 'uns' and steered straight for the enemy's starboard mainchains through the heavy smoke, convinced that Clonfert's party would board on the other side. He heard the answering cheer, but it was the cheer of spectators rather than of participants: Clonfert's boats did not intend to stir. Jack realized this in the last fifty yards, but he was committed and it was too late to do anything but race on. The privateersmen fought hard: they killed several Agamemnons,

57

among them a midshipman to whom Jack was much attached, and wounded many more. For some minutes it was doubtful who should drive whom over the side – a cruel, bitter little action, vicious hand-to-hand murder in the fading light – and then the French captain, flinging his empty pistols at Jack's head, leapt the rail and swam for it, followed by most of his remaining men. It was not the safety of the shore that he was seeking, however, but the second battery of guns that he had mounted there; and these he turned straight on to the ship, to sweep her deck with grape at point-blank range. Although Jack had received a shrewd rap on the head, his wits were about him still, and before the first discharge he had cut the cables and let fall the foretopsail to the nascent land-breeze, so that there was already way upon her when the fire began. With the luck that never deserted him in those days he steered her through the one channel in which she would not ground, and the light air took her out; though not before the grapeshot had wounded another man, cut away the crossjack halliards, and scored him across the ribs with a wound like a blow from a red-hot poker, knocking him flat into a pool of blood. They picked up the other boats and returned to the *Agamemnon*, Clonfert taking over.

Jack was scarcely conscious of going up the side. He grieved extremely for the boy who had been killed; his mind was dulled by pain and by the fever that followed so quickly in that climate; and Clonfert's eager explanation – 'he was right up against a mudbank – he was pinned down by the shore-battery – it would have been suicide to move – he was in the very act of landing to take it from behind when Aubrey made his gallant dash' – seemed to him uninteresting and unimportant. Later, when he was fit for duty again, it did seem to him a little strange that the official letter should have omitted his name and have given Clonfert quite so much credit; though indeed Clonfert was senior to him at that time; and then again half a dozen privateersmen, unable to swim, had taken refuge below, where they had had to be overcome after Clonfert's taking over. But by that time

Clonfert had exchanged into the *Mars*; and Jack, homeward-bound in the *Agamemnon*, soon forgot the incident, retaining only an inward conviction that Clonfert was either singularly muddle-headed and unenterprising or that he was somewhat shy. None of the other officers in the wardroom offered an opinion – their silence was significant – and in the turmoil of the succeeding years Jack would scarcely have remembered Clonfert but for the noise he made sometimes in the newspapers, as when he was cast in damages for criminal conversation with Mrs Jennings, or on the occasion of his court-martial for striking another officer on the quarterdeck of HMS *Ramillies*, and sometimes more creditably in the Gazette. His court-martial had led to his being dismissed the service, and although after some time he had been reinstated by order-in-council he necessarily lost seniority: on the other hand, during the interval he took service with the Turks, and the experience proved uncommonly useful when, as a King's officer once more, he attached himself to Sir Sydney Smith. He was with that somewhat flamboyant gentleman at Acre when Smith forced Buonaparte to retire, and in other creditable actions, mostly on shore; and Smith praised him highly in his public letters: indeed Clonfert and the Admiral agreed well together – they were both seen walking about London wearing Oriental robes – and it was due to him that Clonfert was made a commander, his present rank. Jack was well aware that Gazettes might suppress truth and suggest falsehood, but he knew that they could not possibly invent victories such as the destruction of a Turkish squadron or the spiking of the guns of Abydos; and on these occasions it occurred to him that he might have been mistaken about Clonfert's want of courage. The reflection did not linger, however: quite apart from the fact that Clonfert was not a man whom Jack had taken to, he was a follower of Smith; and Smith, though dashing, was a vain, showy man who had given Nelson much uneasiness in the Mediterranean. Jack's admiration and respect for Nelson was such that his opponents could find no friend in Captain Aubrey. His mind ran on to admirals, their rivalries, the ill-effect of these rivalries, the problems of high and necessarily remote command.

'Why, brother, what a study you are in,' said Stephen. 'We shall certainly row clean through my weed, if you go on at this unconsidered pace. Pray, what is in your mind? Dread of the French, no doubt?'

'Certainly,' said Jack shipping his oars, 'they make my heart die within me. But what concerns me most, as we get nearer to the Cape, is the possibility of a pennant, and what comes with it.'

'I do not understand you – a little to the left, if you please; I believe I see a cephalopod among the wrack. He is gone, the thief. Row gently, joy, and I shall trail my little net. I do not understand you: the ship has a perfectly good pennant at this moment; surely you must have noticed it.' He nodded towards the *Boadicea*, from whose masthead dropped the long streamer that showed she was in commission.

'What I mean is the broad pennant.' Stephen looked stupid. 'The *broad* pennant, Stephen, that shows you are a commodore: and what comes with it is high command. For the first time you are as who should say a flag, an admiral; and you have an admiral's responsibilities of command.'

'What of it, my dear? To my certain knowledge you have always exercised command efficiently: I doubt I could have done much better myself. You say belay, and he belayeth. What more can you desire, for all love?' Stephen spoke with only a small part of his attention: all the rest was concentrated upon the cephalopod, though indeed he did murmur something about commodores – he remembered them perfectly – the chief Indiaman of the fleet that had succoured them so providentially after their affray with Monsieur de Linois had been called the commodore.

'Why, don't you see,' cried Jack, his mind fixed upon this question of command, 'it has always been the command of a single ship. You are bred up to it – it comes natural. But high command is something you come to suddenly, with no experience. There are captains under you; and handling the captains of a squadron, each one of them God the Father of his own quarterdeck, is a very different matter from handling a ship's company under your own eye. You can rarely choose them and you can rarely get rid of them; and if you do not handle them right, then the squadron is inefficient, and there's the devil to pay with tar. A good understanding is more important than I can tell you. Nelson could do it as easy as kiss my hand . . . the band of brothers, you know . . .' His voice trailed away, and as he watched Stephen grubbing among the weed he thought of cases where admirals or commodores had lacked the Nelson touch: a melancholy list – bitter ill-feeling, indecisive actions, golden opportunities thrown away for lack of support, strict obedience to the letter of the Fighting Instructions, courts-martial, and above all the enemy roaming about the sea unchecked. 'Corbett's reputation is sound enough, so is Pym's,' he said almost to himself, and then louder, 'But now I come to think of it, Stephen, you should know all about Clonfert. He is a countryman of yours, an eminent chap, I dare say, in Ireland.'

'Sure, it is an Irish title,' said Stephen, 'but Clonfert is as much an Englishman as you are yourself. The family name is Scroggs. They have some acres of bog and what they call a castle near Jenkinsville in the bleak north – I know it well; *anthea foetidissima* grows there – and a demesne south of the Curragh of Kildare, forfeited Desmond land; but I doubt he has ever set foot on it. A Scotch agent looks after what rents he can rack out of the tenants.'

'But he is a peer, is he not? A man of some real consequence?'

'Bless your innocence, Jack: an Irish peer is not necessarily a man of any consequence at all. I do not wish to make any uncivil reflection on your country – many of my best friends are Englishmen – but you must know that this last hundred years and more it has been the practice of the English ministry to reward their less presentable followers with Irish titles; and your second-rate jobbing backstairs politician, given a coronet of sorts and transplanted into a country where he is a stranger, is a pitiful spectacle, so he is; a flash Brummagem imitation of the real thing. I should be sorry if the Irish peers, for the most part of them, were Irishmen. Apart from certain naval lords, that the ministry dare not have in the English House, they are a shabby crew, upon the whole, out of place in Ireland and ill-at-ease in England. I do not speak of your Fitzgeralds or Butlers, you understand, still less of the few native families that have survived, but of what is commonly called an Irish peer. Clonfert's grandfather, now, was a mere – Jack, what are you about?'

'I am taking off my shirt.'

'To swim so soon after dinner, and such a dinner? I cannot advise it. You are very corpulent; full of gross, viscous humours after these weeks and months of Poirier's cooking. And now we are come to the point, my dear, it is my clear duty to warn you against gule, against ungoverned appetite . . . a brutish vice, inductive mainly to the sin of Eve . . . bulimy, bulimy . . . dinners have killed more men than ever Avicenna healed . . .' he prosed away while Jack took off his trousers. 'So you are determined on your bathe?' he said, looking at his naked companion. 'Will you let me see your back, now?' He ran his fingers over the dull-blue scar and asked, 'Do you feel it, these days?'

'Just a trifle, this morning,' said Jack. 'But otherwise, from the time we cleared the Channel until yesterday, never a twinge. A swim,' he said, slipping over the side and plunging deep into the pure blue water with his long yellow hair streaming out behind him, 'is the very thing for it,' he continued, rising to the surface and blowing hard. 'God, it is so refreshing, even though it is as warm as milk. Come on, Stephen, bathe while you may. For tomorrow we reach the cold current setting north, the green water and the westerlies, I trust; you will have your mollymawks and your pintadoes and maybe your albatrosses, but there will be no more swimming till the Cape.'

Chapter Three

Ever since the *Boadicea* had made her landfall all hands had been in a state of feverish activity, putting the last touches to her beauty: now it was almost over, and she stood into False Bay with a fair breeze rounding her studdingsails and wafting the reek of fresh paint along with her. The only stage still to obscure her spotless black and white Nelson chequer was that occupied by the carpenters' mates, applying carmine with anxious care to the lips, cheeks and bosom of the opulent though insipid British queen.

Jack, already fine in his best uniform, stood by the starboard rail of the quarterdeck with Mr Farquhar beside him. A little farther forward the gunner blew on his slow-match by the brass nine-pounder: all the other guns were housed, ranged with the perfection of the Guards on parade, their breeching pipeclayed. Seymour was a conscientious first lieutenant, and the deck was a pleasure to behold – the gleaming pallor of the wood, the ebony of the seams new-laid with pitch, the falls precisely flemished, a series of exact helices that no man dared disturb, the few pieces of brass the captain would permit blazing in the sun, no speck of dust to be seen from stem to stern, the hen-coops, the surviving swine struck down into the hold together with the goat, which, in the general silence, could be heard bleating angrily for its long-overdue tobacco. The general silence, for all hands were on deck in their Sunday frocks, and they gazed earnestly, mutely at the shore, upon which people could now be seen walking about – walking about on dry land, among trees! – most of them perceptibly black: the only sounds to be heard, apart from the goat, were the bark of the master conning the ship from the forecastle, the ritual answers of the timoneer, the chant of the leadsman in the chains: 'By the mark, fifteen: by the mark, fifteen: and a half, fifteen: by the deep, sixteen: and a half, fifteen', and the conversational voice of the Captain as he pointed out various objects to his guest.

'That flat rock is what we call Noah's Ark, and far over there is Seal Island – the Doctor will like that. And beyond the Ark where you see the white water is the Roman Rock: we shall pass between the two. Indeed, we shall open Simon's Bay at any minute now. Mr Richardson, pray see if the Doctor has finished – whether he can come on deck – he would be sorry to miss all this. Yes, there we are,' he went on, with his telescope to his eye as the inner harbour came into full view. '*Raisonable*, do you see? The two-decker. Then *Sirius*: *Néréide* lying inside her, a very pretty berth: then a brig I cannot make out at all. Mr Seymour, what do you make of the brig with her topmasts on deck?' At this point Stephen appeared, blinking in the strong light, wiping his bloody hands on a woollen nightcap and looking squalid. 'Ah, there you are, Doctor,' cried Jack. 'Have you finished sawing up poor young Francis? How is he coming along? Prime, I dare say?' Francis, until today the most popular topman in the ship, endeavouring to gild the *Boadicea*'s main topgallant truck, had lost his hold, making a most spectacular fall from that giddy eminence, missing the deck (and certain death) by the grace of the frigate's roll, but grazing her number twelve portlid with such force as to play havoc with his thoracic cage and above all to smear the bleeding paintwork, the grass-combing bugger.

'He may do,' said Stephen. 'These young fellows are made of steel and a particularly resilient leather. So that is Africa.' He looked greedily at the shore, the known haunt of the aardvark, the pangolin, the camelopard; of birds without number, roaming at large amidst a flora of extraordinary wealth, headed by the ostrich. 'And that,' pointing towards a remote headland, 'is the all-dreaded Cape of Storms itself, I make no doubt?'

'Not exactly,' said Jack. 'The Cape is far astern: I am

sorry you did not see it. We came round precious close while you was busy. But before that you did see the Table Mountain, did you not? I sent a messenger.'

'Yes, yes. I felt most obliged to you, in spite of the unchristian hour. It might also be compared with Ben Bulben.'

'Curious, ain't it? And now here on the larboard bow – no, the larboard – you have Simon's Bay, a sweet anchorage. And there's *Raisonable*, wearing the flag.'

'Would that be a line-of-battle ship?' asked Farquhar. 'A most imposing vessel.'

'I doubt any sixty-four would ever lie in the line nowadays,' said Jack. 'In any case, the *Raisonable* was built fifty years ago, and if she fired a full broadside she might fall to pieces; but I am glad she looks imposing. Then comes *Sirius*, a much more powerful ship in fact, although she has but one tier of guns; thirty-six eighteen-pounders, much the same broadside weight of metal as ours. Then another frigate, do you see? *Néréide*, thirty-six; but only twelve-pounders. Then that odd little brig-of-war.'

'Pray, sir, why are they not at sea?' asked Farquhar. 'As I understand it, those and a smaller vessel called the *Otter* are almost all we have to guard the Indian trade. I ask out of mere curiosity.'

'Oh,' said Jack, 'this is the tail-end of the hurricane season up there. They could hardly be blockading the Mauritius in the hurricane season. They are probably in to refit and to take in stores – nothing for them up there, two thousand miles to the north . . . Mr Johnson, I believe you may begin to reduce sail.'

His eyes were fixed to his glass: the *Boadicea* had made her number and he was watching for the master-attendant's boat to put off. There it was, just leaving the pier. Although the frigate was now under fore and main topsails alone, still she glided in, heaved on by the moderate south-east swell and the making tide, and the shore came fast towards him. The moment he had the Admiralty House square on he would begin his salute; and while he waited for that moment to come he had the strangest feeling that at the first gun

England and his whole voyage south would vanish into the past.

'Carry on, Mr Webber,' he said, and as he spoke the nine-pounder bawled out its respects with a tongue of fire in a cloud of smoke.

'Fire one,' said the gunner; and the echoes came hurrying back from the mountains. 'Fire two. Fire three . . .' By the seventeenth gun the great bay was alive with crossing reverberations, and before they had died away a puff of smoke appeared on the *Raisonable*'s side, followed a second later by the deep report. Nine guns she fired, the reply due to a captain, and after the ninth the *Boadicea*'s signal-midshipman, young Weatherall, piped, 'Flag signalling, sir.' Then his voice broke to a harsh bass as he went on, '*Captain repair aboard flag.*'

'Acknowledge,' said Jack. 'Lower away the gig. Where's my coxswain? Pass the word for my coxswain.'

'I am sorry, sir,' said Johnson, blushing. 'Moon is drunk.'

'Damn him,' said Jack. 'Crompton, jump into the gig. Mr Hill, are these all my papers? Every last one?' Clasping the packet of sealed, canvas-covered documents to his bosom he ran down the side, caught the heaving gig on the height of its rise, and said, 'Shove off.'

It was many, many years since he had last been here, a midshipman, an oldster, in the *Resolution*, yet how exactly he remembered it all; there were a few more civilian houses in the village at the bottom of the bay, but everything else was just the same – the steady beat of the surf, the mountains, the men-of-war's boats crossing to and fro, the hospital, the barracks, the arsenal: he might himself have been a lanky boy, returning to the *Resolution* after catching Roman-fish off the rocks. He was filled with a pleasurable excitement, with countless memories, yet at the same time with an apprehension that he could not define.

'Boat ahoy?' asked the *Raisonable*.

'*Boadicea*,' replied the acting coxswain in a voice of brass; and then more quietly he said, 'Rowed of all.' The gig kissed against the tall flank of the flagship, the sideboys ran down

66

with their scarlet man-ropes, the bosun started his call, and Jack was piped aboard. As he took off his cocked hat he realized with a shock that the tall bowed white-haired figure who answered his salute was the Admiral Bertie he had last seen in Port of Spain as the lithe, lively, wenching captain of the *Renown*; and some part of his busy mind said to him, beneath all the rest, 'Perhaps you are not so very young yourself, either, Jack Aubrey.'

'Here you are at last, Aubrey,' said the Admiral, shaking his hand. 'I am very happy to see you. You know Captain Eliot?'

'Yes, sir; we were shipmates in the *Leander* in 'ninety-eight. How do you do, sir?'

Before Eliot could reply with anything more than an extension of the friendly smile that he had worn ever since Jack's face appeared, the Admiral went on, 'I dare say those papers are for me? Come along; let's have a look at them in the cabin.' Splendour; opulence; carpets; a portrait of Mrs Bertie, looking plump and comfortable. 'Well,' he said, wrestling with the outer covers, 'so you had a tedious passage of it: but did you have any luck on your way down? They used to call you Lucky Jack Aubrey in the Mediterranean, I remember. God damn these seals.'

'We saw barely a sail, sir; but we did have a little brush off the Dry Salvages, and retook the old *Hyaena*.'

'Did you? Did you, indeed? Well, I am heartily glad of it . . .' The papers were free now, and as he glanced through them he said, 'Yes. I have been expecting these. We must take them along to the Governor at once. But you have a politico aboard, I see? A Mr Farquhar? He must come too: I shall send my barge, by way of compliment; you cannot be too careful with these political gents. You had better order some cool clothes, too; it is a twenty-mile ride to Cape Town. The Governor will not object to nankeen trousers and a round jacket.' He gave his orders and called for a bottle of wine. 'This is the right Diamant of the year one, Aubrey,' he said, sitting down again. 'Too good for you young fellows but you did retake the old *Hyaena*. . . I was a midshipman in her. Yes.' His washed-out blue eyes looked back over forty-five years, and he observed, 'That was in the days before carronades.' Returning to the present he drank his wine, saying, 'I trust your luck will hold, Aubrey: you need it, on this station. Well, and so we shall have to fag over that damned mountain, a wearying ride in this infernal dust – dust everywhere, rain or shine; a whole nation of swabbers would never come to an end of it. I wish we did not have to go. If it were not for the political side, I should get you to sea the minute you had your water aboard. The situation is far worse than ever it was before you left England – far worse than when these orders were written. The French have snapped up two more Indiamen, this side of the Ten Degree Channel, the *Europe* and the *Streatham*: homeward-bound Indiamen, worth a mint of money.'

'Lord, sir, that is very bad,' cried Jack.

'Yes, it is,' said the Admiral, 'and it is going to get even worse unless we bring it up with a round turn, and smartly at that. That is what we must do: it is feasible, and it must be done. Oh, yes, it is feasible, with a certain amount of initiative . . . and maybe I should add good fortune too, though luck don't bear talking about.' He touched wood, considered for a while, and then said, 'Listen, Aubrey, before your Mr Farquhar comes aboard – before we start getting entangled in political considerations – I shall lay the position before you as clearly as I can. There are four French frigates based on Mauritius and Réunion, in addition to the force they had there last year: they can use Port Louis or Port South-East in Mauritius and Saint-Paul in Réunion, and separately or in pairs they can range out as far as the Nicobars and beyond – the whole Indian Ocean. You can't catch them out there; we can't convoy all the Eastern trade – we do not possess the ships; and you can't blockade them for ever. So you must either destroy them in detail in their home waters or eventually you must take their bases away from them. Now with this in mind, we have seized and garrisoned Rodriguez with part of the 56th and some Bombay sepoys, for your water in the first place, and in the second as a base for the reinforcements that are supposed to come from India in time. There are only about four hundred men on the island at present, but we hope for more next year – it is a question of transports. You know Rodriguez?'

'Yes, sir. I have not touched there, however.' Rodriguez: a remote and tolerably barren speck of land alone in the ocean, three hundred and fifty miles eastward of Mauritius: he had viewed it from the masthead of his dear *Surprise*.

'So at least you have your water. As for ships, you have *Boadicea*, of course; *Sirius*, with a good steady captain in Pym, as regular as a clock; *Néréide* – she is only a twelve-pounder, and getting on in years, but Corbett keeps her in very good order though he is rather undermanned; *Otter*, a fast, useful eighteen-gun sloop, in very good order too. Lord Clonfert has her: she should be in any moment now. And I can let you have *Raisonable* except in the hurricane months, for she cannot bear a hard blow. She is not all she was when I was a boy, but we careened her a few weeks ago, and she is quite fast. At least she is a match for the *Canonnière*, who is older still; and she makes a show. I might conceivably be able to add the *Magicienne* from Sumatra, in time, and the *Victor*, another sloop. But even without them, I conceive that, *Raisonable* cancelling out *Canonnière*, three well worked-up frigates and a powerful sloop would not be reckoned out of the way for dealing with four Frenchmen.'

'Certainly not, sir,' said Jack. The Admiral was speaking as though Jack's pennant were a certainty.

'No one will pretend it is an easy task, however. The Frenchmen are *Vénus*, *Manche*, *Caroline* – it was she who took the last two Indiamen – and *Bellone*, all new forty-gun frigates. As for the rest, they have the *Canonnière*, as I have said, still mounting her fifty guns, our brig the *Grappler*, several avisoes and a few smaller things. And I warn you, Aubrey, if you hoist your pennant, I cannot let you have a captain under you. If you shift into the *Raisonable* for the time being, Eliot can replace you in *Boadicea*; but I cannot let you have a captain under you.' Jack bowed. He had scarcely relied upon it: on the remoter stations there were few post-captains to spare; and then again if a commodore did have a captain under him, that commodore was entitled to a third of the Admiral's share of prize-money.

'May I ask whether we have any intelligence of their land forces, sir?' he said.

'Yes, but I wish it were more exact. On Mauritius General Decaen has the best part of two regiments of the line, and his militia may amount to ten thousand or so. Our information from Réunion is more scanty, but it seems that General Desbrusleys has much the same. Oh, it is a tough nut to crack, I grant you; but cracked it must be, and at the earliest possible moment. You have to strike hard and fast with your forces concentrated while theirs are dispersed: in a word, you have to go in and win. Government will be in a rare old taking when the news of the *Europe* and the *Streatham* reaches England, and this is the kind of situation where you must produce results at once. I do not mention the country's interests, of course; but I do say that from a purely personal point of view there is probably a knighthood or even a baronetcy if you succeed; and if you don't, why it is the beach and half-pay for the rest of your life.'

A midshipman darted in. 'The captain's duty, sir,' said he, 'and should you wish a compliment to the gentleman in the barge?'

'Certainly,' said the Admiral. 'As to a flag.' In the pause that followed he gazed abstractedly at his wife's portrait. 'Should you not like a baronetcy, Aubrey? I am sure I would. Mrs Bertie fairly longs to wipe her sister's eye.'

The unofficial part of Simon's Town, though little more than a hamlet, had drinking-booths, wine-shops and places of entertainment enough for a town of moderate size; and into one of those, at dusk, walked Stephen Maturin, bearing a bunch of orchids. He was tired, thirsty, and covered from head to foot with African dust; but he was happy, having spent his first half-day ashore walking up a mountain clothed with a vegetation largely unknown to him and inhabited by remarkable birds, some of which he recognized from their published descriptions: he had also seen three-quarters of a female spotted hyaena, and he found the remaining piece, including its wistful face, removed to some distance, in the act of being devoured by his old friend the bearded vulture – a pleasant combination of the present and the past, of two far-distant worlds.

He called for wine and water, mingled them in proportion to his thirst, placed his orchids in the water-jug, and drank until at last he began to sweat again. Apart from the landlord and three pretty Malay girls at the bar, there were only two other people in the twilit room, a very large officer in a uniform he could not make out, a vast gloomy man with a great deal of dark whisker, not unlike a melancholy bear, and his smaller, inconspicuous companion, who sat at his ease in shirtsleeves, with his breeches unbuttoned at the knee. The sad officer spoke a fluent though curious English devoid of articles: the smaller man's harsh and grating accent was clearly that of Ulster. They were discussing the Real Presence, but he had not made out the thread of their discourse before they both burst out, 'No Pope, no Pope, no Pope,' the sad officer in the deepest bass that Stephen had ever heard. At the bar the Malay girls politely echoed, 'No Pope,' and as though it were a signal they brought candles and set them about the room. The light fell on Stephen's orchids and upon the contents of his handkerchief, fourteen curious beetles, collected for his friend Sir Joseph Blain, formerly the chief of naval intelligence; he was considering one, a buprestid, when he became aware of a darkness by his side, the melancholy bear, gently swaying. 'Golovnin, fleet-lieutenant, captain of Imperial Majesty's sloop *Diana*,' said he, clicking his heels.

Stephen rose, bowed, and said, 'Maturin, surgeon of Britannic Majesty's ship *Boadicea*. Please to take chair.'

'You have soul,' observed Golovnin, nodding at the orchids. 'I too have soul. Where did you find them, flowers?'

'In mountain,' said Stephen.

Golovnin sighed; and taking a small cucumber from his pocket he began to eat it. He made no reply to Stephen's proffer of wine, but after a while he said, 'What is their name, flowers?'

'*Disa grandiflora*,' said Stephen, and a long silence fell. It was broken by the Ulsterman, who, tired of drinking alone, brought his bottle over and set it on Stephen's table without the least ceremony. 'I am McAdam, of the *Otter*,' he remarked, sitting down. 'I saw you at the hospital this morning.' Now, by the light of the candle, Stephen recognized him, not from that morning but from many years ago: William McAdam, a mad-doctor with a considerable reputation in Belfast, who had left Ireland after the failure of his private asylum. Stephen had heard him lecture, and had read his book on hysteria with great applause. 'He will not last long,' observed McAdam, referring to Golovnin, now weeping on to the orchids.

'Nor will you, colleague,' thought Stephen, looking at McAdam's pallid face and bloodshot eye.

'Will you take a wee drink?'

'Thank you, sir,' said Stephen, 'I believe I shall stay with my negus. What is it that you have in your bottle, pray?'

'Och, it's a brandy they distil hereabouts. Raw, rot-gut stuff; I drink it experimentally, not from indulgence. He' – pointing an unsteady finger at Golovnin – 'drinks it from nostalgia, as the nearest to his native vodka; I encourage him.'

'You alluded to an experiment?' said Stephen.

'Yes. Strobenius and others allege that a man dead drunk on grain-spirits falls backwards: on brandy he falls forwards. And if that is true, it tells us something about the motor centres, if you understand the expression. This gentleman here is my corpus vile. Yet it is wonderful how he holds out. This is our third bottle, and he has drunk glass for glass with me.'

'I honour your devotion to science, sir.'

'I do not give a fart in hell for science,' said McAdam. 'Art is all. Medicine is an art or it is nothing. Medicine of the mind, I mean; for what is your physical medicine, apart

72

from purges and mercury and bark, what your murderous chirurgical tricks? They may, with luck, suppress symptoms: no more. On the other hand, where is the true *fons et origo* of nine-tenths of your vicious constitutions of body? The mind, that's where it is,' he said, tapping his forehead. 'And what heals the mind? Art: nothing else. Art is all. That is my realm.'

It occurred to Stephen that McAdam was perhaps a somewhat seedy practitioner of this or any other art; a man furthermore whose inward torments were clearly printed on his face. But as they talked of the interaction of mind and body, of interesting cases they had seen – false pregnancies – inexplicable remissions – their experience afloat – the inverse relationship of constipation and courage – the proved efficacity of placebos – his opinion of McAdam rose: indeed, a mutual esteem came into being, and McAdam's arrogant, didactic tone grew even civil. He was telling Stephen about his patients aboard the *Otter* – most of the Otters were, *sensu stricto*, mentally deranged, and there was one case that McAdam would describe and name, were it not for professional secrecy, a fascinating and particularly subtle chain of symptoms – when without any warning Golovnin fell off his chair, grasping the orchids. He lay motionless, still in the attitude of sitting; but he fell sideways, a wholly inconclusive result. At the sound of the crash the landlord paced to the door and whistled. Two enormous sailors walked in, and murmuring, 'Come, Vasily Mikhailovitch; come, little father,' they carried their captain out into the darkness.

'He has not hurt my flowers, however,' said Stephen, smoothing their petals. 'They are, in their essentials, quite intact. You have no doubt remarked the curious spiral convolution of the ovary, so typical of the whole order. Though perhaps your realm does not extend to botany, at all?'

'It does not,' said McAdam. 'Though twisted ovaries are well within it; and twisted testicles too – I speak in figure, you understand: I am jocose. No. The proper study of mankind is man. And I may observe, Dr Maturin, that this eager

73

prying into the sexual organs of vegetables on your part seems to me . . .'

What it seemed to Dr McAdam did not appear, for his tide too had now reached the full. He rose; his eyes closed, and he pitched straight into Stephen's arms, falling, as Stephen noted, forwards.

The landlord brought one of the wheelbarrows that he kept under the porch, and with the help of a black, Stephen wheeled McAdam towards the pier, passing several bodies of cheerful liberty-men as he went. He hailed each party in turn, asking for any Otters; but no man chose to leave the sheltering darkness and sacrifice a moment of his shore-leave, and Stephen heard nothing but facetious replies – '*Otter*'s bound for the Rio Grande' – '*Otter*'s paid off at the Nore' – '*Otter* was broke up for firewood last Wednesday week' – until he met a group of Néréides. A familiar voice cried, 'It's the Doctor,' and there was the powerful form of Bonden at his side, Jack Aubrey's coxswain from his earliest command.

'Bonden, sir. Do you remember me?'

'Of course I remember you, Bonden,' said Stephen, shaking his hand. 'And am delighted to see you again. How do you do?'

'Pretty spry, thank you, sir; and I hope I see you the same? Now just you shove off, Darkie' – to the black – 'I'll take care of this here barrow.'

'The question is, Bonden,' said Stephen, giving the black two stuivers and a penny, 'the question is, how shall I find the means of conveying my charge to his ship, always supposing that his ship is here at all, which seems to be a matter of some doubt? He is the surgeon of the *Otter*, Bonden, a learned man, though somewhat original; and at the moment disguised in drink.'

'*Otter*, sir? She come in on the turn of the tide, not ten minutes ago. Never you fret, I'll square our boat-keeper directly and take him out.' He hurried away: a little later the *Néréide*'s jolly-boat appeared at the step, and Bonden carried the body into it. In spite of the dimness Stephen

74

noticed that Bonden moved stiffly; and this stiffness became more apparent as he pulled out across the harbour towards the distant sloop.

'You are stiff, Barret Bonden,' said Stephen. 'In another man I should say he had certainly been flogged; but that can scarcely be the case with you. I trust this is not a wound, or a rheumatism from the falling damps?'

Bonden laughed, but without much mirth, and said, 'Oh, it was four dozen at the gangway, all right, sir, and two more for luck: brass on the lock of the number seven gun not bright enough.'

'I am amazed, Bonden: amazed,' said Stephen, and indeed he was. Bonden had never been flogged to his knowledge; and even in a flogging ship fifty lashes was a savage punishment for anything but a most serious crime. 'And grieved. Let us row over to the *Boadicea*, and I shall give you some salve.'

'It's all right now, sir, thanking you kindly. I was aboard you this afternoon, but it was not for no salve: you will find the letter we wrote, a-laying there in your cabin.'

'What is it all about, tell?'

'Well, sir,' said Bonden, resting on his oars: but by this time they were close to the larboard side of the *Otter*, and in reply to her hail Bonden called, 'Your doctor coming aboard: request a line.' The *Otter* was perfectly used to this: a whip with a bowline appeared over the side; Bonden slipped it under McAdam's arms; and the surgeon vanished upwards.

'Well, sir,' said Bonden again, pulling slowly towards the *Boadicea*, 'this is the way of it. When me and Killick, on the Leeward Islands station, heard the Captain was afloat again, we went to join him, in course: and there was plenty more in other ships did likewise – old Sophies, old Surprises, even an old Polychrest, Bolton, that slab-sided cove the Captain pulled out of the sea. Oh, was he to new-commission a ship, he'd have no trouble finding a ship's company: not like some –' He swallowed the coarse expression with a cough and went on, 'Howsoever, we put in our request, and

Captain Dundas, a very affable gent and a friend of the Captain's as you know full well, sir, discharged us into *Néréide*, Captain Corbett, for the Cape: which he was so kind as to say he was sorry to lose us, and give Killick a pot of guava-jelly for the Captain. But *Néréide*'s short-handed: because why? because the men run whenever they can. There was Joe Lucas, of our mess, as swam three mile, with bladders, off St Kitts, sharks and all: was brought back, flogged, and swum it again, with his back like a raw steak. And today, with only twelve liberty-men out of the whole crew, two of 'em are off for the mountain, in spite of all them wild beasts, I know for certain fact, leaving thirty-eight months' pay and their prize-money. So, do you see, we are afraid, Killick and me and the rest, that Captain Corbett will not discharge us into the *Boadicea*; and so we wrote this letter to you, sir. Because not liking to put ourselves in the Captain's way, being that he's to hoist his pennant any minute as they say, and therefore too busy, we hoped you might put in a good word, just casual, at the right moment.'

'Of course I shall. But you could very well have addressed Captain Aubrey himself; he has the kindest recollection of you – often speaks of his real coxswain, and much regrets your absence.'

'Does he, though?' said Bonden, with a chuckle of satisfaction. 'But even so, we'd take it very kind in you to say a word: it would come more proper, like, from you. And we are main anxious to be out of *Néréide*.'

'She is not altogether a happy ship, I collect?'

'No, sir, she ain't.' He rested on his oars again, and looking a little sideways at Stephen he added, 'She's a shot-rolling ship: that's what she is.'

Stephen knew nothing about the sailing of ships, theoretical or practical; but he did know that when a crew started trundling cannon-balls about the deck under the cover of darkness, then something was very much amiss; for the next stage was mutiny. He also knew that in any normal ship it would be unthinkable for an unusually steady, sober man like Bonden to be flogged.

'I'm not complaining, mark you,' said Bonden. 'Nor I'm not setting up in judgment: there are some right bastards in the *Néréide*, before the mast and elsewheres; and when things reach a certain pitch, in such a ship the cat falls on the just and the unjust alike. I can take fifty lashes as well as the next man, I hope; though I may say as how it was the first time the cat and me came acquainted – oh, I was beat like a drum when I was a little chap in the *Thunderer*, but that was only the master-at-arms' admonition, as we say. His cane, sir. No. What I mean is, that in the first place me and Killick and the rest want to get back to our own captain: and in the second, we want to get out before things turn nasty. And at the gait they are going now – well, I shouldn't give much for Captain Corbett's life, nor some of his officers, come an action, or even maybe a dirty night with no moon; and we want no part in it.'

'Ugly, Bonden, very ugly,' said Stephen, and no more until they were alongside the *Boadicea*, when he said, 'Good night, now; and thank you for rowing me home.'

He turned in with Leguat's *Voyage*, with its fascinating account of the solitaire, and Sparmann; and late in the middle watch he heard Jack come aboard. But it was not until quite late in the morning that they met, Stephen having been called to the sick-bay to deal with an alcoholic coma that had suddenly started to gush blood at the ears; and when they did meet it was clear to him that both his crapulous night and his crapulous morning (the sick-bay had smelt like a distillery) were to be prolonged. Captain Aubrey had the yellow, puffy look of one who has drunk far too much – so much indeed that his twenty-mile ride back had not worked it off. 'Twenty miles, *more* than twenty miles, on a damned screw that flung me down three times, and spoilt my best nankeen trousers,' he said. His steward had broken the coffee-pot: his French cook had gone ashore with Bretonnière to join the other prisoners of war, and never more would there be brioche for breakfast. But infinitely more galling than even the missing coffee was the fact that the Admiral had promised Jack his orders and had not produced them. An interminable, inconclusive conference with the Governor, Mr Farquhar and two general officers of a stupidity remarkable even for the army: then an equally long supper with the soldiers, determined to make their guest drunk. And all this while no orders. By the time Jack set off on his glandered mare the Admiral had long since gone to bed; the flag-lieutenant knew nothing about any orders, written or even contemplated. So here he was, as he told Stephen in the cabin, not knowing *where* he was: there had been no word about his pennant at any time. So here he was, left hanging up in the air: perhaps the expedition would not take place at all: and if it did, after months of delay, perhaps he was not intended to command at all – there had been a furtive, evasive look in the eye of the Admiral's secretary, an ill-looking, untrustworthy swab, for all he was a parson. There had been no mention of higher command in his original sailing orders, and although the Admiral had certainly spoken as though the matter were settled, the appointment no doubt lay at his discretion: the Admiral might have changed his mind: he might have been influenced by the opinion of the council. And then earlier there had been that ominous '*if* you hoist your pennant'.

'Let us take a turn on deck,' he said. 'My head seems to be made of hot sand. And Stephen, might I beg you, implore you, not to smoke those vile things in the cabin? It is your pot-house all over again, like that soldiers' mess last night.'

They reached the quarterdeck in time to see an odd figure come up the side, a young man dressed in a gaudy coat and a little gaudy hat. He had come up the starboard side, the officers' side, and as he advanced towards Mr Seymour he saluted. The first lieutenant hesitated: not so Jack. 'Turn that fellow off the ship,' he roared. Then, in a lower voice, holding his hand to his aching forehead, 'What the devil does he mean by it, prancing about the deck of a King's ship improperly dressed, like a jack-pudding?' The young man got into a boat, and was rowed away by a crew of merry-andrews, all in much the same kind of rig.

Jack's steward cautiously sidled near, muttering something about 'the gun-room's pot', and Stephen said, 'I believe he means that coffee's up.'

It was: and as they drank it benignity returned, helped by fresh cream, bacon, eggs, pig's fry, the last of the true French short bastards, toasted, and Sophie's orange marmalade.

'I am sorry I was so cursed snappish just now, about your cigar,' said Jack, pushing back his chair at last and undoing his waistcoat. 'Pray smoke, Stephen. You know I like the smell.'

'Ay,' said Stephen. He broke a cigar in three, crumbled one piece, moistened it with a few drops of coffee, rolled it in paper, and lit it with a voluptuous indraught. 'Listen, now, will you?' he said. 'Bonden, Killick and some others are aboard the *Néréide*, and wish to return to you. All tastes are to be found in nature, we are told; and it is to be presumed that they like the brutal, arbitrary, tyrannical exercise of power.'

'Oh,' cried Jack, 'how very, very pleased I am! It will be like old times. I have rarely regretted anything so much as having to part with them. But will Corbett ever let them go? He's devilish short-handed; and it's only a courtesy, you know, except to a flag. Why, a man like Bonden is worth his weight in gold.'

'Corbett does not seem to be aware of his value, however: he gave him fifty lashes '

'Flogged Bonden?' cried Jack, going very red. 'Flogged my cox'n? By God, I . . .'

A nervous young gentleman brought the news that the Commander-in-chief's flag-lieutenant had been seen putting off from the shore and the captain of the *Otter* from his sloop, and that Mr Seymour thought Captain Aubrey might like to know.

'Thank you, Mr Lee,' said Jack, and he went on deck: Lord and Lady Clonfert had been far, far from his mind, but they came back with a rush as he saw the *Otter*'s gig, pulled by the same merry-andrews of just before breakfast, approaching the *Boadicea*. It was at about the same distance as the *Raisonable*'s barge, but the flag-lieutenant paused by the flagship to exchange a bellowed and apparently very amusing conversation with a friend on her poop, and before it was over the gig was alongside.

Clonfert was piped aboard, a slight, strikingly handsome, youthful-looking man in full uniform with a star on the bosom of his coat and a singular expression of expectation and uneasiness on his face. He flushed as Jack shook his hand, saying, 'I am happy to see you again, Clonfert; but I heartily wish I had better news for you. Come into my cabin.' Once there he went on, 'I am very much concerned to tell you, that because of an unfortunate misunderstanding about the time, I was obliged to leave Plymouth without Lady Clonfert.'

'Oh,' said Clonfert, with a look of bitter contrariety on his mobile face. 'I was afraid that might be so. I sent early to inquire, but it seems that the message I sent by one of my officers could not be received.'

'An officer?' cried Jack. 'I had no notion – an officer, in that rig?'

'I am sorry it did not meet with your approval, sir,' said Clonfert stiffly. 'But it is my custom to dress my gig's crew in my own colours – it is usual enough in the service, I believe – and the gentlemen under my command fall in with my humour. I confess it is irregular, however.'

'Well, it can lead to misunderstanding. Still, it is cleared up now, and I have delivered my damned unwelcome news – I regret it extremely, but I am sure that Lady Clonfert will have taken the next Indiaman. She will have travelled in much greater comfort, and she should be here within the next week or so, for we made but a slow passage of it. You will dine with me? We have a sucking-pig, and I recall you was fond of sucking-pig in the *Agamemnon*.'

Clonfert flushed again at the name of the ship: he darted an intensely suspicious glance at Jack, and then with an artificial air he said he must beg to be excused – with infinite reluctance he must plead a previous engagement – but that in taking his leave he must be allowed to express his sense of Captain Aubrey's great politeness in having intended to bring Lady Clonfert to the Cape; he was *pénétré, pénétré.*

He brought it off well enough to make Jack, whose conscience was far from easy on that score, feel something of a scrub; and if he had not tripped on his way out of the cabin the performance would have been well-nigh perfect. The flag-lieutenant was already on deck, talking and laughing with Seymour, when Jack saw his visitor to the side; and Jack's searching eye saw that the jolly young man was the bearer not of the unimportant inconclusive temporizing verbal order that he had so dreaded – that he had so reasonably dreaded, from the tone of last night's conference – but of an important folder bound up with tape, red official tape.

In the cabin once more he received the folder; but first he had to listen to the flag-lieutenant's message. 'The Admiral desires me to say, sir, that he was taken unwell just after the meeting; that he was unable to give you your orders as he had intended; but that he dictated them from his bed at the earliest possible moment. In fact, sir, he dictated them to me, the secretary not being in the way.'

'So you know what is in them, I dare say?'

'Yes sir; and may I be the first to wish you joy of your pennant, sir?'

'Thank you, Mr Forster,' said Jack, with the full sun lighting up his heart and bowels, his whole being. 'Thank you very much indeed. I trust the Admiral's indisposition causes him no pain or distress? I could wish him restored to the most amazing health and happiness immediately.' The flag-lieutenant thought that perhaps the Admiral had eaten something; for his part he had recommended a dose of rhubarb; and Jack listened to him with an appearance of steady solicitous attention. Jack looked decently solemn, but his mind was swimming in happiness, a happiness made all the more wholly concrete, real and tangible when the flag-lieutenant's recollections of an occasion upon which he too had eaten something came to an end and Jack could cut the tape and see that his orders were addressed to Commodore Aubrey. Yet underlying this pure felicity there was another level of consciousness, a hard, sober determination to come straight into direct contact with the 'real thing', to see exactly what it amounted to, to gauge the limits of his possible initiative, to weigh up the forces in presence, and to start dealing with the situation at once.

The orders were clear, concise, and urgent: the Admiral had obviously had his way. Commodore Aubrey was directed and required to repair aboard the *Raisonable*; to hoist his pennant; to take the ships and vessels named in the margin under his command; to proceed to sea with the utmost dispatch; to seek out and destroy the French cruisers operating south of 10°S and west of 70°E, and, with the cooperation of the officer commanding the land forces on Rodriguez (which were to be reinforced at the appropriate juncture), to undertake the reduction of the French possessions of the Ile Bourbon, otherwise Ile de la Réunion, otherwise Ile Buonaparte, and of the Mauritius, otherwise Ile de France, together with that of the French ships and vessels in the seas thereto adjacent: he was to attend to the general directions in the attached schedules A and B; and in all political matters or those having a bearing on contact with the civil population he was to seek the advice of William Farquhar, Esquire, H.M. Governor-Designate, and in the absence of Mr Farquhar then that of Dr Stephen Maturin.

The schedules, together with various appreciations, charts, hydrographical notes, and estimates of the French strength, mostly derived from the American merchantmen that passed to and fro, were in separate packets; and among them was a paper bearing the superscription Lieutenant Johnson, R.N., *Boadicea*. 'What is this?' asked Jack.

'The Admiral has confirmed your acting-order for Mr Johnson,' said the flag-lieutenant. 'It is his commission.' Jack nodded, a fresh jet of pleasure overcoming the underlying gravity for a moment, and the flag-lieutenant went on, 'I am also to say, sir, that the Admiral desires you will use your own discretion entirely as far as *Raisonable* is concerned, and shift your pennant just as you see fit: he knows her condition only too well. He asks for this list of followers and servants to be sent to him in Cape Town, and he hopes you will see proper to maintain the following appointments. He much regrets that time and his present indisposition do not allow him to communicate the confidential remarks upon your captains personally, in the usual manner, and begs you will forgive this hasty scribble.' He passed a half-sheet of paper, folded and sealed, and said, 'I believe that is all, sir, apart from Mr Shepherd's message: he says that since you will need a commodore's secretary he begs to recommend his cousin, Mr Peter. Mr Peter has been several months on this station and is thoroughly *au courant*. He is in Simon's Town at the moment – rode over with me – if you choose to see him.'

'I should be happy to see Mr Peter,' said Jack, strongly aware of the importance of these civilities, of the importance of good relations throughout the squadron.

Decency required Jack to refresh the flag-lieutenant; decency required the flag-lieutenant to see his share of the bottle out within ten minutes, in order to leave the new commodore free for the innumerable tasks awaiting him; but although the young man did his best, no period of Jack's life had ever passed so slowly.

When Mr Forster had gone at last, Jack summoned Johnson and said, 'I wish you joy of your commission, Mr Johnson. Here it is. The Admiral has confirmed your acting-order, and I am very sure you deserve it.' He handed over the precious document, even more precious perhaps to Johnson than his pennant was to Jack – certainly less loaded with responsibility – and both to cut short the flood of thanks and to gain a few minutes he said, 'Pray be so good as to send the bosun as soon as possible,' while to the bosun he said, 'Mr Fellowes, I do not suppose we have a broad pennant in the colour-chest? If not, I should be obliged if you would have one run up directly.'

'Aye aye, sir,' said the bosun, trying to suppress a grin, 'broad pennant it is.' Out of piety, a dread of offending fate by presumption, Jack had never ordered one to be made: he had felt the temptation very strongly – he had longed to cherish it in private – but he had waited until it should be certain. On the other hand the Boadiceas had turned the matter over in their heads well north of the line, ferreting about and fitting odd scraps together; they had become convinced of the need for such an object, and it had been lying by these last four thousand miles.

The bosun hurried off forward: Jack broke the Admiral's seal and read: 'Captain Pym of the *Sirius* is a thoroughly reliable, conscientious officer, but wanting in initiative; Captain Corbett of the *Néréide*, though he keeps an excellent discipline and is of outstanding value as a fighting commander, has a tendency to irascibility that is to be regretted; he is on bad terms with Captain Lord Clonfert of the *Otter*, and the two should not be sent together on detached service if it can be avoided. Lord Clonfert has distinguished himself recently in several minor actions of a most dashing nature; and he, like Captain Corbett, has a considerable acquaintance with the waters off Réunion and Mauritius.' The confidential remarks told Jack perhaps rather more about the Admiral than the captains; but he had scarcely formulated this reflection before Fellowes came hurrying back, bearing the beautiful pennant in his arms. Jack looked at it with an affectation of detachment that could scarcely have deceived his daughters, far less the bosun. 'Thank you, Mr Fellowes,' he said. 'Pray put it on the locker, and then ask the Doctor, with my compliments, whether he can spare a moment.'

He was drawing on the breeches of his best full-dress uniform when Stephen walked in. 'I thought you might like to see something new,' he said, adding, not without pride, '*Ex Africa surgit semper aliquid novo – novi*, eh?'

'To what do you refer?' asked Stephen, gazing about the cabin.

'Cannot you see anything that strikes you dumb with awe, the mark of a living commodore, very nearly the most exalted being on the face of the earth?'

'The ornamental cloth? Oh, that: I had understood you

84

to say something new. That cloth I saw daily in the bosun's cabin when his bowels were disturbed, long ago: I took it for a sign of his office, or perhaps the banner of some bosuns' guild.' Then, feeling obscurely that he had not quite fulfilled his friend's expectations, he added, 'But it is an amazingly handsome flag, upon my honour; and so neatly sewn. I dare say you will hang it up, presently; and sure it will do us all great credit, the pretty thing.'

If there had been little secrecy aboard the frigate, there was even less in the squadron. No one had failed to remark the flag-lieutenant's arrival, nor his prolonged stay in the *Boadicea*, nor the subsequent desertion of the flagship by a troop of the Admiral's servants and followers, nor yet Captain Aubrey's passage across the harbour: when the swallow-tailed pennant broke out at the *Raisonable*'s masthead, therefore, not a ship or vessel present let a second go by before starting the thirteen-gun salute due to the man it symbolized. The salutes merged with one another and with their echoes, filling the bay with a sullen roar and a cloud of smoke that drifted over Jack as he stood there on the poop, not directly looking at his pennant, but feeling its presence with oh such intensity: the moment his thunderous reply was done, he returned to the signal-lieutenant and said, '*All captains*, Mr Swiney.'

He received them in the Admiral's great cabin: the *Raisonable* was not the *Hibernia* nor yet the *Victory*, but still this was a noble room, full of dappled reflected light, and as they filed in their blue and white and gold made it look nobler still. Pym of the *Sirius* came first, a big man, as tall as Jack and fatter; his congratulations were as frank and unreserved as his fine friendly open face, and Jack's heart warmed to him. Corbett followed, a small dark round-headed man whose set expression of determined, angry authority was now softened into a look of the deference and the pleasure proper to this occasion. He had fought several most creditable actions in the West Indies, and in spite of Bonden Jack looked at him with respect: with hopeful anticipation, too. Corbett's good wishes were almost as cordial as Pym's, although there might have been the slightest hint of resentment, of merit and local knowledge passed over: but in any event they were far more hearty than Clonfert's formal 'Allow me to offer my felicitations, sir.'

'Now, gentlemen,' said Commodore Aubrey, when this stage was over, 'I am happy to tell you that the squadron is to proceed to sea with the utmost dispatch. I should therefore be obliged for a statement of each ship's readiness, her condition: not a detailed statement, you understand – that can come later – but a general notion. Lord Clonfert?'

'The sloop I have the honour to command is always ready to put to sea,' said Clonfert. That was mere rodomontade: no ship was always ready to put to sea unless she never used up any water, stores, powder or shot; and the *Otter* had just come in from a cruise. They all knew it, Clonfert as well as any once the words were out of his mouth. Without allowing the awkward pause to last more than a moment, however, Jack went straight on, receiving a more rational account from Pym and Corbett, from which it appeared that the *Sirius*, though well-found in general, badly needed careening, and that she was having great trouble with her water-tanks, new-fangled iron affairs that had been wished on her in Plymouth and that leaked amazingly. 'If there is one thing that I detest more than anything,' said Captain Pym, staring round the table, 'it is innovations.' The *Sirius* had rummaged her hold to come at the tanks, so even with the best will in the world, and working double tides, she could scarcely be ready for sea before Sunday. The *Néréide*, though apparently fit to sail the moment she had filled her water, was really in a much sadder way: she was old, as the Commodore knew, and according to Captain Corbett's carpenter her navel-futtocks could be removed with a shovel; while she was certainly iron-sick fore and aft, if not amidships too; but far worse than that, she was shockingly undermanned. Captain Corbett was sixty-three hands short of his complement: a shocking figure.

Jack agreed that it was a very shocking figure, to be sure.

'But let us hope that the next homeward-bound Indiaman to put in will solve the difficulty with sixty-three prime hands and a few supernumaries.'

'You are forgetting, sir, that ever since their disagreement with Government about the running of the colony the Company's ships no longer touch at the Cape.'

'Very true,' said Jack, with a covert glance at Clonfert. He covered his lapse by saying that he should visit their ships in the course of the afternoon, when he would hope to see their detailed statements of condition, and suggested that they should now discuss some claret that he had taken from a Frenchman on his way down. The last of the Lafite appeared, together with something in the farinaceous line from the *Boadicea*'s galley.

'Capital wine,' said Pym.

'As sound as a nut,' said Corbett. 'So you found a Frenchman, sir?'

'Yes,' said Jack, and he told them about the *Hébé*: it was not much of an action, but the mere talk of banging guns, the *Hyaena* restored to the list, the prize neatly salvaged, caused the formal atmosphere to relax. Reminiscence flowed with the claret: comparable actions and old shipmates were called to mind: laughter broke out. Jack had never served with either Pym or Corbett, but they had many acquaintances in common throughout the service: when they had spoken of half a dozen, Jack said, 'You knew Heneage Dundas in the West Indies, of course, Captain Corbett?' thinking that this might jog his mind.

'Oh, yes, sir,' said Corbett: but no more.

'That will not wash, however,' said Jack within: and aloud, 'Lord Clonfert, the bottle stands by you.'

All this time Clonfert had been sitting silent. A shaft of light, falling on his star, sent a constellation of little prismatic dots flashing high: now, as he leant forwards to the bottle, they all swept down. He filled his glass, passed the bottle on, and moved perhaps by some notion of repairing his unpleasant relationship with Corbett and possibly at the same time of winning an ally in this meeting where he could not but feel at a disadvantage, he said, 'Captain Corbett, a glass of wine with you.'

'I never drink a glass of wine with any man, my lord,' replied Corbett.

'Captain Corbett,' said Jack quickly, 'I was astonished to learn about the Russian brig lying inside the *Néréide*, and even more astonished when the Admiral told me that her captain had served under you.'

'Yes, sir, he was in the *Seahorse* when I had her, serving as a volunteer to learn our ways: and he picked them up pretty well, I must confess. His people are scarcely what we should rate ordinary, but I dare say he will knock some seamanship into them in time. They have a fine sense of discipline in those parts: a thousand lashes are not uncommon, I believe.'

The talk ran on about the unfortunate *Diana* – her sailing from the Baltic on a voyage of discovery at a time of peace between England and Russia – her arrival, all unsuspecting, in Simon's Town to learn that war had been declared – her curious status – her curious build – her people's curious ways ashore.

Eight bells struck: they all stood up. Jack detained Corbett for a moment and said, 'Before I forget it, Captain Corbett, my coxswain and some other men are aboard the *Néréide*. Here, I have jotted down their names. You will oblige me by having 'em sent over.'

'Certainly, sir,' said Corbett. 'Of course . . . But I beg you will not think I intend the least disrespect if I venture to repeat that I am cruelly short-handed.'

'So I understand,' said Jack. 'But I do not mean to rob you: far from it. You shall have an equal number from the *Boadicea*, and I believe I may even be able to let you have a few more. We pressed some good men among the *Hébé*'s prisoners.'

'I should be most uncommon grateful, sir,' said Corbett, brightening at once. 'And I shall send your men back the moment I reach the ship.'

It was with his own coxswain at his side, therefore, that

the Commodore put off for his tour of the squadron. 'This is like old times, Bonden,' he said, as they approached the *Sirius*. 'Yes, sir; only better,' murmured Bonden: and then, in answer to the frigate's hail, he roared, 'Pennant,' in a voice to wake the dead.

It did not startle the *Sirius*, however: from the moment of Captain Pym's return all hands had turned to – dinner cut short, grog gulped down – in order to give her an entirely artificial and fallacious appearance, designed to make her appear what she was not. They had done so with a will, being proud of their ship, and although there had been no time for any lavish repainting, the *Sirius* that the Commodore beheld was as unlike her workaday self as the concentrated effort of two hundred and eighty-seven men and several women (some regular, others less so) could make her. Seeing that she was virtually disembowelled because of her tanks, they had not been able to turn her into a larger version of a royal yacht, as they could have wished; but apart from the pyramids of nameless objects on deck, decently shrouded with awnings and tarpaulins, she was very presentable, and Jack was pleased with what he saw. He did not believe it, of course; nor was he expected to believe it: the whole thing, from the whitewashed coal in the galley to the blackened balls in the shot-garlands, was a ritual disguise. Yet it had a relationship to the facts, and he gained the impression of a fine steady ship in moderately good order with competent officers and a decent crew largely composed of man-of-war's men – she had been in commission these three years and more. Captain Pym had set up a splendid array of bottles and cakes in his cabin, and as Jack lowered a Bath bun whose specific gravity somewhat exceeded that of platinum he reflected that its consistency was in all likelihood a fair symbol of the ship – steady, regular, rather old-fashioned, reliable; though perhaps not apt to set the Indian Ocean in a blaze.

Next the *Néréide*. She had had no real need to turn to in order to achieve the full effect that the *Sirius* had aimed at, yet from the mute, weary sullenness of her crew and the anxious, jaded, harassed look of her officers, every man jack aboard had been hard at it, gilding the lily for this occasion. Jack liked a taut ship, and of course a clean ship, but the total perfection of the *Néréide*'s vast expanse of brass alone oppressed him: he went through with his inspection, that being due to those who had toiled so hard and to so little purpose, but he made his tour of the silent, rigid frigate with no pleasure at all. His real business lay below, however, among the navel-futtocks; and there in the depths with the captain, his nervous first lieutenant and his nervous carpenter, he found that Corbett had not exaggerated greatly. Her timbers were indeed in a bad way: yet, he reflected as he prodded about with a spike, the Simon's Town surveyor might be right in saying that they would last another two or three seasons, whereas unless Jack was out in his reckoning the rot on the upper deck would spread more rapidly than that. As a young fellow, a midshipman in those very waters, he had been disrated for misconduct, for venery, and turned before the mast: infinitely against his will he had been a foremast jack for six months. That ship's standard of spit and polish had been nothing remotely like the *Néréide*'s, but she had had a tartar of a captain and a driving first lieutenant, and he knew to his cost just what it took in labour to produce even half this result. And those months, so wretched at first and indeed for most of the time, had also given him something that few officers possessed: an intimate understanding of life at sea from the men's point of view, a comprehension from within. He knew their language, spoken and silent; and his interpretation of the looks he had seen before coming below, the constraint, the veiled sideways glances, the scarcely perceptible nods and signs, the total lack of anything resembling cheerfulness, depressed him extremely.

Corbett was a brisk man with figures, however: he produced his detailed statement of the *Néréide*'s condition, neatly ruled in black and red, at the same time as his Madeira and sweet biscuits. 'You are very well found in powder and shot, I see,' Jack remarked, glancing over the columns.

'Yes, sir,' said Corbett. 'I don't believe in flinging it into the ocean: besides, your genuine recoil does so plough up the deck.'

'It does; and the *Néréide*'s deck is a most remarkable sight, I must confess. But do you not find it answers, to have your men handy with the guns – accurate at a distance?'

'Why, sir, as far as my experience goes, it don't make much odds. I have always engaged yardarm to yardarm, when they could not miss if they tried. But I don't have to tell *you* anything about close engagement, sir, not after your action with the *Cacafuego*, ha, ha.'

'Still, there is something to be said for the other school of thought – something to be said for knocking away the enemy's sticks from a mile off and then lying athwart his hawse,' observed Jack mildly.

'I am sure you are right, sir,' said Corbett, without the least conviction.

If the *Néréide* had been as like a royal yacht as a man-of-war could very well be, the *Otter*, at first glance, was the yacht itself. Jack had never, in all his life, seen such a display of gold leaf; and rarely had he seen all shrouds and stays wormed with vermilion yarn and the strops of the blocks covered with red leather. At second glance it seemed perhaps a little much, touching on the showy, just as the perfection of tailoring on Clonfert's quarterdeck – even the midshipmen had laced cocked hats, breeches, and Hessian boots with gold tassels – had a hint of costume rather than of uniform about it: and as he stood there Jack noticed to his surprise that Clonfert's officers appeared rather a vulgar set. They could not help their undistinguished faces, of course, but their stance, now too rigid, like tailor's dummies, now too lounging and easy by far, was something else again; so was their under-bred open staring, their direct listening to what their captain had to say to him. On the other hand, no great perspicacity was required to see that the atmosphere aboard the *Otter* was as unlike that in the *Néréide* as possible: the lower-deck Otters were a cheerful, smiling crew, and it was clear that they liked their captain; while the standing officers, the bosun, the gunner and the carpenter (those essential pillars), seemed steady, valuable, experienced men. The *Otter*'s decks, rigging and gingerbread-work had surprised him; her cabin surprised him even more. Its not inconsiderable size was much increased by looking-glasses in gilt frames; these reflected a remarkable number of cushions piled up on a Turkish sofa, and the Arabian Nights were even more strongly called to mind by scimitars hanging on the bulkhead against a Persian carpet, a gilt mosque-lamp swinging from the beam, and a hubblebubble. Among all this the two twelve-pounders looked homely, brutish, drab, and ill-at-ease.

The ritual offerings appeared, brought in by a black boy in a turban, and Jack and Clonfert were left alone: a certain awkwardness became manifest at once. With advancing years Jack had learnt the value of silence in a situation where he did not know what to say. Clonfert, though slightly older in spite of his youthful appearance, had not, and he talked – these baubles were from his Syrian campaign with Sir Sydney – the lamp a present from Dgezzar Pasha – the scimitar on the right from the Maronite Patriarch – he had grown so used to Eastern ways that he could not do without his sofa. Would not the Commodore sit down? The Commodore had no notion of lowering himself to within inches of the deck – what could he do with his legs? – and replied that he should as soon keep an eye on the *Boadicea*'s boats as they pulled briskly between the arsenal and the frigate, filling her magazines and shot-lockers with what he hoped would prove a most persuasive argument. Then the Commodore would surely taste a little of this Constantia and toy with an Aleppo fig: Clonfert conceived that they made an interesting combination. Or perhaps a trifle of this botargo?

'I am infinitely obliged to you, Clonfert,' said Jack, 'and I am sure your wine is prodigious good; but the fact of the matter is, that *Sirius* gave me a great deal of capital port and *Néréide* a great deal of capital Madeira; so what I should really prize beyond anything at this moment is a cup of coffee, if that is possible.'

It was not possible. Clonfert was mortified, chagrined, desolated, but he drank no coffee; nor did his officers. He really was mortified, chagrined and desolated, too. He had already been obliged to apologize for not having his statement of condition ready, and this fresh blow, this *social* blow, cast him down extremely. Jack wanted no more unpleasantness in the squadron than already existed; and even on the grounds of common humanity he did not wish to leave Clonfert under what he evidently considered a great moral disadvantage; so pacing over to a fine narwhal tusk leaning in a corner he said, in an obliging manner, 'This is an uncommonly fine tusk.'

'A handsome object, is it not? But with submission, sir, I believe horn is the proper term. It comes from a unicorn. Sir Sydney gave it to me. He shot the beast himself, having singled it out from a troop of antelopes; it led him a tremendous chase, though he was mounted on Hassan Bey's own stallion – five and twenty miles through the trackless desert. The Turks and Arabs were perfectly amazed. He told me they said they had never seen anything like his horsemanship, nor the way he shot the unicorn at full gallop. They were astounded.'

'I am sure they were,' said Jack. He turned it in his hands, and said, with a smile, 'So I can boast of having held a true unicorn's horn.'

'You may take your oath on it, sir. I cut it out of the creature's head myself.'

'How the poor fellow does expose himself,' thought Jack, on his way back to the *Raisonable*: he had had a narwhal tusk in his cabin for months, bringing it back from the north for Stephen Maturin, and he was perfectly acquainted with the solid heft of its ivory, so very far removed from horn. Yet Clonfert had probably thought that the first part was true. Admiral Smith was a remarkably vain and boastful man, quite capable of that foolish tale: yet at the same time Admiral Smith was a most capable and enterprising officer. Apart from other brilliant actions, he had defeated Buonaparte at Acre: not many men had such grounds for boasting.

Perhaps Clonfert was of that same strange build? Jack hoped so with all his heart – Clonfert might show away with all the unicorns in the world as far as Jack was concerned, and lions too, so long as he also produced something like the same results.

His meagre belongings had already come across from the *Boadicea*; they had already been arranged by his own steward as he liked them to be arranged, and with a contented sigh Jack sat easy in an old Windsor chair with arms, flinging his heavy full-dress coat on to a locker. Killick did not like seeing clothes thrown about: Killick would have to lump it.

But Killick, who had dashed boiling water on to freshly-ground coffee the moment the *Raisonable*'s barge shoved off from the *Otter*, was a new man. Once cross-grained, shrewish, complaining, a master of dumb and sometimes vocal insolence, he was now almost complaisant. He brought in the coffee, watched Jack drink it hissing hot with something like approval, hung up the coat, uttering no unfavourable comment, no rhetorical 'Where's the money going to come from to buy new epaulettes when all the bullion's wore off, in consequence of being flung down regardless?' but carried on with the conversation that Jack's departure had interrupted. 'You did say, sir, as how they had no teeth?'

'Not a sign of them, Killick. Not a sign, before I sailed.'

'Well, I'm right glad on it' – producing a handkerchief with two massive pieces of coral in its folds – 'because this will help to cut 'em, as they say.'

'Thank you, Killick. Thank you kindly. Splendid pieces, upon my word: they shall go home in the first ship.'

'Ah, sir,' said Killick, sighing through the stern-window, 'do you remember that wicked little old copper in the back-kitchen, and how we roused out its flue, turning as black as chimney-sweeps?'

'That wicked little old copper will be a thing of the past, when next we see the cottage,' said Jack. 'The *Hébé* looked after that. And there will be a decent draught in the parlour, too, if Goadby knows his business.'

'And them cabbages, sir,' went on Killick, in an ecstasy

of nostalgia. 'When I last see 'em, they had but four leaves apiece.'

'Jack, Jack,' cried Stephen, running in. 'I have been sadly remiss. You are promoted, I find. You are a great man – you are virtually an admiral! Give you joy, my dear, with all my heart. The young man in black clothes tells me you are the greatest man on the station, after the Commander-in-chief.'

'Why, I am commodore, as most people have the candour to admit,' said Jack. 'But I did mention it before, if you recollect. I spoke of my pennant.'

'So you did, joy; but perhaps I did not fully apprehend its true significance. I had a cloudy notion that the word 'commodore' and indeed that curious little flag were connected with a ship rather than with a man – I am almost sure that we called the most important ship in the East India fleet, the ship commanded by the excellent Mr Muffit, the commodore. Pray explain this new and splendid rank of yours.'

'Stephen, if I tell you, will you attend?'

'Yes, sir.'

'I have told you a great deal about the Navy before this, and you have not attended. Only yesterday I heard you give Farquhar a very whimsical account of the difference between the halfdeck and the quarterdeck, and to this day I do not believe you know the odds between . . .' At this point he was interrupted by the black-coated Mr Peter with a sheaf of papers, by a messenger from the general at Cape Town, and by Seymour, with whom he worked out a careful list of those men who could be discharged into the *Néréide*, either in the light of their own crimes or in that of the frigate's more urgent needs, and lastly by the Commander-in-chief's secretary, who wished to know whether his cousin Peter suited, to say that Admiral Bertie, now much recovered, sent his compliments: without wishing to hurry the Commodore in any way, the Admiral would be overjoyed to hear that he had put to sea.

'Well, now, Stephen,' said Jack at last, 'this commodore

lark: in the first place I am not promoted at all – it is not a rank but a post, and J. Aubrey does not shift from his place on the captains' list by so much as the hundredth part of an inch. I hold this post just for the time being, and when the time being is over, if you follow me, I go back to being a captain again. But while it lasts I am as who should say an acting temporary unpaid rear-admiral; and I command the squadron.'

'That must warm your heart,' said Stephen. 'I have often known you chafe, in a subordinate position.'

'It does: the word is like a trumpet. Yet at the same time . . . I should not say this to anyone but you, Stephen, but it is only when you have an enterprise of this kind on your hands, an enterprise where you have to depend on others, that you understand what command amounts to.'

'By others you mean the other commanders, I take it? Sure, they are an essential factor that must be thoroughly understood. Pray open your mind upon them, without reserve.' Jack and Stephen had sailed together in many ships, but they had never discussed the officers: Stephen Maturin, as surgeon, had messed with them, and although he was the captain's friend he belonged to the gun-room: the subject was never, never raised. Now the case altered: now Stephen was Jack's political colleague and adviser; nor was he bound in any way to the other commanding officers. 'Let us begin with the Admiral; and Jack, since we are to work openly together, we must speak openly: I know your scruples and I honour them, yet believe me, brother, this is no time for scruples. Tell me, do you look for full, unreserved support from Mr Bertie?'

'He is a jolly old boy,' said Jack, 'and he has been as kind and obliging to me as I could wish: he confirmed my acting-order for Johnson at once – a most handsome compliment. As long as all goes well, I make no doubt he will back us to the hilt; apart from anything else, it is entirely in his interest. But his reputation in the service – well, in Jamaica they called him Sir Giles Overreach, from the fellow in the play, you know; and he certainly over-reached poor James.

A good officer, mark you, though he don't see much farther through a brick wall than another man.' He considered for a while before saying, 'But if I made a mistake, I should not be surprised to be superseded: nor if I stood between him and a plum. Though as things stand, I cannot see how that could come about.'

'You have no very high opinion of his head, nor of his heart.'

'I should not go as far as that. We have different ideas of what is good order in a ship, of course . . . no, I shall tell you one thing that makes me uneasy about his sense of what is right. This Russian brig. She is an embarrassment to everybody. The Admiral wishes her away, but he will not take the responsibility of letting her go. He will not accept the responsibility of making her people prisoners, either – among other things they would have to be fed, with everything charged against him if Government disapproved. So what he has done is to make the captain give his word not to escape and has left him lying there, ready for sea: he is trying to starve Golovnin out by allowing no rations for his men. Golovnin has no money and the merchants will not accept bills drawn on Petersburg. The idea is that he will break his word and disappear some dirty night when the wind is in the north-west. His word means nothing to a foreigner, said the Admiral, laughing; he wondered Golovnin had not gone off six months ago – he longed to be rid of him. He took it so much as a matter of course – did not hesitate to tell it – thought it such a clever way of covering himself – that it made my heart sink.'

Stephen said, 'I have noticed that some old men lose their sense of honour, and will cheerfully avow the strangest acts. What else affects your spirits, now? Corbett, I dare say? In that case the beadle within has quite eaten up the man.'

'Yes: he is a slave-driver. I do not say a word against his courage, mark you; he has proved that again and again. But by my book his ship is in very bad order indeed. She is old too, and only a twelve-pounder. Yet with the odds as they are, I cannot possibly do without her.'

'What do you say to the captain of the *Sirius?*'

'Pym?' Jack's face brightened. 'Oh, how I wish I had three more Pyms in three more *Siriuses*! He may be no phoenix, but he is the kind of man I like – three Pyms, and there would be your band of brothers for you. I should have to do myself no violence, keeping on terms with three Pyms. Or three Eliots for that matter: though he will not be with us long, more's the pity. He means to invalid as soon as ever he can. As it is, I shall have to humour Corbett to some degree, and Clonfert; for without there is a good understanding in a squadron, it might as well stay in port. How I shall manage it with Clonfert I can hardly tell: I must not get athwart his hawse if I can avoid it, but with that damned business of his wife I am half way there already. He resented it extremely – refused my invitation, which is almost unheard-of in the service, previous engagement or not: and there was no previous engagement. This is an odd case, Stephen. When we talked about him some time ago, I did not like to say I had my doubts about his conduct – an ugly thing to say about any man. But I had, and I was not the only one. Yet maybe I was not as wise as I supposed, for although he still looks like a flash cove in a flash ship, he did distinguish himself up the Mediterranean with Admiral Smith.'

'That, I presume, was where he came by his star? It is an order I have never seen.'

'Yes, the Turks handed out quite a number, but they were thought rather absurd, and not many officers asked permission to wear them: only Smith and Clonfert, I believe. And he has also carried out some creditable raids and cutting-out expeditions in these waters. He knows them well, and he has a native pilot; the *Otter* draws little water, even less than the *Néréide*, so he can stand in among the reefs; and according to Admiral Bertie he might almost be setting up as a rival to Cochrane in the matter of distressing the enemy.'

'Yes: I have heard of his enterprise, and of his ship's ability to go close to the shore. I shall no doubt have to be with him from time to time, to be landed and taken off. But just now you spoke of the odds. How do you see them at present?'

'Simply in terms of ships and guns, and only from the point of view of fighting at sea, they are rather against us. Then if you allow for the fact that we shall be more than two thousand miles from our base while they are in their home waters, with supplies at hand, why, you might say that they are in the nature of three to five. In the Channel or the Mediterranean I should put it nearer evens, since we are at sea all the time in those parts, and they are not: but their heavy frigates have been out the best part of a year now, plenty of time to work up their crews, given competent officers; and upon the whole the French officers are a competent set of men. But all this is very much up in the air – there are so many unknowns in the equation. For one thing, I know nothing of their captains, and everything depends on them. Once I catch sight of them at sea I shall be able to reckon the odds more accurately.'

'Once you have had a brush with them, you mean?'

'No. Once I have seen them, even hull-down on the horizon.'

'Could you indeed judge of their abilities at so remote a view?'

'Of course,' said Jack a little impatiently. 'What a fellow you are, Stephen. Any sailor can tell a great deal from the way another sailor sets his jib, or goes about, or flashes out his stuns'ls, just as you could tell a great deal about a doctor from the way he whipped off a leg.'

'Always this whipping off of a leg. It is my belief that for you people the whole noble art of medicine is summed up in the whipping off of a leg. I met a man yesterday – and he was so polite as to call on me today, quite sober – who would soon put you into a better way of thinking. He is the *Otter*'s surgeon. I should probably have to cultivate his acquaintance in any event, for our own purposes, since the *Otter* is, as you would say, an inshore prig; but I do not regret it now that I have met him. He is, or was, a man of shining parts. But to return to our odds: you would set them at five to three in favour of the French?'

'Something of that kind. If you add up guns and crews and tonnage it is a great deal worse; but of course I cannot really speak to the probability until I see them. Yet although I have sent a hundred Boadiceas to lend a hand aboard the *Sirius*, and although I know Pym is doing his utmost to get her ready for sea, our own ship has to take in six months' stores, and I should love to careen her too, the last chance of a clean bottom for God knows how long – I cannot see how we can sail before Saturday's tide. I shall keep the people hard at it, and harry the arsenal until they wish me damned, but apart from that there is nothing I can do: there is nothing that the Archangel Gabriel could do. So what do you say to some music, Stephen? We might work out some variations on "Begone Dull Care".'

Chapter Four

The squadron, standing north-east with the urgent trade-wind on the beam, made a noble sight; their perfect line covered half a mile of sea – and such a sea: the Indian Ocean at its finest, a sapphire not too deep, a blue that turned their worn sails a dazzling white. *Sirius*, *Néréide*, *Raisonable*, *Boadicea*, *Otter*, and away to leeward the East India Company's fast-sailing armed schooner *Wasp*, while beyond the *Wasp*, so exactly placed that it outlined her triangular courses, floated the only bank of cloud in the sky, the flat-bottomed clouds hanging over the mountains of La Réunion, themselves beneath the horizon.

The Cape and its uneasy storms lay two thousand miles astern, south and westward, eighteen days' sweet sailing; and by now the crews had long since recovered from the extreme exertion of getting their ships ready for sea three tides before it seemed humanly possible. But once at sea new exertions awaited them: for one thing, the perfection of this line, with each ship keeping station on the pennant at exactly a cable's length, could be achieved only by incessant care and watchfulness. The *Sirius*, with her foul bottom, kept setting and taking in her topgallants; the *Néréide* had perpetually to struggle against her tendency to sag to leeward; and Jack, standing on the poop of the *Raisonable*, saw that his dear but somewhat sluggish *Boadicea* was having an anxious time of it – Eliot was fiddling with his royals – while only the pennant-ship, fast in spite of her antiquity, and the *Otter* were at ease. And for another, all the ships except the *Boadicea* were disturbed, upset and harassed by the Commodore's passion for gunnery.

He had begun as soon as they sank Cape Agulhas, and

although they were by no means reconciled to the exercise they were used to his ways; they were quite sure what the Commodore would be at at this point in the afternoon watch when they saw the *Raisonable* signal to the *Wasp* and then bid the squadron wear together. Up and down the line the bosuns' calls shrilled high and clear, the hands stood poised upon their toes (for the competition between the ships was very keen, the horror of public disgrace very great), and the moment the *Raisonable* deviated from her line the others began their turn: round they came, as trim as could be, forming the line with their larboard tacks aboard, the wind one point free, a reversed line, with the *Otter* leading. They had no great press of sail and this was a simple manoeuvre; even so, it was well executed; there was not much amiss with their seamanship, reflected Jack, looking over the taffrail at the *Néréide*'s masts, all in one line, eclipsing those of the *Sirius*, her next astern. Meanwhile the schooner had cast off the targets, and she was making sail with remarkable diligence, being eager to run out of range as soon as possible.

It was an understandable eagerness, for as usual the *Otter* opened a fine brisk fire a little before her guns could really be said to bear, and her wilder shot whipped up the sea between the schooner and the target. Her second broadside was nearer the mark, and might have hit it if the Otters had waited for the top of the roll: her third resembled the first, except that one ball did skip over the target: and she did not manage a fourth. Jack, watch in hand, was calling the figures to the mathematical midshipman he had brought with him when the *Boadicea* spoke out, pitching her shot a trifle high but sweeping the hypothetical deck; her second broadside struck the enemy square amidships, and with rapturous cries her third and fourth demolished the floating wreckage. 'One minute fifty-five seconds,' wrote Spotted Dick upon his slate, following it with two points of admiration. 'As they bear, Mr Whittington,' called Jack. The *Raisonable* was understood to play no competitive role in all this: because of her age she could not blaze away with the single, timber-shattering roar of a younger ship, but every third gun of her lower deck, half charged, and several of her lighter pieces produced a slow rolling fire that would have done a certain amount of damage. Far more damage than the full but almost comically inept broadsides of the *Néréide*: two broadsides only, and those fired so high that no more than a single shot went home – a shot almost certainly fired by one of the quarter-gunners that Jack had most reluctantly sent into her. Then came *Sirius*, with two deliberate broadsides and then her five aftermost guns as the battered target went astern: slow but quite accurate at this moderate range.

Jack had neither the time nor the powder for any more. As soon as the guns were housed he signalled *Tack in succession* and called the schooner under his lee. From the moment they weighed from Simon's Town he had watched the sailing of the ships under his command with a very close attention, but never had he kept his glass so fixedly upon any one of them as now he kept it upon the *Wasp* as she came racing up close-hauled, throwing white water right down her lee-rail. She was a beautiful craft, beautifully handled, and she sailed closer to the wind than he would have thought possible; yet his anxious, worn expression did not lighten when she rounded to and lay there under the *Raisonable*'s quarter, her captain looking up at her lofty poop with an inquiring face.

Jack nodded absently to the schooner, told the signal lieutenant to summon the captain of the *Sirius*, stepped aft with a speaking-trumpet and hailed the *Boadicea*, desiring her acting-captain to come aboard. The Commodore received them rather formally in the fore-cabin, where Mr Peter handed Eliot written orders to proceed to the Mauritius in company with the *Sirius*, there to lie off Port-Louis, the capital and the chief port, in the north-west of the island, and to rendezvous with the rest of the squadron on that station: in the intervening time they were to watch the motions of the enemy and to gain all the information they could. To these orders Jack added a clear direction not to engage in any action unless the odds were heavily in their favour, together with some advice about arriving off Sable Point after dark and sending in boats to look into the harbour at crack of dawn, so that they could pull out against the sea-breeze. Then, in his care for the *Boadicea*, he was going on to beg Eliot not to carry too great a press of sail, not to set his royals – a spar carried away in these latitudes was a terrible loss – she must be humoured, not drove – when he realized that he sounded more like a mother-hen than was quite right. He stifled his recommendation about the *Boadicea*'s starboard cathead, saw them over the side, watched their ships steer north, and went below again, going right aft to the great cabin, where Stephen sat at a table, encoding letters on paper of surprising thinness.

'The great advantage of these ark-like vessels,' observed Stephen, 'is that one can at least speak in privacy. The Admiral, with his luxury of dining-room, bedroom, ante-chamber, fore-cabin, and then this magnificence with the balcony behind, could riot at his ease; the Commodore can freely speak his mind. A mind that is, I fear, oppressed by melancholy thoughts?'

'Yes: commodious, ain't it?' said Jack, stepping out on to the stern-gallery, from which he could see the *Wasp*, rising and falling ten feet on the long smooth swell and shivering her foretopsail from time to time to keep her pace down to that of the two-decker. Coming back he said, 'Stephen, I do so hate this vile scheme of yours.'

'I know you do, my dear,' said Stephen, 'You have frequently mentioned it. And each time I have replied, that in the first place the contacts and the information I seek are of essential importance; and in the second, that the risk is negligible. I walk two hundred paces along a strand clearly defined by palm-trees; I call at the second house I see – a house of which I have an accurate drawing – I make a contact of inestimable value, receive my information, deliver these documents, whose extreme tenuity, you see' – holding them out – 'renders them edible, as tradition doth require – I walk back to the boat and so to your swift-sailing machine, to join you, with the blessing, for breakfast. I promise not to linger, Jack, though La Réunion is another Ophir, to the philosophic mind.'

Jack paced up and down: all that Stephen said was perfectly reasonable. Yet not so many years ago Jack had fetched him out of Port Mahon more dead than alive, Port Mahon in Minorca, where he had been caught on a secret mission, interrogated with all the barbarity of the Inquisition, and very nearly destroyed.

'Minorca was entirely different,' said Stephen. 'In that case I had been undermined at home. Here the possibility does not exist.'

'It is not only that,' said Jack, coming to a halt in front of a chart of the coast of La Réunion. 'Just look at these God-damned reefs. Think of the surf. I have told you again and again, Stephen, these inshore waters are hellish dangerous – reefs everywhere, half of 'em uncharted, the most tremendous surf. I know what I am talking about. I was here as a boy. There is scarcely a beach where you can land in safety, even when the swell is more moderate by half. To get into your Petite Anse you must run through a gap in the reef not a cable's length across even at high tide, by moonlight. And what if this Company's chap don't find it? He is no pilot for these waters: admits it candidly.'

'The alternative is to go in the *Otter*. Clonfert does know these shores; and he has a native pilot. And since I shall have to spend some time in the *Otter* sooner or later, I am eager to know her captain. Much will depend upon our understanding.'

'Certainly he knows this coast,' said Jack, 'but then the coast knows him. He has been in and out a score of times on this east side alone. The *Otter* is very recognizable, and if any fishing-boat or aviso or watchman on the cliffs sees her standing in, then every soldier and militiaman on the island will be running about, shooting the first thing that stirs. No: if it has to be, then the schooner is the right choice. Her captain is a steady young fellow and a good seaman; nothing flash or gimcrack about him or his *Wasp*. Besides, there is the time.'

'Sure, I should prefer the schooner. She leaves us at Rodriguez for Bombay, as I understand it, and that will preserve my character a little longer.'

'Well,' said Jack in the most unwilling voice. 'But I tell you, Stephen, I shall give him absolute orders to return immediately if he cannot make out his leading marks at once, or at the least sign of movement ashore. And Stephen, I must tell you this, too: if the scheme goes wrong, I cannot land a party to bring you off.'

'It would be madness to attempt any such thing,' said Stephen placidly; and after a slight pause, 'Honest Jack, would it be uncivil to remind you, that time waits for no man? This also applies, they tell me, to the tide.'

'Then at least,' cried Jack, 'I can send Bonden with you, and have a carronade mounted in the boat.'

'That would be kind; and might I suggest that black men for the boat's crew would be a diabolically cunning stroke, by way of amusing the enemy? For we must assume that he sees in the dark, the creature.'

'I shall attend to it this minute,' said Jack, and he left Stephen to his encoding.

A little before four bells in the afternoon watch Dr Maturin was lowered like a parcel on to the heaving deck of the *Wasp*, where Bonden seized him, cast off the five fathoms of stout line that had held him motionless (no one had the least opinion of his powers of self-preservation, at sea) and led him aft, whispering, 'Don't forget to pull off your hat, sir.'

It was a round hat of French manufacture, and Stephen took it off to the schooner's quarterdeck and to her captain with something of an air; then turning about with the intention of waving it to Jack he found that he was gazing over a broad lane of sea at the *Raisonable*'s stolid figurehead. The schooner had already crossed the two-decker's bows, and she was now flying goose-winged towards the clouds that hung over La Réunion.

'If you will step this way, sir,' said the captain of the *Wasp*, 'I believe we shall find our dinner ready.'

At the same moment Killick mounted to the poop of the *Raisonable*, where Jack was staring after the schooner, and stated, with something of his old acerbity, that 'the gentlemen were treading on one another's toes in the halfdeck this ten minutes past: and his honour still in his trousers.' Abruptly Jack realized that he had forgotten his invitation to the wardroom, that he was improperly dressed – north of Capricorn once more he had reverted to the free and easy ducks – and that he was in danger of committing unpunctuality. He darted below, huddled on his uniform, and shot into the great cabin just as five bells struck. Here he received his guests, the sailors in their best blue coats, the soldiers in their scarlet, and all of them red-faced in the heat, for they had had their finery on for the last half-hour at least: presently he led them to the dining-table, where the skylight admitted the rays of the ardent sun, and they grew redder still. At the beginning of a cruise, and often right through it, these feasts, theoretically the gathering of equals for social intercourse but in fact the almost obligatory attendance of men belonging to different steps of a rigid and never-forgotten hierarchy, tended to be ponderous affairs. Jack was perfectly aware of it, and he exerted himself to give some semblance of spontaneity to his entertainment. He tried very hard, and at one point, feeling for the sufferings of the Marine captain whose stock was bringing him nearer and nearer to a cerebral congestion, he even thought of bidding them take off their heavy coats: but that would never do – a disproportioned thought indeed – for although he naturally liked his guests to enjoy themselves, he must not conciliate their goodwill by the least improper concession; they must enjoy themselves within the limits of naval convention, and these limits certainly did not extend to turning the cabin into a bawdy-house. He confined himself to ordering the awning, removed for Stephen's aerial voyage, to be rigged again, and water to be dashed upon the deck.

Although his heart was not in it, he laboured on: yet

artificial conviviality is rarely infectious, and still they sat, hot, prim, polite. Convention required that no man but Jack Aubrey should initiate any conversation, and since they had not yet taken the measure of their new Commodore they obeyed it religiously. Presently he began to run short of topics, and he was reduced to urging them to eat and drink. For his own part he could only go through the motions of eating – his stomach was quite closed – but as a grateful coolness began to come down from the shaded skylight, wafted by the unvarying south-east trade, the bottle went about more briskly. Even before the port came to the table each man had a shining, glazed appearance, a tendency to stare and hold himself very straight, and each man behaved with even greater care as the decanter went its rounds – tolerably dismal rounds, as Jack could not but inwardly confess.

Dinner in the *Wasp*'s low triangular cabin was a very different matter. Since this coming night's activity called for a mind as clear as it could be Stephen had begged for thin cold coffee: Mr Fortescue drank no wine at any time, so the bottle he had provided for his guest stood untouched between the lime-juice and the tall brass pot while the two of them devoured a great mound of curry so Vesuvian that it paled the tropic sun. Each had early discovered the other's passionate concern with birds; and now, after a modest though fully-detailed account of petrels he had known, Mr Fortescue observed that there was nothing like a sailor's life for bringing a man acquainted with the world.

'Sir, sir,' cried Stephen, waving a Bombay duck, 'how can you speak so? Every ship I have sailed upon might have been called the Tantalus. They have carried me to remote countries, within reach of the paradise-bird, the ostrich, the sacred ibis; they have set me down in a variety of smelly and essentially identical havens; and then, almost without exception, they have hurried me away. The wealth of the Indies is within my grasp, and I am hurried away to another stinking port a thousand miles away, where exactly the same thing occurs. In candour I must not deny that the intervening ocean may reveal wonders that more than compensate the tedium of one's confinement, the Judaic ritual of life aboard – I have beheld the albatross! – but these are fleeting glimpses: we know nothing of the birds' economy, the interesting period of their loves, their solicitude for their young, their domestic tasks and cares. Yet all this is just at hand, attained by enormous expense of spirit and of the public treasure: and it is thrown away. No: I can conceive of no more deeply frustrating life for a naturalist than that of a sailor, whose lot it is to traverse the world without ever seeing it. But perhaps, sir, you have been more fortunate?'

Mr Fortescue, though freely admitting the justice of Dr Maturin's observations in general, had indeed been more fortunate, particularly in respect of the great albatross, *Diomedea exulans*, to which the Doctor had so feelingly referred: he had been cast away on Tristan da Cunha, where he had lived with and upon albatrosses, thousands and thousands of albatrosses, to say nothing of the penguins, terns, skuas, prions, the indigenous gallinule and a hitherto nondescript finch. He had sat with albatrosses right through their incubation; he had weighed, measured, and eaten their eggs; he had attended to their nuptial ceremonies; and, having been cast away with a piece of pencil and the *Complete Practical Navigator*, whose blank pages served for notes and measurements, he had, to the best of his poor abilities, drawn them.

'And were you indeed able to make illustrated notes?' cried Stephen, his eyes gleaming. 'How I wish, oh how I wish, that you might be persuaded to communicate them, at some not too distant time!'

As it happened, said Mr Fortescue, reaching for the book, they were just at hand, entirely at Dr Maturin's service; and he rather thought that there might be some specimens – eggs, skins, and bones – in the locker upon which he sat.

They were still with their albatrosses at nightfall, when the chaotic mountains of La Réunion stood black against the afterglow, and when Jack, with the taste of brass in his mouth and an aching head, began his pacing of the poop, glancing westward at each turn, although there could not be the slightest chance of seeing the *Wasp* much before dawn. It was a pacing that continued as the stars swept widdershins round the southern sky and watch succeeded watch: nervous and uneasy at first, it settled into a mechanical to and fro of his body, leaving his mind to run clear. By this stage he was fairly peaceful, and between watching the stars he ran over his calculations, always coming up with the same comforting result: La Réunion lay at the apex of a triangle whose base was the squadron's course during the afternoon and then the night, its southern arm the *Wasp's* path taking Stephen in, an arm some fifty miles long. He had kept the squadron under topsails alone, and having checked the rate of sailing each time the log was heaved he was confident that they would have run off eighty miles at about four bells in the morning watch, reaching the point at which the northern arm of the triangle, that of the schooner bringing Stephen back, should meet the base, making a neat isosceles of the whole. In these seas, with their perfectly steady wind, such calculations could be made with remarkable accuracy; and here the only important variable was the time Stephen spent ashore, which Jack provisionally set at three hours.

The middle watch wore on: once a flying squid struck against the great stern-lantern: otherwise the quiet night-routine of the ship moved along its invariable course. The wind sang an even note in the rigging, the water slipped along the side, the phosphorescent wake stretched out, a straight line broken by the bow-wave of the *Otter*, two cables' lengths astern; and at each stroke of the bell the sentinels called out from their stations, 'All's well', 'All's well', right round the ship and up and down the squadron.

'I hope to God they are right,' said Jack. He stepped down to the quarterdeck and looked at the log-board again. He was strongly tempted to go up into the top or even to the masthead; but that would singularize the whole thing too much – draw too much attention to it – and he returned to his lonely poop, only desiring the officer of the watch to send a good man aloft with a night-glass and bid him keep a sharp lookout.

He was still on the poop when the eastern stars began to pale: the morning watch had been called long since and men were moving about the dim deck, sprinkling sand. Jack's certainties had vanished an hour ago: his neat isosceles triangle had fled down the wind, routed by a thousand fresh unknown quantities. He stood still now, leaning on the rail and searching the horizon from the west to south-west. The blazing rim of the sun thrust up; light shot into the eastern sky; and the lookout hailed, 'Sail ho.'

'Where away?' cried Jack.

'On the starboard beam, sir. *Wasp*. A-lying to.'

And there indeed she was, hull-down, well to the east, her triangular sails just nicking the rising sun. Jack called down to the quarterdeck, 'Make sail to close her,' and resumed his pacing. The steady grind of holystones, the slap of swabs: full day-time life returned to the *Raisonable* as she set her topgallants and ran fast along the line that should cut the schooner's path. When his powerful glass had shown him Stephen walking about far over there, Jack went below, said, 'Breakfast in the after-cabin, Killick,' and stretched himself out on his cot for a while. Presently he heard the officer of the watch call for a bosun's chair, agitated cries of 'Handsomely, handsomely, there. Boom him off the backstay,' and a little later Stephen's familiar step.

'Good morning, Stephen,' he said. 'You look as pleased as Punch – the trip was to your liking, I hope and trust?'

'The most delightful trip, I thank you, Jack; and a very good morning to you too. Most delightful . . . look!' He held out his two hands, opened them cautiously and disclosed an enormous egg.

'Well, it is a prodigious fine egg, to be sure,' said Jack: then, raising his voice, 'Killick, light along the breakfast, will you? Bear a hand, there.'

'Other things have I brought with me,' said Stephen, drawing a green-baize parcel from his pocket and a large cloth bag. 'But nothing in comparison with the truly regal gift of that most deserving young man Fortescue. For what you see there, Jack, is nothing less than the concrete evidence of the albatross's gigantic love. Whereas this' – pointing to the gently heaving parcel – 'is no more than a poll-parrot of the common green, or West African, species, too loquacious for its own good.' He undid the baize, snipped the band confining the parrot's wings, and set the bird upon its feet. The parrot instantly cried, 'A bas Buonaparte. Salaud, salaud, salaud,' in a metallic, indignant voice, climbed on to the back of his chair, and began to preen its ruffled feathers. 'The cloth bag, on the other hand, contains some of the finest coffee I have ever tasted; it grows to great advantage upon the island.'

Breakfast appeared, and when they were alone again Jack said, 'So you did not spend all your time ashore bird's nesting, I collect. Would it be proper to tell me anything about the rest of your journey?'

'Oh, that,' said Stephen, setting his egg sideways upon a butter-dish to see it at a better angle. 'Yes, yes: it was a straightforward piece of routine, perfectly simple, as I told you. Fruitful, however. I shall not tell you about my interlocutor – far better to know nothing in these cases – apart from saying that I take him to be a wholly reliable source, exceptionable only in his prolonged retention of this indiscreet fowl, a fault of which he was himself most sensible. Nor shall I trouble you with the political aspect: but I have a clear notion of the military side. I believe it to be a true statement of the position, and am not without hope that it will give you pleasure. In the first place, our accession of strength is as yet unknown: in the second, the two most recently captured Indiamen, the *Europe* and the *Streatham*, are in St Paul's road, on the other side of the island, together with their captor, the frigate *Caroline*, whose inward parts are alleged to require some attention that will keep her there for perhaps a fortnight. In fact her captain, a most amiable young man called Feretier, is attached to the wife of the Governor, General Desbrusleys, a passionate gentleman who is at odds with Captain Saint-Michiel, the commandant of St Paul's, and with most of the other officers on La Réunion. At present he is at Saint-Denis: his forces amount to something over three thousand men, including the militia; but they are stationed at various points, twenty and even thirty miles apart over difficult mountain country; and although St Paul's is strongly defended by batteries and fortifications mounting, let us see, nine and eight is seventeen – I write seven and I retain one; five and five is ten, and with the one that I retained, eleven – mounting a hundred and seventeen guns, you may consider it practicable, in spite of the difficulty of landing on these shores, to which you have so frequently adverted. This rude sketch shows the approximate location of the batteries. This the disposition of the troops. You will forgive me for labouring the obvious when I say, that if you do decide to act, then celerity is everything. "Lose not a minute", as you would put it.'

'Lord, Stephen, how happy you make me,' said Jack, taking the paper and comparing it with his chart of St Paul's roadstead and the shore. 'Yes, yes: I see. A crossing fire, of course. Forty-two-pounders, I dare say; and well served, no doubt. There is no possibility of cutting the Indiamen or the frigate out, none at all, without we take the batteries. And that we cannot do with our Marines and seamen: but three or four hundred soldiers from Rodriguez would just tip the scale, I do believe. We could not hold the place, of course, but we might take the ships – there is a fair chance that we take the ships.' He stared at the paper and at his chart. 'Yes: a tough nut, to be sure; but if only I can persuade the soldiers on Rodriguez to move at once, and if only we can get our men ashore, I believe we can crack it. St Paul's is on the leeward side, where the surf is not so wicked unless the wind lies in the west . . . but I quite take your point about losing no time, Stephen . . .' He ran out of the cabin, and a few moments later Stephen, turning the egg over in his hands, heard the *Raisonable* begin to speak as she bore up for Rodriguez, spreading sail after sail: the masts complained, the taut rigging sang with a greater urgency, the sound of the water racing along her side mounted to a diffused roar; the complex orchestra of cordage, wood under stress, moving sea and wind, all-pervading sound, exalting to the sea-borne ear – a sound that never slackened day or night while the squadron made good its five hundred miles with the strong, steady south-east wind just abaft the beam.

Rodriguez: the low dome of the island lay clear on the starboard bow at dawn on Thursday, a greenish dome, its skyline stuck with palm-trees, in a green lagoon; all round the immense surrounding reef the white of breakers, and beyond it the intense blue of the open sea, uninterrupted for five thousand miles to windward. A man-of-war bird passed a few feet overhead, its long forked tail opening and closing as it glided through the swirling currents about the forestaysail and the jibs, but neither Jack nor Stephen moved their steady gaze from the land. On a flat tongue of land with a large house upon it and some huts, neat rows of tents could already be seen: no great number of them, but enough to shelter the three or four hundred soldiers that might make the descent on La Réunion a possibility, if only their commanding officer could be induced to stir. Jack had seen combined operations by the score, few of them a pleasant memory; and the likelihood of miserable jealousies between army and navy, the divided command, to say nothing of divided councils, were clear in his mind. He was superior to Lieutenant-Colonel Keating in rank, but that gave him a mere precedence, no right to issue orders: it would have to be a true, willing cooperation or nothing. He must rely upon his powers of exposition: and as though an unremitting glare might carry conviction, he kept the glass trained on the house, moving it only occasionally to glance at the gap in the surf that showed the narrow passage into the lagoon.

Stephen's mind was largely taken up with the same considerations; yet part of it was also aware, vividly aware, that the island gliding towards him was the home of an enormous land tortoise, not perhaps quite so vast as *Testudo aubreii*, discovered and named by himself on a comparable island in this same ocean, but even so one of the wonders of the world;

and, more important still, that until recently it had been the home, the only home, of the solitaire, a bird in some ways resembling the dodo, equally extinct alas, but still less known to science, even in fragmentary remains. He turned over a number of approaches to this subject, none wholly satisfactory, given Jack's gross insensibility to all science without an immediate application: for Captain Aubrey, as for the rest of brute creation, there were only two kinds of birds, the edible and the inedible. Even after prolonged meditation, during which the squadron reduced sail for the first time in fifty-two hours, he could produce no more than a timid 'Were we compelled to stay a short while . . .' that passed unnoticed, for as he spoke Jack raised his speaking-trumpet and hailed the *Néréide*, saying, 'Lead in, if you please, Captain Corbett. And preserve us from evil.'

'Amen,' said a forecastleman automatically, glancing at the Commodore with horror as soon as the word was out of his mouth.

'. . . perhaps I might be allowed a party,' continued Stephen, 'a very small party, consisting only of ambulant cases . . .' He would have added 'to look for bones', if the Commodore's eager determined expression had not convinced him that he might as well have pleaded with the ship's figurehead.

The barge splashed down into the calm waters of the lagoon, its crew stretched out as they were bid, and this same eager determined expression advanced with long strides up the coral beach to meet Colonel Keating. They exchanged salutes, shook hands, and the soldier said, 'You will not remember me, sir, but I was at a dinner given in your honour at Calcutta after your magnificent defence of the China fleet.'

'Certainly I remember you, sir,' said Jack, who had indeed some recollection of this tall, lean figure – a long-nosed, capable face that raised his hopes, 'and am very happy to see you again.'

The Colonel looked pleased, and as he led Jack through a double hedge of his men, Englishmen of the 56th Foot on the one side, turbaned sepoys of the 2nd regiment of Bombay

Infantry on the other, he observed, 'How delighted we were to see you coming in. We have been so cruelly bored on this dismal rock, these last few months – reduced to tortoise-races – nothing to look forward to except the arrival of the main body next year – nothing to shoot except guinea-fowl.' Jack instantly seized upon the opening and said, 'If we are of the same mind, Colonel, I believe I can do away with your boredom. I can offer you something better than guinea-fowl to shoot at.'

'Can you, by God?' cried the soldier, with a look as keen as Jack's. 'I rather hoped something might be afoot, when I saw you come ashore so quick.'

In the tents, drinking tepid sherbet, Jack stated the case: he felt almost certain that the Colonel, though mute, was with him, but even so his heart thumped strangely as he spoke the words that must bring the answer, positive, negative, or temporizing: 'And so, sir, I should value your appreciation of the position.'

'Sure, I am of your mind entirely,' said Keating straight away. 'There are only two things that make me hesitate – hesitate as the officer commanding the troops on Rodriguez, I mean, not as Harry Keating. The first is that I have barely four hundred men here, a mere advance-party to build the fort and prepare the lines. It was never imagined that I should move until the arrival of the main body with the next monsoon, and I might be broke for stirring, for leaving my command. Yet as against that, I know the Company loves you like a son, so I might equally well be broke for not falling in with your plan of campaign. As far as that goes, then, I should choose to follow my own inclination, which is the same as yours, sir. The second is this question of landing through the surf – the choice of our disembarkation. As you pointed out so candidly, there lies the crux. For with no more than your Marines and what seamen you can spare – say six hundred men with my few companies – it must necessarily be nip and tuck. My men, and particularly the sepoys, are not clever in boats: if we do not land cleanly and carry their works out of hand, a neat *coup de main*, there will be the devil to pay, once their columns start coming in from Saint-Denis and the other places. If I could be satisfied on that point, I should cry "done directly".'

'I cannot pretend to be well acquainted with the western side of the island myself,' said Jack, 'but I have two captains here with a vast deal of local knowledge. Let us hear what they have to say.'

Colonel Keating's conscience longed to be satisfied, and it would have taken far less to do so than Corbett's vehement assertion that landing on the west side, north of St Paul's, so long as the wind stayed in the south-east, which it did three hundred days in the year, was as easy as kiss my hand, particularly when this was reinforced by Clonfert's still more positive statement that even with a westerly wind he would undertake to set a thousand men ashore in a sheltered cove accessible through gaps in the reef known to his black pilot. But the Colonel was less pleased when the two captains disagreed violently upon the best place for the landing, Clonfert maintaining that the St Giles inlet was the obvious choice, Corbett that no one but a blockhead would attempt anything but the Pointe des Galets, adding, in reply to Clonfert's objection that it was seven miles from St Paul's, that he conceived the opinion of a post-captain with a *real* knowledge of these waters, acquired over many years of service on the station during this war and the last, was likely to carry more weight than that of a very young commander. The Colonel retired into a grave, formal absence while the captains wrangled, the veiled personalities growing more naked until the Commodore called both to order, not without asperity. And somewhat later Keating's delight in the company of the sailors was damped again when Lord Clonfert abruptly excused himself before the end of dinner and left the tent as pale as he had been red at the beginning of the meal – a redness attributable to the Commodore's words, delivered in what was meant to be the privacy of the nascent fort: 'Lord Clonfert, I am exceedingly concerned that this display of ill-feeling should have taken place, above all that it should have taken place in the presence of Colonel

Keating. You forget the respect due to senior officers, sir. This must not occur again.'

'Lord, Stephen,' cried Jack as he came into the stern-gallery of the *Raisonable*, where Dr Maturin sat gazing wistfully at the land, 'what a capital fellow that Keating is! You might almost think he was a sailor. "When do you wish my men to be aboard?" says he. "Would six o'clock suit?" says I. "Perfectly, sir," says he; turns about, says to Major O'Neil, "Strike camp," and the tents vanish – the thing is done, with no more words bar a request that his Hindus should be given no salt beef and his Mahometans no salt pork. That is the kind of soldier I love! In three hours we shall be at sea! *Néréide* is preparing to receive them at this minute. Are you not delighted, Stephen?'

'Oh, excessively delighted; delighted beyond measure. But Jack, am I to understand that no shore-leave is to be allowed – that we are to be hurried from this place as we were hurried from the parturient whale off Cape Agulhas? I begged Mr Lloyd for a boat, a small boat, but he declared that it was as much as his skin was worth to suffer me to go without an order from you, adding, with an inhuman leer, that he thought the Commodore would have anchors atrip before the ebb. Yet surely it would be of immeasurable benefit to all hands, to be indulged in running about and frolicking, if no farther than the strand?'

'Bless you, Stephen,' said Jack, 'you shall have your boat, for what bugs you may gather in two hours and a half; for two hours and a half it is, mark you well, not a minute more; and I shall send Bonden with you.'

Stephen was making his laborious way down the stern-ladder, his searching foot was already poised over the boat itself, when the *Otter*'s yawl pulled alongside and a midshipman said, 'Dr Maturin, sir?'

Stephen writhed his neck round, directing a grim look at the young man: all his professional life ashore had been haunted by these vile messengers; innumerable concerts, theatres, operas, dinners, promised treats had been wrecked or interrupted by fools, mooncalves, who, to gain some private end, had broken a leg, had fits, or fallen into a catalepsy. 'Go and see my mate, Mr Carol,' he said.

'Dr McAdam's particular compliments to Dr Maturin,' went on the midshipman, 'and would be most grateful for his present advice.'

'Hell and death,' said Stephen. He crept up the ladder, flung some medical objects into a bag, and crept down again, holding the bag in his teeth.

A worried, perfectly sober McAdam received him aboard the *Otter*. 'You wished to see this case in its crisis, Doctor: pray step below,' he said in public; and in private, 'This is the crisis, God damn me, and a tear-my-guts-out crisis too. I am relieved to have you to consult with, colleague – am in three minds at the least.' He led him into the captain's cabin, and there, on the sofa, lay Lord Clonfert, doubled up with pain. He made a real attempt at mastering it to greet Stephen and to thank him for coming – 'Most benevolent – vastly obliged – *désolé* to receive him in these conditions' – but the strong gripes cut him very short.

Stephen examined him carefully, asked questions, examined him again, and the doctors withdrew. The attentive ears that hung about the neighbourhood could make precious little of their Latin, but it was understood that Dr Maturin would have nothing to do with Dr McAdam's iliac passion, still less his Lucatellus' balsam; that he slightly inclined to a colonic spasm; that he believed Dr McAdam might do well to exhibit *helleborus niger* in the heroic dose of twenty minims, together with forty drops of thebaic tincture and sixty of antimonial wine, accompanied, naturally, with a little Armenian bole, as a temporary expedient; he had known it answer in tormina of much the same kind (though less intense) that afflicted a purser, a wealthy purser who dreaded detection when the ship paid off; but this was a particularly difficult, interesting case, and one that called for a more prolonged consultation. Dr Maturin would send for the other lenitives he had mentioned, and when the enemata had had their effect, Dr McAdam might choose to walk on the island to discuss the matter at greater length: Dr Maturin always thought more clearly when walking. The ears dispersed during the coming and going of the messenger; they made nothing of the administration of the drugs other than the fact that the groans in the cabin stopped; but they did catch some words about 'delighted to attend the opening of the body, in the event of a contrary result' that earned Dr Maturin some brooding glances as the two medical men went over the side, for the Otters loved their captain.

Up and down they strolled among the hurrying soldiers, then through the tortoise-park, where the disconsolate French superintendent stood thigh-deep among some hundred of his charges, and so towards the interior, until at last the rollers crashing on the reef were no more than a continuous, half-heard thunder. Stephen had seen a flight of parrots that he could not identify, some francolins, a kind of banyan tree which, rooting from its branches, made dark arcades that sheltered countless fruit-bats the size of a moderate dove: and some promising caves; yet his professional mind had also followed McAdam's long and detailed account of his patient's habit of body, his diet, and his mind. He agreed with his colleague in rejecting physical causes. 'This is where the trouble lies,' repeated McAdam, striking the dome of his head, bald, naked and disagreeably blotched with ochre against the pallid, sweating scalp.

'You were not so sure of your diagnosis a little while ago, my friend, with your iliac passion and your strangulation,' said Stephen inwardly; and outwardly, 'You have known him a great while, I collect?'

'Sure, I knew him as a boy – I treated his father – and I have sailed with him these many years.'

'And *peccatum illud horribile inter Christianos non nominandum*, can you speak to that? I have known it produce strange sufferings, though mostly of a cutaneous nature; and none as extreme as this.'

'Buggery? No. I should certainly know it. There is repeated venereal commerce with the other sex, and always has been. Though indeed,' he said, standing while Stephen grubbed up a plant and wrapped it in his handkerchief, 'it is the wise man that can always separate male and female. Certainly men affect him far more than women; he has more women than he can do with – they pursue him in bands – they cause him much concern – but it is the men he really minds: I have seen it again and again. This crisis, now: I know it was brought on by your Captain Aubrey's checking him. Corbett is bad enough, but Aubrey . . . I had heard of him often and often, long before he ever came out to the Cape – every mention of him or of Cochrane in the Gazette, every piece of service gossip, analysed, diminished, magnified, praised, decried, compared with his own doings – cannot leave them alone, any more than a man can leave a wound in peace . . . Och, be damned to his whimsies – why does he have to be Alexander? Do you want a drink?' asked McAdam, in a different voice, pulling out a case-bottle.

'I do not,' said Stephen. Until now the decent conventions of medical conversation had restrained McAdam's language and even his harsh, barbarous dialect; but spirits worked very quickly upon his sodden frame, and Stephen found the liberated McAdam tedious. In any event, the sun was no more than a hand's-breadth above the horizon. He turned, walked quickly through the almost deserted camp, down the now empty beach with McAdam blundering after him, and into the boat.

'I beg you will take notice, Commodore,' he said, darting on to the poop, 'that I am come aboard seven minutes before my time, and desire it may be made up, whenever the requirements of the service next permit.'

For the time being the service required Stephen, his shipmates, and three hundred and sixty-eight soldiers to bowl along the twentieth parallel, and to cover the hundred leagues between Rodriguez and the rest of the squadron as briskly as ever the *Néréide*, with her heavy load, could be induced to pass through the sea. It would have been far more convenient to stow the troops in the spacious *Raisonable*, but here everything depended upon speed, and Jack dreaded the loss of time in transferring them to the *Néréide*, perhaps with the sea running high: for he had fixed upon Corbett's landing-place, and the *Néréide*, replete with local knowledge and drawing little water, was to set them ashore at the Pointe des Galets; she therefore ran westward horribly crowded and trailing a smell of Oriental cooking.

Cracking on as though yards, booms, gaffs and even top-masts were to be had for the asking in the nearest port, they ran off the distance in two days, and on the evening of the second they found the *Boadicea* and *Sirius* north-east of Mauritius, exact to the rendezvous and, as far as could be told, undetected from the land. This Jack learnt from the soaking Captain Pym, whom he summoned aboard the *Raisonable* in the most pitiless way through an ugly cross-sea, with a close-reef topsail wind sending warm green water over the waist of the two-decker. Pym had some solid intelligence, gained from two separate fishing-boats taken far off shore: the *Canonnière*, condemned by the surveyors as a man-of-war, had had all her guns but fourteen taken out and was refitting to carry a commercial cargo back to France in a month or so; on the other hand, only one of the powerful new frigates, the *Bellone*, was in Port-Louis, the *Manche* and the *Vénus* having sailed north-eastwards some time before, with six months' provisions aboard.

The heavy sea, the increasing wind, the sudden tropical darkness made it impossible to gather a council of war; and having seen the half-drowned Pym regain his ship, Jack called the *Boadicea* under his lee and in a voice that carried loud and clear over the general roar he desired Captain Eliot to proceed to St Paul's with the utmost dispatch, *the utmost dispatch*, to lie there in the offing, and to 'bottle 'em up until we join you – never mind about carrying away a spar or two.' The *Boadicea*, with her fire-power, would hold them if there was any attempt at getting away.

By the next day the squadron had left Saint-Louis far astern; they were clear of the disturbed winds and currents to the leeward of Mauritius, and in the moderate sea the Marines and a hundred seamen went aboard the *Néréide* to join the rest of the landing-party. The captains gathered with the Colonel and his staff in the great cabin of the *Raisonable*, and the Commodore ran over the plan of attack once more. Stephen was there, and Jack presented him, as casually as possible, as the political adviser to the governor-designate: this earned him a broad stare from Corbett and a curiously agreeable smile from Clonfert, but it aroused no emotion in the others, taken up as they were with the coming event. Lord Clonfert was looking pale and drawn, but much stronger than Stephen had expected: before the conference he had taken Dr Maturin aside and had thanked him for his care with an obliging warmth that was evidently intended to convey more than common civility. For most of the meeting he sat silent: only towards the end, moved by some impulse that Stephen could not make out, did he put forward the suggestion that he should lead the detachment of seamen – he had some knowledge of the country, and he spoke French. It made sense: Jack agreed, looked round the table, asked whether anyone had any further point to make, caught Stephen's eye, and said, 'Dr Maturin?'

'Yes, sir,' said Stephen. 'I have only this to say: in the event of the capture of St Paul's, it is of the first political consequence that the inhabitants should be well treated. Any looting, rape, or disorderly conduct would have the most prejudicial effect upon the political ends in view.'

They all looked grave, murmuring a general agreement, and shortly afterwards Jack stood up. He wished them all a very good night's sleep, he said, 'for it will be a busy day tomorrow, gentlemen; and if this blessed wind holds, it will start precious early. For my part I shall cut quarters and turn in the minute hammocks are piped down.'

He turned in, but it was not to sleep. For the first time in his sea-going life he lay awake, listening to the wind, watching the tell-tale compass over his cot, and going on deck every hour or so to look at the sky. The blessed wind never faltered, still less did it veer into the dreaded west; indeed it strengthened so much that early in the middle watch he reduced sail.

At the change of the watch he was on deck again. He

could feel the loom of the land somewhere on the larboard bow, and as his eyes grew used to the darkness he could in fact see the mountains of La Réunion clear against the starlit sky. He looked at his watch by the binnacle lamp; paced up and down the quarterdeck; called out, 'Sharp the bowlines, there,' and heard the answering 'One, two, three, belay oh!' 'Bowlines hauled, sir,' said the officer of the watch, and the hands returned to their cleaning of the decks. 'I wonder what Corbett will do about it,' he thought, 'with seven hundred people aboard and not an inch to shove a swab.' He looked at his watch again, stepped into the master's day-cabin to check it with the chronometer, checked his reckoning once more, and said, 'Signal *Néréide carry on.*' The coloured lanterns soared up, *Néréide* acknowledged and a few moments later he saw the dim form of the frigate shake out her reefs, set her topgallantsails, haul her wind two points, and stretch away for the land, away from the squadron, trailing her string of boats.

According to the plan she was to go in alone to avoid suspicion: the landing-parties were to take the batteries commanding the roadstead, and the squadron was then to sail in and deal with the men-of-war and the town. So far the timing was perfect. Corbett would have just light enough to see: Jack disliked the man, but he believed in his knowledge of the coast. But the waiting was going to be hard and long, since the troops had seven miles to march: he resumed his pacing. Seven miles to march, and all he could do in the meantime was to stand in quietly for St Paul's under topsails alone. He watched the sand in the half-hour glass: the top emptied, the glass was turned, the bell rang clear; again the sand began its busy journey, tumbling grain by grain, millions of grains. If all had gone well they should be on their way by now. The glass turned and turned again, and slowly the sky lightened in the east. Another turn, another bell: 'You may pipe the hands to breakfast, Mr Grant, and then clear the ship for action,' he said, and with a fair show of unconcern he walked into his cabin, into the smell of toast and coffee. How had Killick guessed?

Stephen was already up, sitting there clean, shaven and respectably dressed under the swinging lamp. He said, 'There is the strange look about you, brother?'

'A strange feeling, too,' said Jack. 'Do you know, Stephen, that in about one hour's time the dust will begin to fly, and what I shall do is just lie there in the road and give orders while the other men do the work? It has never happened to me before, and I don't relish it, I find. Though to be sure, Sophie would approve.'

'She would also beg you to drink your coffee while it is hot: and she would be in the right of it. There are few things more discouraging to the mind that likes to believe it is master in its own house, than the unquestionable effect of a full belly. Allow me to pour you a cup.'

The banging of the carpenters' mallets came closer as the bulkheads went down and the cabins vanished to give a clean sweep fore and aft: not that the poor old *Raisonable* could do much, clean sweep or not; but even so the familiar sound, the coffee and the toast brought his heart back to something like a natural state. The carpenter himself appeared at the door, begged pardon, hesitated. 'Carry on, Mr Gill,' said Jack pleasantly. 'Don't mind us.'

'It is irregular, sir, I know,' said the carpenter, not carrying on at all but advancing towards the table, 'and I beg you will forgive the liberty. But I fair dread the notion of a battle, sir. Man and boy I've been in the *Raisonable* these six and twenty year; I know her timbers, and I know her butt-heads; and with respect, sir, I make so bold as to say, the firing-off of they old guns will start 'em.'

'Mr Gill,' said Jack, 'I promise you I will use her reasonable. Reasonable, eh, you smoke it?' A ghost of his old merriment showed for a moment; a ghost of a smile appeared on the carpenter's face; but not much conviction.

On deck again, and now the world was full of growing light. The squadron was already right into the broad shallow bay: on the larboard quarter the cape stretched out far westwards into the sea; at the bottom of the bay stood the town of St Paul's, now no more than five miles away; behind rose the savage mountains of La Réunion, barring the eastern horizon; and in the offing lay the *Boadicea*. The wind was steady in the south-east out here, but the different patterns of the sea inshore showed odd local breezes blowing. Jack took his glass, searching for the *Néréide*: he swung it along the cape, the Pointe des Galets – a moderate surf on the outer reef, far less on the beach itself – and all at once he saw her, almost becalmed in the lee of the headland, working slowly out from behind an island against the send of the sea. At the same moment the signal-lieutenant caught sight of her, made out her hoist, and reported, '*Néréide*, sir: *troops on shore.*'

'Very good, Mr –' The young man's name escaped him. His glass ran along the coast, along the causeway that traversed a long stretch of flat watery ground, farther and farther along, and there they were: three bodies of them: first an exact column of red; then the seamen in a smaller, irregular, but compact blueish mass; and then the sepoys. Already they were much nearer to St Paul's than he had dared to hope: but could they ever take the batteries by surprise? Viewed from the sea, the red coats were horribly conspicuous.

'*Boadicea* signalling, sir,' said the lieutenant again. '*Enemy in sight, bearing due east.*'

That meant that the *Caroline* had not slipped out. 'Thank you, Mr Graham,' said Jack – the name came to him this time – 'Reply *Stand in*: and to the squadron *Make more sail.*' As he spoke a flaw in the wind shivered the *Raisonable*'s jib: he and every other man on board glanced up at the clouds gathering over the island: the dark masses had a look that none of them much cared for. Was the wind going to come foul at last? But in a moment the gust had passed, and the squadron, *Sirius, Raisonable* and *Otter*, ran fast and true straight for St Paul's and the powerful batteries guarding the port. And as they ran, so every eye aboard, furtively or openly, watched that distant progress on the land, for a long, long half-hour.

The trim columns far over there were losing shape: they

were advancing at the double now, closer and closer to the first battery guarding St Paul's, the Lambousière, closer and closer until they were hidden from Jack by a screen of trees. In a barely tolerable suspense he waited for the sound of the heavy French guns sending grape into the close-packed companies; but what he heard was a remote crackle of musketry, a faint wind-borne cheering. The red coats were swarming all over the battery, and already the sailors were beyond it, racing for the next, La Centière. Still in their dead silence the three ships stood on, *Boadicea* converging upon them from the west, *Néréide* tearing up from the north. In five minutes they would be within the extreme range of the third battery, La Neuve, right by the town, with its forty guns: now the harbour was wide open; there lay the *Caroline*, and there lay the Indiamen; and Jack could see boats plying between the frigate and the shore. She was landing troops. Beyond her the two Indiamen, a brig-of-war, several smaller vessels – total confusion there. Confusion too just outside the town, where the musket-fire was spreading fast, two distinct lines of fire, as though the French soldiers had formed at last, and were standing firm. Musketry, and then Jack saw the *Caroline* begin to turn; there had been some order amidst all that turmoil, for she had evidently laid out a spring: in his glass he could see the hands at her capstan, slewing her; and as her guns bore so she fired at the English troops, a steady, rapid independent fire. The brig was firing too. Yet scarcely had her first guns spoken but there was an answer from the Lambousière battery: the seamen had turned the guns on the shipping in the port, and they had sent up the union flag. Immediately afterwards the musket-fire round the Centière reached a paroxysm; the British colours ran up on the battery, and its guns joined in. The smoke drifted wide, a cloud with flashes in its heart.

Jack glanced up and down his line. The *Boadicea* had reached her station ahead: the *Néréide* was still half a mile astern. He must stand on past the guns of the third battery, tack and stand closer in. Although his guns would easily fetch the town by now he dared not fire into the mêlée at this range; even a broadside at the *Caroline* meant the risk of hitting his own people, directly behind. The inaction, the passive waiting, was extraordinarily painful, above all as the English soldiers seemed to be falling back. Slowly, slowly on, and silently; they were coming abreast of La Neuve. The waiting would not last much longer: round-shot would be all about their ears at any moment now. The battery glided by, full on the beam, and he could see the mouths of the guns. But not one spoke, and not a man was there to serve them: the gunners had either run, or they had joined the defenders. The confusion in the town now had a pattern, the French line had broken, and they were retreating up the hill. Yet for all that the round-shot came flying from the harbour. The *Caroline*, still firing fast from her starboard broadside, now gave the squadron her whole tier of larboard guns. She concentrated her fire on the pennant-ship, and at her first discharge she hulled the *Raisonable* three times and struck her maintop. Wreckage, a studdingsail-boom, and some blocks came hurtling down into the splinter-netting over the quarterdeck. The next sent a dozen hammocks flying amidships; yet still the squadron could not reply.

'You have noted the time, Mr Peter?' asked Jack, knotting a stray signal-halliard.

'Immediately, sir,' cried Peter. The secretary was a yellowish white, made all the more evident by his black clothes: his morning's beard showed strongly against his skin. 'Seventeen minutes after eight,' he said.

How the *Caroline* pasted them! She was completely shrouded in her own smoke, but still the twenty-four-pound shot came crashing home. 'Admirable practice,' observed Jack to the secretary. Still another steady broadside, and the ship's bulwark of hammocks had great ragged gaps in it; three men were down. The glass turned; the bell struck one. 'Mr Woods,' said Jack to the master, as he stood conning the ship, 'as soon as the church and the tower are in line, we shall go about. Mr Graham, to the squadron: *Tack in succession at the gun.* And then *Close engagement.*' The minutes dropped by, then at last the signal-gun. The squadron went about as smoothly as a machine, *Boadicea, Sirius, Raisonable, Otter, Néréide*; smoothly, but slower, close-hauled on the failing inshore breeze, into the reach of the French guns again. Nearer still, and now the Indiamen let fly, together with the brig and every armed vessel in the port. But now in the town the situation was clear enough. Union flags were flying from all the batteries but one, and at this close range the squadron's guns could at last tell friend from foe. In succession their forward guns began to speak: *Boadicea* fired some deliberate sighting shots, *Sirius* her half-broadside, and the *Raisonable*, a moderate rolling fire; *Otter* and *Néréide* nothing but their bow-guns yet. Eliot had a fine notion of close engagement, observed Jack to himself. The *Boadicea* had stopped firing and she was standing straight in to cross the bows of the *Caroline* as she lay there within twenty-five yards of the shore. At this rate she would surely ground in the next few minutes.

'*Boadicea* signalling: *Permission to anchor, sir,*' said a voice in his ear.

'*Affirmative,*' said Jack, and he turned to the waiting carpenter.

'Five foot of water in the well, sir,' reported Mr Gill, 'and we sprung a butt-end, with them old guns.'

'Mr Woods, haul your wind,' said Jack, never moving his eye from the *Boadicea*. 'Ship the pumps.' He saw her small bower splash down, followed by her stream-anchor: there she lay, her sails clewed up, right athwart the *Caroline*, within pistol-shot of the shore. And now her crew's long training showed itself: in a furious eruption of fire and smoke she played with both broadsides on the frigate, the Indiamen, and the remaining battery. The *Sirius*, the *Otter*, and from some distance, the *Néréide* supported her: the *Raisonable*, lying to, said nothing apart from a few symbolic shots from her stern-chaser. But Jack's spirit was entirely aboard the *Boadicea*, in the true heart of the battle, approving her every stroke; and when, in less than half a glass, the *Caroline's* colours came down, followed by those of all the other ships and of the last battery, his heart leapt as though she had struck to him. They came down, and a universal cheer went up from the entire squadron, echoed by a roaring from the land.

'My barge, Mr Warburton,' said Jack to the first lieutenant. 'And my compliments to Dr Maturin: we are going ashore.'

The town had suffered very little, and the square in which they met Colonel Keating, with a group of officers and civilians, might have been living in deep peace – windows open, stalls of bright fruit and vegetables displayed, the fountain played – but for the dead silence, all the heavier for the recent warlike thunder, and the total absence of inhabitants. 'Give you joy, Colonel,' said Jack in an unnaturally loud voice as they shook hands. 'You have done wonders, sir: I believe the place is ours.'

'For the moment we may say so, sir,' said Keating with a beaming smile, 'but they are rallying on the hills above, and Desbrusleys' column from Saint-Denis is likely to be here by nightfall. We must go to work at the double.' He laughed very cheerfully, and catching sight of Stephen he said, 'There you are, Doctor: a glorious good morning to you, sir. You politicoes will be pleased with us – we have behaved like lambs, sir, like Sunday-going lambs – not a maiden has been put to the blush, so far, and my men are all well in hand.'

'Might I beg for an officer and a few soldiers, Colonel?' said Stephen. 'I must find the mayor and the chief of police.'

'Certainly you may, sir. Captain Wilson will be delighted to accompany you. But please to remember, that we are likely to be bundled out in less than twelve hours' time; a couple of regiments, with their artillery playing on us from the heights, would make the place untenable.' He laughed again, and from some odd contagion the whole group laughed too: cautious faces peered at the mirth from behind window-curtains; a number of small black boys crept closer under the market stalls. 'Oh, Commodore,' he went on, 'where are my wits? Here are the captains of the Indiamen.'

'I am happy to see you, gentlemen,' said Jack, 'and beg you will go aboard your ships at once. We knocked them about a little, I fear, but I trust they will be ready for sea before . . .' His words were cut off by an earth-shaking explosion, the upward flight of dark lumps of masonry, their corresponding downward crash, as the Lambousière battery disintegrated.

'That will be your friend Lord Clonfert,' remarked the Colonel, chuckling. 'A very active officer. Now, Commodore, shall we attend to the public property?'

They attended to it, and to a great deal besides. Theirs was an enormously busy day, for not only had the more dangerous fortifications to be destroyed, a large number of English prisoners to be released, still more French prisoners to be secured, the wounded seamen from the *Caroline* – half the crew, headed by their captain – to be carried to the hospital, and committees of anxious citizens, clergy and merchants to be reassured, but the wind had fulfilled its earlier threat. It now lay somewhat to the west of south, and the surf was increasing every hour. The *Caroline*, the Indiamen, the *Grappler* brig, and several other vessels having cut their cables at the last moment, had to be heaved off; the *Raisonable* was obliged to be laid in a mud berth at the ebb for the angry Mr Gill to come at her sprung butt-end; while every officer, every bosun and carpenter that could possibly be spared from a thousand other urgent tasks was furiously busy in the French naval yard, an undreamt-of Tom Tiddler's ground strewn with cordage, sailcloth, and spars of every dimension. Stephen had an equally strenuous time with the mayor, the vicar-general, and the chief of police; while at the same time he made a large number of private contacts. His was a less physically active day than most, but at sunset, when the senior officers gathered at Keating's headquarters, a carefully-chosen cabaret by the port, and sat there refreshing themselves with white wine and an admirable local fish, he was as tired as any of them. The weariness was apparent in their drawn faces, the frequent yawns, the relaxed posture, but not in their expressions, and their spirits: they were still a band of grigs. Colonel Keating was as merry as ever when he passed Jack his little spy-glass and pointed out the French soldiers gathering on the heights above the town. 'They tell me the main column is to be led by General Desbrusleys himself,' he said, speaking loud to be heard above the surf. 'Yet I wonder a man of such spirit has not placed his artillery before this; there are some capital places up there, you know, for a plunging cross-fire. But no doubt he means to come by another route.'

A frantic Company's supercargo darted by, in search of hands to reload his precious silk. He plunged through the gathering maidens lining the port and vanished with a low, frustrated howl. The maidens resumed their vigil, clasping one another and giggling: none had yet been caused to blush, even by this late hour; but hope was not altogether dead, though the last boats were putting off.

'Make the good woman understand we mean to pay, would you, Stephen? She does not seem to understand French very well,' said Jack privately; and aloud, 'I do not wish to hurry you, gentlemen, but I believe it would be as well to go aboard. Weather permitting, we shall come ashore tomorrow and finish our task. The hands will be rested, and' – nodding at Stephen – 'in daylight they will be out of temptation.'

The weather did not permit. The wind settled into the west, blowing right on the land, and although the squadron, together with its captures and recaptures, rode easily far beyond the breakers, with a fine holding-ground and two cables veered out on end, and although the swell did not prevent a numerous gathering for breakfast in the *Raison-able*, it seemed evident that the thunderous surf, a quarter of a mile deep along the shore as far as eye could reach, must prevent any communication with the town. It was an uncommonly cheerful breakfast, with yesterday's action on shore fought over point by point, with kind words from the soldiers about the Navy's versatility, discipline and enterprise, and it was a breakfast that made surprising inroads on Jack's mutton hams from the Cape and his soft tack from

St Paul's; yet there was not an officer aboard who did not know that they had left a great deal undone in the town, partly from want of time and partly from want of an authoritative list of government as opposed to private property: Stephen had obtained the list a little before dark, but until that time he had strongly insisted that nothing but the most obvious military stores and equipment should be touched. Then again, all the sailors and most of the soldiers knew that if the wind kept in the west the squadron would be in a most uncomfortable position. Desbrusleys would bring his artillery from Saint-Denis under the cover of darkness and lob mortar-shells on to them from behind the nearest hill while they lay like sitting ducks, unable to beat out to sea: for the moment, however, the French seemed disinclined to move. Their forces could be seen on the mountain-ridge above St Paul's; but there they stayed, and their immobility contributed not a little to the gaiety of the meal.

It was not until well after dinner that a column was reported to be advancing over the causeway from Saint-Denis. A remarkably large column, too, with artillery. 'He will never get his guns across the marsh without fascines, however,' observed Colonel Keating, 'because we destroyed the bridge; and it will take him the best part of the day to cut them. The most tedious, wearing task I know, getting guns across a marsh.'

'The surf is growing less,' said Captain Corbett. 'In my opinion we shall be able to land tomorrow – look at the westward sky. Soon come, soon go: that's my experience.'

'Earlier than that, I trust,' said Jack. 'I should never rest easy again, was we not to blow up at least the first three buildings in Dr Maturin's list.'

'And from the political point of view,' said Stephen, 'I should rejoice to see the archives go up in flames: such an invaluable confusion.'

'If I may speak, sir,' said Lord Clonfert, 'I believe it could be attempted now, or at least before the evening. I brought away a couple of surf-boats, and there are more alongside the *Sirius*, if I am not mistaken. My men are used to handling them, and I will undertake to put a party of Marines and seamen ashore.'

'Perhaps in two or three hours,' said Jack, staring at the sea. How much was this Clonfert's desire to outdo Corbett? Even after yesterday's joint action their relationship was obviously still as bad as ever: even worse, maybe. Yet there was the importance of the objective; and these surf-boats, well managed, could do surprising things. But was Clonfert merely showing away? What kind of capers would be cut on shore? On the other hand, he had certainly done well yesterday . . . Jack felt that Clonfert's mental processes were foreign to him: there was something about the man that he could not make out, either at this point or after some hours of reflection, when he came to his pragmatic decision, gave the order, and stood on the *Raisonable*'s poop, watching the surf-boats pull away. They were on the edge of the whiteness, waiting for the huge roller: it came, sweeping the sea, rose again black against the white water, and again they shot forward: again and again, and the last wave pitched them high on the beach.

Now they were busy. A tower to the left of the town gave a great jerk, its parapet flying bodily into the air: smoke and dust surrounded it, the whole building settled into a low shapeless heap, and the vast boom reached the ship. A long pause, and then smoke appeared behind the administrative buildings. 'Those are my tax-gatherer's records,' said Stephen, beside him. 'If that does not render us beloved, the Bourbonnais are hard to please. General Desbrusleys seems sadly bogged down,' he added, shifting his glass to the far-distant stationary column in the marsh.

They watched: they watched. At one time Jack remarked that the surf was certainly diminishing; and at another he said, 'You know, Stephen, I am growing almost used to being a spectator: yesterday I thought I should hang myself from mere misery . . . I suppose it is what you pay for command. Look at the smoke, over beyond the arsenal. What now, Mr Grant?'

'I beg pardon, sir, but Mr Dale of the *Streatham* Indiaman

is in a great taking. He says they are burning his silk – begs you to see him.'

'Let him up, Mr Grant.'

'Sir, sir,' cried Mr Dale. 'They are burning our silk! Pray sir, signal them to stop. Our silk – our chief cargo – half a million pounds' worth of silk – the French stored it in that warehouse. Oh, pray, sir, signal them to . . . oh Lord, Lord' – clasping his hands – 'it is too late.' The smoke gave way to flame, to a great sheet of flame; and all the signals in the world would not put it out.

'Pray, Clonfert,' said Jack, when the captain came to report, 'why did you burn the store behind the arsenal?'

'Behind the arsenal, sir? I was assured it was government property. A most respectable man, a priest, assured me it was government property. Have I done wrong?'

'I am sure you acted with the best intentions, but it seems that the Indiamen's silk was there, to the tune of half a million.' Clonfert's face fell, he looked utterly wretched, and suddenly quite old. 'Never mind it,' said Jack. 'I dare say they exaggerate; and anyhow we have saved them three millions, as they themselves acknowledge. You have done nobly, nobly – how I envied you on shore! It was no doubt a necessary stroke, for if we are drove off, pretty foolish we should look, leaving all that in enemy hands. But come, you are soaking wet: should not you like to shift your clothes? I have plenty in my sleeping-cabin.'

It was no use. Clonfert retired, sad, cast down, his glory quite put out. Nor did he revive the next day, when, the sea almost calm again, the south-east wind re-established, and all the squadron's forces ready in the boats to oppose Desbrusleys, one of Stephen's new acquaintances put off from the shore with the news that the Saint-Denis column was retreating, and that Captain Saint-Michiel, the commandant of St Paul's, was willing to treat for a suspension of arms.

The news was visibly true: the column could be seen withdrawing. All hands turned to their ships, and presently the commandant's emissaries appeared. General Desbrusleys, it seemed, had blown out his brains; but whether this was the outcome of the unhappy gentleman's military or marital reverses, or of the two combined, did not appear. At all events, for the moment the French army command was in a state of hopeless confusion, and Saint-Michiel made no difficulty about signing an agreement that gave the British squadron a long, peaceful week in St Paul's. Peaceful, but active: they were able to destroy or take away a hundred and twenty-one guns and an immense quantity of powder and shot, to blow up the remaining fortifications, to reduce the naval yard to a mere desolation with not so much as a paint-pot in it, and to do wonders for that fine frigate the *Caroline*: while the Commodore and the Colonel had time to write their despatches, a most arduous and delicate undertaking. When Jack's were finished at last, stripped of all humanity and copied fair in Mr Peter's hand, together with the very moderate casualty-list, an exact amount of the captured ships and vessels, a somewhat less exact account of the government stores and provisions taken, and many other documents, he came to his difficult decision.

He sent for Corbett and Clonfert, receiving them in some state with his secretary beside him. To the first he said, 'Captain Corbett, since we already have a *Caroline* in the service, I have provisionally renamed her the *Bourbonnaise*; but there is nothing provisional in my offering you the command of her, and at the same time desiring you to proceed forthwith to the Cape with my despatches. I have no doubt the Admiral will send you straight home with them, so I will burden you, if I may, with my own personal letters. I have manned her with something near her complement, barring Marines of course, from the merchant-seamen released at St Paul's, so I must ask you to be very moderate in the article of followers. Here is your order, and this is my private packet.'

Corbett's habitually angry face was ill-suited for the expression of pleasure, but even so it cracked and expanded with delight. The man who carried these despatches – the news of the neatest, completest little victory in his experience – would be much caressed at the Admiralty: would be certain of the next plum going.

'I shall be moderation incarnate, sir,' he said. 'And may I say, sir, that nothing could increase my sense of this command more than the obliging manner in which it has been given?'

To the second he said, 'Lord Clonfert, it gives me great pleasure to appoint you to the *Néréide*, Vice Captain Corbett. Tomkinson, your first lieutenant, may have the *Otter*.' Clonfert too flushed bright at the news, the entirely unexpected news, of this decisive step in his career, the vital change from a sloop to a post-ship; he too made his acknowledgments, and more gracefully by far than Corbett; and for a while the full shining glory of the first day on La Réunion returned, indeed a greater glory. Yet it seemed to have some slight bitter aftertaste, for as he was taking his leave he said, with a smile not wholly of unmixed happiness, 'I never thought, sir, when we were lieutenants together, that it would be you that made me post.'

'He is an odd fish, Clonfert,' said Jack to Stephen, between two peaceful duets. 'You might almost think I had done him an injury, giving him his step.'

'You did so advisedly, not from any sudden whim? It is the real expression of your sense of his deserts, and not an alms? He should in fact be made a post-captain?'

'Why,' said Jack, 'it is rather a case of *faute de mieux*, as you would say. I should not like to have to rely upon him at all times; but one of them had to go, and he is a better captain than Corbett. His men will follow him anywhere. Perhaps he may lay out popularity more than I think right, but whether or no, your foremast Jack dearly loves a lord; and I must take advantage of that just as I should take advantage of a tide or a shift in the wind; I shall let him take most of his Otters into the *Néréide*, and scatter the Néréides about the squadron. That was a damned unhealthy ship.' He shook his head, looking grave, and played a series of deep notes: they changed however, promising a happy development; but before he reached it his dry bow refused its duty, and he reached out for the rosin.

'When you have done with my rosin, Jack – *my* rosin,

I say – would you be prepared to reveal our immediate destination?'

'It will please you, I believe. We must take Keating back to Rodriguez first, and you shall have a romp with your tortoises and your vampires; then, while the rest of the squadron is blockading Mauritius, down to the Cape to leave Eliot and the poor old *Raisonable*; then back in the *Boadicea*, which is taking the Indiamen south. Back to these waters, to see what can be done about the remaining frigates, unless you and Farquhar have further designs on La Réunion. I will not say I am sanguine, Stephen, because that might not be very clever; but I remember when you asked me how I should set the odds some weeks ago, I said three to five against us. Now I should say they are evens, or slightly in our favour.'

Chapter Five

The Admiral was pleased with the Commodore, as well he might be, for not only had Jack captured one of the four powerful French frigates that so disturbed Mr Bertie's peace of mind, and retaken two Indiamen together with a useful eighteen-gun sloop, not only had he destroyed one of the strongest French bases in the Indian Ocean, doing so with such briskness that the Admiral's dispositions would be admired even in Whitehall, which always called for quick results, but he had also enriched Mr Bertie to the extent of several thousand pounds. Just how many thousand it was impossible to say until a tribe of officials six thousand miles away should have set a value on a prodigious number of objects such as the three hundred and twenty pikes, forty rammers and forty sponges taken at St Paul's; but in any case Admiral Bertie would eventually receive one twelfth of the total sum that they arrived at: without having stirred hand or foot, without having given any advice more valuable than a general exhortation to 'go in and win', he had acquired a considerable addition to his fortune; and ever since his first charming conference with Captain Corbett, the fore-runner of the squadron, he had spent the chief of his time in drawing up detailed plans for new stabling and a pine-house at Langton Castle, where he lived, while in default of the coronet for which she longed, Mrs Bertie should have a suit of lace.

Yet although the Admiral was perhaps a little devious beneath his bonhomie he had a grateful heart – a fairly grateful heart; at least he was no gripe-farthing; and the moment the *Raisonable* was signalled he began to lay on a feast, sending two boats away to the westward for lobsters, his favourite dish.

As he led the Commodore towards this glowing spread, which was attended by almost all the eminent men and all the beautiful women of Cape Town, so long as they were white, he said, 'How happy I am to see you back so soon, Aubrey, and how very well things have turned out! I sent Corbett straight home with your splendid news, as soon as I had dashed off my covering letter: you will have a Gazette to yourself, I am sure. What a pretty ship she is, too, your *Bourbonnaise* – fine narrow entry, and as stiff as a steeple. I wish our yards could turn 'em out like that: yet after all, if you young fellows take 'em ready made, it saves our ship-wrights' time, eh? Ha, ha. I confirmed her new name, by the by, and shall confirm all your appointments: I am glad Clonfert is made post, though that was a sad unlucky stroke with the Company's silk: I dare say you keel-hauled him for it at the time. Still, 'tis of no use crying over spilt milk, as I always tell Mrs Bertie; and all's well that ends well. Clon-fert is made post, and you have taken four thumping prizes and half a dozen little ones. You did not see anything else on your way down, I suppose, just for the *bonne bouche*, as they say, ha, ha?'

'Well, sir, we sighted that Russian sloop *Diana* beating about off Rodriguez; but I thought I should best fall in with your views by disregarding her.'

The Admiral did not seem to hear. After a momentary absence he went on, 'Well, and so you knocked their batteries about their ears. I am glad of it, and Farquhar is cock-a-hoop, as far as a dry stick of a man like that can be cock-a-hoop – drinks no wine, and the water has rotted all the joy out of him – I did not ask him to this dinner: in any case, he declines all invitations. He is longing to see you, however, and your Dr Maturin; for the next bite, once Rodriguez is reinforced, is Bourbon for good and all. Or La Réunion, or Ile Buonaparte, as they call it. Damned fools: this chopping and changing is typical of your foreigner, don't you find, Aubrey? That should be with the next monsoon, as long as transports can be provided for three or four thousand men. What kind of man is this Dr Maturin, may I ask? Is he to be trusted? He looks something of the foreigner to me.'

'Oh, I believe he is quite trustworthy, sir,' said Jack, with an inward grin. 'Lord Keith has a great opinion of him: offered him to be physician of the fleet. And the Duke of Clarence called him in, when the whole faculty was at a stand. He thinks the world of Dr Maturin.'

'Oh, indeed?' cried the Admiral, deeply impressed. 'I shall have to take care of him, I find. Not that these clever politicoes can really be trusted, you know. You must take a long spoon to sup with the devil, I always say. However, let us get to our lobsters. You can trust my lobsters, Aubrey, ha, ha. I sent a couple of boats to the westward for 'em, the moment you made your number.'

The lobsters were trustworthy, so were the oysters, so was the rest of the enormous meal, which carried on, remove after remove, until the cloth was drawn at last and the port appeared, when Admiral Bertie called out, 'Fill up, gentlemen. Bumpers all round. Here's to Lucky Jack Aubrey with three times three; and may he thump 'em again and again.'

A week later the Governor of the Cape also honoured the Commodore with a feast. It consisted of game – blauwbok, springbok, steinbok, klipspringer, hartebeest, wildebeest, the black and the blue – no lobster at all, and it took even longer to eat; but this was as far as the Governor's originality could take him; once more the meal ended with cabinet pudding, and once more the guests drank their port wishing that Jack might thump them again and again.

At the time of this second toast Stephen was eating bread and cold meat with Mr Farquhar and Mr Prote, his secretary, in an upper room of the government printing-house, a secluded place from which the workmen had withdrawn. They were all of them more or less black, for in the light of Stephen's most recent intelligence they had been recasting a proclamation to the people of La Réunion, as well as a number of handbills and broadsheets that painted, in glowing colours and fluent French, the advantages of British rule, promising respect for religion, laws, customs and property, pointing out the inevitably disastrous consequences of resistance, and the rewards (perhaps a little imprecise and rhetorical) of cooperation. There were similar documents, though in a less forward state of preparation, addressed to the inhabitants of Mauritius; and all these were to be printed as secretly as possible, with the help of two confidential journeymen. Yet since neither of these knew a word in French, Farquhar and Prote had been perpetually in and out of the house, and both had grown fascinated by the technical processes of printing. In their eagerness to show Stephen their proficiency they corrected three long texts in the galley, reading by means of a little looking-glass that they tended to snatch from one another, plucking out letters, inserting others, prating about upper case, lower case, formes, coigns and composing-sticks, setting-rules and justification, and gradually smearing themselves, and him, with an unreasonable quantity of printer's ink.

They were no longer talking about the act of printing, however, not even about their insidious printed warfare: that, together with Stephen's detailed report of the promising state of public feeling on La Réunion and his account of the agents he had acquired, was far behind them; and now, as they ate their blotted meat, they discussed the poetry of the law, or rather poetry in the law, a subject to which they had been led by considerations on the inheritance of landed property in Mr Farquhar's future kingdom.

'The French system, their new French code, is very well on paper,' observed Farquhar, 'very well for a parcel of logical automata; but it quite overlooks the illogical, I might say almost supra-logical and poetic side of human nature. *Our* law, in its wisdom, has preserved much of this, and it is particularly remarkable in the customary tenure of land, and in petty serjeanty. Allow me to give you an example: in the manors of East and West Enbourne, in Berkshire, a widow shall have her free-bench – her *sedes libera*, or in barbarous law-Latin her *francus bancus* – in all her late husband's copyhold lands *dum sola et casta fuerit*; but if she be detected in amorous conversation with a person of the opposite sex – if she grant the last favours – she loses all, unless she appears in the next manor-court, riding backwards on a black ram, and reciting the following words:

> 'Here I am
> Riding on a black ram
> Like a whore as I am;
> And for my crinkum-crankum
> Have lost my binkum-bankum;
> And for my tail's game
> Am brought to this worldly shame.
> Therefore good Mr Steward let me have
> my lands again.

'My uncle owns one of these manors, and I have attended the court. I cannot adequately describe the merriment, the amiable confusion of the personable young widow, the flood of rustic wit, and – which is my real point – the universal, contented acceptance of her reinstatement, which I attribute largely to the power of poetry.'

'There may be a significant statistical relationship between the number of black ram-lambs suffered to reach maturity,' said Prote, 'and that of personable young widows.'

'And 'tis no isolated case,' continued Farquhar. 'For in the manor of Kilmersdon in Somerset, for example, we find what is essentially the same purgation, though in an abbreviated form, since no more than this distich is required:

> 'For mine arse's fault I take this pain.
> Therefore, my lord, give me my land again.

'Now is it not gratifying, gentlemen, to find our black rams – unprofitable creatures but for this interesting ceremony – so far apart as Berkshire and Somerset, with no record of a white ram's ever having been admitted? For your black ram, gentlemen, is, I am persuaded, intimately connected with the worship of the Druids . . .'

Mr Farquhar was a man with a good understanding and a great deal of information, but at the first mention of Druids, oak-groves or mistletoe a wild gleam came into his eye, a gleam so wild on this occasion that Stephen looked at his watch, rose to his feet, said that he must regretfully leave them, and gathered up his book.

'Should you not like to wash before you go?' asked Farquhar. 'You are somewhat mottled.'

'Thank you,' said Stephen. 'But the being upon whom I am about to wait, though eminent for precedence, does not stand on ceremony.'

'What can he have meant by eminent for precedence?' asked Mr Prote. 'Anyone who is anyone, apart from us, is at the Governor's.'

'He may well mean a black magus, or a potentate among the Hottentots. Now the Druids, I say . . .'

In fact the being's precedence was merely alphabetical: for in the gaiety of his heart Dr Maturin had referred to the aardvark. It stood before him now, a pale creature with a bulky hog-backed body close on five feet long, a broad tail, an immense elongated head ending in a disc-like snout, short stout legs and disproportionately long translucent ass's ears; it was partially covered with sparse yellowish hair that showed the unwholesome nightwalker's skin below; it blinked repeatedly. The aardvark was acutely conscious of its position and from time to time it licked its small tubular lips, for not only had it been measured and weighed, while a tuft of bristles that could ill be spared had been clipped from its flank, but now it was being looked at through a diminishing-glass and drawn. It was a meek, apologetic animal, incapable of biting and too shy to scratch; and it grew lower and lower in its spirits: its ears drooped until they obscured its weak, melancholy, long-lashed eyes.

'There, honey, it is done,' said Stephen, showing the aardvark its likeness: and calling upwards through the ceiling he said, 'Mr van der Poel, I am infinitely obliged to you, sir. Do not stir, I beg. I shall lock the door and leave the key under the mat: I am going back to the ship, and tomorrow you shall see the egg.'

Some hours later he beheld Simon's Town again, its inner anchorage scattered with Jack's prizes: it reminded him of Port Mahon long ago, when the *Sophie*'s captured feluccas, trabacaloes and xebecs lined the quay. 'That was very well,' he said, 'and Minorca a delightful island; but even Minorca could never boast the aardvark.' The street was filled with liberty-men, a cheerful crew, for not only had Jack ordered a modest advance of prize-money – two dollars a nob paid down on the capstan-head – but Dr Maturin's words on loot had not been obeyed quite as strictly as he could have wished, and pieces of the finest Oriental silk, slightly charred, covered the little forms, the infinitely seductive bosoms of the sailors' companions. He was hailed on all sides; kind hands led his hired nag away; and a Boadicean midshipman, smelling strongly of patchouli, rowed him out to the *Raisonable*. At ease in his spacious cabin he opened his book and looked at the picture again. 'It is perhaps the most gratifying beast I have ever figured,' he said, 'and it displays a touching affection for the good Mr van der Poel; I believe I shall attempt to colour it.' He turned back through the pages. Most were covered with the small close-written text of his diary, but there were several drawings – the Rodriguez tortoise, the seals of False Bay – some washed with water-colour. 'Perhaps not,' he said, considering them. 'My talents scarcely seem to lie that way.' He converted the Dutch weight of the aardvark into avoirdupois, sharpened his pen to a finer point, reflected for a while, gazing out of the scuttle, and began to write in his personal cipher.

'I cannot trace the chain of thought or rather of associations that leads me to reflect upon Clonfert and Jack Aubrey. Conceivably the aardvark plays a part, so ill-at-ease: but the links are obscure. Clonfert's tormina exercise my mind; for by whatever private scale of pain one may measure them, they must come tolerably high. It seems ludicrously facile to regard them as the direct transposition of his state of mind; yet McAdam is no fool except to himself; and in some not dissimilar cases that Dupuytren and I dissected we were able to eliminate any direct physical cause. The vermiform appendix, so often the villain in these apparent strangulations, as pink as a healthy worm, the whole tract from the oesophagus downwards, devoid of lesion. Clonfert is more of an Irishman, with the exacerbated susceptibilities of a subject race, than I had supposed; more indeed than I gave Jack to understand. I find that as a boy he did not attend a great English public school, as did most of his kind I have known; nor did he go early to sea and thereby wash away the barrier: the first years of his nominal service were book-time, as they call the amiable cheat by which a complaisant captain places an absent child upon his muster-roll. Far from it: he was brought up almost entirely by the servants at Jenkinsville (a desolate region). Squireen foster-parents too for a while, his own being so mad or so disreputable: and he seems to have sucked in the worst of both sides. On the one hand he derived his notion of himself as a lord from people who have had to cringe these many generations to hold on to the odd patch of land that is their only living; and on the other, though half belonging to them, he has been bred up to despise their religion, their language, their poverty, their manners and traditions. A conquering race, in the place of that conquest, is rarely amiable; the conquerors pay less obviously than the conquered, but perhaps in time they pay even more heavily, in the loss of the humane qualities. Hard, arrogant, profit-seeking adventurers flock to the spoil, and the natives, though outwardly civil, contemplate them with a resentment mingled with contempt, while at the same time respecting the face of conquest – acknowledging their greater strength. And to be divided between the two must lead to a strange confusion of sentiment. In Clonfert's case the result of this and of other factors seems to me an uneasy awareness of his own distinction (he often mentions it), a profound uncertainty of its real value, and a conviction that to validate its claims he should be twice as tall as other men. In spite of his high heels, both literal and figurative, he is not twice as tall as other men: Jack, in particular, tops him by a head and more. He has surrounded himself with a strikingly inferior set of officers, which I do not remember to have seen done in the Navy, where the aristocratic captains are almost always accompanied by aristocratic officers and midshipmen, just as a

Scotch commander will gather Scotchmen around him: no doubt they provide him with the approval he longs for; but how much can a man of his understanding value their approval? And if Lady Clonfert and Mrs Jennings are a fair example of his women, to what degree can their favours really gratify him?

'Upon this foundation, and upon what McAdam tells me, I could build up a moderately convincing Clonfert whose entire life is an unsatisfactory pretence: a puppet vainly striving to be another puppet, equally unreal – the antithesis of Jack, who has never played a part in his life, who has no need for any role. It would not satisfy me, however, for although it may have some truth in it and although it may go far towards pointing at the origin of the tormina and some other symptoms I have noted (McAdam did not appreciate the significance of the asymmetric *sudor insignis*), it does not take into account the fact that he is *not* a puppet. Nor, which is far more important, does it take into account the affection of his men: Jack asserts that sailors love a lord and no doubt that is profoundly true (apart from anything else, the fancied difference diminishes the servitude); but they do not go on loving a lord if he is worthless. They did not go on loving Prince William. No: a continued affection over a long period must be based upon the recognition of real qualities in the man, for a ship at sea, particularly a small ship on a foreign station, is an enclosed village; and whoever heard of the long-matured judgment of a village being wrong? The communal mind, even where the community is largely made up of unthinking and illiterate men, is very nearly as infallible as a Council. And the qualities valued by a community of men are commonly good nature, generosity and courage. Courage: here I am on the most shifting ground in the world. For what is it? Men put different values on their lives at different times: different men value approval at different rates – for some it is the prime mover. Two men go through the same motions for widely different reasons; their conduct bears the same name. Yet if Clonfert has not performed these actions I am very sure that his men would not esteem him as they do. Farquhar's illogicality may well render their affection for Lord Clonfert greater than it would be for Mr Scroggs, but that is merely an addition; the esteem is already there, and so are the actions upon which it is founded. I saw him storm a battery at St Paul's; and in the result his outward gestures, his élan, and indeed his success were indistinguishable from Jack Aubrey's.

'Jack Aubrey. The lieutenant of long ago is still visible in the grave commodore, but there are times when he has to be looked for. One constant is that indubitable happy courage, the courage of the fabled lion – how I wish I may see a lion – which makes him go into action as some men might go to their marriage-bed. *Every man would be a coward if he durst*: it is true of most, I do believe, certainly of me, probably of Clonfert; but not of Jack Aubrey. Marriage has changed him, except in this: he had hoped for too much, poor sanguine creature (though indeed he is sick for news from home). And the weight of this new responsibility; he feels it extremely: responsibility and the years – his youth is going or indeed is gone. The change is evident, but it is difficult to name many particular alterations, apart from the comparative want of gaiety, of that appetence for mirth, of those infinitesimal jests that caused him at least such enormous merriment. I might mention his attitude towards those under his command, apart from those he has known for years: it is attentive, conscientious, and informed; but is far less personal; his mind rather than his heart is concerned, and the people are primarily instruments of war. And his attitude towards the ship itself: well do I remember his boundless delight in his first command, although the *Sophie* was a sad shabby little tub of a thing – the way he could not see enough of her meagre charms, bounding about the masts, the rigging, and the inner parts with an indefatigable zeal, like a great boy. Now he is the captain of a lordly two-decker, with these vast rooms and balconies, and he is little more than polite to her; she might be one set of furnished lodgings rather than another. Though here I may be mistaken: some aspects of the sailor's life I do not understand. Then again there is the diminution not only of his animal spirits but also of his appetites: I am no friend to adultery, which surely promises more than it can perform except in the article of destruction; but I could wish that Jack had at least some temptation to withstand. His more fiery emotions, except where war is concerned, have cooled; Clonfert, younger in this as in many other ways, has retained his capacity for the extremes of feeling, certainly the extremity of pain, perhaps that of delight. The loss is a natural process no doubt, and one that prevents a man from burning away altogether before his time; but I should be sorry if, in Jack Aubrey's case, it were to proceed so far as a general cool indifference; for then the man I have known and valued so long would be no more than the walking corpse of himself.'

The sound of the bosun's call, the clash of the Marines presenting arms, told him that Jack Aubrey's body, quick or dead, was at this moment walking about within a few yards of him. Stephen dusted sand upon his book, closed it, and waited for the door to open.

The officer who appeared did indeed resemble Commodore rather than Lieutenant Aubrey, even after he had flung his coat and with it the marks of rank on to a nearby locker. He was bloated with food and wine; his eyes were red and there were liverish circles under them; and he was obviously far too hot. But as well as the jaded look of a man who has been obliged to eat and drink far too much and then sit in an open carriage for twenty miles in a torrid dust-storm, wearing clothes calculated for the English Channel, his face had an expression of discouragement.

'Oh for some more soldiers like Keating,' he said wearily. 'I cannot get them to move. We had a council after dinner, and I represented to them, that with the regiments under their command we could take La Réunion out of hand: the *Raisonable* would serve as a troop-carrier. St Paul's is wide open, with not one stone of the batteries standing on another. They agreed, and groaned, and lamented – they could not move without an order from the Horse-Guards; it had always been understood that the necessary forces were to come from the Madras establishment, perhaps with the next monsoon if transports could be found; if not, with the monsoon after that. By the next monsoon, said I, La Réunion would be bristling with guns, whereas now the French had very few, and those few served by men with no appetite for a battle of any kind: by the next monsoon their spirits would have revived, and they would have been reinforced from the Mauritius. Very true, said the soldiers, wagging their heads; but they feared that the plan worked out by the staff must stand: should I like to go shooting warthogs with them on Saturday? And to crown all, the brig was not a packet but a merchantman from the Azores – no letters of any kind. We might as well be at the back of the moon.'

'It is very trying, indeed,' said Stephen. 'What say you to some barley-water, with lime-juice in it? And then a swim? We could take a boat to the island where the seals live.'

To a cooler, fresher Jack he offered what comfort he could provide. He left the stolid torpor of the soldiers to one side – neither had really believed in the possibility of stirring them, after the dismal end of the unauthorized expedition to Buenos Aires from this very station not many years before – and concentrated on the changed perception of time during periods of activity; these busy weeks had assumed an importance unjustified by their sidereal, or as he might say their absolute measure; with regard to exterior events they still remained mere weeks; it had been unreasonable to expect anything on their return to the Cape; but now a ship might come in any day at all, loaded with mail.

'I hope you are right, Stephen,' said Jack, balancing on the gunwale and rubbing the long blue wound on his back. 'Sophie has been very much in my mind these last few days, and even the children. I dreamt of her last night, a huddled, uneasy dream; and I long to hear from her.' After a considering pause he said, 'I did bring back some more pleasant news, however: the Admiral is fairly confident of being able to add *Iphigenia* and *Magicienne* to the squadron within the next few weeks; he had word from Sumatra. But of course they will be coming from the east – not the least possibility of anything from home. The old *Leopard*, too, though nobody wants *her*: iron-sick throughout, a real graveyard ship.'

'The packet will come in from one day to the next, and it will bring a budget of tax-demands, bills, and an account of the usual domestic catastrophes: news of mumps, chicken-pox, a leaking tap; my prophetic soul sees it beneath the horizon.'

The days dropped by while the *Boadicea*, her holds emp-tied and herself heaved down with purchase to bollards on the shore, had her foul bottom cleaned; Jack set up his tele-scope with a new counterbalance that worked perfectly on land; Stephen saw his lion, a pride of lions; and then, although it had mistaken the horizon, his prophetic soul was shown to have been right: news did come in. But it was not domestic news, nor from the west: the flying *Wasp* had turned about in mid-ocean and had come racing back to the Cape to report that the French had taken three more Indiamen, HM sloop *Victor*, and the powerful Portuguese frigate *Minerva*.

The *Vénus* and the *Manche*, already at sea when the squad-ron looked into Port-Louis, had captured the *Windham*, the *United Kingdom*, and the *Charlton*, all Indiamen of the high-est value. The *Bellone*, slipping out past the blockade by night, had taken the eighteen-gun *Victor*, and then she and her prize had set about the *Minerva*, which mounted fifty-two guns, but which mounted them in vain against the fury of the French attack. The Portuguese, now *La Minerve*, was at present in Port-Louis, manned by seamen from the *Canonnière* and some deserters: the Indiamen, the *Vénus* and the *Manche* were probably there too, but of that the *Wasp* was not quite sure.

Before the turn of the tide Jack was at sea, the warthogs, the soldiers, and even his telescope left behind: he had shifted his pennant into the *Boadicea*, for the hurricane months were not far away, and the *Raisonable* could not face them. He was back in his own *Boadicea*, driving her through variable and sometimes contrary winds until they reached the steady south-east trade, when she lay over with her lee-rail under white water, her deck sloping like the roof of Ashgrove Cottage, and began to tear off her two hundred and fifty and even three hundred nautical miles between one noon observation and the next; for there was some remote hope of catching the Frenchmen and their prizes, cutting them off before they reached Mauritius.

On the second Sunday after their departure, with church rigged, Jack was reading the Articles of War in a loud, official, comminatory voice by way of sermon and all hands were trying to keep upright (for not a sail might be attempted to be touched). He had just reached article XXIX, which dealt with sodomy by hanging the sodomite and which always made Spotted Dick and other midshipmen swell purple from suppressed giggling at every monthly repetition, when two ships heaved in sight. They were a great way off, and without interrupting her devotions, such as they might be with every mind fixed earnestly upon the masthead, the *Boadicea* edged away to gain the weather-gage. But by the time Jack had reached *All crimes not capital* (there were precious few), and well before he cleared the ship for action, the windward stranger broke out the private signal. In answer to the *Boadicea*'s she made her number: the *Magicienne*; and her companion was the *Windham*.

The *Magicienne*, said Captain Curtis, coming aboard the Commodore, had retaken the Indiamen off the east coast of Mauritius. The *Windham* had been separated from her captor, the *Vénus*, during a tremendous sudden blow in 17°S; the *Magicienne* had snapped her up after something of a chase, beating to windward all day, and had then stood on all night in the hope of finding the French frigate. Curtis had found her at sunset, looking like a scarecrow with only her lower masts standing and a few scraps of canvas aboard, far away right under the land, creeping in with her tattered forecourse alone. But unhappily the land to which she was creeping was the entrance to Grand-Port; and when the land-breeze set in, blowing straight in her teeth, the *Magici-*

enne had the mortification of seeing the *Vénus* towed right under the guns of the Ile de la Passe, at the entrance to the haven.

'By the next morning, sir, when I could stand in,' said Curtis apologetically, 'she was half way up to the far end, and with my ammunition so low – only eleven rounds to a gun – and the Indiaman in such a state, I did not think it right to follow her.'

'Certainly not,' said Jack, thinking of that long inlet, guarded by the strongly fortified Ile de la Passe, by batteries on either side and at the bottom and even more by a tricky, winding fairway fringed with reefs: the Navy called it Port South-East, as opposed to Port-Louis in the north-west, and he knew it well. 'Certainly not. It would have meant throwing the *Magicienne* away; and I need her. Oh, yes, indeed, I need her, now they have that thumping great *Minerva*. You will dine with me, Curtis? Then we must bear away for Port-Louis.' They passed the Indiaman a tow, and lugging their heavy burden through the sea they stood on, the wind just abaft the beam.

Stephen Maturin had been deeply mistaken in supposing that Jack, older and more consequential, now looked upon ships as lodgings, more or less comfortable: the *Raisonable* had never been truly his; he was not wedded to her. The *Boadicea* was essentially different; he entered into her; he was one of her people. He knew them all, and with a few exceptions he liked them all: he was delighted to be back, and although Captain Eliot had been a perfectly unexceptionable officer, they were delighted to have him. They had in fact led Eliot a sad life of it, opposing an elastic but effective resistance to the slightest hint of change: 'The Commodore had always liked it this way; the Commodore had always liked it that; it was Captain Aubrey that had personally ordered the brass bow-chasers to be painted brown.' Jack particularly valued Mr Fellowes, his bosun, who had clung even more firmly than most to Captain Aubrey's sail-plan and his huge, ugly snatch-blocks that allowed hawsers to be instantly set up to the mastheads, there to withstand the strain of an extraordinary spread of canvas; and now that the *Boadicea*'s hold had been thoroughly restowed, her hull careened, and her standing-rigging rerove with the spoils of St Paul's, she answered their joint hopes entirely. In spite of her heavy burden she was now making nine knots at every heave of the log.

'She is making a steady nine knots,' said Jack, coming below after quarters.

'How happy you make me, Jack,' said Stephen. 'And you might make me even happier, should you so wish, by giving me a hand with this. The unreasonable attitude, or lurch, of the ship caused me to overset the chest.'

'God help us,' cried Jack, gazing at the mass of gold coins lying in a deep curve along the leeward side of the cabin. 'What is this?'

'It is technically known as money,' said Stephen. 'And was you to help me pick it up, instead of leering upon it with a stunned concupiscence more worthy of Danae than a King's officer, we might conceivably save some few pieces before they all slip through the cracks in the floor. Come, come, bear a hand, there.'

They picked and shovelled busily, on all fours, and when the thick squat iron-bound box was full again, Stephen said, 'They are to go into these small little bags, if you please, by fifties: each to be tied with string. Will I tell you what it is, Jack?' he said, as the heavy bags piled up.

'If you please.'

'It is the vile corrupting British gold that Buonaparte and his newspapers do so perpetually call out against. Sometimes it exists, as you perceive. And, I may tell you, every louis, every napoleon, every ducat or doubloon is sound: the French sometimes buy services or intelligence with false coin or paper. That is the kind of thing that gives espionage a bad name.'

'If we pay real money, it is to be presumed we get better intelligence?' said Jack.

'Why, truly, it is much of a muchness: your paid agent and his information are rarely of much consequence. The real jewel, unpurchasable, beyond all price, is the man who hates tyranny as bitterly as I do: in this case the royalist or the true republican who will risk his life to bring down that Buonaparte. There are several of them on La Réunion, and I have every reason to believe there are more on the Mauritius. As for your common venal agents,' said Stephen, shrugging, 'most of these bags are for them; it may do some good; indeed it probably will, men rarely being all of a piece. Tell me, when shall you be able to set me down? And how do you reckon the odds at present?'

'As to the first,' said Jack, 'I cannot say until I have looked into Port-Louis. The odds? I believe they are still about evens for the moment. If they have gained the *Minerve*, we have gained the *Magicienne*. You will tell me that the *Minerve* is the heaviest of the two, and that the *Magicienne* only carries twelve-pounders; but Lucius Curtis is a rare plucked 'un, a damned good seaman. So let us say evens for the moment. For the moment, I say, because the hurricane-season is coming, and if they lie snug in port and we outside, why, there is no telling how we shall stand in a few weeks' time.'

During the night they brought the wind aft as they went north about Mauritius, and when Stephen woke he found the *Boadicea* on an even keel; she was pitching gently, and the urgent music that had filled her between-decks these last days was no longer to be heard. He washed his face perfunctorily, passed his hand over his beard, said, 'It will do for today,' and hurried into the day-cabin, eager for coffee and his first little paper cigar of the day. Killick was there, gaping out of the stern-window, with the coffee-pot in his hand.

'Good morning, Killick,' said Stephen. 'Where's himself?'

'Good morning, sir,' said Killick. 'Which he's still on deck.'

'Killick,' said Stephen, 'what's amiss? Have you seen the ghost in the bread-room? Are you sick? Show me your tongue.'

When Killick had withdrawn his tongue, a flannelly object of inordinate length, he said, paler still, 'Is there a ghost in the bread-room, sir? Oh, oh, and I was there in the middle watch. Oh, sir, I might a seen it.'

'There is always a ghost in the bread-room. Light along that pot, will you now?'

'I durs'nt, sir, begging your pardon. There's worse news than the ghost, even. Them wicked old rats got at the coffee, sir, and I doubt there's another pot in the barky.'

'Preserved Killick, pass me that pot, or you will join the ghost in the bread-room, and howl for evermore.'

With extreme unwillingness Killick put the pot on the very edge of the table, muttering, 'Oh, I'll cop it: oh, I'll cop it.'

Jack walked in, poured himself a cup as he bade Stephen good morning, and said, 'I am afraid they are all in.'

'All in what?'

'All the Frenchmen are in harbour, with their two Indiamen and the *Victor*. Have not you been on deck? We are lying off Port-Louis. The coffee has a damned odd taste.'

'This I attribute to the excrement of rats. Rats have eaten our entire stock; and I take the present brew to be a mixture of the scrapings at the bottom of the sack.'

'I thought it had a familiar tang,' said Jack. 'Killick, you may tell Mr Seymour, with my compliments, that you are to have a boat. And if you don't find at least a stone of beans among the squadron, you need not come back. It is no use trying *Néréide*; she don't drink any.'

When the pot had been jealously divided down to its ulti-mate dregs, dregs that might have been called dubious, had there been the least doubt of their nature, they went on deck. The *Boadicea* was lying in a splendid bay, with the rest of the squadron ahead and astern of her: *Sirius*, *Néréide*, *Otter*, the brig *Grappler* which they had retaken at St Paul's, and a couple of fore-and-aft-rigged avisoes, from the same source: to leeward the *Windham* Indiaman, with parties from each ship repairing the damage caused by the blow and the violence of the enemy, watched by the philosophical French prize-crew. At the bottom of the deep curve lay Port-Louis, the capital of Mauritius, with green hills rising behind and cloud-capped mountains beyond them.

'Shall you adventure to the maintop?' asked Jack. 'I could show you better from up there.'

'Certainly,' said Stephen. 'To the ultimate crosstrees, if you choose: I too am as nimble as an ape.'

Jack was moved to ask whether there were earthbound apes, as compact as lead, afflicted with vertigo, possessed of two left hands and no sense of balance; but he had seen the startling effect of a challenge upon his friend, and apart from grunting as he thrust Stephen up through the lubber's hole, he remained silent until they were comfortably installed among the studdingsails, with their glasses trained upon the town.

'You have the white building with the tricolour flying over it?' said Jack. 'That is General Decaen's headquarters. Now come down to the shore and a little to the right, and there is the *Bellone*: she is swaying up a new foretopmast. Another foot – he holds up his hand – he bangs home the fid: neatly done, most seamanlike. Inside her lies the *Victor*. Do you see the French colours over ours? The dogs; though indeed she was theirs before she was ours. Inside again, the French colours over the Portuguese: that is the *Minerva*. A very heavy frigate, Stephen; and no sign of her having been roughly handled that I can see. Then comes the *Vénus*, with the broad pennant, alongside the sheer-hulk. They are giving her a new mizzen. Now she *has* been handled rough – bowsprit done in the gammoning, headrails all ahoo, not a deadeye left this side, hardly; and very low in the water; pumps hard at it: I wonder they managed to bring her in. Yet it was early in the year for that kind of blow: she must have been in the heart of it, the Indiaman on the edge, and the *Magicienne* quite outside, for Curtis never even struck his topgallant masts.'

'Your hurricano has a rotatory motion, I believe?'

'Exactly so. And you can be taken aback just when you

think you have rode it out. Then over to the right you have the *Manche* and a corvette: the *Créole*, I believe. A very tidy squadron, once they have put the *Vénus* to rights. What a match it would be, was they to come out and fight their ships as well as that gallant fellow at St Paul's fought his. What was his name?'

'Feretier. Do you suppose they mean to come out?'

'Never in life,' said Jack. 'Not unless I can amuse them – not unless I can make their commodore believe we are no longer in the offing, or only one or two of us. No: it looks like Brest or Toulon all over again: steady blockade until we are down to salt horse and Old Weevil's wedding-cake. We used to call it polishing Cape Sicié in the Mediterranean. But at least it means that I can send you down to La Réunion with the *Grappler*, if you really have to go: she can convoy the *Windham* that far, in case of the odd privateer, and be back the next day. It is barely thirty leagues, and with this steady wind . . . Forgive me, Stephen, it is time for my captains. There is Clonfert's gig putting off already, with his damn-fool boat's crew. Why does he have to make such a raree-show of himself?'

'Other captains dress their boat's crew in odd garments.'

'Still, there is such a thing as measure. I do not look forward to this meeting, Stephen. I shall have to call for an explanation – they will have to tell me how the *Bellone* got out. However, it will not be long. Shall you wait for me here?'

The conference was longer than Jack had expected, but Stephen, cradled in his top as it swung fore and aft on the long even swell, scarcely noticed the passage of time. He was warm through and through, so warm that he took off his neck-cloth; and while his eye dwelt on the motions of the seabirds (noddies, for the most part), the routine work on the deck below, the repairs carrying on aboard the *Windham*, and the boats moving to and fro, his mind was far away on La Réunion, following a large number of schemes designed to overcome the French reluctance to becoming British by means less forthright, and less murderous, than a yardarm-to-yardarm engagement with both broadsides roaring loud. He was therefore almost surprised to see the Commodore's large red face heave up over the edge of his capacious nest; while at the same time he was concerned to see its heavy, anxious expression, the comparative dullness of that bright blue eye.

'This is a damned awkward harbour for a close blockade,' observed the Commodore. 'Easy enough to slip out of, with the wind almost always in the south-east, but difficult to enter, without you are lucky with the sea-breeze and the tide – that is why they use St Paul's so often – and difficult to bottle up tight in the dark of the moon. Still, come down into the cabin, if you would like a wet: Killick has discovered a few pale ancient beans that will just provide our elevenses.'

In the cabin he said, 'I do not blame them for letting the *Bellone* slip between them and the cape; and the *Canonnière* was gone before ever they reached their stations. But I do blame them for falling out over it. There they sat like a couple of cross dogs, answering short and glaring at one another. It was Pym's responsibility as the senior captain, of course; but whose fault it was in fact I could not make out. All I am sure of is that they are on wretched terms. Clonfert seems to have a genius that way, but I am surprised at Pym, such an easy, good-natured fellow. However, I have invited all captains to dine, and let us hope that will smooth things over. It is a miserable business, these rivalries in a squadron. I thought I had got rid of them with Corbett.'

Although this dinner, whose main dishes were a four-hundred-pound turtle and a saddle of mutton from the Cape, was eaten in a humid ninety degrees, it did restore a semblance of civility, if no more. Pym was no man to keep up a resentment, and Clonfert could command the social graces; they drank wine together, and Jack saw with relief that his entertainment was going fairly well. Curtis of the *Magicienne* was a lively, conversable man, and he had much to tell them about the French squadron and its depredations in the Company's far eastern settlements: Hamelin, their commodore, was a savage, Jacobin fellow, it seemed, though a good seaman, while Duperré of the *Bellone* had a fine, swift-sailing ship, and he fought her with great determination; and the French crews were in a surprisingly high state of efficiency. Curtis's account carried the dinner over the first formal stage, and soon there was plenty of animated talk; although indeed Clonfert addressed almost all his conversation to his neighbour, Dr Maturin, and the two young commanders, Tomkinson of the *Otter* and Dent of the *Grappler*, did not feel it proper to open their mouths except to admit calipash and calipee, fat-tailed sheep and Cape Madeira.

'You and Clonfert got along very well together,' observed Jack, when his bloated guests had gone. 'What did you find to talk about? Is he a reading man?'

'He reads novels. But most of the time we spoke of his exploration of these coasts. He has charted many of the inlets, rowing in with his black pilot; and he has a surprising fund of information.'

'Yes. I know. He outdoes Corbett in that, I believe. He has real abilities, if only . . . What now?'

'All ready, sir,' said Bonden.

'Show me the pockets.'

'Number seven canvas, sir, double-sewn,' said Bonden, spreading his jacket and displaying an array of pouches. 'With flaps.'

'Very good. Now stow these away, and button 'em up tight.'

As he received the little heavy bags Bonden's visage took on a glassy, know-nothing look: he said no word; he extinguished the gleam of intelligence in his eye. 'There we are,' said Jack. 'And here is a chit for Captain Dent. He will ask you if you can make out the leading-marks for the cove where *Wasp* put the Doctor ashore, and if you can *not* – mark me, Bonden, if you are not dead certain of both marks and soundings – you are to say so, whether they think you a jack-pudden or no. And Bonden, you will take great care of the Doctor. Hammer his pistol-flints, d'ye hear me, and do not let him get his feet wet.'

'Aye, aye, sir,' said Bonden.

A few minutes later the boat pulled away; Bonden, though unnaturally stout in his close-buttoned jacket, sprang up the side of the *Grappler* and hauled Stephen aboard; and the brig headed south-west, followed by the Indiaman.

Jack watched them until they were hull-down, and then he turned his gaze to the shore, with its fortifications sharp and clear against the bright green of sugar-cane. He could almost feel the answering gaze of the French commanders training their telescopes on the squadron, particularly that of Hamelin, his equivalent on the other side; and as he gave the orders that would set the long blockade in motion he turned over the possibilities of amusing them and of bringing them out to fight.

He had tried several before the *Grappler* came back, bearing Stephen, loaded with intelligence, a chest of the best coffee in the world, and a new machine for roasting it: he had tried open provocation and lame-duck ruses, but Hamelin would not bite, the cunning dog; the French lay there at their ease, and the squadron was obliged to be content with its steady routine of beating to and fro with only the prospect of Christmas to encourage them.

By no means all the news that Stephen brought was good: the frigate *Astrée* was expected from France; the disaffection of the commandant of St Paul's had much diminished since General Desbrusleys' death; and an important body of regulars with fervently Buonapartist officers had arrived. La Réunion would be much harder to take with the promised three thousand troops from India than it would have been with half that number from the Cape some weeks earlier. In the opinion of the French officers it could not be successfully attacked, even with good weather for landing, by less than five thousand men. On the other hand, he had learnt a great deal about Mauritius, the more important island of the two by far, with its splendid ports: among other things, a considerable part of the French garrison was made up of Irish troops, prisoners of war or volunteers who still believed in Buonaparte. And Stephen had many contacts to make, some that might be of the greatest value. 'So,' said he, 'as soon as you can let me have the *Néréide*, with Clonfert's local knowledge and his black pilot, I should like to begin the work of preparation. Apart from other considerations, our broadsheets need time to have their effect; and some well-chosen rumour, some indiscretion in the proper place, might conceivably bring your French frigates out.'

Jack freely admitted the importance of the task in hand. 'Yet do you think me weak, Stephen, when I say how I regret the days when we were of no account – when we cruised by ourselves, pretty busy at times, but often free for our hand of piquet in the evening and our music. You shall have *Néréide* tomorrow, if you choose, since *Vénus* has chosen this moment to heave down, and the *Manche* shows signs of doing much the same, so I can spare a ship; but at least let us have this evening to ourselves. While you were away I transposed the Corelli for violin and 'cello.'

The music tied them back to what seemed a very distant past, one in which no commodore's secretary with his heap of papers had to be kept away for a few hours' peace; a past where no susceptible captains had to have their feelings managed, and where what little administration the first lieutenant left to his captain could be settled out of hand, among people he knew intimately well. But the morning brought Mr Peter back with a score of documents; the *Magicienne* was very much afraid that she would have to ask for a court-martial upon her yeoman of the sheets for an almost unbelievable series of offences, starting with drunkenness and ending with a marlin-spike struck into the ship's corporal's belly; and the *Sirius* was running short of wood and water. Stephen crossed to the *Néréide* after no more than the briefest farewell.

He found Clonfert in high spirits, delighted to be away on his own, delighted to be away from the Commodore's rigid discipline: for although there were many things in which Jack and Lord St Vincent did not see eye to eye, including politics and free speech, they were at one in their notions on keeping station and on prompt, exact obedience to signals. They walked the quarterdeck in the forenoon, and as they strolled up and down the windward side, with the high wooded shore of Mauritius gliding by and shimmering in the heat, Stephen took in the atmosphere of the ship. There were few original Néréides left, since Clonfert had brought all his officers together with most of the *Otter*'s crew, and there was the same feeling in the frigate as there had been in the sloop. In many ways it was much like that in any man-of-war: that is to say, the hands' activities, the employment of their strictly-regulated time, the almost fanatical regard to neatness, were much the same as he had observed in other ships. Yet in none of Jack Aubrey's commands had he ever heard the captain's orders followed by suggestions that things might be better otherwise; and this as it were consultation appeared to be customary right down the hierarchy, from the officer of the watch to Jemmy Ducks, who looked after the poultry. With his limited experience, Stephen could not say that it was wrong: everybody seemed brisk and cheerful and when a manoeuvre was decided upon it was carried out promptly: but he had supposed this loquacity and tergiversation to be confined to the navy of the French, that lively, articulate nation.

The exception seemed to be the warrant-officers, the master, the bosun, the gunner and the carpenter, grave men who adhered to the Royal Navy's tradition as Stephen had seen it, particularly the magnificent granite-faced Mr Satterly, the elderly master, who appeared to regard his captain with a veiled affectionate indulgence and to run the ship with scarcely a word. The commissioned officers and the young gentlemen were far less mute; they obviously desired Clonfert's favour and attention, and they competed for it partly by activity and partly by a curious mixture of freedom and something not far from servility. The words 'my lord' were always in their mouths, and they pulled off their hats with a marked deference whenever they addressed him; yet they addressed him far more often than was usual in any ship that Stephen had known, crossing to his side of the quarterdeck unasked and volunteering remarks of no great consequence, unconnected with their duty.

Perhaps high spirits did not suit Clonfert quite so well as low. When he led Stephen to his cabin he showed its furnishings with a somewhat tiresome exultation, though insisting that this arrangement was merely temporary: 'not quite the thing for a post-captain – passable in a sloop, but a trifle shabby in a frigate.' The cabin, like most of those in rated ships, was a strikingly beautiful room: in Corbett's time it had been bare scrubbed wood, gleaming brass, shining windows, and little more; now that Spartan interior, rather too large for Clonfert's possessions, looked as though a brothel had moved into a monastery, and as though it had not yet settled down. The size of the room was increased by two large pier-glasses that Clonfert had brought with him from the *Otter*, one to port, the other to starboard: he strode to and fro between them telling Stephen the history of the hanging lamp in some detail; and Stephen, sitting cross-legged upon the sofa, noticed that at each turn Clonfert automatically glanced at his reflection with a look of inquiry, doubt, and complacence.

During dinner the Captain ran on about his Turkish and Syrian experiences with Sir Sydney Smith, and at some point Stephen became aware that for Clonfert he had ceased to be a table-companion and had turned into an audience. It was quite unlike their friendly discourse of some days before, and presently Stephen grew sadly bored: lies or half-lies, he reflected, had a certain value in that they gave a picture of what the man would wish to seem; but a very few were enough for that. And then they had a striving, aggressive quality, as though the listener had to be bludgeoned into admiration; they were the antithesis of conversation. 'They can also be embarrassing,' he thought, looking down at his plate, for Clonfert was now astride that unfortunate unicorn: it was a handsome plate, with the Scroggs crest engraved broad and fair upon the rim; but it was a Sheffield plate, and the copper was showing through. 'Embarrassing and hard work; since in common humanity one must keep the man in countenance. What a state of nervous excitement he is in, to be sure.'

Yet although Stephen kept Clonfert decently in countenance, mutely acquiescing in the unicorn and a variety of unlikely feats, he did not put such violence upon himself as to encourage a very long continuation; eventually Clonfert grew conscious that he had somehow missed the tone, that his audience was not impressed, was not with him, and an anxious look came into his eye. He laid himself out to be more agreeable, speaking once again of his gratitude for Stephen's care of him during his seizure. 'It is a wretched unmanly kind of disease,' he said. 'I have begged McAdam to use the knife, if it would do any good, but he seems to think it nervous, something like a fit of the mother. I do not suppose the Commodore ever suffers from anything of that kind?'

'If he did, I should certainly not speak of his disorder, nor the disorder of any other patient under my hands,' said Stephen. 'But,' he added more kindly, 'you are not to suppose that there is anything in the least discreditable in your malady. The degree of pain exceeds anything I have seen in any tormina, whatever their origin.' Clonfert looked pleased, and Stephen went on, 'It is a grave matter, indeed; and you are fortunate in having such an adviser as Dr McAdam in daily reach. I believe, with your leave, that I shall wait upon him presently.'

'Honest McAdam, yes,' said Clonfert, with a return to his former manner. 'Yes. He may be no Solomon, and we must overlook certain frailties and an unfortunate manner; but I believe he is sincerely devoted to me. He was somewhat indisposed this morning, or he would have paid his respects when you came aboard; but I believe he is up and about by now.'

McAdam was in his sick-bay, looking frail. Fortunately for the Néréides his mate, Mr Fenton, was a sound practical ship's surgeon, for McAdam had little interest in physical medicine. He showed Stephen his few cases, and they lingered a while over a seaman whose inoperable gummata were pressing on his brain in such a manner that his speech followed an inverted logic of its own. 'The sequence is not without its value,' said McAdam, 'though it is scarcely in my line. For that matter there is little scope for my studies in a ship of war. Come away below, and we will take a drop.' Far below, in the smell of bilge-water and grog, he went on, 'Mighty little scope. The lower deck is kept far too busy for much to develop apart from the common perversions. Not that I would have you understand that I agree for a moment with the wicked old Bedlam chains and straw and cold water and whipping; but there may be some fancies that in the egg cannot stand a wee starting with a rope's end, nor close company. At any rate I have not had a decent melancholia from the lower deck this commission. Manias, yes; but they are two a penny. No: it is aft that you must look for your fine flower of derangement, not forgetting the pursers and clerks and schoolmasters, all mewed up more or less alone; but above all your captains – that is where the really interesting cases lie. How did you find our patient?'

'In a high flow of spirits. The hellebore answers, I believe?'

For some time they discussed valerian, polypody of the oak, and stinking gladwin, their effects, and Stephen recommended the moderate use of coffee and tobacco; then McAdam branched off to ask, 'And did he speak of Captain Aubrey, at all?'

'Barely. In the circumstances it was an omission that I found remarkable.'

'Aye, and significant too, colleague, most significant. He has been on about Captain Aubrey these last days, and I took particular notice of the *sudor insignis* that you pointed out. It coincides within an hour or so. He was obliged to shift his coat after every bout: he has a chestful, and the right side of each one is pale from scrubbing away the salt, the right side alone.'

'It would be interesting to analyse that salt. Belladonna would suppress the sweat, of course. No more grog, I thank you. But it appears to me that for our patient truth is what he can persuade others to believe: yet at the same time he is a man of some parts, and I suspect that were you to attack him through his reason, were you to persuade him to abandon this self-defeating practice, with its anxiety, its probability of detection, and to seek only a more legitimate approval, then we should have no need for belladonna or any other anhidrotic.'

'You are coming into my way of thinking, I find: but you are not come far enough. The trouble lies much deeper, and it is through unreason that the whole nexus must be attacked. Your belladonna and your logic are pills from the same box: they only suppress the symptom.'

'How do you propose to attain this end?'

'Listen now, will you,' cried McAdam, slopping out a full tumbler and drawing his chair so near that his breath wafted in Stephen's face, 'and I will tell you.'

In his diary that night Stephen wrote, 'if he could carry out a reconstruction of the Irish political and social history for the last few ages which has formed our patient, and then a similar rebuilding of his mind from its foundation in early childhood to the present day, McAdam's scheme would be admirable. Yet even for the second part, what tools does he dispose of? A pickaxe is all. A pickaxe to repair a chronometer, and a pickaxe in drunken hands at that. For my part I have a higher opinion of Clonfert's understanding if not of his judgment than has my poor sodden colleague.'

This higher opinion was confirmed the next evening, when the *Néréide* made her way through a wicked series of reefs off Cape Brabant and the gig put Stephen and the captain ashore in a little creek; and the next, when the black pilot not only took them into a still lagoon but also guided them through the forest to a village where Stephen had a conversation with a second potential ally; and again some days later during a stroll behind Port South-East with a packet of subversive papers.

As he told Jack on rejoining the *Boadicea*, 'Clonfert may not be his own best friend in some ways, but he is capable of a steadiness and a resolution that surprised me; and I must observe, that he perpetually took notes of the depth of the water and of the bearings in what I am persuaded you would call a seamanlike manner.'

'So much the better,' cried Jack, 'I am delighted to hear it, upon my word and honour. I have been doing something in that line myself, with young Richardson: he promises to be a capital hydrographer. We have laid down most of the nearby coast, with double angles and any number of soundings. And I have discovered a watering-place on Flat Island, a few leagues to the northwards; so we shall not have to be perpetually fagging out to Rodriguez.'

'No Rodriguez,' said Stephen in a low voice.

'Oh, you shall see Rodriguez again,' said Jack. 'We still have to put in there for stores, turn and turn about; but not quite so often.'

Turn and turn about they went, while the French remained obstinately at peace in their deep harbour, fitting themselves out anew to the last dump-bolt; and turn by turn, when he was not away in the *Néréide* down the coast, Stephen moved into each departing ship. His limestone caves on Rodriguez fulfilled all their golden promise; Colonel Keating was kindness itself, providing fatigue-parties and draining a small marsh; and by the third turn Stephen was able to report that from the bones found in the mud alone he could almost promise Jack the sight of a complete skeleton of the solitaire within the next two months, while at the same time he might partially clothe it with feathers and pieces of skin found in the caves.

For the rest of the time it was plain blockade, inshore at night, off the capes by day, but never far, lest a Frenchman should slip out on the land-breeze, go north about in the darkness and bear away for the rich waters of the Indian Ocean, leaving the squadron a great way to leeward. Up and down, up and down, and all the time their thin canvas grew thinner in the tropical sun and the sudden prodigious down-pours, their running rigging, incessantly passing through the countless blocks as they trimmed sail, gradually wasted away in those wisps called shakings, and the weed accumulated on their bottoms, while through the gaps in their copper the teredos thrust their augers through the oak.

Christmas, and an immense feast on the upper deck of the *Boadicea*, with a barrel of providently salted penguins from off the Cape serving as geese or turkeys, according to the taste and fancy of the mess, and plum-duff blazing faint blue under the awnings spread against the fiercer blaze of the Mauritian sun. New Year, with a great deal of ship-visiting; Twelfth Night, and the midshipmen's berth regaled the gunroom with a two-hundred-pound turtle – an unfortunate experiment, for it was the wrong kind of turtle: the shell turned into glue, and all who had eaten of the creature pissed emerald green; and now Jack began to consult his barometer every watch.

It was a handsome, heavily-protected brass instrument hanging in gimbals by the table on which they breakfasted, and he was unscrewing its bottom when Stephen observed, 'I shall soon have to think of another trip to La Réunion. This Mauritius brew is sad stuff, in comparison.'

'Very true,' said Jack. 'But drink it while you may. *Carpe diem*, Stephen: you may not get another cup. I unscrewed this shield, because I thought the tube must have broke. But here is the quicksilver, do you see, lower than I have ever seen it in my life. You had better stow your bones in the safest place you can think of. We are in for an uncommon hearty blow.'

Stephen swept the vertebrae he had been sorting into his napkin and followed Jack on deck. The sky was pure and innocent, the swell rather less than usual: on the starboard bow the familiar landscape lay broad and green under the eastern sun. '*Magicienne* is at it already,' said Jack, glancing at the busy hands over the water, setting up double preventer-stays. '*Néréide* has been caught napping. Mr Johnson: *Squadron make sail*; *course due west*; *prepare for heavy weather*.' He turned his glass to Port-Louis: yes, there was no fear of the French slipping out. They too could read a barometer, and they too were making all fast.

'Might this portend a hurricano?' asked Stephen privately in his ear.

'Yes,' said Jack, 'and we must have all the sea-room we can win. How I wish Madagascar were farther off.'

They won forty miles of sea-room; the boats on the booms could scarcely be seen for frappings; the guns were double-breached, bowsed up against the side until they made it groan; topgallantmasts were down on deck; storm-canvas bent; spare gaskets, rolling-tackles, spritsailyard fore and aft – all that a great deal of activity and experienced seamanship could accomplish was done: and all under the same pure sun.

The swell increased long before a darkness gathered in the north. 'Mr Seymour,' said Jack, 'tarpaulins and battens for the hatchways. When it comes, it will blow across the sea.'

It came, a curved white line racing across the sea with inconceivable rapidity, a mile in front of the darkness. Just before it reached them the *Boadicea*'s close-reefed topsails sagged, losing all their roundness; then a tearing wall of air and water ripped them from their bolt-tops with an enormous shrieking howl. The ship was on her beam-ends, the darkness was upon them and the known world dissolved in a vast omnipresent noise. Air and water were intermingled; there was no surface to the sea; the sky vanished; and the distinction between up and down disappeared. Disappeared momentarily for those on deck, more durably for Dr Maturin, who, having pitched down two ladders, found himself lying on the ship's side. Presently, she righted and he slid down; but on her taking a most furious lee-lurch on wearing round, he shot across the deck, through all his remaining stock of Venice treacle, to land on hands and knees upon the other side, clinging to a suspended locker in the darkness, puzzled.

In time gravity reasserted itself; he climbed down, still mazed from the prodigious din and by his tumbles, and groped his way forward to the sick-bay. Here Carol, nominally his assistant but in fact the virtual surgeon of the frigate, and the loblolly-boy had preserved their lantern, by whose light they were disentangling their only patient, a poxed member of the afterguard, whose hammock, twirling in the violent motion, had enveloped him like a cocoon.

Here they remained, hooting lugubriously to one another for a while. Rank had little significance in this pandemonium, and the loblolly-boy, an ancient man once sailmaker's crew and still good at sewing, told them in his shrill, carrying voice that in Jamaica as a boy he had known seven ships of the line founder with all hands in a blow not half as hugeous as this here. Presently Stephen shouted, 'Come aft, Mr Carol, and let us take all the lanterns we can find. The casualties will soon be coming down.'

They crept aft through the darkness – deadlights shipped long since, and the air that came blasting down was charged with shattered water, not light – and to them were brought the injured men: one from the wheel, his ribs cracked by the flying spokes; a small, light reefer dashed by the wind against the hances, and now limp, insensible; Mr Peter, who had made the same plunge as Stephen, though less luckily; more ribs, some broken limbs. Then, as lightning struck the ship, three men quite dazed and one with a shocking burn, dead before they brought him below.

Bandaging, splinting, operating in a space that heaved through forty-five degrees in all directions and on chests that shifted and slid beneath them, they worked on and on. At one point a messenger from the quarterdeck came with the Commodore's compliments and was all well, together with something about 'eight hours'; and then, much, much later, when the ship had been on a comparatively even keel for some time, with no new cases coming below and the last of the fractured clavicles reduced, there was the Commodore himself, streaming wet, in his shirt and breeches. He looked round, spoke to those casualties in any condition to hear him, and then in a hoarse voice he said to Stephen, 'If you have a moment at any time, Doctor, you will find a curious sight on deck.'

Stephen finished his bandage with a neat double turn and

made his way up through the small hole in the canvas-covered hatch. He stood blinking in the extraordinary orange-tawny light, bracing himself against the flying air, as solid as a wall. 'The lifeline, sir,' cried a seaman, putting it into his hand. 'Clap on to the lifeline for all love.'

'Thank you, friend,' said Stephen, gazing about him, and as he spoke he realized that the enormous universal roar had diminished: it was now slightly less than that of continuous battle at close quarters. The *Boadicea* was lying to under a scrap of mizzen staysail, riding the tremendous seas nobly, shouldering them aside with her bluff bows: her fore and main topmasts had gone by the board; wild ropes by the score stretched horizontally aft from the wrecked tops, sometimes cracking as loud as a gun; her remaining shrouds were packed with scraps of seaweed and pieces of terrestrial vegetation – a palm-frond was clearly recognizable. But this was not the curious sight. From the drowned forecastle aft, and particularly on the quarterdeck, wherever there was the slightest lee, there were birds. Seabirds for the most part, but right by him a little creature like a thrush. It did not move as he approached it, nor even when he touched its back. The others were the same, and he looked into the lustrous eye of a bosun-bird within a few inches. In this unearthly lurid glow it was hard to make out their true colours or their kind, but he did distinguish a white-headed noddy, scarcely to be seen within five thousand miles of the Mauritius. As he was struggling towards it a sort of growl in the orange clouds immediately above overcame the general roar, and in a second it was followed by a thunder so intolerably vast that it filled all the air about him; and with the thunder a blaze of lightning struck the ship again. He was flung down, and picking himself up with a confused recollection of a triple stroke, of a forward gun having gone off, blasting out its portlid, he crawled below to wait for the wounded.

There were no wounded. Instead there appeared a piece of jellied veal, brought by Killick with the message that 'the thunderbolt had made hay of the best bower anchor, but otherwise all was well; that unless they were taken aback in the next hour or so, the Commodore thought they might be through the worst of it; and that he hoped Dr Maturin might see better weather in the morning.'

Having slept like a corpse through the middle watch, and having attended his urgent cases at first light, Dr Maturin did indeed see better weather when he came on deck. The sky was the most perfect blue, the sun delightfully warm, the gentle south-east wind refreshing: there was an enormous swell, but no white water, and apart from the desolation of the deck, the steady gush of the pumps, and the worn look of all hands, yesterday might have been a nightmare out of time. Yet there were other proofs: Mr Trollope, the second lieutenant, limped up to him and pointed out two ships of the squadron, far, far to leeward: the *Magicienne*, with her mizzen gone, and the *Sirius*, with no topmast standing.

'Where is the Commodore?' asked Stephen.

'He turned in half a glass ago. I begged him to get some sleep. But before he went below he told me to take care to show you the best bower, a most amazing philosophical sight.'

Stephen considered the fused, distorted metal, and said, 'We seem to be heading south?'

'South-west as near as ever we can, with our compasses run mad because of the lightning; south-west for the Cape to refit. And don't we wish we may get there, ha, ha!'

Chapter Six

There were no banquets at the Cape for Jack Aubrey; there were few kind words from the Admiral, either, although the Commodore had brought in all his squadron safe after one of the worst blows this last decade; and there were less, if less were possible, when an American barque arrived with the news that the *Bellone*, *Minerve*, and *Victor* were out – she had spoken them off the Cargados Garayos, standing north-east under a press of sail to cruise for Indiamen in the Bay of Bengal.

Not that Jack had any leisure for feasting in Cape Town or for comfortable chat with Admiral Bertie: it was an anxious, hurried time for him, with five ships to be refitted by a small yard with scarcely a spare frigate-topmast in it – supplies were expected from India – and no fit timber much nearer than Mossel Bay. A small, ill-furnished yard, and one governed by men of a rapacity that Jack had never seen equalled in all his long experience: the squadron was known to have done well for itself at St Paul's, and the yard was going to have a proper share come Hell or high water, regardless of the fact that all this wealth depended on leisurely decisions to be taken far away at some future date – that the squadron had very little cash in hand, and could only take it up by bills at a usurious rate of interest. An anxious time, with the Frenchmen out; and one rendered more anxious still, as far as Jack was concerned, by a host of factors. By the steady obstruction of those in control of spars, cordage, paint, block, copper, iron-work, and the countless other objects the squadron cried out for. By the Admiral's apparent indifference to very gross corruption: Aubrey must be aware that dockyard people were not plaster saints, observed Mr Bertie, nor yet choir-boys; these things should be settled as they were usually settled in the Navy; and for his part he did not give a straw how the Commodore set about it, so long as the squadron was ready for sea by Tuesday sennight at the latest. By the discovery that his own Mr Fellowes, seduced by the bosun of the *Sirius* and a desire to be rich now rather than at some later period when he might be dead, had not only looked upon the thunder-struck best bower as a perquisite, but had done the same by the kedge, fifty fathom of two-inch rope, and an unreasonable quantity of other stores – a court-martial quantity. By contention among his captains as to who should be served first from the meagre supplies whose existence the dockyard could not conceal. And above all by the loss of one vessel carrying mail and by the arrival of another so thoroughly soaked by rain-storms under the line that all letters apart from those wrapped in waxed sailcloth had mouldered and partly coalesced; Sophie had never learnt to use waxed sail-cloth, nor to number her letters, nor to send copies in another bottom.

Immediately after the arrival of this blotting-paper packet, Jack snatched an interval between visits to the master-attendant and the rope-walk and tried to disentangle the sequence with the help of such dates as 'Friday' or 'after church'. But this interval was also seized upon by Mr Peter, whose great sheaf of documents reminded Jack of his duty as a commodore: all that he had told the Commander-in-chief by word of mouth had to be cast into official, written form, carefully read over and considered. Very carefully, for although Jack was the least suspicious creature afloat, Stephen was not, and he had pointed out that it might be wise to regard Mr Peter as a functionary with loyalties on land rather than as a confidential ally. And then there was his duty as captain of the *Boadicea*: although his first lieutenant saw to the daily running of the ship, Mr Seymour was now exceedingly busy with the refitting, and in any case there were several things that necessarily fell to the captain. It was he who persuaded Mr Collins, now at eighteen the senior master's mate, that he was not absolutely required to marry the young lady who alleged that, as a direct consequence of Mr Collins' attentions, all her girdles were now too tight; still less to marry her at once. 'A fortnight is not enough, in these affairs,' he said. 'It may be only an indigestion, a pound or two of beefsteak pudding. Wait until we come in from the next cruise. And until then, Mr Collins, I desire you will not leave the ship. Though indeed,' he added, 'was you to marry every girl you play love-tokens with, when ashore, the place would very soon come to look like Abraham's bosom.'

It was he who patiently listened to an indignant, rambling account of sharp practice far away, delivered by Matthew Bolton, forecastleman, starboard watch, in his own name and in that of three mute companions unnaturally shaved and scraped. Bolton had refused Mr Seymour's help, on the grounds that as the Commodore had pulled him out of the sea when they were shipmates in the *Polychrest*, it obviously fell to him to do the same throughout the length of Bolton's natural life.

This was a logic that seemed convincing to Bolton, the first lieutenant and the Commodore; and when Jack had extracted the facts from the circumstantial details, a description of the grass-combing bugger that had tried this guardo-move, and an account of Mrs Bolton's state of health, he reached for a pen, and, watched very closely indeed by the four seamen, wrote a letter, which he then read out to them in a harsh, all-hands-to-punishment voice that gave the utmost satisfaction:

'*Boadicea*,
Simon's Town

Sir,
Conformably to the wishes of the men named in the margin, late of the *Néréide*, and now on board of His Majesty's ship under my command, I acquaint you that unless the prize-money due to them for Buenos

Ayres and Monte Video, and received by you under their power of attorney, is forthwith paid, I shall state the case to the Lords Commissioners of the Admiralty, with a request that their solicitor may be directed to sue for the same.

I am, etc.

'There,' he said, 'that will clap a stopper over his antics. Now, Bolton, if the Doctor is aboard, I should like to see him when he is at leisure.'

As it happened the Doctor was not on board. He was half way between Cape Town, where he had left Mr Farquhar, and False Bay, sitting in a sparse grove of proteas in a dust-storm, clasping a loose portfolio of plants to be dried for his herbal, and dividing what attention he had left between a small flock of crested mouse-birds and a troop of baboons. Presently he came down to the harbour, where he washed away some of the dust at his usual tavern and received from the landlord (an obliging African of Huguenot descent) the foetus of a porcupine: and here, as he had expected, he found McAdam, sitting in front of a bottle that would have preserved the foetus almost indefinitely. Little of it had been drunk, however, and McAdam entertained him with a reasonable account of their patient's extraordinary activity and flow of spirits. Lord Clonfert, it appeared, was up well before dawn every day (a rare occurrence), inspiring all hands with a sense of extreme urgency; he had bleared Pym's eye over a couple of topgallant yards by means of a thumping bribe; and he was now negotiating with a known receiver of stolen goods for a gig. 'Sure it will break his heart if he is not the first that is ready for sea,' said McAdam. 'He has set his soul on outdoing the Commodore.'

'May we not in part attribute his activity to the roborative, stimulating use of coffee, and to the general soothing effect of mild tobacco, which has set his humours *in equilibrio*? Tobacco, divine, rare, superexcellent tobacco, which goes far beyond all their panaceas, potable gold, and philosopher's stones, a sovereign remedy to all diseases. A good vomit, I confess, a virtuous herb, if it be well qualified and opportunely taken, and medicinally used, but as it is commonly abused by most men, which take it as tinkers do ale, 'tis a plague, a mischief, a violent purger of goods, lands, health; hellish, devilish and damned tobacco, the ruin and overthrow of body and soul. Here, however, it *is* medicinally taken; and I congratulate myself upon the fact, that in your hands there is no question of tinkers' abuse.'

The flying dust, the incessant wind, had made McAdam more gross than usual; he had never cordially liked Stephen's prescription of coffee and tobacco; and from his wavering, red-rimmed eye it seemed that he was meditating a coarse remark. Indeed, he began, 'A fig for . . .' but having belched at this point he reconsidered his words, fixed his gaze on the bottle, and continued, 'No, no: you do not have to be a conjuror to see it is all emulation. If the one is your dashing frigate-captain, t'other will be your dashing frigate-captain to the power of ten, whether or no. He will outdo the Commodore though he burst.'

It would not be difficult to outdo the Commodore in his present state, the creature, reflected Stephen as he walked into the cabin: not, at least, in the article of speed. Captain Aubrey was completely surrounded by papers, including those of the courts-martial that were to be held over the next few days – the usual offences of desertion and violence or disobedience or both when drunk: but time-consuming – and upon them all he had laid out the mildewed sheets of his private correspondence.

'There you are, Stephen,' he cried. 'How happy I am to see you. What have you there?'

'An unborn porcupine.'

'Well, there's glory for you. But Stephen, you are a rare one for making out a secret hand, I am sure. Would you help me try to find out the sequence of these letters, and perhaps even the sense?'

Together they pored over the sheets, using a magnifying-glass, intuition, crocus of antimony, and a little diluted copperas; but to small effect.

'I do make out that the Old Nonpareils we planted had three apples apiece, and that the strawberries failed,' said Jack, 'and she obviously heard from Ommaney, because here is the parlour chimney drawing fit to turn a mill, and a Jersey cow – the children have hair, and teeth, any number of teeth, poor little souls. Hair: with all my heart, though she does say it is straight. Straight or frizzled, 'tis all one: they will look far better with some hair – Lord, Stephen, it must have been their hair I blew away, thinking it was shakings that had got into the cover.' He crept about for some time and came up with a little wisp. 'Very little shakings, however,' he said, folding it into his pocket-book and returning to the letters. 'Neighbours most attentive: here is another brace of pheasants from Mr Beach last Thursday. But in this one she says she is well, surprisingly well, underlined twice: says it again in what I take to be the last. I am heartily glad of it, of course, yet why *surprisingly*? Has she been ill? And what is this about her mother? Could the second word be palsy? If Mrs Williams has been sick, with Sophie looking after her, that might explain the *surprisingly*.'

They pored again, and Stephen almost certainly deciphered a hare, a present from Captain Polixfen, eaten jugged on Saturday or Sunday or both; and something about the rain. All the rest was mere conjecture.

'I think old Jarvie was altogether wrong in saying that a sea-officer had no business to marry,' said Jack, carefully gathering the sheets. 'Yet I can see what he meant. I should not be unmarried for the world, you know; no, not for a flag; but you cannot conceive how my mind has been going back to Ashgrove Cottage these days, when I should be thinking about getting the squadron to sea.' He jerked his head over his shoulder and stared out of the scuttle for a while before adding, 'These God-damned courts-martial: and what to do about the land-sharks in the yard. To say nothing of the bosun and his infernal capers.'

During supper he picked at his mutton, setting out the difficulty of dealing with Mr Fellowes: disposing of His Majesty's property was an immemorial practice among His

Majesty's servants – if the objects were damaged it was almost legitimate by length of custom – and in the Navy it went by the name of cappabar. Pursers, carpenters, and bosuns stole most, having more to steal, and better opportunities; but there were limits, and Fellowes had not confined himself to damaged goods, nor to those of slight value. He had carried cappabar too high by far – the thing was flagrant – and Jack could bring him before a court-martial and have him broke tomorrow. It was Jack's duty to have him broke. On the other hand, it was also his duty to keep his ship in the highest possible fighting-trim: for that he needed a first-rate bosun: and first-rate bosuns did not grow on trees, at the Cape. First-rate bosuns were not twelve a penny. He grew a little heated on the subject, cursing Fellowes for a half-witted zany, a mad lunatic, a fling-it-down-the-gutter sodomite; but his heart was not in it; his epithets lacked real warmth and inventiveness; and his mind was clearly still far away in Hampshire.

'Come,' said Stephen, 'if ever the Madras establishment fulfils its undertakings, and we move on La Réunion, which I begin to doubt, Mr Farquhar will be with us, and that will be an end to our music. Let us play my old lament for the Tir na n-Og; I too am mighty low, and it will serve as a counter-irritant. Like will be cured by like.'

Jack said that he would be very happy to lament with Stephen until the moon went down, but with messengers expected from Cape Town and from every official in the yard, he did not expect they would reach any very high flow of soul before they were interrupted. In the event they had not even tuned their strings when Spotted Dick appeared, to state, with Mr Johnson's duty, that *Iphigenia* was off the point, had made her number, and was standing in.

With a brisk south-east wind and the making tide she had dropped anchor before moonrise, and the news that Captain Lambert brought drove all thoughts of England and of music from Jack Aubrey's head. The *Iphigenia*, that fine thirty-six-gun eighteen-pounder frigate, escorting a small fleet of transports, had reinforced Colonel Keating at Rodriguez to the extent of two regiments of European troops, two of Indian, and some auxiliaries: the numbers were fifteen hundred short of what had been hoped for, but the soldiers had done their best: they had kept very nearly to their time, and the definitive attack on La Réunion was now a possibility, though a hazardous one, above all if the French had moved fresh forces into the island. They would certainly have had time to remount their batteries.

The first thing to do was to find out what ships Governor Decaen had in Mauritius, and, if it could be done, to shut them up in their harbours. 'Captain Lambert,' he said, 'what is the state of the *Iphigenia?'*

He did not know Lambert at all, a recently-promoted young man, but he liked the look of him – a small round jolly sailor with a capable air – and he fairly loved him when he took a paper from his pocket and said, 'These are my officers' reports, sir, made as we were standing in. Purser: provisions for nine weeks in full, of all species, except rum: of that, only thirty-nine days. Master: one hundred and thirteen tons of water; beef very good, pork sometimes shrinks in the boiling; the rest of the provisions very good. I should add, sir, that we watered, wooded, and tortoised at Rodriguez. Gunner: eighteen rounds of powder filled; plenty of wads; forty rounds. Carpenter: hull in good state; knees of the head supported by two cheeks; masts and yards in good state; pretty well stored. Surgeon: in the sick list, three men, objects for invaliding; portable soup, fifty-seven pounds; other necessaries to the nineteenth of next month only. And as for my people, sir, we are only sixteen short of complement.'

'Then I take it you can sail at once, Captain Lambert?'

'The moment we have won our anchors, sir, unless you wish me to slip. Though I should be happy to take in a little powder and shot, and some greenstuff: my surgeon is not quite happy about his lime-juice.'

'Very good, very good, Captain Lambert,' said Jack, chuckling. 'You shall certainly have your powder and shot. Never trouble with that damned yard at this time of night:

I have more than we can safely stow, from St Paul's, and my gunner will have to disgorge the surplus. And you may have six of our bullocks that are waiting on the beach. As for your greenstuff, my purser has an excellent unofficial man on shore, will rouse you out any quantity in half an hour. Mr Peter, be so good as to prepare a letter to the Admiral, to go at once: Mr Richardson is our best jockey, I believe – tell him to never mind the lions and tigers on the road; they are all gammon, for the most part. Then, an order for Captain Lambert – proceed to sea on the ebb, rendezvous off Port-Louis, copies of private signals, alternative rendezvous at Rodriguez after the – let me consider – the seventeenth. And let all captains come aboard. Killick, pass the word for the gunner, and bring a bottle of the Constantia with the yellow seal. The yellow seal, d'ye hear me?'

Between the signing of papers and the interview with the reluctant gunner they drank their bottle, the best bottle in the ship, and the captains began to arrive: their coxswains could be heard answering the sentry's hail in quick succession: '*Néréide*', '*Sirius*', '*Otter*', '*Magicienne*'.

'Now, gentlemen,' said the Commodore, when they were all assembled, 'when can your ships proceed to sea?'

If it were not for Pym's vile newfangled iron tanks, the *Sirius* could be ready in a couple of days: if it had not been for the yard's incomprehensible delay over the long-promised iron horse, the *Otter* might say the same. '*Néréide* will be ready for sea in thirty-six hours,' said Clonfert, smiling with intent at Captain Pym: but the smile changed to a look of surprised vexation when Curtis said, 'The *Magicienne* can sail this minute, sir, if I may have leave to water at Flat Island. We are no more than thirty ton shy.'

'I am delighted to hear it, Captain Curtis,' said Jack. 'Delighted. *Magicienne* and *Iphigenia* will proceed to Port-Louis with the utmost dispatch. Mr Peter will give you your orders; and with this wind you might be well advised to warp out into the fairway to catch the first minute of the ebb.'

They received their orders; they warped out into the fairway; and dawn saw the two frigates beating out of the bay, to vanish, close-hauled, round the Cape of Good Hope by the time the cabin's breakfast of eggs and mutton-ham came aft in a cloud of fragrance. Shortly afterwards Captain Eliot arrived with a formal order from the Admiral directing the Commodore to convene his court-martial, and a letter in which he congratulated Jack on this splendid accession of force at Rodriguez, from which the country might confidently expect wonders in a very short time indeed, particularly as for the next few weeks the squadron would have the use of the *Leopard*. The horrible old *Leopard*.

Jack changed into his full-dress uniform; the ominous union flag broke out at the *Boadicea*'s peak; the captains gathered; and with Mr Peter acting as deputy judge-advocate they set about the unpleasant business of trying poor Captain Woolcombe for the loss of the *Laurel* of twenty-two guns, captured by the *Canonnière* – the Frenchman's last fight – off Port-Louis before Jack came to the Cape: for until this time a sufficient number of senior officers had never been in Simon's Town long enough for the court to be formed, and poor Woolcombe had been under nominal arrest ever since he had been exchanged. Everyone knew that in the circumstances, with the *Canonnière* in sight of her home port, carrying an enormous land-based crew and mounting more than twice the number of far heavier guns, no blame could be attached to the *Laurel*'s captain; everyone knew that there must be an honourable acquittal – everybody except Woolcombe, for whom the issue was far too important for any certainty whatsoever and who sat throughout the long proceedings with a face of such anxiety that it made the members of the court very thoughtful indeed. Each of them might find himself in the same position, faced perhaps with ill-disposed judges, differing from him in politics or service loyalties or bearing him some long-nourished grudge: a court of amateur lawyers, from whose decision there was no appeal. Illogically, perhaps, since they themselves had framed the verdict, every member of the court shared in Woolcombe's glowing relief when the judge-advocate read it out, and when Jack handed back the captain's sword with an elegant if somewhat studied formal speech. They were happy with Captain Woolcombe, and the sentences for some of the desertions and embezzlements that followed were quite remarkably light. Yet for all that the sentences took a great while to reach: the stately process went on and on. In his own ship a captain could deal with any delinquent foremast hand so long as the offence did not carry the death-sentence, but he could not touch any officer holding a commission or a warrant; they had to come before the court; and at times it seemed to Jack, on the boil with impatience to get to sea, to make the most of the situation before the French knew of the forces on La Réunion, that no warrant-officer in the squadron had found any better use for his time than getting drunk, overstaying his leave, disobeying, insulting, and even beating his superiors, and making away with the stores entrusted to his care. Indeed, a steady diet of courts-martial gave a most unpleasant impression of the Royal Navy: crime, oppression, complaints of illegal conduct, sometimes justified, sometimes fabricated or malicious (one master charged his captain with keeping false musters, on the grounds that he had a friend's son on the ship's books when in fact the young gentleman was at school in England, a perfectly normal practice, but one which would have wrecked the captain's career if the court had not performed some singular acrobatics to save him), brawling in the wardroom, against officers, evidence of long-standing ill-will; and all the bloody violence of the lower deck.

Between these grim sessions the presiding judge turned sailor again, and he drove on the refitting of his ships, fighting a most determined battle against obstruction and delay. But having all the time in the world, the dockyard won hands down; they had gauged his needs and his impatience quite exactly, and he had not only to bleed borrowed gold at every vein, but even to thank his extortioners before the last sack of thirty-penny nails and ten-inch spikes came aboard. These actions took place at dawn and dusk, for at dinner-time the president of the court necessarily entertained the other members.

'Pray, Commodore, do you not find passing sentence of death cut your appetite?' asked Stephen, as he watched Jack carve a saddle of mutton.

'I cannot say I do,' said the Commodore, passing Captain Woolcombe a slice that dripped guiltless blood. 'I don't like it, to be sure; and if the court can possibly find a lesser offence, I think I should always give my vote for it. But when you have a straightforward case of cowardice or neglect of duty, why, then it seems to me plain enough: the man must be hanged, and the Lord have mercy on his soul, for the service will have none. I am sorry for it, but it don't affect my appetite. Captain Eliot, may I help you to a little of the undercut?'

'It seems to me perfectly barbarous,' observed Stephen.

'But surely, sir,' said Captain Pym, 'surely a medical man will cut off a gangrened limb to save the rest of the body?'

'A medical man does not cut off the limb in any spirit of corporate revenge, nor *in terrorem*; he does not make a solemn show of the amputation, nor is the peccant limb attended by all the marks of ignomiy. No, sir: your analogy may be specious, but it is not sound. Furthermore, sir, you are to consider, that in making it you liken the surgeon to a common hangman, an infamous character held in universal contempt and detestation. And the infamy attaching to the executioner arises from what he does: the language of all nations condemns the man and *a fortiori* his act: which helps to make my point more forcibly.'

Captain Pym protested that he had not intended the least reflection upon surgeons – a capital body of men, essential in a ship, and on shore too, no doubt: he would not meddle with analogies any more; but still perhaps he might adventure to say that it was a hard service, and it needed a hard discipline.

'There was a man,' remarked Captain Eliot, 'who was sentenced to death for stealing a horse from a common. He said to the judge, that he thought it hard to be hanged for stealing a horse from a common; and the judge answered, "You are not to be hanged for stealing a horse from a common, but that others may not steal horses from commons." '

'And do you find,' asked Stephen, 'that in fact horses are not daily stolen from commons? You do not. Nor do I believe that you will make captains braver or wiser by hanging or shooting them for cowardice or erroneous judgment. It should join the ordeal of the ploughshare, floating or pricking to prove witchcraft, and judicial combat, among the relics of a Gothic past.'

'Dr Maturin is quite right,' cried Lord Clonfert. 'A capital execution seems to me a revolting spectacle. Surely a man could be . . .'

His words were drowned in the general flow of talk that Stephen's word 'shooting' had set going; for Admiral Byng had been shot to death on his own quarterdeck. Almost everybody was speaking, except for Captain Woolcombe, who ate in wolfish silence, his first meal without anxiety; and the names of Byng and Keppel flew about.

'Gentlemen, gentlemen,' cried Jack, who saw the far more recent Gambier and Hervey and the unfortunate engagement in the Basque roads looming ahead, 'let us for Heaven's sake keep to our humble level, and not meddle with admirals or any other god-like beings, or we shall presently run foul of politics, and that is the end of all comfortable talk.'

The noise diminished, but Clonfert's excited voice could be heard carrying on, '. . . the possibility of judicial error, and the value of human life – once it is gone, it cannot be brought back. There is nothing, nothing, so precious.'

He addressed himself to his neighbours and to those sitting opposite him; but none of the captains seemed eager to be the recipient, and there was the danger of an embarrassing silence, particularly as Stephen, convinced that two hundred years of talk would not shift his kind, bloody-minded companions an inch, had taken to rolling bread pills.

'As for the value of human life,' said Jack, 'I wonder whether you may not over-estimate it in theory; for in practice there is not one of us here, I believe, who would hesitate for a moment over pistolling a boarder, nor think twice about it afterwards. And for that matter, our ships are expressly made to blow as many people into Kingdom Come as possible.'

'It is a hard service, and it requires a hard discipline,' repeated Pym, peering through his claret at the enormous joint.

'Yes, it is a hard service,' said Jack, 'and we often call our uniform buttons the curse of God; but a man – an officer – enters it voluntarily, and if he don't like the terms he can leave it whenever he chooses. He takes it on himself – he knows that if he does certain things, or leaves them undone, he is to be cashiered or even hanged. If he has not the fortitude to accept that, then he is better out of the service. And as for the value of human life, why, it often seems to me that there are far too many people in the world as it is; and one man, even a post-captain, nay' – smiling – 'even a commodore or a jack-in-the-green, is not to be balanced against the good of the service.'

'I entirely disagree with you, sir,' said Clonfert.

'Well, my lord, I hope it is the only point upon which we shall ever differ,' said Jack.

'The Tory view of a human life . . .' began Clonfert.

'Lord Clonfert,' called Jack in a strong voice, 'the bottle stands by you.' And immediately afterwards, aiming at bawdy, in which all could share, and quickly attaining it, he spoke of the striking increase – the potential increase – in the population of the colony since the squadron's arrival: 'a single member of my midshipmen's berth has already contrived to get two girls with child: one brown, the other isabella-coloured.' The others turned with equal relief to similar accounts, to reminiscences of burning wenches in Sumatra, at Port-au-Prince, in the Levantine ports; to rhymes, to conundrums; and the afternoon ended in general merriment.

The *Néréide*, her topgallantmasts and her new gig on board at last, left Simon's Town for Mauritius that evening:

and as they stood watching her out of the bay, Stephen said to Jack, 'I am sorry I started that hare; it gave you some uneasiness, I am afraid. Had I recollected, I should not have asked it in public, for it was a private question – I asked for information's sake. And now I do not know whether the public answer was that of the Commodore or of the plain, unpennanted Jack Aubrey.'

'It was something of both,' said Jack. 'I do in fact dislike hanging more than I said, though more for myself than for the hanged man: the first time I saw a man run up to the yardarm with a nightcap over his eyes and his hands tied behind his back, when I was a little chap in the *Ramillies*, I was as sick as a dog. But as for the man himself, if he has deserved hanging, deserved it by our code, I find it don't signify so very much what happens to him. It seems to me that men are of different value, and that if some are knocked on the head, the world is not much the poorer.'

'Sure, it is a point of view.'

'Perhaps it sounds a little hard; and perhaps I came it a little over-strong and righteous, when I was speaking, speaking as a commodore, to Clonfert.'

'You certainly gave him an impression of unbending severity and perfect rectitude.'

'Yes, I was pompous: yet I did not speak far beyond my own mind. Though I must confess he vexed me with his tragic airs and his human life – he has a singular genius for hitting the wrong note; people will accept that kind of thing from a learned man, but not from him; yet he will be prating. I hope he did not resent my checking him: I had to, you know, once he got on to Whigs and Tories. But I did it pretty civil, if you remember. I have a regard for him – few men could have got the *Néréide* out so quickly. Look, she is going about to weather the point. Prettily done – stays as brisk as a cutter, stays in her own length – he has a very good officer in his master: and he would be one himself too, with a little more ballast – a very good officer, was he a little less flighty.'

'It is curious to reflect,' wrote Stephen in his diary that

night, 'that Jack Aubrey, with so very much more to lose, should value life so very much more lightly than Clonfert, whose immaterial possessions are so pitifully small, and who is partly aware of it. This afternoon's exchange confirms all I have observed in my acquaintance with both. It is to be hoped, if only from a medical point of view, that some resounding action will soon give Clonfert a real basis – a sounder basis than his adventitious consequence. Nothing, as Milton observes, profits a man like proper self-esteem: I believe I have mangled the poor man; but here is Mr Farquhar, the all-knowing, who will set me right. If only there were another thousand men on Rodriguez, I might write Governor Farquhar with some confidence even now.'

Mr Farquhar came aboard, but with no ceremony and with so small a train – one secretary, one servant – that it was clear he had been listening to the military men in Cape Town, who had little opinion of the sepoy in his own country and none at all of his fighting qualities elsewhere. Their considered opinion was that the French officers were right when they said that five regiments of European troops, supported by artillery, would be needed for a successful attack; that the hazards of landing on such a shore were so great that even five regiments were scarcely adequate, particularly as communication between the sea and the land might be cut off from one day to the next, and with it the troops' supplies; and that perhaps it would be better, all things considered, to wait for further reinforcements at the next monsoon.

'I wish I could share your sanguine outlook,' he said to Stephen, when at last he was in a fit condition to say anything at all (the *Boadicea* had had heavy weather until she reached the twenty-fifth parallel), 'but perhaps it is based upon more information than I possess?'

'No: my reports were tolerably complete,' said Stephen. 'But I am not sure that you or the soldiers attach the same weight to our present superiority in ships. If, as it appears likely, two of their frigates are away from the scene of action, our local advantage is five to two; a very great advantage, and in this I do not count the *Leopard*, which is, I am told, only a smaller *Raisonable*, the kind of vessel that is facetiously termed a coffin-ship by the sailors, of questionable use even as a transport. It was long before I came to appreciate the prodigious force represented by a man-of-war of the larger kind: we can all envisage the dreadful power of a battery, of a fortress belching fire; but a ship seems so peaceful an object, and to the untutored eye so very like the Holyhead packet writ large, that perhaps one does not easily see it as a vast battery in itself, and what is more a moveable battery that can turn its resistless fire in various directions, and then, its work of destruction completed, glide smoothly off to begin again elsewhere. The three frigates, my dear sir, the three frigates by which we presumably outnumber our adversaries, represent an enormous train of artillery, a train that is not painfully dragged by innumerable horses, but is borne by the wind. I have seen them in action upon this very coast, and I have been amazed. There are also the enemy's lines of supply to be considered: superiority at sea means that they may readily be severed.'

'I take your point,' said Farquhar. 'But the decisive battle must be fought on land; and the few regiments we possess must be put down on that land.'

'Yes,' said Stephen. 'What you say is very true. And I admit that these considerations would make me more doubtful of the issue than in fact I am, were I not supported by what you would perhaps term an illogical source of hope.'

'It would be benevolent in you to share your comfort.'

'As you may know, in the service our Commodore is known as Lucky Jack Aubrey. I am not prepared to enter into the concept of luck, as it is vulgarly called: philosophically it is indefensible; in daily experience we see it to exist. All I will say is, that Captain Aubrey seems to possess it in an eminent degree; and it is that which cheers my sometimes pensive nights.'

'How I hope you are right,' cried Farquhar. 'How sincerely I hope you are right.' After a pause he added, 'For countless reasons: among them the fact that I do not touch emolument or allowance until I enter into my functions.' He paused again, passed his hand over his eyes, and swallowed painfully.

'Let us take a turn on deck,' said Stephen. 'The greenish pallor is invading your face again, no doubt induced by melancholy thoughts as much as by the motion of the ship. The brisk trade-wind will blow them away.'

The brisk trade-wind instantly picked off Mr Farquhar's hat and wig. They flew forward, to be caught – a miracle of dexterity – by the bosun, who rose from the new best bower, seized the one in his right hand, the other in his left, and sent them aft by a midshipman. For his own part Mr Fellowes had preferred to keep the full length of the gangway between himself and the quarterdeck ever since a memorable day in Simon's Town, when the Commodore had had a private word with him, if private is quite the term for an explosion of honest rage that resounded from the after-cabin to the cutwater, filling the ship's company with mirth, glee, and apprehension, evenly mingled.

Covered once more, Mr Farquhar hooked himself into the rigging at Stephen's side; and as he gazed about him the corpse-like appearance faded from his face: the *Boadicea* was leaning over so that her lee chains were under the tearing white water and her weather side showed a broad streak of new copper; ahead of her the *Sirius*, under the same cloud of sail, kept as precisely to her station as though the two ships were joined by an iron bar; and together they were racing away to the north-east in the track of the *Néréide* to join the *Magicienne* and the *Iphigenia* off Port-Louis. They had already passed the *Leopard*, which had had two days' start (and which, since her captain was related to the Admiral, was strongly suspected of being present only to share in any prize-money that might be going), and they were cracking on as though they meant to run off the two thousand miles and more in under a fortnight – a real possibility, they having picked up the powerful trade so soon. 'Celerity is everything, in these operations,' he said, 'and here we have celerity given form. How we fly! It is exhilarating! It is like a race for a thousand pound! It is like wrestling with a handsome woman!'

Stephen frowned; he disliked Mr Farquhar's warmer similes. 'Sure celerity is all,' he said. 'Yet a great deal also depends upon our finding the other ships at the rendezvous. The sea is so uncommonly vast, the elements so capricious, the instruments for finding the latitude so imperfect, or so imperfectly used, that I have known a vessel cruise ten days and more without finding her consorts.'

'Let us put our trust in the Commodore's mathematical powers,' said Mr Farquhar. 'Or his luck: or both. I believe, Dr Maturin, that if you would so far indulge me, I could relish a little, a very little, of your potable soup again, with just a sippet of toast; and I promise that if ever I come to govern my island, my first care, after the new constitution, shall be to repay you in turtle.'

Their trust was not misplaced. The day after they had seen the mountains of La Réunion piercing the white trade-clouds far to the leeward the two frigates went north about Mauritius, and there, true to the appointed coordinates, they found the rest of the squadron. Lambert, the senior captain, came aboard at once: the position in Port-Louis was just what they had expected, with the *Vénus*, the *Manche*, and the *Entreprenant* corvette lying snug in port and the *Bellone* and *Minerve* still far away; but on the other hand Clonfert, sent to cruise off the south-east of the island, had discovered a new French frigate, the thirty-eight-gun *Astrée*, moored under the batteries of the Rivière Noire in an impregnable position, obviously aware of the blockade of Port-Louis and unwilling to emerge. He had also cut out a four-hundred-ton merchantman from Jacotet, spiking the guns of the little batteries and taking some officers prisoner. It was true that the ship had proved to be a neutral, an American, one of the many Americans who used these seas, almost the only neutrals and almost the only source of casual information available to either side: but even so, said Lambert, it was a most dashing affair.

'This is a damned unfortunate object for dashing at and a damned odd moment to choose for dashing,' said Jack afterwards. 'If the *Néréide* had been knocked about in this cutting-out lark (for it was no more), we should have been put to our shifts to cover the landing, above all now that they have the *Astrée*. I wonder at Lambert, sending him off alone: though indeed it is plain that he knows these waters, and that he don't want conduct. Jacotet is a hellish awkward anchorage to get into. However, I think we must take Clonfert with us to Rodriguez as soon as we have watered, to keep his ardent spirits out of the way of temptation until there is a proper scope for 'em. He may dash till he goes blue in the face, once the real battle is engaged.'

They watered at Flat Island, and the *Boadicea* and the *Néréide* stretched away to the east for Rodriguez, leaving Pym in command with orders to fade imperceptibly away by night with the *Iphigenia* and *Magicienne*, leaving the *Leopard* and two avisoes off Port-Louis to bring instant warning if the *Bellone* and *Minerve* should return from the Bay of Bengal. 'For there's the rub,' said Jack. 'If those two heavy frigates, together with *Vénus*, *Manche* and *Astrée*, were to fall on our rear at the wrong moment, with the troops half on shore and half off, we should be like Jackson, hard up in a clinch, and no knife to cut the seizing.'

Ordinarily Rodriguez presented the appearance of a desert island; perhaps somewhat larger than the ideal desert island, being a good ten miles long, and perhaps somewhat greyer and more sterile inland than might have been wished, though pleasant enough after a long voyage with no sight of land; but now the bay was crowded with shipping, and on the shore exactly squared streets of tents stretched away in all directions, while in these streets hundreds and even thousands of men moved about, their red coats visible from a great way off.

Jack was first ashore, taking Stephen and Farquhar with him: to his intense relief he found that Keating was still in command – no glum, over-cautious general had superseded him. The two commanders instantly and with great goodwill plunged into the details of moving soldiers, ammunition, stores, provisions, arms, and even some howitzers in due order to the scene of action, and Stephen slipped silently away. 'The solitaire could never have borne this,' he reflected as he made his way through the crowded camp. 'And even the tortoise-park is sadly diminished.'

He had not gone a hundred yards before a voice behind him called out, 'Doctor! Doctor!'

'Not again?' he muttered angrily, walking faster among the screw-pines and drawing his head down between his shoulders. But he was pursued, run down; and in his overtaker he instantly recognized the tall, lank, and still very boyish form of Thomas Pullings, a shipmate from his first day at sea. 'Thomas Pullings,' he cried, with a look of real pleasure replacing the first malignant glare. 'Lieutenant Pullings, upon my word and honour. How do you do, sir?'

They shook hands, and having inquired tenderly after the Doctor's health and the Commodore's, Pullings said, 'I remember you was the first that ever called me Lieutenant P, sir, back in dear old Pompey. Well, now, if you chose to tip it the most uncommon civil, you could say Captain.'

'You do not tell me so? And are you indeed a captain already?'

'Not by land, sir; I am not Captain P by land. But at sea I am the captain of the *Groper* transport. You can see her from here, if you stand from behind the tree. Hey, you, the lobster there,' he called to an intervening soldier, 'your dad worn't no glazier. We can't see through you. There, sir: the brig just beyond the snow. She's only a transport, but did you ever see such lovely lines?'

Stephen had seen just such lines in a Dutch herringbuss, but he did not mention the fact, saying no more than 'Elegant, elegant'.

When her captain had gloated over the squat, thick object for a while he said, 'She's my first command, sir. A wonderful brig on a bowline; and she draws so amazing little water, she can run up the smallest creek. Will you honour us with a visit?'

'I should be very happy, Captain,' said Stephen. 'And since you are in command, might I beg the favour of a shovel, a crowbar, and a stout man of fair average understanding?'

The Commodore and the Colonel worked on their plan of campaign; the staff-officers worked on their lists; the soldiers polished their buttons, formed in squares, formed in fours, and marched off by the right into the boats, filling the transports and the frigates until the harassed sailors could scarcely holystone the decks, let alone come at the rigging; and Dr Maturin, with two Gropers of fair average understanding dug out the remains of the solitaire from the caves into which she had retired from hurricanes, only to be overwhelmed by the ensuing deluge of now rock-like mud.

The last soldier left the beach, a crimson major in charge of the operation; and as he set his weary foot on the *Boadicea*'s quarterdeck he looked at his watch and cried, 'One minute fifty-three seconds a man, sir: that beats Wellington by a full two seconds!' A single gun to windward from the Commodore, the signal *Make sail*, and the fourteen transports began to file through the narrow opening in the reef to join the men-of-war.

By the evening they had sunk the island. They were sailing towards the setting sun with a fine topgallantsail breeze on the larboard quarter; and nothing but open sea lay between them and the beaches of La Réunion. The enterprise was now in train. Jack was far too busy with Colonel Keating and his maps for anything but the living present, but Stephen felt the long hours of gliding towards the inevitable future more than he had expected. He had been intimately concerned in matters of greater moment, but none in which the issue would be so clear-cut – total success, or total failure with a shocking loss of life – in a matter of hours.

He was not altogether happy about the plan to attack, which assumed that they would be expected at St Paul's, a restored, strengthened St Paul's, and which required a feint and then a landing at two points, the one east and the other south-west of Saint-Denis, the capital, the second being designed to cut off communication between Saint-Denis and St Paul's; nor was Jack, who feared the surf. But since Colonel Keating, a man in whom they had great confidence, and one who had fought over some of the terrain, strongly urged its strategic importance, and since he was supported by the other colonels, the Commodore had yielded, neither Stephen nor Farquhar saying anything, except when they stressed the importance of respect for civilian and ecclesiastical property.

The hours dropped by. At every heave of the log La Réunion was seven or eight miles nearer. Mr Farquhar was busy with his proclamation, and Stephen paced the quarterdeck, silently hating Buonaparte and all the evil he had brought into the world. 'Good only for destruction – has destroyed all that was valuable in the republic, all that was valuable in the monarchy – is destroying France with daemonic energy – this tawdry, theatrical empire – a deeply vulgar man – nothing French about him – insane ambition – the whole world one squalid tyranny. His infamous treatment of the Pope! Of this Pope and the last. And when I think of what he has done to Switzerland and to Venice, and to God knows how many other states, and what he might have done to Ireland – the Hibernian Republic, divided into departments – one half secret police, the other informers – conscription – the country bled white –' A subaltern of the 86th caught his pale wicked glare full in the eye and backed away, quite shocked.

In the afternoon of the day after the council three ships were sighted from the masthead: *Sirius*, *Iphigenia* and *Magicienne*, exact to the rendezvous, having seen no sign of the *Bellone* or *Minerve*, nor any hint of movement in Port-Louis. That evening they began to take chosen troops aboard over an easy, gentle sea: and Jack summoned the captains to explain the course of action. While the main force made a demonstration before Sainte-Marie, the *Sirius* was to land Colonel Fraser's brigade and the howitzers at Grande-Chaloupe, a beach on the leeward side of the island between Saint-Denis and St Paul's. At the same time part of the brigades under Colonel Keating were to be landed at the Rivière des Pluies, thus placing Saint-Denis between two fires; and here the other troops should also be landed as the transports came in; for the frigates were now to press on alone under all the sail they could bear.

They pressed on, still over this long easy swell, in a gentle breeze with studdingsails aloft and alow: a magnificent sight in their perfect line stretching over a mile of sea, the only white in that incomparable blue. They pressed on, never touching a sail except to make it draw better, from sunset until the morning watch; and all the time the Commodore took his sights on the great lambent stars hanging there in the velvet sky, checking his position again and again with the real help of Richardson and the nominal help of Mr Buchan the master, calling for the log at every glass, and perpetually sending below for the readings of the chronometers and the barometer. At two bells in the morning watch he gave orders to reduce sail; and coloured lanterns, with a leeward gun, bade the squadron do the same.

Dawn found him still on deck, looking yellow and unshaved and more withdrawn than Stephen cared to see. La Réunion lay clear on the larboard bow, and the soldiers, coming sleepily on deck, were delighted to see it: they clustered on the forecastle, looking at the land with telescopes; and more than one cried out that he could find no surf upon the reefs, nothing but a little line of white. 'They may not be so pleased in twelve hours' time,' said Jack in a low voice, answering Stephen's inquiring look. 'The glass has been sinking all through the night; still, we may be in before it comes on to blow.' As he spoke he took off his coat and shirt, and then, having given his orders to Trollope, the officer of the watch, his breeches: from the rail he pitched head-first into the sea, rose snorting, swam along the line of boats that each frigate towed behind her, made his way back along them, and so went dripping below: the Boadiceas were perfectly used to this, but it shocked the redcoats, as savouring of levity. Once below and free of good mornings right and left, he went straight to sleep, with barely a pause between laying his long wet hair on the pillow and unconsciousness; and fast asleep he remained, in spite of the rumbling boots of a regiment of soldiers and the din inseparable from working the ship, until the faint tinkle of a teaspoon told some layer of his mind that coffee was ready. He sprang up, looked at the barometer, shook his head, dipped his face into a kid of tepid water, shaved, ate a hearty breakfast, and appeared on deck, fresh, pink, and ten years younger.

The squadron was coasting along just outside the reef, a reef upon which the sea broke mildly: three lines of rollers that a well-handled boat could manage easily enough.

'Upon my word, Commodore, the weather seems to serve our turn,' said Colonel Keating; and then in a louder voice and waving his hat to a young woman who was gathering clams on the reef, 'Bonjour, Mademoiselle.' The young woman, who had already been greeted by the three leading frigates, turned her back, and the Colonel went on, 'How do you think it will stay?'

'It may hold up,' said Jack. 'But then again it may come on to blow. We must move smartly: you will not object to a very early dinner, at the same time as the men?'

'Never in life, sir. Should be very happy – indeed I am sharp-set even now.'

Sharp-set he might be, reflected Jack, but he was also nervous. Keating set about his very early dinner with a decent appearance of phlegm, yet precious little went down his gullet. He had never had such an important command; nor had Jack; and in this waiting period they both felt the responsibility to a degree that neither of them would have thought possible. It affected them differently, however; for whereas Keating ate very little and talked a good deal, Jack devoured the best part of a duck and followed it with figgy-dowdy, gazing thoughtfully out of the stern-window as the not very distant landscape slipped by: far off, the harsh, precipitous mountains; nearer to, cultivated land, the occasional house: forest, plantations, a hamlet, and some carts creeping against the green. Their dinner did not last long: it was first interrupted by the report of two sail bearing east a half south – they later proved to be the leading transports, *Kite* and *Groper* – and then cut short entirely by the appearance of the little town of Sainte-Marie before Jack had quite finished his first attack upon the figgy-dowdy.

Here the reef trended in towards the coast, and the squadron turned with it, heaving to at the Commodore's signal. Already the town was in a state of turmoil: people were running about in all directions, pointing, screeching audibly, putting up their shutters, loading carts. They had plenty to screech about, for there, right off their anchorage, where the fresh water of the stream made gaps in the coral, and well within gunshot, lay five ships, broadside on, with their ports open and a frightful array of cannon pointing straight at Sainte-Marie. Even worse, large numbers of boats with soldiers in them were rowing about, evidently determined to land, to take, burn, raze, and sack the town. The sergeant's guard from the little post was lined up on the beach, but they did not seem to know what to do, and every man who could command a horse had long since galloped off to Saint-Denis to give the alarm and to implore instant succour from the military there.

'This is going very well,' said Colonel Keating some time later, as he watched the vanguard of the succour through his telescope. 'Once their field-pieces are across the stream, they will have a devil of a time getting them back again. Their horses are quite done up already. See the company of infantry at the double! They will be pooped, sir, pooped entirely.'

'Aye,' said Jack. 'It is very well.' But his mind was more on the sea than on the land, and it appeared to him that the surf was growing: the rollers, perhaps from some blow far to the east, were coming in with more conviction. He looked at his watch, and although it wanted forty minutes of the stated time he said, 'Make *Sirius*'s signal to carry on.'

The *Sirius* paid off heavily, filled, and bore away for Grande-Chaloupe, carrying close on a thousand men and the howitzers. As she moved off, her place was taken by the

Kite, the *Groper*, and two other transports, increasing the alarm on shore.

The plan had been unable to allot any precise interval between the two landings, since obviously that must depend on the time the *Sirius* should take to pass Saint-Denis and reach the agreed point between that town and St Paul's; but they had hoped for something in the nature of two hours. With the failing breeze, however, it now looked as though at least three would be required: and all the while the surf was growing. The waiting was hard, and it would have been harder still if the newly-arrived French field-pieces, drawn up on a hill behind the post, had not seen fit to open fire. They threw no more than four-pound balls, but they threw them with striking accuracy, and after the first sighting shots one passed so close to Colonel Keating's head that he cried out indignantly, 'Did you see that, sir? It was perfectly deliberate. Infernal scrubs! They must know I am the commanding officer.'

'Do you not shoot at commanding officers in the army, Colonel?'

'Of course not, sir. Never, except in a mêlée. If I were on land, I should send a galloper directly. There they go again. What unprincipled conduct: Jacobins.'

'Well, I believe we can put a stop to it. Pass the word for the gunner. Mr Webber, you may fire at the field-pieces by divisions: but you must point all the guns yourself, and you must not damage any civilian or ecclesiastical property. Pitch them well up beyond the town.'

With the great guns going off one after another in a leisurely, deliberate fire, and the heady smell of powder swirling about the deck, tension slackened. The soldiers cheered as Mr Webber sent his eighteen-pound balls skimming among the Frenchmen on their knoll, and they roared again when he hit a limber full on, so that one wheel sprang high into the air, turning like a penny tossed for heads or tails. But such an unequal contest could not last long, and presently the French guns were silenced: and all the time the swell increased, sending white water high on the reef and surging through the gap to break in great measured rollers on the strand.

Yet after the lull the breeze had strengthened too, with every sign of blowing hard before the night, and at length Jack said, '*Sirius* should be at Grande-Chaloupe by now. I think we may move on.'

Their move took them briskly past another shallow gap in the reef, where more fresh water broke the coral, and to another anchorage (though still indifferent) off the mouth of the Rivière des Pluies.

'This is it,' said Colonel Keating, map in hand. 'If we can go ashore here, the landing will be unopposed. It will be at least an hour before they can get round: probably more.'

'My God,' thought Jack, looking at the broad belt of surf, the steep-to beach of rounded boulders. He stepped to the taffrail and hailed, '*Néréide*, ahoy. Come under my stern.' The *Néréide* shot up, backed her foretopsail, and lay pitching on the swell: there was Lord Clonfert on her quarterdeck; and Stephen noticed that he was wearing full-dress uniform – no unusual thing in a fleet-action, but rare for a skirmish.

'Lord Clonfert,' called Jack, 'do you know the deep-water channel?'

'Yes, sir.'

'Is a landing practicable?'

'Perfectly practicable at present, sir. I will undertake to put a party ashore this minute.'

'Carry on, Lord Clonfert,' said Jack.

The *Néréide* had a little captured schooner among her boats, a local craft; and into this and some of her boats she poured an eager party of soldiers and seamen. The squadron watched the schooner run down to the edge of the surf, followed by the boats. Here she took to her sweeps, backing water and waiting for the master-wave: it came, and she shot in through the breaking water, on and on, and they thought she was through until at the very last she struck, ten yards from the shore, slewed round, and was thrown on to the beach, broadside on. As the wave receded all the men leapt ashore, but the backdraught took her into the very curl of the next, which lifted her high and flung her down so hard that it broke her back at once and shattered her timbers. Most of the other craft fared the same: the boats beaten to pieces, the men safe. Only four bodies were to be seen, dark in the white water, drifting westwards along the shore.

'It is essential to carry on,' cried Colonel Keating in a harsh voice. 'We must take Saint-Denis between two fires, whatever the cost.'

Jack said to Mr Johnson, 'Make *Groper*'s signal.'

While the transport was coming up he stared at the beach and the floating wreckage: as he had thought, it was only the last stretch that was mortal at this stage. Anything of a breakwater would allow boats to land; and the *Groper* was the only vessel with a draught shallow enough to go in so far. When she was under the *Boadicea*'s lee he called, 'Mr Pullings, you must shelter the boats: take your brig in, drop your stern-anchor at the last moment, and run her ashore as near as you can heading south-west.'

'Aye, aye, sir,' said Pullings.

The *Groper* bore up in a volley of orders, made her way slowly towards the land while her people were busy below, rousing a cable out of a stern-port, and then much faster: into the surf, on and on through it. In his glass Jack saw the anchor drop, and a moment later the *Groper* ran hard aground right by the shore. Her foretopmast went by the board with the shock, but the hands at the capstan took no notice: they were furiously heaving the cable in, forcing her stern round so that she lay just south-west, braced against the seas and creating a zone of quiet water right in by the shore.

'Well done, Tom Pullings, well done indeed: but how long will your anchor hold?' muttered Jack, and aloud, 'First division away.'

The boats ran in, landed and hauled up, half-swamped in most cases but rarely overset: the beach was filling with redcoats, forming neatly in line as they came ashore. Some, with Colonel McLeod, had taken up position a few hundred yards inland. Then the *Groper*'s cable parted. A tall comber took her stern, wrenched it round, and flung her on that unforgiving beach: and since her bows were already stove, she went to pieces at once, leaving the surf the full sweep of the shore. The wave that broke her was the first of a growing series; and presently the belt of surf grew wider and wider, thundering louder still.

'Can another ship be sent in, Commodore?' asked Keating.

'No, sir,' said Jack.

On the road that led from Sainte-Marie to Saint-Denis, and that here curved inland from the coast to avoid a swamp, three separate bodies of French troops could be seen, moving slowly from east to west, towards Saint-Denis. Colonel McLeod's party on shore had already thrown up drystone breastworks between the beach and the road, and had formed behind them in good order. To the left of their line the seamen and the Marines had done much the same; but being on wetter ground they had made a broad turf wall, upon which stood Lord Clonfert, conspicuous with his star and his gold-laced hat.

The first body came abreast of the landing-party at a distance of two hundred yards: they halted, loaded, levelled their pieces, and fired. Clonfert waved his sword at them, reached behind him for a Marine's musket, and returned the fire. It was almost the only shot in reply to the French discharge: clearly the landing-party had spoilt nearly all its powder.

As the squadron watched, too far for accurate fire on this heaving sea but near enough for telescopes to show every detail, two cavalrymen came galloping down the road from Saint-Denis, spoke to an officer and rode on. The troops shouldered their muskets, reformed, and set off towards Saint-Denis at the double. The second and third bodies, also given orders by the horsemen, came fast along the road: each halted long enough for a volley or two, and each was saluted by Clonfert from the top of his wall. He was eating a biscuit, and each time he put it down on his handkerchief to shoot. Once he hit an officer's horse, but most of the time his musket missed fire.

Still more horsemen came riding fast from Saint-Denis, one of them probably a field-officer, urging the troops to hurry. The inference was as clear as the day: Colonel Fraser had landed in force from the *Sirius*, and these men were being called back to protect the capital.

'*Magicienne* and the *Kite* and *Solebay* transports must go and support him at once,' said Jack. 'The rest of the squadron will stay here, in case the sea goes down by the morning.' Colonel Keating agreed: he seemed glad of the authoritative statement, and Stephen had the impression that he had lost his sense of being in control of the situation – that this impossibility of communicating with the visible shore was something outside his experience.

Throughout this time Stephen and Farquhar had stood by the hances, out of the way, two figures as unregarded as they had been at the time of the military councils, where they sat virtually mute, dim among the splendid uniforms; but now, after a hurried consultation with Farquhar, Stephen said to Jack, 'We are agreed that if Colonel Fraser has a firm footing on the other side of the island, I should be put ashore there.'

'Very well,' said Jack. 'Mr Fellowes, a bosun's chair, there. Pass the word for my coxswain. Bonden, you go aboard *Magicienne* with the Doctor.'

What remained of this anxious day off the Rivière des Pluies was taken up with watching the surf. A little before sunset half an hour's downpour of a violence rare even for those latitudes deadened the white water of the breakers so that the channel was a little clearer, and a subaltern of the 56th, born in the West Indies and accustomed to surf from his childhood, volunteered to swim ashore with Colonel Keating's orders to Colonel McLeod. He launched himself into the rollers with the confidence of a seal, vanished, and reappeared on the crest of a wave that set him neatly on his feet at high-water-mark: shortly afterwards McLeod, covering the subaltern's nakedness with a plaid, marched off at the head of his men to seize the little post at Sainte-Marie, deserted by its occupants, to hoist the British colours, and to regale upon the stores left by the sergeant's guard.

Yet darkness fell with its usual suddenness in the tropics, and it was impossible to send boats in through the reviving turmoil. The ships stood off and on all night, and in the morning the combers were still roaring up the beach. There might, Jack agreed, be a slight improvement, but it was nothing like enough; and his strongly-held opinion was that they should proceed at once to Grande-Chaloupe to reinforce the troops landed from the *Sirius* and *Magicienne*, leaving the *Iphigenia* and some transports to land at the Rivière des Pluies later in the day if the sea went down. Happily Colonel Keating shared this opinion to the full, and the *Boadicea* made sail, passed Saint-Denis, where the soldiers swore they could distinguish gunfire on the far side of the town, rounded Cape Bernard, and stretched south-south-west under a cloud of canvas for the beach of Grande-Chaloupe, obvious from miles away by the congregation of shipping and the now unmistakeable gunfire in the hills above.

They stood in, and here, on the leeward side of the island, what a different state of things was seen! Calm beaches, lapping billows, boats plying to and fro: and up in the hills companies of redcoats regularly formed; companies of turbans; guns at work, and still more guns being dragged up by ant-like lines of seamen.

The Colonel and his staff raced ashore, all weariness forgotten; troops, guns, heavy equipment began to pour from the frigate. Jack's duty bound him to the ship, however, and he stood watching through his telescope. 'This is a damned poor way of being present at a battle,' he said to Mr Farquhar. 'How I envy Keating.'

Colonel Keating, provided with a captured horse on the beach itself, spurred his mount up the paths to Colonel Fraser's forward post, where they both surveyed the scene. 'You have a charmingly regular attack here,' said Keating with great satisfaction, directing his spy-glass right and left.

'And a most judicious defence: the French have made a very proper disposition of their forces.'

'Yes, sir. It is as regular as one could wish, except for the blue-jackets. They will rush forward and take outworks before they are due to fall: though I must confess, they have done wonders in getting the howitzers up. But on the whole it *is* pretty regular: over on the right, sir, beyond the signal-post, Campbell and his sepoys have made the prettiest set of approaches. They are only waiting for the word to charge: that will carry us two hundred yards nearer their demi-lune.'

'Then why don't you give it, Mother of God? They have clearly outflanked the enemy already. Where is your galloper?'

'He is just behind you, sir. But if you will forgive me, there is a parley in train. The political gentleman from the ship came up with a clergyman and a party of tars and said he must speak to the French commanding officer. So knowing he was the Governor's adviser, we beat a chamade and sent him across with a flag of truce. It seemed to me proper; and yet now I half regret it . . . Can he be quite right in the head, sir? He desired me to keep this bone for him, saying he would not trust it to the French for the world.'

'Oh, these politicoes, you know, Fraser . . .' said Colonel Keating. 'It will come to nothing, however. They are very strongly entrenched on the hill; and even if McLeod comes up from the east, it will take us a good week of regular approaches to press them to their main works.'

They were studying the main works with great attention through their telescopes when an aide-de-camp said, 'I beg your pardon, sir, but Dr Maturin is approaching with a French officer and a couple of civilians.'

Colonel Keating walked forward to meet them. Stephen said, 'Colonel Keating, this is Colonel Saint-Susanne, who commands the French forces on the island. These gentlemen represent the civil administration.' The two soldiers saluted one another: the civilians bowed. Stephen went on, 'From a desire to avert the effusion of human blood, they wish to know the terms upon which you will grant a capitulation covering the whole island: and I have taken it upon myself to assure them that the terms will be honourable.'

'Certainly, sir,' said Colonel Keating, with an icy glare at Stephen. 'Gentlemen, pray step this way.'

Jack and Farquhar, prosaically eating an early elevenses and wondering vaguely, repetitively, why there was no longer any firing in the hills, were interrupted first by cheering on the shore and then by an ensign bearing a scribbled note. 'Forgive me, sir,' said Jack; and he read, 'My dear Commodore – Your friend has disappointed us – he has *done us out* of our battle, as neat a battle as you could wish to see. We had driven in their piquets – outflanked their right wing – and then quite out of order a capitulation is proposed, *to avert the effusion of human blood* forsooth – they accept the usual terms – honours of war, side-arms and baggage, personal effects and so on – so if you are satisfied, please come ashore to sign together with your obliged humble servant, H. Keating, Lieut.-Col.'

The Commodore laughed aloud, beat his massive thigh, held out his hand and said, 'Governor, I give you joy. They have surrendered, and your kingdom awaits you. Or this island of it, at the least.'

Chapter Seven

His Excellency the Governor of La Réunion sat at the head of his council table: he now wore a uniform as splendid as that of the gold and scarlet colonels on his left hand, more splendid by far than the weather-worn blue of the sea-officers on his right; and now there was no question of his sitting mute. Yet there was no trace of hauteur to be seen on his eager, intelligent face as he tried to guide the meeting towards a unanimous approval of the Commodore's revolutionary scheme, his plan of an instant attack upon Mauritius, with simultaneous landings from Flat Island off Port-Louis and in the neighbourhood of Port South-East at the other end of the island. Colonel Keating had been with him from the first; but a distinct inclination to enjoy the fruits of victory for a while, 'to allow the men a little rest', and, more creditably, a desire to prepare the campaign with due deliberation, so that mortars for example did not arrive without their shells, had yet to be overcome; for if so ambitious and risky an operation as this were to fail, the attempt could be justified only by a unanimous vote.

'I shall echo the Commodore's words, gentlemen,' said Mr Farquhar, 'and cry, "Lose not a moment." This is the moment at which we have a superiority of five to three in frigates, when we possess a fleet of transports, troops in the first flush of victory, and exact intelligence of the enemy's strength and dispositions on the Mauritius, supplied by their own records here.'

'Hear him, hear him,' said Colonel Keating.

'With command of the sea we may concentrate our forces wherever we choose. Furthermore, my colleague' – bowing to Stephen at the far end of the table – 'assures me that at this juncture, this very favourable juncture, our efforts at sapping the enemy's morale are more than likely to be crowned with success; and we are all aware of Dr Maturin's powers in that direction.' It was not the most fortunate stroke: some of the colonels who had toiled and sweated extremely in the hope of glory turned a sombre gaze upon Dr Maturin. Feeling this, Mr Farquhar hurried on, 'And perhaps even more important, this is the moment at which our hands are free. The *Leopard* has taken our despatches to the Cape: she will not return. No orders from any authority unacquainted with the exact state of local conditions can take the guidance of operations from the hands of those who *are* acquainted with them – no new set of staff-officers can, for the moment, arrive with a plan of campaign matured in Bombay, Fort William, or Whitehall. This is a state of affairs that cannot last.'

'Hear him, hear him,' said Colonel Keating, Colonel McLeod and Colonel Fraser; and the fatter, more cautious staff-officers exchanged uneasy glances.

'Far be it from me to decry patient laborious staff-work,' said the Governor. 'We have seen its gratifying results on this island: but, gentlemen, time and tide wait for no man; and I must remind you that Fortune is bald behind.'

Walking away from the Residence through streets placarded with the Governor's proclamation, Jack said to Stephen, 'What is this that Farquhar tells us about Fortune? Is she supposed to have the mange?'

'I conceive he was referring to the old tag – his meaning was, that she must be seized by the forelock, since once she is passed there is no clapping on to her hair, at all. In the figure she ships none abaft the ears, if you follow me.'

'Oh, I see. Rather well put: though I doubt those heavy-sided lobsters will smoke the simile.' He paused, considering, and said, 'It don't sound very eligible, bald behind; but, however, it is all figurative, all figurative . . .' He gazed with benign approval at a strikingly elegant woman accompanied by an even more willowy black slave-girl, stepped into the gutter to let them pass, then looked haughty, unconscious, a thousand miles away, and continued, 'Still, I am glad they have come to see reason. But Lord, Stephen, what an infernal waste of time these councils are! If it had dragged on another day the squadron would have been dispersed – *Sirius* is gone already – and I should have had to follow my own scheme. My first duty is to the sea, and I must get at Hamelin before the *Bellone* and *Minerve* are back. But as it is, I can combine the two. Pullings!' he exclaimed.

On the other side of the street Pullings cast off the girl at his side and crossed, blushing a reddish mahogany yet beaming too. 'Did you find anything you liked, Pullings?' asked Jack. 'I mean, in the professional line?'

'Oh, yes, sir – I was only looking after her for a minute, for Mr – for another officer, sir – but I don't suppose you will let me have her, sir – far too pretty, except for a trifle of worm in her futtocks, her ground-futtocks.' Pullings had been sent to St Paul's in the *Sirius* when the frigate tore down immediately after the capitulation to snap up all the shipping in the road; he had been told to make his own choice of a replacement for the *Groper*, and he had done himself as proud as Pontius Pilate. They watched the young woman attach herself to the arm of Mr Joyce of the *Kite* transport, and as they walked along, Pullings, more coherent now that he was relieved of a sense of guilt – for very strangely his officers looked upon Jack Aubrey as a moral figure, in spite of all proofs to the contrary – expatiated on the merits of his prize, a privateer schooner, copper-fastened, wonderfully well-found.

At the gates of the government stable-yard they parted, and while Bonden led forth a powerful black horse, once the pride of the French garrison, Stephen said, 'This is not the moment to ask how you mean to combine the two schemes; yet I admit that I am curious to know. Bonden, I advise you, in your own best interest, not to stand behind that creature's heels.'

'If you will ride over to St Paul's with me,' said Jack, 'I will tell you.'

'Alas, I have an audience of the Bishop in half an hour, and then an appointment at the printing-shop.'

'Maybe it is just as well. Things will be clearer in the morning. Bonden, cast off afore.'

Things were indeed clearer in the morning: the Commodore had seen all the officers concerned; he had all the facts distinctly arranged; and he received Stephen in a room filled with charts and maps.

'Here, do you see,' he said, pointing to an island three or four miles off Port South-East, 'is the Ile de la Passe. It lies on the reef at the very edge of the only deep-water channel into the port: a devilish channel, narrow, with a double dog-leg and any number of banks and rocks in its bed. The island is pretty strongly held – it mounts about twenty heavy guns – but the town is not. They expect us in the north, where we have been blockading all this while, and most of their forces are around Port-Louis: so if we knock out the Ile de la Passe – and a couple of frigates should be able to manage it –'

'In spite of the intricate navigation? These are very alarming shoals, brother. I see two and three fathoms marked for a couple of miles inside the reef; and here is a vast area with the words *Canoe-passage at high-tide*; while your channel is a mere serpent; a lean serpent at the best. But I am not to be teaching you your business.'

'It can be done. Clonfert and his black pilot know these waters perfectly. Look, here is the Jacotet anchorage just at hand, where he cut out the American. Yes, they should manage it well enough; though of course it must be done by boats and in the night; ships could not stand in against that fire, without being sadly mauled. Then once the island is seized, the French cannot easily retake it: their batteries cannot reach across the inner bay and since they have no ship of force in Port South-East, nor even gunboats, they have no means of getting their artillery any nearer. Nor can they starve it out, so long as we victual it from the sea. So if we hold the Ile de la Passe we deny the French their best harbour after Port-Louis; we have a base for our landing;

and we open up all the country out of range of the batteries for your handing-out of broadsheets and culling simples. For their little garrisons in the town and along the coast will scarcely stir outside the reach of their own guns.'

'This is a very beautiful plan,' said Stephen.

'Ain't it?' said Jack. 'Keating has already sent some Bombay gunners and European troops into the *Néréide*, to garrison the place when we have taken it: for obviously the *Néréide* possesses more local knowledge than all the rest of the squadron put together.'

'You do not feel that Clonfert's oversetting of the little ship off the Rivière des Pluies throws a certain shade on his qualifications?'

'No, I do not. It could have happened to anyone in those circumstances, with the soldiers ready to call us shy. I should have tried it myself. But I am not going to give him his head at the Ile de la Passe; I do not want him to be coming it the Cochrane: Pym shall command. Pym may not be very wise, but he is a good, sound man, as regular as a clock; so *Néréide*, *Iphigenia* and perhaps *Staunch* –'

'What is this *Staunch*?'

'She is a brig: came in last night from Bombay. A useful little brig, and in excellent order. Narborough has her, a most officer-like cove: you remember Narborough, Stephen?' Stephen shook his head. 'Of course you do,' cried Jack. 'Lord Narborough, a big black man with a Newfound-land dog, third of the *Surprise*.'

'You mean Garron,' said Stephen.

'Garron, of course: you are quite right. Garron he was then, but his father died last year, and now he is called Narborough. So *Néréide*, *Iphigenia*, and perhaps *Staunch* if she can get her water in quick enough, are to run up to Port-Louis, where Pym is watching Hamelin's motions. *Iphigenia* will stay, and *Sirius* and *Néréide* will come south for the Ile de la Passe.'

'The *Néréide* is not to come back here, so?'

'To wait for the dark of the moon, you mean? No; we cannot afford the time.'

'Then in that case I had better go aboard her now. There is a great deal to be done in the Mauritius, and the sooner I get there the better. For I tell you, my dear, that though they are less lethal, my broadsheets are as effective as your – as your round-shot.'

'Stephen,' said Jack, 'I am convinced of it.'

'I had almost said, as effective as your broad*sides*, but I was afraid the miserable play upon words might offend an embryonic baronet; for Farquhar tells me that if this second campaign should succeed as well as the first the happy commander will certainly be so honoured. Should you not like to be a baronet, Jack?'

'Why, as to that,' said Jack, 'I don't know that I should much care for it. The Jack Aubrey of King James's time paid a thumping fine not to be a baronet, you know. Not that I mean the least fling against men who have won a great fleet-action – it is right and proper that *they* should be peers – but when you look at the mass of titles, tradesmen, dirty politicians, moneylenders . . . why, I had as soon be plain Jack Aubrey – Captain Jack Aubrey, for I am as proud as Nebuchadnezzar of my service rank, and if ever I hoist my flag, I shall paint *here lives Admiral Aubrey* on the front of Ashgrove Cottage in huge letters. Do not think I am one of your wild democratical Jacobins, Stephen – do not run away with that notion – but different people look at these things in different lights.' He paused, and said with a grin, 'I'll tell you of one chap who would give his eye-teeth to be a baronet, and this is Admiral Bertie. He puts it down to Mrs Bertie, but the whole service knows how he plotted and planned for the Bath. Lord,' he said, laughing heartily, 'to think of crawling about St James's for a ribbon when you are an ancient man, past sixty. Though to be sure, perhaps I might think differently if I had a son: but I doubt it.'

In the afternoon of the next day, Dr Maturin, preceded by two bales of handbills, proclamations and broadsheets, some printed in Cape Town and others so recently struck off in Saint-Denis that they were still damp from the press, came alongside the *Néréide*, six hours late. But the Néréides were not used to his ways; they were in a fuming hurry to be off in pursuit of the *Iphigenia*, which had sailed at crack of dawn; and they let him drop between the boat and the ship's side. In his fall he struck his head and back on the boat's gunwale, cracking two ribs and sinking stunned down through the warm clear water: the frigate was already under way, and although she heaved to at once not a man aboard did anything more valuable than run about shouting for some minutes, and by the time she had dropped her stern-boat Stephen would have been dead if one of the bale-carrying black men had not dived in and fetched him out.

He had had a shrewd knock, and although the weather was so kind, the sun so warm, an inflammation of the lungs kept him pinned to his cot for days. Or rather to the captain's cot, for Lord Clonfert moved from his own sleeping-cabin and slung a hammock in the coach.

Stephen therefore missed their rapid voyage north, the meeting of the ships off Port-Louis, and their return south-wards through heavy seas to carry out the Commodore's plan of attack on the Ile de la Passe; he missed all but the sounds of their first abortive attempt at gathering the boats for the assault in a pitch-black night with the wind blowing a close-reef topsail gale, when even the *Néréide*'s pilot could not find the channel and when the weather forced them back to Port-Louis; but on the other hand, in these circumstances of particular intimacy he did grow more closely acquainted with Clonfert and McAdam.

The captain spent many hours at Stephen's bedside: their conversation was desultory and for most part of no great consequence; but Clonfert was capable of an almost female delicacy – he could be quiet without constraint, and he always knew when Stephen would like a cooling drink or the skylight opened – and they talked about novels, the more recent romantic poetry, and Jack Aubrey, or rather Jack Aubrey's actions, in a most companionable way; and at times Stephen saw, among the various persons that made up his host, a gentle, vulnerable creature, one that excited his affec-tion. 'His intuition, however,' reflected Stephen, 'though so nice in a tête-à-tête, does not serve him when three or more are gathered in a room, nor when he is anxious. Jack has never seen him in his quasi-domestic character. His women have, no doubt; and it may be this that accounts for his notorious success among them.'

These reflections were prompted by the visit of his old shipmate Narborough, before whom Clonfert pranced away, monopolizing the talk with anecdotes of Sir Sydney Smith, and to whom he behaved with such an aggressive affectation of superiority that the commander of the *Staunch* soon returned aboard her, thoroughly displeased. Yet that same evening, as the *Néréide* and *Staunch* approached the Ile de la Passe once more, coming south about while the *Sirius* took the northern route, to avoid suspicion, Clonfert was as quiet and agreeable and well-bred as ever he had been: particularly conciliating, indeed, as though he were aware of his lapse. And when, at his request, Stephen had once again related Jack's taking of the *Cacafuego*, shot by shot, Clonfert said with a sigh, 'Well, I honour him for it, upon my word. I should die happy, with such a victory behind me.'

With McAdam Stephen's relationship was by no means so pleasant. Like most medical men Stephen was an indifferent patient; and like most medical men McAdam had an authoritative attitude towards those under his care. As soon as the patient had recovered his wits they fell out over the advisability of a cingulum, a black draught, and phlebotomy, all of which Stephen rejected in a weak, hoarse, but passionate voice as 'utterly exploded, fit for Paracelsus, or a quicksalver at the fair of Ballinasloe', together with a fling about McAdam's fondness for a strait-waistcoat. Yet this, even when it was coupled with Stephen's recovery without any treatment but bark administered by himself, would not have caused real animosity if McAdam had not also taken to resenting Clonfert's attention to Stephen, Stephen's ascendancy over Clonfert, and their pleasure in one another's company.

He came into the cabin, only half-drunk, the evening

before the *Néréide* and the *Staunch*, though delayed by head-winds, hoped to rendezvous with the *Sirius* off the Ile de la Passe for the assault, took Stephen's pulse, said, 'There is still a wee smidgeon of fever that bleeding would certainly have cured before this; but I shall allow you to take the air on deck again tomorrow, if the action leaves you any deck to take it upon,' drew his case-bottle from his pocket, poured himself a liberal dram in Stephen's physic-glass, and bending, picked up a paper that had slipped beneath the cot, a single printed sheet. 'What language is this?' he asked, holding it to the light.

'It is Irish,' said Stephen calmly: he was extremely vexed with himself for letting it be seen, for although there was no kind of remaining secrecy about his activities, his in-grained sense of caution was deeply wounded: he was deter-mined not to let this appear, however.

''Tis not the Irish character,' said McAdam.

'Irish type is rarely to be found in the French colonies, I believe.'

'I suppose it is meant for those papisher blackguards on the Mauritius,' said McAdam, referring to the Irishmen who were known to have enlisted in the French service. Stephen made no reply, and McAdam went on, 'What does it say?'

'Do you not understand Irish?'

'Of course not. What would a civilized man want with Irish?'

'Perhaps that depends upon your idea of a civilized man.'

'I'll just give you my idea of a civilized man: it is one thot makes croppies lie down, thot drinks to King Billy, and thot cries – the Pope.' With this McAdam began to sing 'Croppies lie down', and the grating, triumphant noise wounded Stephen's still fevered and over-acute hearing. Stephen was fairly sure that McAdam did not know he was a Catholic, but even so his irritation, increased by the heat, the din, the smell, and his present inability to smoke, rose to such a pitch that against all his principles he said, 'It is the pity of the world, Dr McAdam, to see a man of your parts obnubilate his mind with the juice of the grape.'

McAdam instantly collected his faculties and replied, 'It is the pity of the world, Dr Maturin, to see a man of your parts obnubilate his mind with the juice of the poppy.'

In his journal that night Stephen wrote, '. . . and his blotched face clearing on a sudden, he checked me with my laudanum. I am amazed at his perspicacity. Yet do I indeed obnubilate my mind? Surely not: looking back in this very book, I detect no diminution of activity, mental or physical. The pamphlet on Buonaparte's real conduct towards this Pope and the last is as good as anything I have ever written: I wish it may be as well translated. I rarely take a thousand drops, a trifle compared with your true opium-eater's dose or with my own in Diana's day: I can refrain whenever I choose: and I take it only when my disgust is so great that it threatens to impede my work. One day, when he is sober, I shall ask McAdam whether disgust for oneself, for one's fellows, and for the whole process of living was common among his patients in Belfast – whether it incapacitated them. My own seems to grow; and it is perhaps significant that I can feel no gratitude towards the man who took me from the water: I make the gestures that humanity requires but I feel no real kindness for him: surely this is inhuman? Humanity drained away by disgust? It grows; and although my loathing for Buonaparte and his evil system is an efficient stimulant, hatred alone is a poor sterile kind of a basis. And, laudanum or not, the disgust seems to persist even through my sleep, since frequently it is there, ready to envelop me when I wake.'

The next morning was not one of those occasions, frequent though they were. Having listened in vain at intervals throughout the night for sounds that might herald an action or even a meeting with the other ships, Stephen awoke from a long comfortable dozing state, a wholly relaxed well-being, aware that his fever was gone and that he was being looked at through the crack of the partly open door. 'Hola,' he cried, and a nervous midshipman, opening wider, said, 'The Captain's compliments to Dr Maturin, and should he be awake and well enough, there is a mermaid on the starboard bow.'

She was abaft the beam before Stephen reached the rail, a vast greyish creature with a round snout and thick lips, upright in the sea, staring at the ship with her minute beady eyes. If she was indeed a maid, then she must have had a friend who was none, for in her left flipper she held a huge grey baby. She was going fast astern, staring steadily, but he had time to see her opulent bosom, her absence of neck, hair, and external ears, and to estimate her weight at forty stone, before she dived, showing her broad tail above the wave. He made the fullest acknowledgments for such a treat – had always longed to see one – had searched the Rodriguez lagoons and those of an island near Sumatra but had always been disappointed until this happy moment – and now he found the realization of his wishes even more gratifying than he had hoped.

'I am glad you was pleased,' said Lord Clonfert, 'and I hope it may be some lay-off against my wretched news. *Sirius* has queered our pitch: see where she lays.'

Stephen took his bearings. Four or five miles away on his right hand rose the south-east coast of Mauritius, with the Pointe du Diable running into the sea: also on his right hand, but within a hundred yards, the long reef stretched out fore and aft, sometimes dry, sometimes buried under the white rollers, with the occasional island standing on it or rising from the paler shallow water inside; and at the far end, where Clonfert was pointing, there lay the *Sirius*, close to a fortified island from whose walls, clear in the telescope, flew the union jack.

In spite of his pleasure at Stephen's delight, it was clear that Clonfert was profoundly disappointed and put out. 'They must have gained twenty leagues on us, while we were beating up off the cape,' he said. 'But if Pym had had any bowels he would have waited for tonight: after all, I did lend him my pilot.' However, as an attentive host he checked any bitter reflections that might have occurred to him, and asked Stephen whether he would like his breakfast.

'You are very good, my lord,' said Stephen, 'but I believe I shall stay here in the hope of seeing another siren. They are usually found in the shallow water by a reef, I am told; and I should not miss one for a dozen breakfasts.'

'Clarges will bring it to you here, if you are quite sure you are strong enough,' said Clonfert. 'But I must send for McAdam to survey you first.'

McAdam looked singularly unappetizing in the morning light, ill-conditioned and surly: apprehensive too, for he had some confused recollection of harsh words having passed the night before. But, having beheld the mermaid, Stephen was in charity with all men, and he called out, 'You missed the mermaid, my dear colleague; but perhaps, if we sit quietly here, we may see another.'

'I did not,' said McAdam, 'I saw the brute out of the quarter-gallery scuttle; and it was only a manatee.'

Stephen mused for a while, and then he said, 'A dugong, surely. The dentition of the dugong is quite distinct from that of the manatee: the manatee, as I recall, has no incisors. Furthermore, the whole breadth of Africa separates their respective realms.'

'Manatee or dugong, 'tis all one,' said McAdam. 'As far as my studies are concerned, the brute is of consequence only in that it is the perfect illustration of the strength, the irresistible strength, of suggestion. Have you been listening to their gab, down there in the waist?'

'Not I,' said Stephen. There had been much talk among the men working just out of sight forward of the quarterdeck rail, cross, contentious talk; but the *Néréide* was always a surprisingly chatty ship, and apart from putting this outburst down to vexation at their late arrival, he had not attended to it. 'They seem displeased, however,' he added.

'Of course they are displeased: everyone knows the ill-luck a mermaid brings. But that is not the point. Listen now, will you? That is John Matthews, a truthful, sober, well-judging man; and the other is old Lemon, was bred a lawyer's clerk, and understands evidence.'

Stephen listened, sorted out the voices, caught the thread

of the argument: the dispute between Matthews and Lemon, the spokesmen of two rival factions, turned upon the question of whether the mermaid had held a comb in her hand or a glass.

'They saw the flash of that wet flipper,' said McAdam, 'and have translated it, with total Gospel-oath conviction, into one or other of these objects. Matthews offers to fight Lemon and any two of his followers over a chest in support of his belief.'

'Men have gone to the stake for less,' said Stephen: and walking forward to the rail he called down, 'You are both of you out entirely: it was a hairbrush.'

Dead silence in the waist. The seamen looked at one another doubtfully, and moved quietly away among the boats on the booms with many a backward glance, thoroughly disturbed by this new element.

'*Sirius* signalling, sir, if you please,' said a midshipman to the officer of the watch, who had been picking his teeth with a pertinacity so great that it had rendered him deaf to the dispute. '*Captain to come aboard.*'

'I am anxious to see whether the *Sirius* has any prisoners,' said Stephen, when the Captain appeared, 'and if I may, I will accompany you.'

Pym welcomed them with less than his usual cheerfulness: it had been a bloody little action, one in which he had lost a young cousin, and although the frigate's decks were now as trim as though she were lying at St Helens, there was a row of hammocks awaiting burial at sea, while her boats still lay about her in disorder, all more or less battered and one with a dismounted carronade lying in a red pool. The anxiety of the night had told on Pym and now that the stimulus of the victory was dying he looked very tired. Furthermore, the *Iphigenia* had sent an aviso with word that the three frigates in Port-Louis were ready for sea, and the *Sirius* was extremely busy, preparing her return. Her captain found time to be affable to Stephen, but his preoccupation made his words to Clonfert seem particularly curt and official. When Clonfert, having offered his congratulations, began to say that the *Néréide* felt she might have been allowed to take part, Pym cut him short: 'I really cannot go into all that now. First come first served is the rule in these matters. Here are the French commandant's signals; he did not have time to destroy them. As for your orders, they are very simple: you will garrison the island with a suitable force – the French had about a hundred men and two officers – and hold it until you receive further instructions; and in the meantime you will carry out such operations ashore as seem appropriate after consultation with Dr Maturin, whose advice is to be followed in all political matters. Doctor, if you choose to see the French commandant, my dining-cabin is at your disposition.'

When Stephen returned after questioning poor Captain Duvallier, he gained the impression that Clonfert had been rebuked for his tardiness or for some professional fault to do with the *Néréide*'s sailing; and this impression was strengthened as they pulled back in the barge, together with the black Mauritian pilot; for Clonfert was silent, his handsome face ugly with resentment.

Yet Clonfert's moods were as changeable as a weather-glass, and very shortly after the *Sirius* and *Staunch* had vanished over the western horizon, with Pym flying back to blockade the French frigates in Port-Louis, he blossomed out in a fine flow of spirits. They had cleared up the bloody mess in the fort, blasting holes in the coral rock for the dead soldiers; they had installed the Bombay gunners and fifty grenadiers of the 69th, reordering the heavy guns so that one battery commanded the narrow channel and the other all the inner anchorage that was within their range; they had taken the *Néréide* through the narrow channel into a snug berth behind the fort; and now he was a free man, his own master, with the whole of the nearby coast upon which to distinguish himself. No doubt he was directed to advise with Dr Maturin; but Dr Maturin, having required him to harangue the men on the absolute necessity for good relations with all civilians, black or white, male or female, was quite happy to fall in with his military views, such as an assault upon the battery on the Pointe du Diable and indeed upon any other batteries that might catch his fancy. Dr Maturin's attitude towards these forays was so far remote from the killjoy disapproval Clonfert had at one time feared that he even accompanied the flotilla which crossed the wide lagoon by night to carry the Pointe du Diable in great style at dawn, without the loss of a man. He watched the destruction of the guns, the carrying-off of a beautiful brass mortar, and the prodigious jet of fire as the powder-magazine blew up, with evident complacency, and then walked off into the country to make a variety of contacts and to spread his subversive literature.

Day after day the raids on military installations continued, in spite of the opposition of the French regulars and of the far more numerous militia; for the French had no cavalry, and boats guided by a pilot who knew every creek and passage could reach their goal far sooner than the infantry. Moreover, as Stephen's printed sheets attained a wider circulation, it became apparent that the militia was growing less and less inclined to fight: in fact, after about a week in which the Néréides had traversed the country in all directions, doing no harm to private property, paying for whatever they needed, treating the private Mauritians civilly, and routing all the meagre troops that the southern commander could bring against them, the attitude of the militia came more to resemble a neutrality, and a benevolent neutrality at that. Day after day the soldiers, Marines, and seamen went ashore: the frigate grew steadily more infested with monkeys and parrots, bought in the villages or captured in the woods; and Stephen, though busy with his own warfare, had an interview with an ancient gentlewoman whose grandfather had not only seen, run down and devoured a dodo, perhaps the last dodo to tread the earth, but had stuffed a bolster with its feathers.

Although there was no loot, this was a pleasant interval for all hands, with plenty of excitement and charming weather to say nothing of fresh fruit, fresh vegetables, fresh meat and soft tack: yet Clonfert exultant was a less agreeable companion than Clonfert oppressed. Stephen found his boisterous energy wearisome, his appetite for destruction distasteful, and his continual dashing about the country, often in full dress with his diamond-hilted sword and his foolish star, as tedious as the dinners he gave to celebrate the sometimes important, trivial conquests of his little force. They were conquests in which Stephen could detect no coherent plan: to him they seemed no more than a series of raids determined by the whim of the day; though on the other hand their want of logical sequence puzzled the French commander extremely.

These feasts were attended by Clonfert's officers, and once again Stephen noted the curiously vulgar tone of the *Néréide*'s gun-room and midshipmen's berth, the open flattery of the Captain, and the Captain's appetite for this flattery, however gross. Not a dinner passed without Webber, the second lieutenant, comparing Clonfert with Cochrane, to Clonfert's advantage: the word 'dashing' was in daily use: and once the purser, with a sideways look at Stephen, offered a comparison with Commodore Aubrey – a comparison that Clonfert, with an affectation of modesty, declined to allow. Stephen also observed that when McAdam was invited, which was not always the case, he was encouraged to drink and then openly derided: it grieved him to see a grey-haired man so used by young fellows who, whatever their seamanship and courage might be – and there was little doubt of either – could make no claim to any intellectual powers nor yet to common good-breeding. And he found it still more painful to see that Clonfert never checked their merriment: the Captain seemed more concerned with gaining the approval – even the worship – of his young men than with protecting an old, diminished friend.

It was in the mornings that Stephen found Clonfert's boisterousness more than usually tiresome: and he particularly regretted his company one forenoon, when, in an interval between political activities, he was negotiating with his old lady for the bolster. Clonfert spoke quite good French and he meant to help, but he hit a false note from the beginning. His noisy facetiousness offended and confused her; she began to show signs of incomprehension and alarm and to repeat that 'one never slept so well as upon dodo – sleep was the greatest blessing that God sent to the old – the gentlemen were young, and could do very well on booby-down.' Stephen had almost abandoned hope when Clonfert was called away; but once he was out of the room she reconsidered his argument, and he was paying down the price when the door burst open, a voice shouted, 'Run, run for the boats. The enemy is in sight,' and the village was filled with pounding feet. He laid down the last broad piece, caught the bolster to his bosom, and joined the rout.

Far out at sea, to windward, five ships were standing in towards the Ile de la Passe. Steadying himself in the gig, with his spy-glass to his eye, Clonfert read them off. '*Victor*, the corvette, leading. Then their big frigate, the *Minerve*. I can't make out the next. Then, by God, the *Bellone*. I could almost swear the last is the *Windham* Indiaman again. Stretch out, stretch out, there; pull strong.'

The gig's crew pulled strong, so strong they left the two other boats that had been launched far behind – three more in a farther creek had not yet even gathered their men. But it was a long, long pull, the whole length of the two spreading anchorages between the shore and the island, four miles and more against the wind.

'I shall lure them in,' said Clonfert to Stephen. And then, having glanced impatiently back towards the distant boats, he added, 'Besides, if they go round to Port-Louis, *Sirius* and *Iphigenia* will be no match for them, with Hamelin bringing his three frigates out.' Stephen made no reply.

The exhausted crew ran the gig alongside the *Néréide*. Clonfert told the coxswain to stay there and ran aboard; a few moments later the frigate displayed a French ensign and pennant and Clonfert dropped down into the boat, crying, 'The fort, and stretch out for all you are worth.'

Now the fort too showed French colours, and after a short pause the French signal ran up the flagstaff on the island: '*Enemy cruising north of Port-Louis.*' The leading frigate replied with the French private signal; the island answered it correctly; and each ship made her number. Clonfert had been right: *Victor, Minerve, Bellone*; and the two others were Indiamen, outward-bound Indiamen taken in the Mozambique channel, the *Ceylon* and the unlucky *Windham* again.

On nearing the reef the French squadron reduced sail; it was clear that they were coming in, but they were coming slowly now, and there would be time to make ready for them. Stephen chose a high, remote corner of the fort from which he could survey the whole scene and sat there on his bolster. Above him the white trade-clouds passed steadily over the pure sky; in the warm sunlight the breeze cooled his cheek; and overhead a bosun-bird wheeled in perfect curves: but within the ramparts below he saw far more confusion than he had expected. Aboard the *Néréide*, which had warped in closer to the island and which was now anchored with a spring on her cable, everything seemed to be in order, although so many of her hands were away in the boats; she was clearing for action, her guns were run out already, and her old standing officers had the process well in hand. But in the fort people were running hither and thither; there was a great deal of shouting; and the Indian gunners, whose officer was somewhere in the boats or perhaps on shore, were arguing passionately among themselves. Soldiers and sailors were at cross purposes: and even among the seamen there was none of that quiet, efficient cheerfulness that marked the actions Stephen had seen with Jack Aubrey – no impression of a machine moving smoothly into place. No food was served out, either: a small point, but one that Jack had always insisted upon. And the remaining boats, with at least a hundred and fifty soldiers and seamen in them, were still a great way off: as far as he could make out, the launch had run aground on the horn of a bank, and since the tide was on the ebb the others were having great difficulty hauling it off.

In the fort and on the lagoon time seemed to stagnate, in spite of the strenuous activity: out at sea it flowed steadily, perhaps faster than its natural pace, and Stephen felt a large, ill-defined apprehension fill the back of his mind, like that which accompanies a nightmare. Now men could be distinguished aboard the ships: now their faces were becoming visible, and orders came clear upon the wind. The French ships had formed a line to enter the channel, the *Victor* first, then the *Minerve*, then the *Ceylon*. The corvette steadied, hauled up her courses, and led in under topsails alone, the lead going in the chains on either side. The noise in the fort had given place to dead silence, with the smell of slow-match wafting on the breeze, drifting from the spare tubs and those beside each gun. The corvette entered the narrows, glided nearer and nearer, her bell flashing in the sun; came abreast of the fort, where the turbaned gunners crouched behind the parapet, and passed it, still in this dead silence. Her master's order to the helmsman brought her round in a tight curve behind the fort, into the deep water, and within twenty yards of the *Néréide*. The *Néréide*'s French ensign came down, the English colours ran up with a cheer, and her side vanished in a great cloud of smoke as her broadside roared out in a single vast prolonged explosion. Another and another, with incessant cheering: the corvette dropped her anchor under the *Néréide*'s starboard quarter, still under her full traversing fire, and an officer ran aft along her shattered deck, calling out that she had struck.

At this point the powerful *Minerve* was already in the channel, well within the channel, with the *Ceylon* close behind her: now they were right under the heavy guns of the fort; they could not turn nor bear away nor move any faster. This was the deadly moment, and every man was poised for the order. At the flagstaff the tricolour raced down to make place for the union flag; but the cheering fool who hauled it down flung it wide on to a tub of burning match near the upper magazine. Flame leapt across and with a crash far louder than a broadside and more blinding than the sun a hundred charges exploded all together. At the same second the Bombay artillerymen, still without an officer to stop them overloading, set off their ill-pointed guns, bursting or dismounting six of them and killing a man in the

Néréide's gig as it was going to take possession of the *Victor*.

Stephen picked himself up in the clearing smoke, realized that shrieks were piercing through his deafness, and hurried to the dead and wounded men scattered all about the flagstaff and the dismounted guns. McAdam's assistant was there and his loblolly-boy, and with the help of a few clear-headed seamen they carried them to the shelter of a rampart. By the time they had done what little they could, dressing horrible burns with their torn-up shirts and handkerchiefs, the scene had changed. The *Victor*, having hoisted her colours again, had cut her cable, and she was following the *Minerve* and the *Ceylon* in towards Port South-East. The *Bellone* and *Windham*, just far enough out to sea, far enough from the narrows, to be able to turn, had hauled their wind. The French ships in the lagoon were standing straight for the narrow pass where the *Néréide*'s other boats were advancing in a confused heap, and it seemed that they must take them in the next few minutes. The *Minerve* showed no obvious damage at all.

Clonfert hailed the fort from the *Néréide*, calling for all the soldiers to come aboard: he was going to attack the *Minerve*, and he needed every man to work his guns. It was not an impossible contest in spite of the *Néréide*'s lighter metal; the *Minerve* was not yet cleared for action, she was approaching the second dog-leg off the Horseshoe bank, where she could not turn, whereas the *Néréide* would still have room in the nearer anchorage to luff up and rake her; and neither the *Victor* nor the *Ceylon* could give her much support. But while the soldiers were in the act of going aboard, the *Bellone* changed her mind. She let fall her topgallantsails and headed for the channel and the island. The moment she was engaged in the narrows there was no doubt of what she meant to do: she must come on. And she did come on, with great determination. As she came, handled no doubt by a man who knew the passage perfectly, for she threw an extraordinary bow-wave for such a dangerous piece of navigation, Stephen looked round to see what Clonfert was at, and to his astonishment he saw that the launch and the cutters were passing, had passed, the French men-of-war without being touched – had passed them in the narrows within a biscuit-toss. It was inexplicable. But in any case there they were, with their men pouring into the *Néréide*, and cheering as they came. The *Néréide* had not yet slipped her cables.

The *Bellone* stood on. She had already cleared her starboard broadside and as she approached the island she fired her forward guns: the smoke, sweeping before her, veiled the fort, and through this veil she fired her full array as she swept by, sending eighteen-pound balls and countless lethal fragments of stone flying among the small remaining garrison. Swinging round into the *Néréide*'s anchorage she sent in another broadside against the other face of the battery: and to all this the demoralized Bombay gunners, deprived of support from small-arms men, unofficered, unused to ships, returned no more than a ragged, ineffectual fire. The *Bellone* went straight for the *Néréide*, as though to run her aboard; but just before they touched the *Bellone* put her helm hard down and shot by. For a moment the two frigates were yardarm to yardarm, almost touching: both broadsides crashed out together, and when the smoke cleared, the *Bellone* was well beyond the *Néréide*, running on, still under her topgallantsails, for the second sharp turn in the channel, apparently undamaged. The *Néréide* had lost her driver-boom and a couple of upper yards, but her turn and a sudden gust had laid the *Bellone* over so that her fire was too high to hurt the *Néréide*'s hull or to kill many of her crew: it had cut the spring to her cable, however, and she slewed round so far and so fast that she could not fire into the Frenchman's stern.

Now the silence fell again. The four French ships – for the *Windham*, shying at the entrance and the fort, had stood out along the coast – moved smoothly down to anchor in twenty-fathom water off the Olive bank, half way to Port South-East, and Clonfert returned to the island with a strong party of soldiers. He was in excellent spirits, hurrying about with the army officers to put the fort into such order that it could withstand an attack by the French squadron. Catching sight of Stephen he called out, 'How did you like that, Dr Maturin? We have them in the bag!'

A little later, when the armourers had set up the dismounted guns and spare carronades had replaced those that had burst, he said, 'If it had not been for that infernal luck with the flag, we should have sunk the *Minerve*. But it was just as well – the *Bellone* would have hauled her wind, and as it is we have both of them hard up in a clinch. I am sending Webber in the launch to tell Pym that if he can spare me just one frigate – *Iphigenia*, or *Magicienne* if she has joined – I will lead in and destroy the whole shooting-match. We have them finely in the bag! They can never get out except on the land-wind just before sunrise. How Cochrane will envy us!'

Stephen looked at him: did Clonfert, in his euphoria or his leaping excitement, really believe that he had done well, that his position was tenable? 'You do not intend sailing away yourself in the *Néréide* to bring down the reinforcements, I collect?' he said.

'Certainly not. Pym ordered me to hold this fort, and I shall hold it to the last. To the last,' he repeated, throwing up his head with a look of pride. At the next word his expression changed. 'And did you see that dog?' he cried. 'The *Victor* struck her colours to me and then hoisted them again and made off like a scrub, a contemptible sneaking little God-damned scrub. I shall send a flag of truce to demand her. See where she lays!'

She lay between the two heavy frigates, and from the fort her crew could be seen busily repairing the damage the *Néréide* had inflicted: the French colours flew at her peak.

'They are too close by far,' said Clonfert. He turned to the artillery officer, haggard and quite wretched at having been separated from his men, at having lost the finest opportunity of his professional career, and said, 'Captain Newnham, will the brass mortar fetch them, do you think?'

'I shall try it, my lord,' said Newnham. He loaded the

piece himself with a thirteen-inch bomb-shell, laid it – a long and delicate operation – set the fuse just so, and fired. The shell soared high in the clean air, a rapidly-diminishing black ball, and burst right over the *Bellone*. A delighted cheer went up: the French ships slipped their cables and stood farther in, to anchor out of range. The last shell, fired at extreme elevation, fell short: and it was the last shot of the day.

The remaining hours of light saw all the precautions taken that should have been taken the day before: by the next morning the Ile de la Passe was capable of sinking any ship that attempted the passage. The *Néréide* had crossed new topgallantyards, had repaired her boom and fished her wounded foremast; and she sent in a boat to demand the surrender of the corvette.

'I hope to God Webber has found the *Sirius*,' said Clonfert, gazing eagerly out to sea. But the day passed, and no sail showed beyond the cape. The night passed too, with boats rowing guard: before sunrise the perilous land-breeze began to blow – perilous because it might bring the powerful ships and a swarm of boats across the lagoon in the darkness, but the French never stirred, and at dawn the reviving south-easter kept them where they lay. So two days went by, with no incident apart from the French commodore's refusal to give up the *Victor*. The soldiers drilled and polished their equipment; the artillerymen exercised their pieces; the master-gunner filled cartridges and checked his stores. Clonfert remained as cheerful and active as ever, and his spirits reached a new height on the third day, when the French ships were seen to move down to the far end of the harbour, right down among the shoals and under the batteries of Port South-East, mooring in a curved line that stretched from one end of the sunken reef that guarded the port's entrance to the other; for this, said he, must mean that Webber had found the *Sirius*. At least some of the blockading force must have disappeared from off Port-Louis, and Governor Decaen, fearing an attack upon the *Minerve* and *Bellone*, had surely sent the news overland to

Port South-East. Clonfert was right. Some hours later the *Sirius* herself rounded the cape under a great press of sail.

'Look sharp with the signal,' said Clonfert, when they had exchanged numbers. The prepared hoist broke out, and he laughed aloud.

'What does it signify?' asked Stephen.

'*Ready for action* and *Enemy of inferior force*,' replied Clonfert with a slightly conscious look; and immediately afterwards, 'Look alive with the book, Briggs. What is she saying?'

The signal-yeoman muttered the answer, and the midshipman spoke up: '*Send Néréide's master aboard*, my lord.'

'Gig's crew,' cried Clonfert. 'Mr Satterly, bring her in as quick as ever you can.'

In she came, and her last signal before she entered the channel told the *Néréide* to get under way. The *Sirius* passed the fort almost as fast as the *Bellone*, and still under her topsails and courses swept by the *Néréide*, Pym leaning over the rail and hailing Clonfert to follow him. Down the long winding channel they went, more cautiously now, but the *Sirius* still with her topsails set, for there was not much daylight left. In the *Néréide* her black pilot was at the con; he had her under staysails, no more, and he was muttering to himself, for after the Horseshoe bank their course would lead them into a region of the inner harbour that they did not know well – a region that they had avoided, it being swept by the guns of Port South-East.

Past the Noddy shoal, with the lead going fast: past the Three Brothers, and a four-point turn to larboard. The leadsman's calls came sharp, quick and clear: 'By the mark ten; and a half ten; by the deep eleven; by the deep eleven; by the mark fifteen.' A good depth of water, a clear channel one would have sworn: yet at the last call the *Sirius*, only just ahead, struck hard on the tail of a bank and ran far up on to the submerged coral.

Yet if she had to go aground at least she had chosen a good place for doing so. The shore-batteries could not reach her, and the wind, blowing right on to the land, pinned the

French frigates to their moorings. The *Sirius* and the *Néréide* carried out their warps undisturbed as the sun set over Mauritius, and they settled down to heaving her off in a seamanlike manner. But she would not come off at the first heave, nor in the first hour of heaving, during which the tide began to ebb: however, tomorrow's flood would be higher and there were great hopes of floating her at about eight in the morning; and in the meantime there was nothing to be done except to ensure that no French boat-attack could succeed.

'What have you to say to our patient's present state of exaltation?' said Stephen to McAdam. 'In these circumstances, does it pass the limits of reasonable conduct? Do you find it morbid?'

'I am at a loss,' said McAdam. 'I have never seen him like this, at all. He may know what he is about, but he may be bent on wiping your friend's eye, and damn the whole world, so he does it. Have you ever seen a man look so beautiful?'

Dawn, and still the French had not moved. For once no holystone was heard aboard the *Sirius* or the *Néréide*; no swabs beat the decks, littered as they were with cables, hawsers, heavy tackles, all the resources of the bosun's art. The tide rose, the capstans turned, slower and slower as the full strain came on and as all hands who could find a place at the bars heaved her grinding off into deep water, where she anchored by the *Néréide* and all the carpenters crowded about her bows, cut deep by the sharp and jagged coral. The exhausted hands were piped to their late breakfast, and they were beginning to set the still-encumbered deck into some kind of fighting-trim when the *Iphigenia* and *Magicienne* were seen in the offing.

Clonfert sent his master to bring them in, for Mr Satterly, though harassed and ashamed, now certainly knew the channel up to this point very well; but he had grown so cautious that it was not until after dinner that they dropped anchor and all captains gathered aboard the *Sirius* to hear Pym's plan of attack. It was clear: it made good plain sense. *Néréide*, with her black pilot, was to lead in and anchor between the *Victor* and the *Bellone* at the northern end of the French line; *Sirius* with her eighteen-pounders was to anchor abreast of the *Bellone*; *Magicienne* between the *Ceylon* and the powerful *Minerve*; and *Iphigenia*, who also carried eighteen-pounders, abreast of the *Minerve*, closing the line on the south.

The captains turned to their ships. Clonfert, who did in fact look extraordinarily gay, young, and lighthearted, as though possessed by some happy spirit, went below to put on a new coat and fresh white breeches; coming on deck again he said to Stephen, with a particularly sweet and affectionate smile, 'Dr Maturin, I believe we may show you something to be compared to what you have seen with Commodore Aubrey.'

The *Sirius* made her signal, and the *Néréide*, slipping her cable, led in under staysails, her pilot conning the ship from the foretopmast yard. The *Sirius* followed her, then the *Magicienne*, then the *Iphigenia*, each falling into line at intervals of a cable's length. On through the winding channel with the steady breeze, the shore coming closer and closer: with successive turns in the channel the intervals grew wider, and the *Sirius*, hurrying to close the gap and misjudging her swing, struck hard and grounded on the rocky edge. At the same moment the French frigates and the shore-batteries opened fire.

Pym hailed his ships to carry on. In five minutes the *Néréide* was out of the narrow pass. The *Magicienne* and the *Iphigenia*, judging the channel by the stranded *Sirius*, pressed on after her but now at a somewhat greater distance; and in the last wind, four hundred yards from the French line, the *Magicienne* took the ground. By now the French broadsides were sweeping high over the *Néréide*'s deck from stem to stern to disable her as she ran down, making for the *Victor*'s bow. 'Warm work, Dr Maturin,' said Clonfert, and then, glancing over the taffrail, '*Sirius* has not backed off; she is hard and fast,' he said. 'We must tackle the *Bellone* for her. Mr Satterly, lay me alongside the *Bellone*. Lay me alongside the *Bellone*,' he said louder, to be heard above the din; for now the bow guns were answering the French. 'Aye, aye, sir,' said the master. For another cable's length she held on, straight through the French fire: another fifty yards, and the master, waving his hand to the watchful bosun, ordered the helm put up.

The *Néréide* swung round, dropped her anchor, and lay there broadside to broadside, abeam of the big Frenchman, and her twelve-pounders roared out at point-blank range. She was firing fast: the Marines and soldiers packed tight on the quarterdeck and forecastle were blazing away over the hammocks with steady pertinacity: stray ropes and blocks fell on to the splinter-netting overhead: smoke hung thick between the ships, continually renewed as it blew away, and through the smoke the *Bellone*'s guns flashed orange – flashes from the *Victor* too, on the *Néréide*'s starboard quarter.

Stephen walked across to the other side: the *Magicienne*, hard aground on her sharp piercing reef with her figurehead pointing at the French line, could nevertheless bring her forward guns to bear and she was hitting the enemy as hard as she could, while her boats worked furiously to get her off: the *Iphigenia* was close alongside the *Minerve*; they were separated by a long narrow shoal but they were not a stone's throw apart and they were hammering one another with appalling ferocity. The volume of noise was greater than anything Stephen had ever experienced: yet through it all there was a sound familiar to him – the cry of the wounded. The *Bellone*'s heavy guns were mauling the *Néréide* most terribly, tearing gaps in her hammocks, dismounting guns: presently she would use grape. He was a little uncertain of his position. In all previous engagements his place as a surgeon had been below, in the orlop; here it was perhaps his duty to stand and be shot at, to stand with nothing to do, like the army officers: it did not move him unduly, he found, though by now grape was screeching overhead. Yet at the same time men were carrying below in increasing numbers, and there at least he could be of some use. 'I shall stay for the present, however,' he reflected. 'It is something, after all, to view an action from such a vantage-point.' The glass turned, the bell rang: again and again. 'Six bells,' he said, counting. 'Is it possible we have been at it so long?' And it seemed to him that the *Bellone* was now firing with far less conviction, far less accuracy – that her ragged broadsides had far longer intervals between them.

A confused cheering forward, and from the *Iphigenia* too: a gap in the cloud of smoke showed him the weakly manned and weakly armed *Ceylon*, battered by the grounded *Magicienne* and by the *Iphigenia*'s quarter-guns, in the act of striking her colours; and in one of those strange momentary pauses without a gun he heard the captain of the *Iphigenia* hail the *Magicienne* in a voice of thunder, desiring her to take possession of the Indiaman. But as the *Magicienne*'s boat neared her, pulling fast through water whipped white with small shot and great, the *Ceylon* dropped her topsails and ran for the shore behind the *Bellone*. The boat was still pursuing her and roaring out when the *Minerve*, either cutting her cable or having it cut for her by the *Iphigenia*'s murderous and continual fire, swung round, got under way, and ran straight before the wind, following the *Ceylon*. She steered better than the *Ceylon* however, for the Indiaman blundered right into the *Bellone*, forcing her too to cut. They all three drifted on shore – a heap of ships ashore, with the *Minerve* lying directly behind the *Bellone* and so near that she could not fire. But the *Bellone*'s broadside still lay square to the *Néréide*, and now men were pouring into her from the land and from the *Minerve* and the *Ceylon*: her fire, which had slackened, now redoubled and grew more furious still, the broadsides now coming fast and true. The *Iphigenia*, directly to the windward of her shoal and only a pistol-shot from it, could not stir, and it was clear that in these last few minutes the face of the battle had totally changed. There was no more cheering aboard the *Néréide*. The gun-crews, for all their spirit, were growing very tired, and the rate of fire fell off. By now the sun had almost gone: and the shore-batteries, which had hitherto played on the *Iphigenia* and the *Magicienne*, now concentrated their fire on the *Néréide*.

'Why do we swing so?' wondered Stephen, and then he realized that a shot had cut the spring on the *Néréide*'s cable, the spring that held her broadside-on to the *Bellone*. Round she came, and farther yet, until her stern took the ground, thumping gently with the swell and pointing towards the enemy, who poured in a steady raking fire. She still fired her quarter-guns and her stern-chaser, but now men were falling fast. The first lieutenant and three of the army officers were dead: blood ran over her quarterdeck not in streams but in a sheet. Clonfert was giving the bosun orders about a warp when a messenger from below, a little terrified boy, ran up to him, pointing at Dr Maturin as he spoke: Clonfert crossed the deck and said, 'Dr Maturin, may I beg you to give a hand in the orlop? McAdam has had an accident. I should be most infinitely obliged.'

McAdam's accident was an alcoholic coma, and his assistant, who had never been in action before, was completely overwhelmed. Stephen threw off his coat, and in the darkness, weakly lit by a lantern, he set to work: tourniquet, saw, knife, sutures, forceps, probe, retractor, dressings, case after case, with the sometimes perilously delicate operations continually interrupted by the huge, all-pervading, sonorous jar of heavy shot smashing into the frigate's hull. And still the wounded came, until it seemed that half and even more than half of the *Néréide*'s company had passed through his bloody hands as she lay there, quite unsupported, her fire reduced to half a dozen guns.

'Make a lane there, make a lane for the Captain,' he heard, and here was Clonfert on the chest before him, under the lantern. One eye was torn out and dangling: maxilla shattered: neck ripped open and the carotid artery laid bare, pulsing in the dim light, its wall shaved almost to the bursting-point. A typical splinter-wound. And the frightful gash across his face was grape. He was conscious, perfectly clear in his mind, and at present he felt no pain, a far from uncommon phenomenon in wounds of this kind and at such a time. He was not even aware of the scalpel, probe and needle, except to say that they were oddly cold; and as Stephen worked over him he spoke, sensibly though in a voice altered by his shattered teeth, he told Stephen that he had sent to ask Pym whether he judged the ship could be towed out or whether the wounded should be put into the squadron's boats and the *Néréide* set on fire. 'She might wreck the *Bellone*, when she blows up,' he added.

His wounds were still being dressed when Webber came back from the *Sirius* with one of her officers and a message from Pym, a message that had to be shouted above the crash of the *Bellone*'s guns. Pym suggested that Clonfert should come aboard the *Sirius*. The *Iphigenia* could not possibly warp off from behind her shoal until daylight and in the meantime the *Néréide* lay between her and the French ships; she could not fire upon them; Lord Clonfert might certainly come aboard the *Sirius*.

'Abandon my men?' cried Clonfert in that strange new voice. 'I'll see him damned first. Tell him I have struck.' And when the officer had gone and the dressing was finished he said to Stephen, 'Is it done, Doctor? I am most truly grateful to you,' and made as though to rise.

'You will never get up?' asked Stephen.

'Yes,' he said. 'My legs are sound enough. I am going on deck. I must do this properly, not like a scrub.'

He stood up and Stephen said, 'Take care of the bandage on your neck. Do not pluck at it, or you may die within the minute.'

Shortly afterwards most of the remaining men came below, sent by the Captain: the routine of the ship was gone – there had been no bells this hour and more – and her life was going. Some clustered in the orlop, and from their low, muted talk and from those who came and went their shipmates learnt what was going on: a boat had come from the *Iphigenia* to ask why the *Néréide* was no longer firing, and would the Captain come aboard of her – was told, had struck, and the Captain would not stir – Captain had sent to *Bellone* to tell her to stop firing, because why? Because he had struck;

but the boat could not reach her nor make her hear. Then there was the cry of fire on deck and several men ran up to put it out: and shortly after the mainmast went by the board.

Lord Clonfert came below again, and sat for a while in the orlop. Although Stephen was still working hard he took a look at him between patients and formed the impression that he was in a state of walking unconsciousness; but after some time Clonfert got up and began moving about among the wounded, calling them by name.

It was long past midnight. The French fire was slackening; the British fire had stopped long since; and now after a few random shots the night fell silent. Men slept where they had chanced to sit or throw themselves down. Stephen took Clonfert by the arm, guided him to the dead purser's cot, well under the waterline, directed him how to rest his head so that he should not endanger his wound, and returned to his patients. There were more than a hundred and fifty of them: twenty-seven had already died below, but he had hopes for about a hundred of the rest: the dear knew how many had been killed outright on deck and thrown over-board. Seventy or so, he thought. He roused Mr Fenton, who was sleeping with his head on his arms, leaning on the chest that formed their operating-table, and together they looked to their dressings.

They were still busy when the sun rose and the *Bellone* began to fire at the *Néréide* again: on and on, in spite of repeated hails. The gunner came below with a gushing splinter-wound in his forearm, and while Stephen applied the tourniquet and tied the artery the gunner told him that the *Néréide*'s colours had not in fact been struck: they were flying still, and they could not be hauled down. There was a rumour that they had been nailed to the mast, but the gunner knew nothing of it, and the bosun, who would have had the true word, he was dead. 'And not a scrap of rigging to come at them,' he said. 'So his lordship's told the carpenter to cut the mizzen away. Thank you kindly, sir: that's a right tidy job. I'm much obliged. And, Doctor,' he said in a low rumble behind his hand, 'if you don't much care for a French prison, there's some of us topping our boom in the cutter, going aboard of *Sirius*.'

Stephen nodded, looked over his worst cases, and made his way through the wreckage to the cabin. Clonfert was not there. He found him on the quarterdeck, sitting on an upturned match-tub and watching the carpenters ply their axes. The mizzenmast fell, carrying the colours with it, and the *Bellone*'s fire ceased. 'There, I have done it properly,' said Clonfert in a barely intelligible murmur, out of the side of his ruined, bandaged face. Stephen looked at his most dangerous wound, found him sensible, though by now at a far remove, and said, 'I wish to go to the *Sirius*, my lord: the remaining boat is fit to leave, and I beg you will give an order to that effect.'

'Make it so, Dr Maturin,' said Clonfert. 'I wish you may get away. Thank you again.' They shook hands. Stephen took some papers from his cabin, destroyed others, and made his way to the boat. It was no great climb down, for the *Néréide* had settled on the sea-bed.

Although Pym received him kindly aboard the stranded *Sirius*, his conduct did not raise Stephen's opinion of him as a commander or as a man of sense. The *Iphigenia*, having at last warped herself free of the long shoal that had stood between her and the *Minerve*, sent to ask permission to stand in, to attack the immobilized French ships, boarding them with extra hands from *Sirius* and *Magicienne*, and not only taking them but rescuing the *Néréide* too. No, said Pym, who needed her help to heave his own ship off, she must go on warping towards the *Sirius*. Twice he sent back this categorical reply, each time as a direct order. With the *Iphigenia* warping out, the French fire concentrated on the *Magicienne*, hard and fast on her reef, badly holed, with nine foot of water in her hold and only a few guns that could be brought to bear. The French shot poured in upon her, and sometimes upon the other ships, and upon the frantically busy, exhausted hands in the remaining boats all that long, appalling, bloody day. It was impossible to get her off; it was impossible that she should swim if she were got off. Her men were ordered into the *Iphigenia*, and after sunset she was set on fire, blowing up in doleful splendour about midnight.

The next day the French had a new battery ready on shore, closer to, and the battery and the ships began to fire on the *Iphigenia* and the *Sirius* as they strove to heave Pym's frigate off her reef. At last, after incessant labour all in vain, and after some ugly scenes with the Captain of the *Iphigenia*, who was utterly convinced (and Stephen, together with many better-qualified observers, agreed with him) that his plan would have meant a total victory and who could barely bring himself to speak civilly to the man who had forbidden it, Pym realized that the *Sirius* could not be saved. Her ship's company were taken into the *Iphigenia* and the *Sirius* too was set on fire, Pym thereby relinquishing his command, twenty-four hours too late; and the now solitary *Iphigenia* returned to her warping.

She was obliged to warp – to carry out an anchor on the end of a cable, drop it, and wind herself up to it by the capstan – because never in the daylight did the wind cease blowing dead on shore. She could make no progress whatsoever in any other way, for when the land-breeze got up before dawn she dared not attempt the dark and unseen channel, and it always died with the rising of the sun. So hour after hour her boats, carrying the ponderous great anchors, dragged out the sodden nine-inch hawsers; and if the anchors held, if the ground was not foul, she then crept a very little way, rarely more than fifty yards, because of the turns. But often the ground was foul, and sometimes the anchors came home or were broken or were lost altogether; and all this exhausting labour had to be carried out in the blazing sun by a dispirited crew. Meanwhile the French ships in Port South-East had been heaved off, and a French brig was sighted beyond the Ile de la Passe, probably the forerunner of Hamelin's squadron from Port-Louis.

However, there was nothing for it, and the *Iphigenia* warped on and on towards the fort, fifty yards by fifty yards with long pauses for the recovery of fouled anchors, the whole length of that vast lagoon. It was two full days before she reached a point about three-quarters of a mile from the island, and here she anchored for the night. The next day, when the *Bellone* and *Minerve* had profited by the land-breeze to advance far into the lagoon whose channels they knew so well, and had there anchored, she set to again; and by eight o'clock, when she was within a thousand feet of the fort, of the open sea and the infinite delight of sailing free, she saw three ships join the French brig outside the reef: the *Vénus*, *Manche* and *Astrée*. They were exchanging signals with the *Bellone* and *Minerve*; and the wind, still right in the *Iphigenia*'s teeth, was bearing them fast towards the Ile de la Passe, where they would lie to, just out of range.

The *Iphigenia* at once sent the soldiers and many of the seamen to the fort and cleared for action. She had little ammunition, however: even before the end of the Port South-East battle she had had to send to the *Sirius* for more, and since then she had fired away so much that half an hour's engagement would see her locker bare. The clearing was therefore largely symbolic, and it was carried out, as her captain told Stephen privately, to let the French see that he would not surrender unconditionally, that he still had teeth, and that if he could not get decent terms he would use them.

'That being so,' said Stephen, 'I must ask you for a sailing-boat before the *Vénus* and her consorts close the entrance to the channel.'

'For Réunion, you mean? Yes, certainly. You shall have the launch and my own coxswain, an old whaling hand, and young Craddock to navigate her: though I should not carry the news that you must take, no, not for a thousand pound.' He gave orders for the preparation of the launch – stores, instruments, charts, water – and returning he said, 'You would oblige me extremely, Dr Maturin, by carrying a letter for my wife: I doubt I shall see her again this war.'

The launch pulled along the wicked channel in the darkness, touching twice for all their care; pulled out well beyond the reef, set her lugsail and bore away south-west. She carried ten days' provisions, but although she had many of the *Iphigenia*'s hungry young gentlemen and ship's boys aboard – their captain could not see them spend those years in a prison – the stores were almost intact when, after a perfect voyage, Stephen made his laborious way up the *Boadicea*'s side as she lay at single anchor in the road of St Paul's, close by the *Windham* and the *Bombay* transport.

'Why, Stephen, there you are!' cried Jack, springing from behind a mass of papers as Stephen walked into the cabin. 'How happy I am to see you – another couple of hours and I should have been off to Flat Island with Keating and his men – Stephen, what's amiss?'

'I must tell you what's amiss, my dear,' said Stephen: but he sat down and paused a while before going on. 'The attack on Port South-East has failed. The *Néréide* is taken; the *Sirius* and *Magicienne* are burnt; and by now the *Iphigenia* and the Ile de la Passe will almost certainly have surrendered.'

'Well,' said Jack, considering, '*Minerve*, *Bellone*, *Astrée*, *Vénus*, *Manche*; together with *Néréide* and *Iphigenia*: that makes seven to one. But we have seen longer odds, I believe.'

Chapter Eight

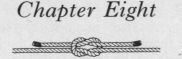

'All hands unmoor ship,' said Jack. The bosun's calls wailed and twittered; the Boadiceas ran to their stations; the fife began its thin piercing tune; 'Stamp and go, stamp and go,' cried the bosun's mates; and in the midst of the familiar din of proceeding to sea Stephen turned from the rail, where he had been staring under his shading hand at the ship lying within the frigate. 'I could almost swear I had seen that vessel before,' he said.

'Oh, not above a hundred times,' said Jack. 'She is the *Windham*. The *Windham* Indiaman again. This time she was outward-bound, and they took her in the Mozambique channel. *Sirius* very neatly retook her when she shied away from Port South-East. Did not Pym tell you?'

'Faith, we had little conversation, Captain Pym and I.'

'No: I suppose not. But, however, Pullings snapped her up in his little schooner just as she was running under the guns of Rivière Noire: a good, seamanlike officer, Tom Pullings . . .'

'Up and down, sir,' called the bosun.

'Thick and dry,' came Jack's answer, as automatic as a response in church; and he continued, '. . . and he brought her in, cracking on regardless. That was the first I knew of the affair. Let fall, there,' he cried, directing his voice upwards.

The topsails flashed out, the frigate's head swung to the north-east and steadied: she heeled, steeper and steeper as the courses, topgallants and staysails were sheeted home in smooth succession and the way came on her, the water slipping fast and faster still along her side. She shaved the cruel reef off Saint-Denis, altered course two points to eastward, and setting a flying-jib she stretched for the Ile de la Passe, making her ten knots watch after watch, her wake a straight green line of phosphorescence in the dark.

Every minute counted. Stephen's voyage had taken so little time that there was a possibility the fort had not yet surrendered, and that the *Iphigenia* still lay under its protection, within the reef. Every minute counted, and although sailcloth and spars were so precious they drove her through the sea as though they had a Spanish galleon in chase: with an even greater zeal indeed; so great that they raised the island before the light of day.

When he had two peaks of the Bamboo Mountain in a line and the Pointe du Diable bearing N17°W Jack reduced sail, carried a night-glass up to the foretop, and took the ship in, ghosting along under topsails on the edge of the land-breeze. His eyes were used to the night, helped as they were by the stars and the sickle-moon: he had made out a good deal of what lay inshore and out to sea, and when the first dawn came up before the sun he was not surprised to see the *Manche* and *Vénus* – but not the *Astrée* – lying two miles off the reef to leeward, the *Iphigenia* just inside it, the *Bellone, Minerve, Néréide* and *Ceylon* Indiaman far over by Port South-East, and the charred wrecks of the *Sirius* and *Magicienne* in the lagoon. But what did give him a shock was the sight of a fifth ship down there, just astern of the shattered *Néréide*. Leaning his telescope on the rim and focusing with care he discovered what she was: the *Ranger* from Bombay. She was only a transport, but she would have been a treasure-ship to the remnant of his squadron, for she carried spare yards and topmasts, besides three hundred tons of invaluable stores, and he had been looking for her arrival at St Paul's these many days – the *Otter*, quite unfit for sea, was heaved down in expectation of what she should bring; the *Staunch* lacked almost everything; and if the *Boadicea* carried away a spar, she would have to whistle for it. And here was the *Ranger* fitting out the enemy. The *Bellone*, which must have suffered terribly in the long action, already had her topgallantyards across. His face took on a harder look.

No colours were flying yet from either the fort or the *Iphigenia*: had they surrendered? If not, conceivably his boats might tow the *Iphigenia* through the channel, covered by the *Boadicea* and the fort, and with even a battered consort he could set about the *Vénus* and the *Manche*; for although he was short of stores, he was rich in men and ammunition. And this was no time for timid defensive measures. He came down on deck, gave orders for the ensign, the private signal, and a hoist stating his intention. The *Boadicea* stood in as the sun came up, signals flying, one eye on the French frigates, the other on the fort and the *Iphigenia*. Farther and farther in, and still no colours, though the sun was now a hand's-breadth over the horizon. Another few minutes and the *Boadicea* would be within random shot.

'A gun to windward, Mr Seymour,' said Jack. 'And shiver the foretopsail.'

In reply the British colours ran up the not so distant flagstaff: yet still the *Boadicea* hung off. Then after a pause in which hoists jerked up and down without the flags breaking out but with a crafty pretence of the halliard's jamming, the private signal.

'Hands about ship,' said Jack, for the island's private signal was ten days out of date.

Not one of the Boadiceas was unprepared for this, and she came about on to the larboard tack as briskly as a smuggling schooner, staying in her own length. The fort's seaward guns sent plumes of white water leaping from the swell two hundred yards short of her; a derisive cheer floated after them, and a little later a line of boats, carrying prisoners, put off the island for the *Manche*.

The *Manche* took them aboard and stood after the *Vénus*, which was already beating up under easy sail as though to get to the windward of the *Boadicea*. As soon as the *Manche* was up, both French frigates set their topgallants. They could be seen clearing for action, and they came on as though they meant it. Jack gazed at them with the utmost intensity, his eye hard to his glass, examining their captains' handling of their ships, gauging their sailing qualities, watching for ruses designed to mask their speed; and all the while he kept the *Boadicea* a little ahead, just out of range. By the time the watch had changed he knew he had the legs of them: he also knew that the *Vénus* could outsail the *Manche* and that if he could induce them to separate . . . but while his mind was running on to the possible consequences of this separation – to a night-engagement – to a boat-landing on the reef behind the fort – the French gave over the chase.

The *Boadicea* wore and pursued them, setting her royals to bring them within the extreme range of her brass bow-chaser, perched on the forecastle, and firing at the *Vénus*, which wore Hamelin's broad pennant. The *Vénus* and the *Manche* replied with guns run out of their gun-room ports, so low as to be ineffectual at this distance; and so the three ships ran, neither side doing the other any damage, until a lucky shot from the *Boadicea*, skipping three times over on the smooth swell, came aboard the *Vénus*. The midshipman high on the foremast jack reported a commotion on the *Vénus*'s quarterdeck: immediately afterwards the French ships went about, and once more the *Boadicea* ran south and west.

All day she ran, trying every kind of ruse and lame-duck trick to lure the faster-sailing *Vénus* ahead of the *Manche*: but nothing would serve. Hamelin had no romantic notions of single combat, and he was determined to fight at an advantage. The two Frenchmen kept within half a mile of one another, doggedly chasing the *Boadicea* over the whole stretch of sea between Mauritius and La Réunion.

'At least we are tolerably well acquainted with our enemies,' said Jack to Seymour and the quarterdeck in general, when the lights of Saint-Denis bore south-west two miles, and all hope was gone.

'Yes, sir,' said Seymour. 'We could have given them topgallants at any time. Dirty bottoms, no sort of doubt.'

'*Manche* was precious slow, shifting her sheets over the stays,' said Trollope. 'I remarked it twice.'

'Surely, sir, they are not what you would call enterprising?' said Johnson.

'Slow-bellies,' said an unidentified voice in the darkness.

In the cabin, over a late supper, Jack said to Stephen, 'Here is Fellowes' list of our requirements. May I beg you to go to Farquhar, tell him how things lie, and ask him to rouse out all that can possibly be found and have 'em down by the waterside at St Paul's in the morning? Make no excuses – I have a thousand things to do – he will understand.'

Before Stephen could answer, Spotted Dick walked in and said, 'You sent for me, sir?'

'Yes. Mr Richardson, you will take the *Pearl* aviso with four good hands and run up to Port-Louis, find the *Staunch*, and bring her down. Mr Peter has her orders ready for you to take.'

'So much responsibility for that pimply lad,' observed Stephen, through his Welsh rabbit.

'Aye,' said Jack, who had brought a prize hermaphrodite into Plymouth from far off Finisterre before his voice had broken. 'We must depend on our small-fry now, men and ships. If we had had the *Otter* or even the *Staunch* with us today, we could have made a dash at that unhandy *Manche*, you know.'

'Could we, indeed?'

'Lord, yes,' said Jack. 'And I trust we shall tomorrow. I have sent Seymour galloping over to St Paul's to bid Tomkinson leave the *Otter* where she lies, shift all his people into the *Windham*, and join me in the roadstead. With this wind getting up, Hamelin will stand off and on tonight, I am very sure.'

Hamelin was more off than on in the light of dawn when the *Boadicea* ran down to St Paul's, and the *Vénus* and the *Manche* were a mere flash of topsails against the western sky. But they were there, and once he had settled that fact beyond any hint of a doubt, Jack Aubrey turned his glass to the distant shipping in the road.

'What in Hell's name is the *Windham* thinking of?' he

cried. 'She has not even crossed her yards. Mr Collins: *Windham proceed to sea immediately*, with a gun; and give her another gun every minute until she weighs. God rot the . . .' He clapped his mouth shut, and clenching his hands behind his back he paced up and down. 'His face is darker than I have ever seen it,' observed Stephen, looking at him from the taffrail. 'Up until now, he has borne these reverses with a singular magnanimity, greater by far than I had looked for. Not a word about Clonfert's disastrous folly; nothing but sympathy for his wounds, and a hope that the French hospital may set him up. No reflection upon Pym's dogged stupidity. Yet there is no greatness of mind without its limits: is this breaking-point?'

'Shot the next gun,' said Jack, stopping short in his stride, with a furious glare at the far-off Hamelin.

'Sir,' said Trollope timidly, 'a transport is rounding the point. The *Emma*, I believe. Yes, sir, the *Emma*.'

The *Emma* she was, and quite apart from her signal it was evident that she wished to speak the *Boadicea* as she hovered there, backing and filling in a black fury of impatience; for the slab-sided transport had already spread a great press of sail.

'*Captain come aboard* pennant, Mr Collins,' said Jack.

The *Emma*'s stern-boat splashed down, pulled across, hooked on, and Pullings came up the side. 'Mr Pullings,' said Jack, 'what is this caper?'

'I beg pardon, sir,' said Pullings, pale with emotion. 'I have *Windham*'s guns aboard: Captain Tomkinson declined the command.'

'Come below and explain yourself,' said Jack. 'Mr Seymour, carry on: course nor'-nor'-west.'

In the cabin it appeared, from Pullings' nervous, involved, embarrassed statement that Tomkinson, having looked into the Indiaman's condition, had refused to take her to sea until she should be made seaworthy, and had returned to the immobilized *Otter*. Pullings, a witness of this, had come to an agreement with the *Emma*'s captain, sick ashore; had moved his men and a score of volunteers into her, she being in a better state than the Indiaman, and by inhuman labour all through the night had shifted the *Windham*'s guns and his own carronades across, helped by Colonel Keating, who had also given him gunners and small-arms men.

'This Tomkinson,' cried Stephen, who could speak openly before Pullings, 'must he not be hanged, or flogged, or at least dismissed the service, the infamous whore?'

'No,' said Jack. 'He is a poor creature, God help him, but he is within his rights. A captain can refuse a command, on those grounds. Tom,' he said, shaking Pullings' hand, 'you are a right sea-officer; I am obliged to you. If you can get eight knots out of your *Emma*, we shall have a touch of those Frenchmen out there, before long.'

The two ships bore away in company, steering a course that would give them the weather-gage in a couple of hours, well north of the island, where the wind came more easterly. But in far less time than that it became apparent to all hands that the *Emma* could not keep up. Six or at the most seven knots was her utmost limit, even with the wind abaft the beam – studdingsails aloft and alow, and even kites, strange sails without a name, all set and drawing – and once they had hauled their wind three points, even six was beyond her power, driven though she was with all the resources of seamanship and an able, willing crew. The *Boadicea* had to take in her topgallants to keep the *Emma* in sight at all; while on the other hand, Hamelin, the necessary complement of a quarrel, kept steadily ahead, with never a sign of reducing sail, still less of heaving to to wait for them.

Yet for all that, Hamelin had now run so far to the westward that he would have to go up to Port-Louis rather than Port South-East, which was something gained, since it would allow Jack to look into the Ile de la Passe again: and the *Emma* was there to perform a most important task that should have fallen to the *Otter*.

'Back the foretopsail, Mr Johnson, if you please,' said Jack, just before the hands were piped to dinner; and when the *Emma* had come labouring up he hailed Pullings, directing him to make for Rodriguez, acquaint the military with the situation, and then to cruise between that island and 57°E to warn any King's or Company's ships he saw, at the same time taking all appropriate measures. 'And Mr Pullings,' he added, in his strong voice, 'I shall not object to your taking one of their frigates, or even two: that will still leave plenty for me.'

The joke was limp enough, in all conscience; but the tone in which it was said, or rather roared, caused Pullings' distressed, tired face to spread in an answering grin.

The *Boadicea* looked at the Ile de la Passe, which greeted her with a roar of heavy guns: she looked beyond it, over the billowing smoke, into Port South-East, and there she saw the *Bellone*, new-rigged and ready for sea. The *Minerve* now had jury topmasts and the *Néréide* something in the way of a main and a mizzen, while caulkers and carpenters were busy about them both: the *Iphigenia* had already sailed. There was nothing to be done, and the *Boadicea* turned about for La Réunion.

'Mr Seymour,' said Jack, in that curiously detached, impersonal tone that had come on him since the news of the defeat, 'when did we last exercise the guns?'

'Several days ago, sir. Much longer than usual,' said Seymour, searching wildly in his mind for the exact date; for this new and somewhat inhuman commodore, though neither fault-finding nor severe, put the fear of God into the quarter-deck. 'It was last Saturday, I believe.'

'Then we will advance quarters by half an hour, and rattle them in and out. We can afford two – no, three – rounds a gun; and I believe we may fire upon targets.'

If Hamelin was the man Jack thought him to be, he would surely have *Astrée* and one or two of his corvettes cruising between Mauritius and Réunion by now, and the sound of gunfire might bring them down: so late that afternoon the sky echoed to *Boadicea's* thunder. The gun-crews, stripped to the waist and gleaming with sweat, plied the massive cannon with even more than their usual diligence, for they too had long since caught their commander's mood: he watched them with a grave satisfaction, a remarkably healthy crew, well fed on fresh meat and garden-stuff, in fine fettle and high training. Good men; a rapid, accurate fire, surpassing anything the *Boadicea* had yet achieved by a clear eight seconds. Although the *Boadicea* was not and never could be an outstanding sailer, he need not fear any single French ship afloat in these waters; nor any two, if only he had the support of a well-handled sloop and if only he could bring them to that perilous thing, an engagement in the darkness, when high discipline and true aim counted for so much. Yet when the guns were housed and cool again the sea remained as empty as it had been before, a vast disc of unbroken blue, now fast darkening to deep sapphire: there was to be no action that night.

Nor the next day either, in the twenty miles of sea before the frigate dropped anchor at St Paul's again. No action at sea, but enormous activity on shore. Jack flung himself into the task of getting the *Otter* and the *Windham* into fighting-trim. He took little notice of Captain Tomkinson, now perhaps the unhappiest man on La Réunion, but directed the work himself: with the Governor's total, intelligent support, he had a sovereign hand in the yards of St Paul's and Saint-Denis, and there, labouring through the night by flares, every artificer in the island did all that could conceivably be done to turn a sixteen-gun sloop and a decayed, cruelly battered Indiaman with no guns but what the soldiers could afford her into honorary frigates, or at least into something that might have some remote chance of standing the enemy's fire, of holding him long enough for the *Boadicea* to run alongside and board.

On the Sunday morning, with the *Otter* in her final stage of refitting but with the *Windham* still heaved down, he was taking a very late breakfast after four hours of the deepest sleep he had known, taking it in the company of Stephen Maturin, whom he saw but rarely these days: he had resolutely dismissed the problems of the dockyard from his mind for twenty minutes, when Stephen involuntarily brought them back by asking the significance of the devil, among those that followed the sea, as in the devil to pay, a phrase he had often heard, particularly of late – was it a form of propitiation, a Manichaean remnant, so understandable (though erroneous) upon the unbridled elements?

'Why, the devil, do you see,' said Jack, 'is the seam between the deck-planking and the timbers, and we call it the devil, because it is the *devil* for the caulkers to come at: in full we say, the devil to pay and no pitch hot; and what we mean is, that there is something hellfire difficult to be done – must be done – and nothing to do it with. It is a figure.'

'A very elegant figure, too.'

'Was you a weak, superficial cove, and feeling low, you might say it described our situation at the moment,' said Jack. 'But you would be wrong. With *Staunch*, and *Otter* and *Windham*, in a day or two . . .' he cocked his ear, and called out, 'Killick, who is that coming aboard?'

'Only an army officer, sir.'

The clash of Marines presenting arms on the quarterdeck: a midshipman to ask whether the Commodore would receive Colonel Fraser, and then the Colonel himself, his face as scarlet as his coat from galloping under the torrid sun.

'Good morning, Colonel,' said Jack. 'Sit down and take a cup.'

'Good morning, sir. Doctor, how d'ye do?'

'Colonel Fraser should instantly drink something cool, and throw off his stock,' said Stephen. 'Your servant, sir.'

'Happy to do so, sir, in one minute; but first I must deliver my despatch – verbal, sir: no time to call for pen and ink. Colonel Keating's compliments to Commodore Aubrey, and HMS *Africaine* is in Saint-Denis. Captain Corbett –'

'Corbett? Robert Corbett?'

'I believe so, sir: a little man, looks rather black and cross when put out – the same that was here before – splendid disciplinarian. Captain Corbett, sir, proceeding to Madras, learnt of the state of affairs here from one of your ships when he was putting in to water at Rodriguez, so he turned off to La Réunion. He had some kind of a small engagement with a schooner on the coast of the Mauritius on the way and he is now landing his wounded: Colonel Keating has given him twenty-five men and an officer to take their place, because, sir, two French frigates and a brig are coming in after him. And Captain Corbett charges me to say, with his duty, that he has taken the liberty of hoisting your broad pennant, to amuse 'em, that he is clearing for action, and will put to sea the moment all his wounded are ashore.'

'Colonel,' said Jack, 'I am infinitely obliged to you. Killick, light along a jug of something cool for Colonel Fraser – sandwiches – mangoes.' These words he called backwards as he ran on to the quarterdeck. 'Mr Trollope, all hands from the yard immediately, and prepare to slip the moment they are aboard. Mr Collins, to *Otter* and *Staunch: proceed to sea immediately* and *enemy cruising east-north-east.* Pass the word for the gunner.' The gunner came running, for the news was spreading fast. 'Mr Webber,' said Jack, 'how much have you filled?'

'Thirty rounds a gun, sir,' said the gunner, 'and twenty-three for the carronades: we been at it all this forenoon.' And then, encouraged by old acquaintance and by the glowing change in the Commodore, 'May I hope to fill some more, sir, for the right true end?'

'Yes, Mr Webber,' said Jack. 'And none of your white letter stuff. Let it all be our very best red large grain.'

Rounding the Pointe des Galets at noon, the *Boadicea,* followed by the *Otter* and the *Staunch*, made out the French ships in the offing: two frigates. The French brig was already topsails down to the northwards, no doubt hurrying off to tell Hamelin what was afoot. There was a general hum of satisfaction, tempered by the fact that the Frenchmen were no longer standing in, but had gone about on the starboard tack, and by the sight of long white lines far out, which meant that the wind, south or south-east to the leeward of La Réunion, was blowing from the east to the north of it, so that the enemy would have the weather-gage. They also saw the *Africaine*, and the actual sight of her raised Jack's heart still higher: she was a thirty-six-gun eighteen-pounder frigate, French-built of course, and one of the finest sailers in the Royal Navy, particularly on a wind. She must have been the plum with which Corbett was rewarded when he brought home the St Paul's despatches. 'He will certainly handle her well,' reflected Jack. 'A capital seaman. Let us hope he has taught his men how to point their guns this time, and that he has made himself more amiable aboard her.' A plum sometimes had that effect upon a disappointed man; and Corbett had often been disappointed.

When he caught sight of her, the *Africaine* was also on the starboard tack, under a press of sail, about eight miles south of the enemy. The two ships exchanged numbers, no more. Jack had no intention of worrying the *Africaine* with signals: Corbett was a fighting captain; he knew very well what to do; there was no doubt that he would do it; and in the meantime he must be left free to concentrate on making up at least seven of those eight miles. The same applied with even greater force to the *Boadicea*: although she could hit harder than the *Africaine*, she could not rival her in speed. Happily one of the Frenchmen was their old *Iphigenia*, now the *Iphigénie* once more, and she was no flyer: the other was probably the *Astrée*, whose qualities he did not know.

He would soon find them out, however, he said, smiling, as he took his glass into the foretop and the six ships settled down to the long chase. An hour later he knew that she had an able captain, that she was faster than the *Iphigenia*, but not faster than the *Boadicea*, while the *Africaine* could give her topgallantsails at least. If the wind held true, the *Africaine* should be up with them before sunset, and the *Boadicea* not long after dark. If the wind held true: that was his chief concern. For were it to back more easterly or even a little north of east as it sometimes did by night, then the *Boadicea* would be dead to leeward of the Frenchmen, and they might be able to run up to Port-Louis before that leeway could be made up. For the *Boadicea* was not at her best on a bowline: and although he would not have it generally known, she could not come up so close to the wind as some other ships, not by half a point, in spite of all his care.

Yet taking thought would neither keep the wind south of east nor improve the *Boadicea*'s sailing: he came down, glanced at the now distant *Staunch* and *Otter*, told Seymour that he was to be called in case the position changed, and went fast to sleep in a hammock slung in the desolate clean sweep fore and aft that had once been his array of cabins, knowing that his officers would sail the ship admirably well and that he must keep his wits as sharp as they could be for what might well be a difficult night-engagement, calling for instant decision.

When he came on deck again the *Otter* and the *Staunch* were barely in sight from the masthead: the *Africaine* was something better than two leagues ahead and she was gaining visibly on the Frenchmen. At his second hail the lookout replied, after a studying pause, that *Staunch* and *Otter* had vanished now: and while the lookout was answering, an unpleasant rattle accompanied his voice: the wind had come too far forward for the studdingsails to set, and they were shivering, in spite of fiddle-taut bowlines. The *Boadicea* took them in: she lost way at once, and presently the *Africaine* was a full eight miles away, pursuing the now invisible French towards the coming night.

A dirty night, though warm, with sudden squalls and a mounting cross-sea that kept forcing the *Boadicea's* head northwards. The best helmsmen in the ship were at the wheel, with Jack behind them, standing by the master at the con. For some little while after full darkness he saw the rockets and the blue lights that showed the *Africaine*'s position. Then nothing. Hour after hour of low driving cloud, very heavy showers of rain, the seas breaking over her starboard bow, the wind in the rigging as she stood on and on; but never the sound that the silent, listening men were waiting for.

Nothing until seven bells in the middle watch, when the breeze turned gusty before dropping to something near a calm: at seven bells and again at the changing of the watch flashes were seen under the cloud to windward, and remote gunfire followed them. 'God send he has not engaged close without me,' murmured Jack, altering course for the flash. That fear had occurred to him in these hours of waiting, together with others, equally wild: but he had put it away – Corbett was no Clonfert; and in any case Corbett knew the *Boadicea*'s rate of sailing perfectly.

The gunfire was louder every glass; but at every glass the breeze grew less; and at last the *Boadicea* had scarcely steerage-way. The short twilight before dawn was veiled by a last sheet of tepid rain. It faded slowly in the still air as the sun rose up; and all at once there was the whole stretch of sea, brilliantly lit, and upon it, four miles away, the *Africaine* with one French ship within pistol-shot on her bow, another on her quarter. She was firing an occasional gun: the enemy answered with full broadsides: then she fell silent.

Four miles away: clear in his telescope Jack saw her colours waver at the peak and come slowly down, down, right down on deck; and still the French kept firing. For a quarter of an hour they kept firing into her silent hull.

Never had he had to master himself with such force: the sight was so horrible that if the breeze had not got up while he was watching it seemed that his heart must break with grief and rage. The royals took it first. The *Boadicea* gave a gentle heave against the sea and the water began to whisper along her side. Jack gave his orders automatically; said, 'Mr Seymour, the slow-match needs renewing,' and took the *Boadicea* down towards the Frenchmen as they lay about their prize, the boats coming and going. 'Masthead, there,' he called. 'What do you see of *Staunch* and *Otter*?'

'Nothing, sir,' came the reply. 'Nothing to windward, nothing to leeward.'

Jack nodded. The breeze was freshening; he could feel it on his cheek, coming beautifully though soft from the south-east and even south of that – the breeze that would have brought him up. The *Boadicea* stood on; and as they watched the *Africaine*'s masts went by the board; first her foremast, then the mizzen, then the main. The *Astrée* and the *Iphigenia* did not appear to have suffered at all.

Whatever it cost, he must resist the temptation to run down and engage them: it would be criminal folly. But the temptation to set the *Boadicea* right between the two, firing both sides, was terribly strong; and with the wind as it lay he might be able to yield just so far and still regard his duty – a quick hard strike and away was allowable: it was even called for.

'Mr Seymour,' said he, 'I am going to run down to within musket-shot of the windward ship. When I give the order, let the starboard guns fire, starting from forwards: deliberate fire at her stern, the smoke to clear between each shot. When the last gun has fired, about ship, and then the larboard broadside as we go about to come up as near as she will lie. Mr Buchan, lay me for the *Iphigenia*.'

The *Boadicea* was bringing up the wind. The Frenchmen had steerage-way, but little more, while she was moving at three knots; and the *Astrée*, behind the *Africaine*, had not run clear before Jack said, 'Fire.' The guns went off in steady, even succession, undisturbed by the ragged broadsides from the *Iphigenia*, the first two wild, the third deadly enough: the *Boadicea*'s was a deliberate fire, aimed with hatred, and hammocks and splinters of rail leapt from the *Iphigenia*'s stern; one fine shot from number twelve struck her between wind and water very near her rudder and a cheer went up. Then the cry 'Helm's a-lee', and the *Boadicea* came up into the wind. She was in stays when the *Astrée*, clear of the *Iphigenia* and the *Africaine* at last, let fly. She hit the *Boadicea* very hard, shattering the stern-boat on its davits and giving her such a blow that for a moment Jack thought she was going to fall off – that he had risked her just that hair's-breadth too far. 'Flat in forward, there,' he cried, felt the fine balance change, and with infinite relief called, 'Mainsail haul.' Round she came and filled, the way still on her: round, round, till her larboard ports stared full at the *Iphigenia*. With one great rippling crash her broadside went off, and she sailed clear of her smoke. At the same moment a shot from the *Astrée* struck the master in the back, cutting him in two at Jack's side. Jack saw his astonished, indignant face jerk forward, knocking the starboard helmsman down. He took the man's place for a moment, bringing the frigate still farther round until her headsails shivered and a quartermaster seized the spokes; then stepping over the body he walked to the taffrail. The *Iphigenia*'s stern had suffered, but her rudder had not gone, nor yet her mizzenmast. She had dropped her foresail and was now before the wind, moving down towards the *Astrée*, masking her fire again: he heard the master's body splash into the sea as he considered her: a scratch crew, no doubt, with not much sense and still less appetite for a close engagement with the *Boadicea*. And as the *Boadicea* stretched away close-hauled and the distance widened, he saw the *Iphigenia* put up her helm and fall foul of the *Astrée*, just as the *Astrée* tried to slip through the gap between her and the *Africaine* to rake the *Boadicea* at extreme range.

He took the frigate some way to windward and there heaved to. In the brilliant sunlight he could see the French ships perfectly, the people on their decks, even the state of their rigging. Sitting on the slide of the aftermost carronade he contemplated the scene; for this was a time for contemplation. No sudden decisions were called for at this point, nor would they be required for some considerable time. The *Astrée* was a formidable ship; she was undamaged; she had disentangled herself from the *Iphigenia* and had worn clear at last; the sea between her and the *Boadicea* was clear. Yet she did not come on. Her shivering foretopsail – her deliberately shivering foretopsail – told him a great deal about her commander, and a score of less obvious details told him more: a competent seaman, no doubt, but he did not mean to fight. He no more meant to fight than Hamelin, at an even greater advantage, had meant to fight; neither this man nor his commodore chose to risk the throw. The conviction, growing stronger as he watched, filled him with grave joy.

On the other hand, said his reason as it compelled his

heart to be quiet, the *Astrée* carried a great broadside weight of metal, her gunnery was accurate, and although she was not faster than the *Boadicea* she could haul closer to the wind: then again, attack and defence were two different things; in a close action the *Astrée* would do tolerably well, and although the *Iphigenia* was handled by a nincompoop, tackling the two of them together by daylight would be unjustifiable in the present balance. Yet he must necessarily retake the the *Africaine* . . .

'On deck, there,' hailed the lookout. 'Two sail right to windward, sir. I think it's *Staunch* and *Otter*.' Some minutes later, 'Yes, sir: *Staunch* and *Otter*.' With this wind it would take them two or three hours to reach him: very well. He stood up smiling and looked across to the lee side, where his first lieutenant, the carpenter and the bosun were waiting to report.

'Three wounded, sir,' said Seymour, 'and of course poor Mr Buchan.' The carpenter had only four shot-holes and eight inches of water in the well: Fellowes gave an account of a fair amount of damage to the sails and rigging forward. 'I reckon an hour will see it to rights, sir,' he added.

'As smartly as ever you can, Mr Fellowes,' said Jack. 'Mr Seymour, let the hands go to breakfast; and the watch below must have some rest.'

He went down into the orlop, where he found Stephen reading in a small book, holding it up to the lantern.

'Are you hurt?' asked Stephen.

'No, not at all, I thank you: I am come down to look at the wounded. How are they coming along?'

'Colley, the depressed cranial fracture, I will not answer for: he is comatose, as you see. We must operate as soon as we have peace and quiet and light – the sooner the better. The two splinter-wounds will do very well. Your breeches are covered with blood.'

'It is the master's. He lost the number of his mess right by me, poor fellow.' Jack went over to the patients, asked them how they felt, told them that things looked very well on deck, that *Staunch* and *Otter* were coming up hand over fist, and that presently the Frenchmen might be served out for what they did to the *Africaine*. Returning to Stephen he said, 'Killick has a little spirit-stove on the go, if you could fancy breakfast.'

And standing by the stern-window while the coffee flowed into them by the pint, he explained the situation, pointing out just how the French lay now and how they had lain at different stages. 'I know you will think it illogical,' he said, his hand firmly gripping the wooden frame, 'and maybe even superstitious, but I have a feeling that the tide has turned. I do not mean to tempt fate, God forbid, but I believe that when the *Staunch* and *Otter* join, we shall retake the *Africaine*. We might even snap up the *Iphigenia*: she is shy; I think we may have hit her hard – look at the people over her side; and the captain of the *Astrée* don't trust her. But I will not go so far as that: the *Africaine* will be enough.'

On deck once more, and a surprisingly respectable deck, with the knotting and splicing almost finished, the swabbers of the afterguard washing the last pale smears from by the wheel, the davits righted, a new foretopsail bent: over the water the French boats were still removing prisoners from the *Africaine*, the *Iphigenia*'s pumps were going hard, and from the look of the feverish activity among the parties inboard and outboard of her, she would be in no way to get under sail for some time. The *Astrée* had moved into a better position to cover her and the *Africaine*: her captain might be no fire-eater, but clearly he meant to cling to his prize if he possibly could. But now from the deck the *Staunch* and *Otter* could be seen hull-up; and the breeze was blowing fresher.

An early dinner, cold, and the grog cut by half; yet there was no grumbling. The Commodore's look of contained pleasure, his certainty, the indefinable change that had come over him, had spread a feeling of total confidence throughout the ship. The hands ate their good biscuit and their execrable cheese, wetted with more watered lime-juice than rum, and they looked at him, they looked at the Frenchmen in their uneasy heap to leeward, they looked at the two ships coming closer every minute, and they talked in low cheerful voices: there was a good deal of quiet laughter in the waist and on the forecastle.

With a piece of chalk the Commodore drew his plan of attack on the deck: the captains of the sloop and the brig watched attentively. The three were to run down in line abreast, the *Boadicea* in the middle, and they were to endeavour to separate the two French frigates; there were many possibilities, depending on the movements of the *Astrée*, and Jack explained them clearly. 'But at all events, gentlemen,' he said, 'in case of the unforeseen, you will not go far wrong by closing with the *Iphigenia*, ahead and astern, and leaving the *Astrée* to me.'

With the wind three points abaft the beam, and under topsails alone for freedom of manoeuvre, they bore down, the brig looking pitifully small on the *Boadicea*'s starboard beam and the sloop a mere wisp to port. Jack had given them plenty of time to feed and rest their hands; he knew that they were thoroughly prepared and well manned, and that their commanders understood his intentions beyond any sort of doubt.

He had foreseen a great many possibilities, and he stood on with a confidence that he had rarely felt so strongly before, a steady rising of his heart; but he had not foreseen what in fact took place. They were still a mile and a half away when the *Astrée* passed the *Iphigenia* a towline and both frigates made sail. Abandoning the *Africaine*, they gathered away, packed on more sail and still more, hauled their wind and stretched to the eastwards as fast as they could go, the fine-sailing *Astrée* keeping the *Iphigenia*'s head right up to the wind, closer than ever the *Boadicea* could lie.

By coming to instantly it was conceivable that since she was somewhat to windward the *Boadicea* might bring them to action at the end of a very long converging chase, in spite of the *Astrée*'s superiority on a bowline; but neither the *Otter* nor the *Staunch* could possibly keep up, and in the meanwhile it was probable that Hamelin's reinforcement, brought by the French brig, would be down for the *Africaine*. No: this, alas, was a time for discretion, and the *Boadicea* stood quietly on for the sad dismantled hulk, which lay wallowing on the swell with no more than her ensign-staff to show the French colours.

The *Boadicea* came alongside: the *Africaine* fired two guns to leeward and the French colours came down, to the sound of immense cheering from the prisoners still aboard her. 'Mr Seymour,' said Jack, with a feeling of anticlimax, yet with a deep glowing satisfaction beneath it, 'be so good as to take possession. What the devil is this?'

This was the sight of a score of Africaines plunging into the sea, swimming across, and swarming up the side of the *Boadicea*. They were in a state of wild enthusiasm, joy and rage strangely mingled: nearly all sense of discipline was gone and they crowded dripping on the quarterdeck, begging the Commodore to renew the action – they would fight his guns for him – they would be happy to serve under Captain Aubrey – not like under some brass-bound buggers – they knew him – and they knew he could serve those French farts out for what they done – take on two of them at any time like kiss your hand – 'I know you can do it, sir,' cried one with a bloody dressing round his upper arm, 'I was ship-mates along of you in *Sophie*, when we fucked the big Spaniard. Don't say no, sir.'

'I am glad to see you, Herold,' said Jack, 'and I wish I could say yes, with all my heart. But you are a seaman – look how they lay. Three hours stern-chase, and five French frigates to northwards ready to come down for the *Africaine*. I understand your feelings, lads, but it's no go. Bear a hand with a towline, and we shall take your barky into St Paul's and refit her: then you shall serve the Frenchmen out your-selves.' They looked longingly at the *Astrée* and the *Iphigenia*, and they sighed; but as seamen they had nothing to say. 'How is Captain Corbett?' asked Jack. 'Did the French take him aboard?'

Silence. Then, 'Don't know, sir.' He looked at them in surprise. In front of him was a row of closed faces: the rare, immediate, man-to-man contact was entirely gone: he had run straight into the brick wall of lower-deck dumbness, the covering-up solidarity he knew so well, often stupid, generally transparent, but always unbreakable. 'Don't know, sir,' was the only answer he would ever get.

Chapter Nine

Slowly the *Boadicea* dragged the *Africaine* southwards through the rising swell: she behaved like a sodden tree-trunk of enormous size, now lagging sullenly so that the *Boadicea*'s masts complained and Seymour's hoarse whisper – all that was left of his voice – desired the hands 'to start that – sheet before everything carried away', now darting unpredictably at the *Boadicea*'s stern and then slewing so that the towline jerked from the sea, a rigid bar of rope on the verge of rupture, squirting water from every strand; and above all she rolled, a dead lurching drunken gunwale-roll that made the surgeons' work even more hazardous and delicate than usual.

Stephen was there, helping poor Mr Cotton, an elderly cripple who had scarcely recovered from a bout of dysentery and who had been overcome with work from the first few minutes of the action. Even now, after a shocking number of deaths below, sixty or seventy cases remained, lying all along the berth-deck: there was plenty of room, at least, since the French had killed forty-nine men outright and had taken fifty prisoners away. The Africaines who remained, helped by a party from the *Boadicea*, were busily lashing what spars they possessed to the stumps of the masts, and towards nightfall they were able to set three staysails, which at once gave the frigate back her life, so that she moved like a sentient being once more, with no more of a roll than a reasonable ship.

'What a relief,' said Mr Cotton, plying his saw. 'At one time I feared I was about to be seasick again – seasick after all these years afloat! A ligature, if you please. Are you subject to the seasickness, Dr Maturin?'

'I have known it in the Bay.'

'Ah, the Bay,' said Cotton, tossing the detached foot into a bucket held by his loblolly-boy, 'that dismal tract. You may let him go,' he said to the patient's messmates, who had been holding him; and into the grey, sweating face he said, 'John Bates, it is all over now. You will do very well, and that foot will earn you a Greenwich pension or a cook's warrant.'

The grey, sweating face murmured in a tiny voice, thanking Mr Cotton, and might he keep the foot, for luck?

'That finishes our urgent cases,' said Mr Cotton, looking round. 'I am infinitely obliged to you, sir. Infinitely obliged; and I wish I had something better to offer you than a dish of tea. But the French stripped us, stripped us like a pack of savages, sir. Fortunately they do not care for tea.'

'A dish of tea would be most welcome,' said Stephen, and they walked aft to the deserted gun-room. 'A bloody action,' he observed.

'I have rarely seen a bloodier,' said Mr Cotton. 'Nor, I suspect, a more unnecessary waste of life. Still, the Captain has paid for it, for what comfort that may be.'

'Killed he was?'

'Killed, or call it what you choose. At all events he is dead,' said Cotton. 'He was brought below at the very beginning – metacarpals of the left foot all abroad. I did what I could, and he insisted on being carried up again – he was a brave man, you know, with all his faults. Then he was hit a second time, but who fired the piece I will not say; nor will I absolutely assert that in the confusion of the night-engagement his own people tossed him over the side; but in any case he disappeared. I dare say you have known similar cases.'

'I have heard of them, of course; and in this particular instance I had some hint of it long ago. Captain Corbett's reputation as a flogging captain had spread pretty wide, I believe.'

'So wide that the hands mutinied when he was appointed to the ship: refused to take her to sea. I was on leave at the time, and when I came back I was surprised to find that the officers sent down from London had persuaded them that he was not as black as he was painted – had persuaded them to return to their duty.'

'Why were you surprised, sir?'

'Because those reputations are never wrong. He *was* as black as he was painted. He flogged those men down to the line, he flogged them across it, and he flogged them all the way up from the Cape.'

'A parenthesis – did you carry any mail for the Cape, any mail for us?'

'Yes; and we were to carry yours on to Rodriguez. But as you know, we never touched there – turned right about the moment we had spoken the *Emma* – and I am sorry to say the Frenchman got it all.'

'Well, well. And yet the men fought with great spirit, I collect?'

'With very great spirit; and that was because they had a decent set of officers. Captain Corbett was scarcely on speaking-terms with any of them: never dined in the gun-room but once, never invited. And the men would have fought her even better if they had been taught how to use the guns: never exercised with them once, all because of that holy deck. It must be in a pretty state at this moment. No: the hands had nothing against the officers, who were a decent set of men, as I say, and game to the last – Tullidge fought the ship after the captain was gone, and he was wounded four times; Forder, the second, had a bullet through the lungs, and Parker's head was shot off. Good officers. Once, when we were off Cape St Roque and Corbett was handing out fifty lashes right and left, they asked me whether they might confine him, and I said no. I was sorry for it afterwards, because although the fellow was sane enough ashore, he was mad at sea: mad with authority.'

'Sure, it is a dangerous draught,' said Stephen. 'Yet some resist it. What is the source of their immunity?'

'What indeed?' replied Mr Cotton. His weariness was too great for speculation, though not for civility, and when

Stephen took his leave he said, 'You were a God-send, Dr Maturin: may I in my turn be of any use to you?'

'Since you are so good,' said Stephen, 'it does so happen that I have a singularly delicate depressed fracture waiting for me tomorrow, and if by then you feel sufficiently recovered, I should be most grateful for your support. My young man has no experience of the trephine, and my hands are not so steady as they were – they do not possess your admirable firmness of grip.'

'I shall be with you, sir, at any hour you choose to name,' said Mr Cotton; and Mr Cotton, long accustomed to the ways of the Navy, was true to his word and exact to his time. At the first stroke of six bells in the forenoon watch he came swarming up the *Boadicea*'s side, using his powerful arms alone and trailing his withered leg. Once aboard he shipped his half-crutch, saluted the quarterdeck, brushed an officious bosun's mate aside, and stumped aft. Everything was ready: under an awning that spread the brilliant light stood an upright chair, made fast to cleats, and in it sat Colley the patient, lead-coloured, snoring still, and so tightly lashed by his friends that he was as incapable of independent movement as the ship's figurehead. The deck and the tops were strangely crowded with men, many of them feigning busyness, for the old Sophies had told their present shipmates of that memorable day in the year two, when, in much the same light, Dr Maturin had sawed off the top of the gunner's head, had roused out his brains, had set them to rights, and had clapped a silver dome over all, so that the gunner, on coming back to life, was better than new: this they had been told, and they were not going to miss a moment of the instructive and even edifying spectacle. From under the forecastle came the sound of the armourer at his forge, beating a three-shilling piece into a flat and gleaming pancake.

'I have desired him to await our instructions for the final shape,' said Stephen, 'but he has already sharpened and retempered my largest trephine.' He held up the circular saw, still gleaming from its bath, and suggested that Mr

Cotton might like to make the first incision. The medical civilities that followed, the polite insistence and refusal, made the audience impatient; but presently their most morbid hopes were gratified. The patient's shaved scalp, neatly divided from ear to ear and flensed away, hung over his unshaved livid snorting face, and now the doctors, poised above the flayed, shattered skull, were talking in Latin.

'Whenever they start talking foreign,' observed John Harris, forecastleman, starboard watch, 'you know they are at a stand, and that all is, as you might say, in a manner of speaking, up.'

'You ain't seen nothing, John Harris,' said Davis, the old Sophie. 'Our doctor is only tipping the civil to the one-legged cove: just you wait until he starts dashing away with his boring-iron.'

'Such a remarkable thickness of bone, and yet the metopic suture has not united,' said Mr Cotton. 'I have never seen the like, and am deeply gratified. 'But, as you say, it confronts us with a perplexing situation: a dilemma, as one might say.'

'The answer, as I conceive it, lies in a double perforation,' said Stephen. 'And here the strength and steadiness of your left forearm will prove invaluable. If you would have the goodness to support the parietal here, while I begin my first cut at this point, and if then we change hands, why, there is a real likelihood that we may lift out the whole in one triumphant piece.'

Had it not been for the need to preserve the appearance of professional infallibility and god-like calm, Mr Cotton would have pursed his lips and shaken his head: as it was he muttered, 'The Lord be with us,' and slid in his flattened probe. Stephen turned back his cuffs, spat on his hands, waited for the roll, placed his point and began his determined cut, the white bone skipping from the eager teeth and Carol swabbing the sawdust away. In the silence the ship's company grew still more intent: the midshipmen's berth, ghouls to a man, craned forward, unchid by their officers. But as the steel bit down into the living head, more than one grew

268

pale, more than one looked away into the rigging; and even Jack, who had seen this grisly performance before, turned his eyes to the horizon, where the distant *Astrée* and *Iphigenia* flashed white in the sun.

He heard Stephen call out the measurements to the armourer as the second cut began; he heard a renewed hammering on the anvil forward; but as he listened a movement far over there to windward seized upon the whole of his attention. Both the Frenchmen were filling: did they mean to edge down at last? He clapped his glass to his eye, saw them come right before the wind, and shut his telescope with a smile: from the busy way they were passing their sheets it was obvious that they were merely wearing once again, as they had done five times since dawn. Yes, they had hauled their wind. Although they had the weather-gage they did not choose to bring him and the crippled *Africaine* to action; and if he was not very much mistaken, this last manoeuvre had put it out of their power, now that the mountains of La Réunion were looming on the larboard bow and the breeze was likely to veer two points inshore. To be sure, the *Africaine* still had all her teeth intact, and the *Staunch* and the *Otter* could give a shrewd nip in a mêlée; but even so . . . He laughed aloud, and at the same moment he heard Mr Cotton cry, 'Oh, pretty. Oh, very prettily done, sir.'

Stephen raised the piece of skull entire and held it up to peer at its underside with a look of sober triumph a moment during which the audience might gaze with fascinated horror into the awful gulf, where Mr Cotton was now fishing for splinters with a pair of whalebone tongs. As he fished, and as a long transverse splinter stirred the depths, an awful voice, deep, slow, thick-tongued and as it were drunk, but recognizable as Colley's, spoke from behind the hanging skin and said, 'Jo. Pass that fucking gasket, Jo.' By this time the audience had dwindled, and many of the remaining ghouls were as wan as Colley himself; they revived, however, when the surgeons placed the silver cover on the hole, fastened it down, restored the patient's scalp to its usual place, sewed it up, washed their hands in the scuttle-butt, and dismissed him below. A pleased murmur ran round the ship, and Jack, stepping forward, said, 'I believe I may congratulate you, gentlemen, upon a very delicate manoeuvre?'

They bridled and said it was nothing so extraordinary – any competent surgeon could have done as much – and in any case, they added, with a sincerity that would have caused Mrs Colley a dreadful pang, there was no call for congratulation until the inevitable crisis had declared itself: after all, it could not be said that any operation was wholly successful unless the patient at least outlived the crisis. After that the cause of death might reasonably be assigned to a host of other factors.

'Oh, how I hope he lives,' said Jack, his eye still on the distant enemy. 'Colley is a prime seaman, a capital, steady hand, and can point his gun as well as any man in the ship. Has a large number of children, too, as I recall.'

All this was very true: Tom Colley, when sober, was a valuable though pugnacious member of his division; he had been bred to the sea and he could hand, reef and steer without having to take thought, and it was a joy to see him dance a hornpipe: the ship would not be the same without him. But beneath this valid reasoning lay a region that the kind observer might have called a sort of mysticism and that others, perhaps more enlightened, would have described as brutish superstition. Jack would not have had it known for the world, but he equated the seaman's recovery with the success of his campaign: and from the behaviour of the *Astrée* and *Iphigenia* over there, Colley was in a fair way to resurrection. If Hamelin had been present, flying his broad pennant aboard the *Astrée* rather than the *Vénus*, would the French attitude have been more determined? Would those two ships have risked the battle, to destroy all his hopes, whatever the cost to themselves? From what he knew of the French commodore, he doubted it.

'An impressive document,' said Governor Farquhar, handing back the copy of Pius VII's excommunication of Buonaparte, the hitherto unpromulgated but effective personal, *greater* excommunication, authenticated by the Bishop's seal, 'and although some of the expressions are perhaps not quite Ciceronian, the whole amounts to the most tremendous damnation that I have ever seen. Were I a Catholic, it would make me extremely uneasy in my mind, if I were obliged to have anything to do with the wretch. The Bishop made no difficulty, I presume?' Stephen smiled, and Farquhar went on, 'How I regret your scruples. This would be of the greatest value to the ministry. Surely we should make another copy?'

'Never concern yourself about the ministry, my dear sir,' said Stephen. 'They know of its existence. They know very well; it is a tolerably open secret, I assure you. But in any event, I must not imperil my source of information: and I have given an undertaking that only three men on the Mauritius shall see it, and that I shall then commit it to the flames.' He lapped the document, heavy with curses, in his handkerchief, and thrust it into his bosom: Farquhar looked wistfully at the bulge, but he only said, 'Ah, if you have given an undertaking . . .' and they both glanced at the slips of paper upon which they had noted the subjects they were to discuss.

Stephen's were all crossed off: one remained on Farquhar's list, but he seemed to find it difficult to broach. He paused, and laughed, and said, 'The form in which I have written this will never do. You would find it offensive. I reminded myself – very unnecessarily, I may add – to beg you to give me an explanation – oh, not in any way an *official* explanation, you understand – for the Commodore's abounding sanguine activity. He really seems to assume that our plans for invading the Mauritius can go forward in spite of this appalling disaster at the Ile de la Passe: he has thoroughly infected or perhaps I should say *convinced* Keating, and the two of them dart from point to point, day and night, flying in the face of the clearest evidence. Naturally I second him with all my power – I scarcely dare do otherwise, now that he has taken on his present heroic Jovian stature. He runs into this room, says, "Farquhar, my good fellow, be so good as to cut all the tallest trees on the island and set all carpenters to work directly. The *Africaine* must have masts by dawn on Thursday at the latest,'' and runs out again. I tremble and obey: but when I reflect that the French possess seven frigates to our one and a pitiful wreck, and when I reckon up the guns at their disposal as opposed to ours, why, I am seized with an amazement.' He stared out of the window, seized with retrospective stupor; and to fill the gap Stephen observed that the number of guns counted for less than the accuracy with which they were pointed and the zeal with which they were served, adding that although the *Africaine* was not yet fit for battle, her guns were available for the other vessels, such as they were.

'Very true,' said the Governor. 'But I will confess that a perhaps unworthy explanation of the Commodore's eager-ness thrust itself into my mind: it occurred to me that he might possibly have some encouraging intelligence that I did not share. Do not take my words amiss, Dr Maturin, I beg.'

'Never in life, my dear sir,' said Stephen. 'No: I have told him nothing that I have not told you. The answer lies on another plane entirely. As I understand it, Commodore Aubrey has arrived at an intimate conviction that we have a moral superiority over our opponents; that the initiative has changed sides; and that, as he puts it himself, although they want neither ships nor seamanship nor conduct, they do lack spirit. They lack an earnest desire to engage, to risk everything on one throw; and he is of the opinion that Hamelin also lacks the sense of the decisive moment in the ebb and flow of a campaign. Furthermore, it is his view that Commodore Hamelin is more interested in snapping up Indiamen than in gathering laurels at the one moment when they lie ready to his hand. He quoted your remark about Fortune with great approval, declaring that Hamelin would find the wench's forelock hellfire hard to grapple, now that she had forged ahead.'

'I made that remark in a very different context,' said

Farquhar; but Stephen, carrying on with his thought, continued, 'I am no strategist, but I know Jack Aubrey well: I respect his judgment in naval matters, and I find his conviction, his military intuition, wholly persuasive. There may also be some illogical factors,' he added, being perfectly aware of the reason for Jack's frequent hurried visits to the hospital and his immoderate delight in Colley's recovery, 'such as seamen's omens and the like, that need not detain a rational mind.'

'So you are persuaded,' said the Governor doubtfully. 'Well then, I too am persuaded; though at one remove. But at least there is no prospect of his stirring until the *Africaine* is ready for sea? No prospect, in this extremely dangerous situation, of his dashing out like a sea-borne Bayard to engage at seven to one?'

'I imagine not, but I would scarcely answer for it. Now, sir,' said Stephen, standing up, 'I must beg to take my leave: the boat is no doubt waiting, and I shall have harsh words if I do not hurry.'

'I shall see you again very shortly?' asked Farquhar.

'Yes, with the blessing. This journey takes me no farther than the south-west tip of the Mauritius, the Morne Brabant, where I see two officers of the Irish troops and another gentleman; and I think I can promise that the Commodore and Colonel Keating will have little trouble with the more Catholic members of General Decaen's garrison, when they come face to face.' As they walked through the hall he said in an undertone, tapping his chest, 'This is so very much more portable than a hundredweight of gold, and so very, very much more effective.'

The great door opened, and in the entrance they were very nearly run down by Mr Trollope, who came bounding up the steps of the Residence four at a time. He recovered himself, cast a reproachful look at Stephen, plucked off his hat, and said, 'I beg your pardon, Your Excellency, but I am charged with the Commodore's respectful compliments and might he have seven hundred and fifty blacks before the evening gun? I was also to remind Dr Maturin that he asked for the aviso at five and twenty minutes past four o'clock precisely.'

Stephen looked at his watch, uttered a low howl, and set off at a shambling run for the harbour, where the *Pearl of the Mascarenes*, the fastest aviso in the island, lay champing at her buoy.

At dawn on Sunday the two quartermasters at the signal-station high above Saint-Denis were weighing the probabilities of duff today: last Sunday they, like all the Boadiceas and all the Africaines, Staunches and Otters, had been deprived of their duff, on account of the furious pace of work in the dockyards; and it looked very much as though the same might happen today. As they leant out to peer at the yard below the strong land-breeze whipped their pigtails forward, obscuring their view: automatically they grasped them with their teeth and peered on: judging by the feverish activity down there, the parties of blacks and seamen and artificers and soldiers already toiling like so many ants, Sunday duff seemed as remote as wedding-cake. Even beef was by no means certain.

'Some foreign mess again,' said William Jenkins, 'and ate cold, no doubt. How Goldilocks does crack on. Slave-driving ain't in it, when you consider two weeks of no duff; and it was much the same in Simon's Town. Hurry, hurry, hurry, and don't you dare sweat the glass.'

Goldilocks was Jack Aubrey's nickname in the service, and the other quartermaster, Henry Trecothick, had sailed with him when the locks were indeed golden, rather than their present dull sun-bleached yellow. He felt that Jenkins was coming it a little high, and he said coldly, 'He's got a job of work to do, ain't he? And dogged does it. Though I must say a man likes a hot dinner, as being more natural and – Bill, what do you make of that craft out there?'

'Where away?'

'Nor'-nor'-east: just coming round the point. Behind the islands. She's dowsed her mainsail.'

'I can't see nothing.'

'What a wall-eyed slab-sided Dutch-built bugger you are, to be sure, Bill Jenkins. Behind the islands.'

'Behind the islands? Why didn't you say so? She's a fisherman, that's what she is. Can't you see they're a-pulling? Ain't you got no eyes?'

'Light along the glass, Bill,' said Trecothick. And having stared fixedly he said, 'She ain't no fisherman. They're pulling like Dogget's coat and badge; pulling right into the wind's eye like it was a race for a thousand pound. No fisherman ever pulled like that.' A pause. 'I tell you what, Bill Jenkins, she's that little old aviso, *Pearl* by name.'

'You and your fancies, Henry. *Pearl* ain't due back this tide, no, nor the next. Was that thunder? A drop of rain would –'

'Christ, she's broke out a signal. Get your fat arse out of the way. *Enemy in sight* – what's red white chequer? – *due north*. Bill, jump down and rouse out Mr Ballocks. I'll fix the hoist. Bear a hand, mate, bear a hand.'

Up flew the signal, out banged the gun: the station above St Paul's repeated within a matter of seconds, and into the dining-cabin of the *Boadicea* darted the midshipman of the watch, who found the Commodore pink and cheerful, surrounded by papers and already dictating to his blear-eyed, unshaved secretary as he devoured his first, or sunrise, breakfast, 'Mr Johnson's duty, sir,' he cried, 'St Paul's repeating from Saint-Denis *enemy in sight, bearing due north*.'

'Thank you, Mr Bates,' said Jack. 'I shall be on deck directly.'

There he found the whole quarterdeck motionless, all faces turned towards the distant flagstaff: he said, 'Prepare to slip, Mr Johnson,' and then he too fixed his eyes on the hill. Two full minutes passed with no further hoist, and he said to the signal-midshipman, 'Repeat to Saint-Denis, *Staunch and Otter proceed to sea immediately: attend to pennant's motions*.' Then stepping to the taffrail he hailed the *Africaine*. 'Mr Tullidge, I have room for fifty volunteers, no more.'

The Africaines were less remarkable for their discipline

275

than their ferocious eagerness to serve the Frenchmen out, and now began a disorderly savage jostling race, whose fifty winners, headed by a powerful master's mate with a face like a baboon, came aboard the *Boadicea* by boat or strong swimming as her buoyed cable ran smoking from her hawse and she cast to the fine land-breeze.

The sails came crowding on; she gathered way, and the good breeze carried them up towards Cape Bernard, the high land that barred out all the ocean due north of Saint-Denis as well as the town itself. With studdingsails on either side, the *Boadicea* threw a bow-wave that came creaming down to the mainchains, but even so the cape moved tediously slow, and Jack found it something of a relief to have his impatience distracted by the ugly scene that developed when it was rumoured that the Africaines were to take over the forward starboard guns. Loud angry voices, rarely raised aboard the *Boadicea*, could be heard on the forecastle, disturbing the holy calm of a well-run man-of-war: the bosun came hurrying aft, spoke to the first lieutenant, and Seymour, crossing the quarterdeck to the rail where Jack was staring at the station in the hope of some more definite signal, coughed and said, 'I beg your pardon, sir, but the men of Mr Richardson's division believe that their guns are to be taken from them, and with the utmost respect they wish to represent that they would find this a little hard.'

'Let the hands come aft, Mr Seymour,' said Jack, with his telescope still trained on the flagstaff, now at the far limit of his view. When he clapped the glass to and turned there they were before him, the whole waist of the ship crowded with men, whose utmost respect (though genuine) was for the moment scarcely discernible beneath their rage at injustice.

'What a precious set of old women you are, upon my word,' he said testily. 'You clap on to a silly buzz with no truth in it and set about one another like a parcel of fish-fags. Look at Eames there, with a bloody nose and on a Sunday too, for shame. And all this before we know whether the enemy is anything more than some stray sloop, or whether he will be so polite as to stay until you have stopped clawing one another. Now I tell you what it is: if we have the good fortune to come into action, every team is going to fight the gun it's used to. That's justice. But if any Boadicea is hurt, then an Africaine takes his place: and if we board, then the Africaines board first. That's flat and that's fair all round. Mr Seymour, be so good as to have cutlasses and boarding-axes served out to the Africaines.'

The general opinion was that this was fair enough: and although for the present the Boadiceas could not be brought to love the Africaines, they did at least treat their guests with a distant civility – no oaths, no blows, little more than a covert kick or nudge, accidental done a-purpose.

Cape Bernard at last, and the frigate rounded it, shaving the reef so close that a lobbed biscuit might have reached the wicked breakers. And as she rounded it, opening new skies, so her people heard the sound of gunfire, the growling of heavy guns a great way off in the north.

'Jump up to the masthead, Mr Richardson,' said Jack, 'and tell me what you see.'

As the midshipman vanished aloft Saint-Denis came into sight: the *Staunch* was still working out of the harbour, and the *Otter* was only a mile ahead of her. Jack frowned; he was about to call the signal-midshipman when he saw fresh canvas break out aboard both of them. It was true that neither had been ready for action, ready to slip at a moment's notice, as the *Boadicea* had been these last twenty-four hours; it was true that they must have had most of their hands ashore or in the yard; but even so he was not pleased, and he meditated a rebuke. 'Am I growing pompous?' he wondered, and the answer 'Probably' had taken disagreeable form in his mind when Spotted Dick, after a scrupulous examination of the distant northern sea, hailed him. 'On deck, there. Sir, I believe I can make out three ships hull-down two points on the larboard bow.' And as if to confirm his words, the distant thunder growled again. Every man aboard listened with all his might, strained ears trying to pierce through the song of the rigging and the slap of the sea to the underlying silence; and every man aboard heard the popping of a musket, weak, but nothing near so remote as the great guns.

Again the masthead hailed the deck, reporting, perhaps a little late, the presence of the aviso a couple of miles away, almost invisible against the reef. She was still pulling strongly against the wind, still announcing that the enemy was in sight, with a musket-shot to underline the signal.

'Close the aviso, Mr Seymour,' said Jack.

As the *Boadicea* swept down the *Pearl* set her jib and mainsail, spun about and ran quartering before the wind, clear of the reef and its islands, so that when the two vessels converged they were both running fast on almost parallel courses – Dr Maturin could be restored to the frigate without the loss of a moment.

His standard of seamanship being tolerably well-known aboard the *Boadicea*, no orders were required for his reception: there was no time for a bosun's chair, but a whip appeared at the mainyardarm; and now, as they tore along together with no more than a few feet of foaming, heaving sea between them, Bonden, poised on the rail of the *Pearl*, seized the line, made Stephen fast, adjured him 'to take it easy', called out, 'Heave away, there: cheerly now', sprang across the gulf and ran up the frigate's side like a cat to receive the Doctor as he came aboard. He had timed the roll exactly, and all would have gone well if Stephen, with some notion of steadying himself, had not grasped at the *Pearl*'s rigging. A slack slabline at once took a turn about his dangling legs and jerked him into a maze of cordage that he could neither name nor disentangle. A fairly heavy swell was running, and for a moment it seemed that Stephen must come aboard in two pieces. A nimble Pearl raced aloft and at great cost to the aviso's rigging cut him free; but this he did at the very moment when the Boadiceas, realizing that they were tearing their surgeon apart, let go; and Stephen therefore swung in a sickening downward curve to strike the frigate's side a little below the waterline. Now, urged by cries, they heaved again, but he stuck under the chains, and the ship's next roll plunged him deep. Unfortunately for Stephen he counted none but friends aboard, and a large proportion of these sprang to his rescue; powerful hands pulled him in different directions by the arms, legs and hair, and only the violent intervention of the Commodore preserved him. He reached the deck at last, more dead than alive, oozing blood from scratches inflicted by the barnacles; they emptied some of the water out of him, carried him below, and plucked off his clothes.

'There, there, take it easy,' said Jack, looking anxiously into his face and speaking in that compassionate protective voice which has vexed so many invalids into the tomb.

'There is not a moment to lose,' cried Stephen, starting up.

Jack pressed him back into the cot with irresistible force, and still in the same soothing voice he said, 'We are not losing any time at all, old Stephen. Not a moment. Do not grow agitated. All is well. You are all right now.'

'Oh, your soul to the devil, Jack Aubrey,' said Stephen, and in an even stronger tone, 'Killick, Killick, you mumping villain, bring in the coffee, will you now, for the love of God. And a bowl of sweet oil. Listen, Jack' – writhing from beneath his hand and sitting up – 'you must press on, crack on, clap on, as fast as ever you can go. There are two frigates out there battering one of ours. And one of them, the *Vénus*, has lost masts, rigging – Bonden will tell you the details – and you may catch her, if only you will make haste, and not sit there leering like a mole with the palsy.'

'Pass the word for my coxswain,' called Jack, and to Stephen he said, 'We are already making haste, you know.' He named the sails that were now urging the *Boadicea* towards the distant battle, and he assured Stephen that the moment she cleared the land-breeze and entered the region of the south-easter offshore, he would let fall his maincourse and set his staysails, for then they would have the wind on the quarter, rather than right aft; and Stephen was to take notice that the presence of the captain on deck was not essential to the progress of the ship, once he was blessed with a seamanlike set of officers. The appearance of Bonden and of Killick bearing the sweet oil cut off Stephen's reply: he groped among the heap of wet clothes, brought out his watch and dipped it in the oil, observing, 'It has survived several grave immersions; let us hope it may survive this. Now, Barret Bonden, I shall give the Commodore a succinct account of the position, and you will supply the technical details.' He collected his mind, and went on, 'Yesterday evening, you must understand, I was standing on the most elevated point of the Morne Brabant, where it overlooks the sea, and conversing with some gentlemen who among other things told me, and this I must not omit, that the *Bellone*, *Minerve* and *Iphigenia* are undergoing heavy repairs, with their guns all out, and will not be fit for sea this fortnight and more: Bonden was at a certain distance –'

'A cable's length, sir,' said Bonden.

'– when I perceived a ship sailing down from Port-Louis in the direction of La Réunion. One of the gentlemen, who had followed the sea for many years, asserted that she was an Indiaman. He pointed out her general mercantile appearance, and the presence of a subsidiary posterior deck, or platform –'

'Poop,' muttered Bonden.

'– the infallible mark of your Indiaman; and he remarked that it would be strange indeed if Monsieur Hamelin, then in Port-Louis, should let such a prize escape him. And in fact shortly afterwards we descried the *Vénus* and a smaller frigate –'

'Pardon me, sir,' said Bonden, '*Wenus* and a *sloop*.'

'The little one had three masts,' said Stephen sharply. 'I counted them.'

'Yes, sir; but she was only a sloop.' And addressing Jack, Bonden went on, 'Sixteen-gun corvette *Victor*, sir.'

'Well, never mind. They pursued the alleged Indiaman, the *Vénus* outsailing her companion: and then to our surprise the Indiaman turned out to be no Indiaman, at all. She took down or folded a number of sails, allowed the *Vénus* to come close, and discharged a number of guns upon her, at the same time displaying a banner indicating she was a man-of-war.'

Jack looked at Bonden, who said, '*Bombay*, sir; a country-built Indiaman bought into the service in the year five. My cousin George, he sailed in her one commission, gunner's mate; said she was a good sea-boat, but mortal slow. Twenty-four eighteen-pounders, two long nines, and fourteen twenty-four-pounder carronades.'

'At this,' said Stephen, 'the *Vénus* drew back, waiting for her consort, and the *Bombay* pressed on. The sun had set: we descended the cliff, made our way to the aviso, and there I resigned the conduct of affairs into Bonden's hands.'

'Well, sir,' said Bonden, 'I knew you would be wishful to know as soon as ever could be, so we nipped through the Dutchman's Passage with barely a scrape, though the tide was out, fetched the *Victor*'s wake, crossed under her stern in the dark just before moonrise, and worked up to windward with all she could wear and well-nigh more. We was well ahead, running nine–ten knots by the time the moon was well up, and we see *Wenus* coming up on the *Bombay* hand over hand, seven knots to her six, maybe; and at the beginning of the middle watch, when we had sunk the land long since, she ranged up alongside and they set to hammer and tongs. I ought to of said, sir, that *Bombay* had a tidy packet of redcoats aboard, and there seemed to be plenty of soldiers in *Wenus* too, her decks were that crowded with men. Well now, *Wenus* didn't care for it overmuch, and presently she wore out of range, new-gammoning her bowsprit, as far as I could judge. Howsoever, in a couple of glasses she perked her spirits up again, and the wind having backed two points she set her stuns'ls and bore down. The action started again in the morning watch, a running fight, with both on 'em under royals and larboard stuns'ls; but by now we was so far ahead I couldn't rightly see how it went. I did see *Wenus* lose her foretopmast and her gaff, and *Bombay*, she lost her main and mizzen topmasts, and her courses were chawed up something cruel; but she was standing on for Saint-Denis and giving as good as she got when last we see her plain, and the sloop was still a league and more astern.'

While he was speaking the *Boadicea* began to heel to larboard; she had run beyond the land-breeze, which came from aft, and she was now in the south-easter, a gentle wind today, untimely gentle. In spite of his words about seamanlike officers Jack went on deck the moment Bonden's account was done. He automatically checked the spread of canvas against the force of the wind, and found something of a disproportion: like so many others, young Johnson still entertained the delusion that more sail meant more speed, and in his eagerness he was pressing her down by the head. Jack did not wish the change to have the appearance of a check, however, and first he hailed the masthead. 'Masthead, there. What do you see?'

'They are hull-up now, sir,' called the lookout. 'Heavy frigate, Indiaman, and a ship-rigged sloop or maybe a jackass frigate, all wearing French colours; pennant aboard the big frigate. No firing since four bells. Frigate's lost her topmasts, all three of them. Indiaman too. Sloop unwounded, I believe.'

Jack nodded, took a turn or so, told Johnson that he might find her labour less with the flying-jib hauled down, slung his glass, set his hands to the shrouds, and swung himself up: up and up, through the maintop, up again to the crosstrees, slower than he would have climbed twenty years before, but still at a respectable pace.

All that the lookout had told him was true; but what the lookout had not been able to tell him was the spirit of the scene far over there to the north, so far over that the shimmering air sometimes gave the distant ships their masts and sometimes took them away; and it was that he had climbed his airy pinnacle to make out. After a backward glance at the *Staunch* and the *Otter*, both of them a couple of miles astern and losing steadily, he settled down to a prolonged study of the position. Between them the *Vénus* and the *Victor* had certainly taken the *Bombay*, having reduced her to her lower masts alone: the *Vénus* had paid heavily, however, losing not only her fore and main topmasts but the greater part of her mizzen too. The sloop had not suffered at all.

There was great activity aboard the *Vénus*, and it appeared to him that they were preparing to send up a new fore-topmast: they had certainly fished a fine great spar of some kind to the stump of the mizzen. Boats were passing between the ships. The distance was too great for any certainty, but it looked as though bodies of men were moving in both directions: as though it were not merely a shifting of prisoners. Did Hamelin intend to man his prize? It was by no means impossible: sailing from his home port he might very well have doubled his crew with seamen drafted from his other ships, to say nothing of all the soldiers in Port-Louis. If he could spare enough men to serve the *Bombay*'s forty guns, and if he had the hardihood to do so, that would change the situation.

Within himself Jack had not the slightest doubt of victory, but it would never do to let this conviction take the form of even unspoken words; it must remain in the state of that inward glow which had inhabited him ever since the retaking of the *Africaine* and which had now increased to fill the whole of his heart – a glow that he believed to be his most private secret, although in fact it was evident to everyone aboard from Stephen Maturin to the adenoidal third-class boy who closed the muster-book. So leaving that to one side he set himself to a cold, professional, objective examination of the factors that might delay or even prevent it.

The first was the wind. The south-easter was slackening; already there were glassy patches of sea on the starboard bow, forerunners of the usual midday lull, which might leave him without steerage-way or compel a very slow advance, head-on, into the combined broadside fire of the *Vénus* and *Bombay*, and which might allow Hamelin time to set up a jury-rig that would at least give him twice his present power of manoeuvring.

The second was the arrival of reinforcements. He had no very high opinion of the French commodore's enterprise, but Hamelin was no half-wit. On finding himself in such a position at dawn, with La Réunion looming large on the south horizon, he would certainly have sent his best cutter racing back to Mauritius for support. In Hamelin's place he would have done so the moment the *Bombay* struck.

While he turned these things over in his mind, the pattern to the northward grew clearer. The boats had been hoisted in; the *Victor*, all sails abroad, had taken the *Bombay* in tow; the *Vénus*, dropping her fore and main courses, had put before the wind. And now a foresail appeared aboard the *Bombay*. They still had a fresh breeze out there, and presently they were moving at about three knots, while the *Boadicea*, with all her noble spread of canvas, was making little better than five and a half. 'However,' he reflected, 'there is nothing much I can do about that.'

What little he could do, he did. Having finished 'Plymouth Point', the surest of tunes for a wind, he was whistling at random when he became aware that Sophie was in his mind, present with an extraordinary clarity. 'Was I a superstitious cove,' he said, smiling with singular sweetness in the direction of England, 'I should swear she was thinking of me.'

The smile was still lingering on his face when he reached the deck, and this encouraged Seymour to ask whether he might start to clear the ship for action.

'As to that, Mr Seymour,' said Jack, looking at the log-board, 'it might be a little premature. We must not tempt fate, you know. Mr Bates, be so good as to heave the log.'

'Heave the log it is, sir,' said the midshipman, darting to the lee-rail with his attendant boy and quartermaster. The boy held the reel, the quartermaster the thirty-second sand-glass; Bates threw the log, watched the mark go clear, called, 'Turn,' and the quartermaster held the glass to his eye, while the boy held up the reel with a hieratic solemnity. The log went astern, the knots in the line passing smoothly through Bates' fingers. 'Nip,' cried the quartermaster. The midshipman nipped, then jerked the line; the boy reeled in, and Bates crossed the deck to announce, 'Just on the five, sir, if you please.'

Jack nodded, glanced up at the frigate's towering array of canvas, at the fire-hose in the tops wetting all the jet could reach, at the buckets hoisting to the crosstrees to damp the topgallants so that they should catch every last ounce of thrust, and said, 'No, Mr Seymour. Without the gods are kind, we have more time on our hands than I could wish. It would be a pity to dowse the galley fires so soon; so let the men be piped to dinner at six bells, and since they went without their duff last Sunday, let there be a double ration of plums today. On the other hand, only half the grog will be served out this spell: and no plush allowed.' The faces of the men at the wheel, the quartermaster conning the ship, the yeoman of the signals and the nearer members of the afterguard took on a stony look. Jack paced fore and aft and continued, "The rest will be kept for supper, wind, weather and the enemy permitting. And Mr Seymour, since we shall be pinched for time, dinner being so early, church will not be rigged today; however, I believe we may proceed to divisions. Mr Kiernan,' he added, nodding towards the baboon-faced officer, 'will muster his Africaines on the forecastle.'

From this moment on time raced by aboard the frigate. Every man, with little notice and even less expectation of this solemn event (practised on every peaceful Sunday, but never, *never* when bearing down on the enemy), had to present himself, an hour earlier than usual, washed, shaved, and in a clean shirt for inspection by his particular midshipman and officer and then by the Commodore himself. Furthermore, there was a general determination to wipe the Africaines' collective eye by a brilliantly striking appearance. All along the gangway and on the forecastle the tie-for-tie pairs swiftly and silently combed and plaited one another's pigtails, while impatient groups clustered round the barber's tubs, urging him to even greater speed, whatever it might cost; and anxious Marines pipeclayed and polished in the blazing sun.

The inspection itself was a creditable affair, with the officers, in full dress and wearing their swords, accompanying the Commodore in his slow progress along the lines of trim seamen in their best; and the hairy Africaines in their dirty shirts were brought suitably low. But the ceremony was marred by an extraordinary degree of distraction:

remarkable things were happening in the north – the *Bombay*'s towline had parted, the *Victor* was having a devilish time passing another, the *Vénus* had first sheered off and had then come up into what wind there was to lend a hand, and above all the vast stretch of ocean between the *Boadicea* and the French had narrowed surprisingly. Even while the Commodore was on deck, few men apart from the rigid Marines could resist glancing northwards and passing remarks; and when he was exploring the galley and the berth-deck with the first lieutenant, Mr Trollope was obliged to call out, 'Silence, fore and aft,' several times, and to take the names of the more loquacious, for future punishment.

The moment divisions was over, the bosun and his mates piped loud and shrill to dinner. Every man aboard knew that the order *clear for action* would follow in a very short time indeed, for the wind had freshened markedly this last half-hour, and that he must make up his mind at once between fighting the ship in his best clothes and missing if not his beef then his double-shotted duff. Most plumped for the duff, which they ate on deck, by their guns, holding it carefully away from their snowy shirts, their silk neckerchiefs, and trousers beribboned at the seams. Scarcely was the last crumb down when the expected order came. Mess-kids vanished and the men, some still chewing, set about the familiar task of making a clean sweep fore and aft: they had done so, and they were standing at their action-stations staring now at the enemy, not far from extreme range, and now astern at the distant *Staunch* and *Otter*, when Stephen appeared on the quarterdeck, bearing a plate of sandwiches.

Dr Maturin was a God-send to the Boadiceas: not only would he accost the Commodore with a freedom impossible to any other man aboard, but he would ask questions that none but he might propound, and receive civil answers rather than a severe set-down. Any gentlemanly reluctance to overhear private conversation had long since died away, and casual chat on the quarterdeck fell silent, in case any word between the Commodore and the Doctor should be lost.

He did not disappoint them now. 'Why, sir,' said he, looking about him, 'what splendour I see: gold lace, breeches, cocked hats. Allow me to recommend a sandwich. And would you be contemplating an attack, at all?'

'It had crossed my mind, I must admit,' said Jack. 'Indeed, I may go so far as to say, that I am afraid a conflict is now virtually inevitable. Did you notice we have cleared for action?'

'Certainly I did. I have not ploughed the ocean all these weary years without learning the significance of this wild disorder, the cabins vanishing, my papers, my specimens, flung upside-down into the nearest recess. That is why I am come out here, for a little peace. Dear me, how close they are! It would be indiscreet, perhaps, to ask what happens next?'

'To tell you the truth, Doctor,' said Jack, 'for the moment I am in two minds. The corvette, do you see, has cast off her tow for good and all, and she is bearing away for the Mauritius under all sail, no doubt on her commodore's orders, while he is coming down towards the *Bombay*. Now if he has manned his prize, if he has sent enough men aboard the *Bombay* to serve her guns, then his plan will be to fight us with both ships in close support; and in that case we must run between 'em, firing both sides. But if he has not manned her, and if he is only covering the *Victor*'s retreat by this manoeuvre, why, then he means to meet us alone. And in that case we must run down on his bow, or his quarter if he wears, and carry him by boarding, so as not to damage his hull nor those precious spars I see on his deck. Another ten minutes will tell us what he means to do. If he don't back his foresail just before reaching the *Bombay*, so as to heave to beside her, you understand, that will mean she is not manned and that he must fight us by himself. Masthead,' he cried, 'what do you see in the north?'

'Nothing, sir, bar the sloop,' replied the masthead. 'A clear horizon all round. Sloop's carried away a kite on the main: is setting another.'

After this there was a prolonged silence aboard the

Boadicea: the men stationed at the guns stared over the barricade of hammocks or out through the open ports at the *Vénus*; the splinter-netting over their heads sent a strange shifting rectangular pattern down on the deck; the wind hummed and sighed through the rigging.

The minutes passed; ten minutes passed; and then a general murmur ran through the ship. The *Vénus* had not backed her foresail and now she was well beyond the *Bombay*. She was ugly, with her stumpy masts, but she was dangerous, determined, and her gunports were all open; she carried heavy metal, and her decks were crowded with men.

'Mr Seymour,' said Jack, 'topsails and forecourse alone, and draw the guns. Reload with grape. Not a shot is to touch her hull. Sweep her decks, but do not touch her hull. D'ye hear me, there?' he cried, raising his voice. 'Any gun-crew that wounds her hull will be flogged. Mr Hall, lay me for the bow.'

Closer and closer. Jack's opinion of Hamelin rose: the Frenchman was staking everything on coming so close before he yawed that his broadside must do the *Boadicea* irreparable damage – staking everything, because after that one turn the *Vénus*, with no more sail than she could spread, would never come up into the wind again, but must lie there to be battered to death.

Closer still in the silence: they were within pistol-shot. The *Vénus*'s bow guns cracked out; the turn began, and the moment before her side came into full view Jack said, 'Hard a-port.' The *Boadicea* moved fast, heeling abruptly, and the thundering broadside from the *Vénus* cut no mast away. The foretopsail yard was wounded, two studdingsail booms had gone, some rigging hung loose; the starboard cathead was shattered and the best bower swung free; but Hamelin had lost his bet.

'Duck up forward,' said Jack, and at once the foresail puckered, checking the frigate's speed as she swept through the enemy's smoke. The *Vénus* turned, turned until she was almost before the wind and stern-on to the *Boadicea*. 'Bear a hand with the clew-line,' said Jack. 'Mr Hall, clear her starboard quarter, and bump me her bows.' The *Boadicea* shot forward, and it was clear that she would range up on the *Vénus* before the Frenchmen had had time to reload. 'Africaines stand by to board over her bow,' he cried. 'Boadiceas, come aft: we go for her quarterdeck. And we give the Africaines one minute's law, mark what I say. Steady there by the guns,' he said, loosening his sword. 'Bonden, where are my pistols?'

There was Killick at his side, holding an old pair of shoes and a coat over his arm. 'You can't go in your best silver-buckled shoes, your honour, nor in your number one coat,' he kept saying in an angry whine. 'It won't take you a minute to change.'

'Nonsense,' said Jack. 'Everyone else is going in his best, so why should I be left out?'

The *Vénus*'s soldiers were firing from her stern, but it was too late. The *Boadicea* ranged alongside, Jack said, 'Fire,' and the *Boadicea*'s grape swept the *Vénus*'s deck at head-height and in the smoke grapnels flew over the side; topmen ran out and lashed the Frenchman's yardarms tight; their bows ground together, and Jack roared, 'Africaines away.' A moment later their sterns swung in, and the two ships lay side by side.

For a full minute he stood at the head of his boarders, while the Marines behind him plied their muskets as though they were on parade and the small-arms men in the tops kept up a fire on the guns. A full minute of vast din and shouting forward, the crackle of pistols and the bellow of a carronade that the Africaines had turned into the waist of the *Vénus*. Then he cried, 'Boadiceas, come along with me,' vaulted on to the torn hammocks, leapt sword in hand across to the shrouds of the mainmast, slashed the boarding-netting, slashed at a head below him, and so down to the *Vénus*'s quarterdeck, followed by a cheering mass of seamen.

Before him stood a line of soldiers – the seamen were in the waist, facing the Africaines' furious attack – and in the second before the wave of Boadiceas broke over them a little terrified corporal lunged at Jack with his bayonet. Bonden caught the muzzle, wrenched the musket free, flogged three men flat with the butt and broke the line. On the deck behind the soldiers lay several bodies – officers – and in the momentary pause Jack thought he saw a French captain's uniform. Then the aftermost group on the larboard gangway, led by a young officer, turned and came for the Boadiceas with such a rush that they were swept back to the wheel, and the next few minutes were a furious confusion of violence, cut and parry, duck the pistol, kick and thrust and hack.

But the Vénuses were no match for the boarders; they were oppressed and hemmed in by their own numbers; they were worn out by their long night's battle and the toil that had followed it; their spirits were crushed by the sight of the *Otter* and the *Staunch* coming up fast, and by the certainty of eventual defeat. A body of Croatian soldiers, who had no real concern with the quarrel, leapt down the now unguarded main hatchway; others followed them, seeking safety below. The remaining Frenchmen on the gangway made a last desperate charge, and a short, broadshouldered seaman with a knife grappled Jack round the waist. Jack dashed his hilt into the seaman's face, trampled him down, broke free; and there in the clear space by the fife-rail stood an officer, offering his sword and pointing aft, where a boy was hauling down the colours.

Through the enormous cheering that spread from the *Vénus*'s quarterdeck to the *Boadicea*, Jack roared out, "Vast fighting, there. Forward there, Africaines, 'vast fighting. She's struck.'

Men fell apart, stared impersonally at one another, and moved slowly away. The extreme tension died with extraordinary speed and within moments a new relationship had established itself, a kind of primitive social contract – men could no longer hit one another.

Jack accepted the officer's sword with a civil bend of his head and passed it to Bonden. The man he had trampled upon got to his feet without looking at him and stumbled away to his shipmates, who were standing where the battle had left them or who had gathered in little groups by the lee-rail, silent, as though the act of surrender had drained their spirit away, leaving them quite numb.

Still the *Boadicea* was cheering, and the exultant din was echoed by the *Bombay*, a quarter of a mile away: she had rehoisted her ensign, and her crew was skipping and waving and roaring all along her side and in her tops.

'Commodore Hamelin?' said Jack to the officer, and the officer pointed to one of the bodies close by the wheel.

'I was sorry about Hamelin, however,' said Jack, as he and Stephen sat over a late dinner. 'Though when you come to think of it, a man could hardly ask better.'

'For my part,' said Stephen, 'I could ask for very much better. A grapeshot in the heart is not my idea of bliss, and I should do my utmost to avoid it. Yet your grief does not affect your appetite, I find: it is the eighth chop you have eaten. Nor, which strikes me with peculiar force, do I find that this battle has produced the melancholy reaction I have so often noticed in you.'

'That is true,' said Jack. 'An action clears your mind amazingly, for the moment; but afterwards the black dog comes down. The butcher's bill, the funerals, the men's widows to write to, the mess to be cleared up, the knotting and splicing, the pumping – you feel done up, hipped, as flat as ditchwater; though there is more to it than that. But this time it is different. To be sure, we have come off scot free or very near, but that is not the point. The point is that this dust-up is only the beginning of the real action. *Africaine* will be ready for sea on Tuesday: with the spars preparing at St Paul's and what we have captured today, *Vénus* and *Bombay* will not take much longer, working double tides – their hulls would already pass a survey, you know. That is four capital frigates, plus the *Windham*, three good sloops, and all our armed transports: while on their side they have only *Astrée* and *Manche* ready for sea. *Bellone* and *Minerve* must certainly be heaved down; and *Iphigenia* and *Néréide* are little use to man or beast even when they are repaired. They have lost their commodore; and the captain of the

Astrée at least is a booby. And where is their spirit? No: I tell you what, Stephen, by the end of the week Keating and I will carry out our plan – that will be the real action, what I call the real action; and I don't care how glum I grow after it.'

'Well, my dear,' said Stephen, 'politically Mauritius was ready to fall like a ripe plum, or mango, even before the Ile de la Passe; and now that you have repaired the disaster and more, I believe you may install Governor Farquhar at Port-Louis within a week of landing your troops.'

Chapter Ten

'You have been very much in my mind these days, sweet-heart, even more than usual,' wrote Jack, continuing his serial letter to Sophie, a letter that he been building up to its present bulk ever since the *Leopard* had sailed from St Paul's for the Cape, his last contact with the flag, 'and I should certainly have wrote, had we not been so uncommon busy. Since Monday morning we have been on the run, with all hands turning to, to make the squadron ready for sea; and such a sawing of carpenters, a thumping of caulkers, and a busyness of bosuns you never heard in your life. Poor Trollope, an active officer but of a bilious turn, was over-come with a sunstroke, while a black blacksmith, that had wrought eighteen hours on a stretch, was carried off in a dead swoon, quite grey. But now it is done. Now we are at sea, sinking the land as the sun comes up' – he looked, smiling, out of the *Boadicea*'s stern-window, and there in her wake, two cable-lengths away, he saw the *Vénus*, her sails pearly in the growing light; beyond her he could make out the *Africaine*, and far to leeward the last three transports. As the pennant-ship, the *Boadicea* was sailing in the middle of the squadron with the *Bombay* and the *Windham* ahead of her, the *Staunch*, the *Otter* and the *Grappler* far up to windward, and under her lee the transports, comfortably full of soldiers – 'and a very respectable body we are. It is true some of our masts would make the dockyard mateys stare, but they will serve: they may not be very pretty, but they will serve. We took many of the spars out of *Bombay* and *Vénus*, and the devil's own job we had to bring them home: I had promised the men the other half of their grog should be served out with their ration for supper, which might have been well enough if they had not found their way into the enemy's spirit-room, too. Lord, Sophie, we rolled back that night like a whole herd of Davey's sows, with seven Boadiceas and seven Africaines in irons, and most of the rest not fit to go aloft. Fortunately the *Otter* had *Bombay* in tow, or I doubt we should ever have brought them both in. As it was, any French brig in her right wits could have snapped us up.

'By the morning most of the hands were sober, and I harangued them on the beastly vice of inebriation; but I am afraid the effect of my words (and thundering good words they were) were quite lost because of the welcome they gave us ashore. Rockets, Bengal lights you could hardly see because of the sun, though kindly intended, salvoes from all the fortifications, and three times three all round the port: the Governor, a capital determined fellow, with a good head on his shoulders, and thoroughly understands cooperation, was so pleased at the sight of two frigates bringing in that he would, though a tea-drinker himself, have made the men drunk again directly, if I had not represented to him, that *we must make hay while the sun shone.* Colonel Keating was positively overjoyed, and expressed himself in the most obliging manner; and he too thoroughly agreed that *we must strike while the iron is hot.*

'Nothing could exceed his zeal in harrying his staff-officers and other slow-bellies and in getting his men aboard with all their proper accoutrements and in the right order: for I will tell you, my dear (since no eye but yours will see this letter, and that only after the event), that we mean to invade the Mauritius the day after tomorrow; and we have a very fair hope of a happy outcome.' He cast a furtive glance at Stephen Maturin as he wrote these words, so offensive to all his friend's principles and so contrary to all his repeated injunctions, and Stephen, catching his eye, said, 'Should you like some encouragement, joy?'

'If you please,' said Jack.

'Then you must know that the captain of the ship the *Jefferson B. Lowell –*'

'The barque, Stephen. The American was a barque; and an amazing fine sailer, too.'

'Bah. Was so good as to tell me of the various rates he and his colleagues trading to St Louis have placed on Mauritius paper money. Before our arrival it was very nearly at par with cash; then it dropped to twenty-two per centum below, and so rose and fell according to the fortunes of the campaign, rising to ninety-three after the Ile de la Passe. But now it is not admitted upon any discount at all, and gold is absolutely insisted upon. There is cool, objective testimony for you.'

'I am delighted to hear it, Stephen: thank you very much,' said Jack. He returned to his letter, and Stephen to his 'cello.

'Keating would, I am sure, have been as busy as a bee in any event, out of zeal for our joint campaign (and never did army and navy work so well together, I believe, since ships were first found out); but in this case he was as busy as two or even more, from an uneasiness in his mind at what he had heard from the army officers we released from the *Vénus*. They spoke of a General Abercrombie, who was to command them and a very considerable force gathered from all parts of India: it is difficult to make much sense of what they said, for their colonel was killed in the action, and the junior officers had only fag-ends of gossip; but the general notion is that they were to rendezvous at Rodriguez with several regiments from Fort William and some troops from the Cape and that they were then to make a descent on La Réunion; which, when you come to think of it, is absurd. Even so, Keating was much concerned: "If any gouty old fool of a general comes along to snatch the bread out of my mouth again the very moment it is buttered," cries he in a great passion, "I shall sell my commission to the highest bidder, and be d—d to the service: to be choused out of the glory when we have done all the work, would be more than flesh and blood can bear." And he told me again of the siege of some Indian city whose name I forget, where he had carried the approaches right up to the walls, had repelled sorties by the score, had made a practicable breach, and was on the eve of storming the place when a general appeared in a palanquin, took over, gave the order to attack, wrote a despatch giving himself all the credit for the victory, was promoted and given the Bath, with an augmentation to his coat of arms. Keating added some pretty severe reflections on the Bath and old men who would do anything for a trumpery piece of ribbon, which I will not repeat, they being somewhat too warm.' Jack paused, meditating a witticism in which *hot water* should combine with *Bath* to produce a brilliant effect, but his genius did not lie that way, and having chewed his pen for some time, he carried on: 'For my own part, I could not make much more sense out of poor Graham of the *Bombay*, either. He had had a cruise after pirates in the Persian Gulf, and when he put in, precious short-handed, he was at once ordered to take a whole heap of soldiers aboard and to rendezvous with the *Illustrious*, 74, just south of the Eight Degree Channel – had nothing but ill-luck all the way – sprang a leak low down under his fore-peak ten days out, had to put back, beating up with the wind in his teeth, pumping hard and his men falling sick – endless delays in the yard – missed his first rendezvous, missed the next, so bore away, sick himself with a low fever, for Port-Louis, where he expected to find us blockading – and was taken, after a long and tolerably bloody running fight. I am afraid the heat and the wear and the anxiety and the action may have sent his wits astray, for the unfortunate wight absolutely struck to a sloop, which he took for a second frigate in the darkness. (It is true she was ship-rigged: our old sixteen-gun *Victor*, but a very mere cockle in fact.) Stephen was of my opinion about his intellects, filled him to the hatches with opium-draughts, shaving and blistering his head just before we left. But in any case, I cannot find that he ever had orders for Rodriguez; so it is a hundred to one that Keating was nourishing a chimaera, as they say. But since it made him so desperate eager to present any lurking general, hungry for honours, with a fait accompli, viz. a conquered island with HM Governor already installed, and since his eagerness chimed in with my eagerness to get to sea before the French had the

Minerve and *Bellone* afloat (there is a rumour that someone, a Royalist or Papist or both, damaged their bottoms with an infernal machine: but I find it hard to believe that even a foreigner could be so wicked) – why, I fairly caressed that chimaera of his. Stephen,' he called, over the growling 'cello, 'how do you spell chimaera?'

'Many people start with ch, I believe. Have you told her about my stink-pot petrel?'

'Is not stink-pot a hellish low expression for a letter, Stephen?'

'Bless you, my dear, a mother that tends her own babies will not boggle at stink-pot. But you may put thalassodrome, if you find it more genteel.'

The pen scratched on; the 'cello sang deep; a midshipman tapped on the door. He reported a sail on the starboard quarter, adding that from a curious patch in her foretopsail she was thought to be the *Emma*.

'Aye, no doubt,' said Jack. 'She has made amazing good time. Thank you, Mr Penn.' The *Emma* had been called in by aviso from her station off Rodriguez, but he had not looked for her sooner than Thursday. 'Tom Pullings will be aboard presently,' he said to Stephen. 'We must keep him for dinner. After all this to and fro-ing off Rodriguez he will be glad of a bite of fresh mutton.' He called out to Killick: the saddle of yesterday's sheep was to be ready at five bells precisely, together with half a dozen of the red Constantia and a drowned baby. They discussed Thomas Pullings, his indifferent prospects, his real deserts, his probable appetite; and the midshipman reappeared, breathless and staring: *Staunch* had just signalled four sail, bearing north-east.

'What says *Emma*?' asked Jack.

'I don't know, sir,' said the midshipman.

'Then be so good as to find out,' said the Commodore, with some asperity.

The *Emma*, it appeared, had nothing to say. No *enemy in sight* flew from her fore; no gun called for her pennant's attention; yet the *Emma*, with a seamanlike captain aboard, was nearer those four sail than the *Staunch*. The conclusion was obvious: the four sails were Indiamen . . . unless, he reflected, with a cold grip in his heart, they were English men-of-war.

Stepping thoughtfully out of the cabin, he took over the deck, hailed the *Africaine* that he was leaving the line, and hauled up to close the *Emma*. Hitherto the *Boadicea* had been proceeding under easy sail, at a pace suited to that of the transports, but now topgallants broke out, and with the fine breeze two points free she began to move like a thoroughbred. Her wake stretched white and long; her bow-wave rose to the bridle-ports and the spray came sweeping aft from her forecastle, making rainbows in the sun. Spirits rose high, and the boys and the younger topmen laughed aloud as they raced aloft to loose the royals: but a few sharp, unusually vehement orders from the quarterdeck did away with their more obvious mirth. The afterguard and the waisters moved as mute as mice, ludicrously tiptoeing when they could not be seen; those forward exchanged covert winks and nudges; and those high above murmured, 'Watch out for squalls, mate,' with a knowing grin. Little passes unnoticed in a man-of-war, and although only the Marine sentry and one or two members of the anchor-watch had seen Jack and Colonel Keating come aboard after Governor Farquhar's farewell dinner, the whole ship's company knew that the skipper 'had taken a glass', that he had been 'as pissed as old Noah', that he had been 'brought down in a barrow, roaring for a woman – for a black girl in his cot', and they smiled indulgently, whispering quotations from his homily on the beastly vice of inebriation, as he called out to know whether that tack was to be brought to the chesstrees this watch or not.

Now the *Boadicea* was really lying down to her work, shouldering the long swell aside with a fine living motion and making her ten knots with no effort, so that for all those untormented by vile premonitions it was a pleasure to feel her sail.

'This is what I had imagined life at sea to be like,' said Mr Peter, a rare visitor to the quarterdeck – he spent most of his days in an airless paper-lined hole beneath the waterline, dividing his time between seasickness and work. 'Do you not find it exhilarating, sir?'

'Sure, it is like a glass of champagne,' replied Stephen; and Mr Peter smiled, looking significantly at Colonel Keating, greyish-yellow and blinking in the sun. It was in fact the Colonel who had been brought down in a wheelbarrow; it was he who had so often cried, 'Let copulation thrive.'

The *Boadicea* and the *Emma* were approaching at a combined rate of sixteen knots, and every few minutes pushed the eastward horizon back another mile. Soon the lookout told the deck of the four sail reported by the *Staunch*: then came another hail – two ships bearing east-north-east, and a hint of topgallantsails beyond them.

Six ships at least: it was almost impossible that so many should be Indiamen. Jack took a few turns, and his face grew more forbidding: he tossed off his coat, borrowed Seymour's telescope, and made his way up to the foretopgallant masthead. He was nearly there, with the shrouds creaking under his weight and the wind sweeping his long hair away to the north-west, when he heard the lookout mutter, 'Sixteen, seventeen . . .'tis a bleeding armada. An invincible bleeding armada. On deck, there . . .'

'Never mind, Lee,' said Jack, 'I can see 'em myself. Shift over.' He settled himself into the crosstrees and trained his glass east and north-east. There they lay, the greatest concentration of men-of-war he had ever seen in the Indian Ocean. And presently, to knock any lingering ghost of hope on the head, he made out the *Illustrious*, a two-decker wearing a vice-admiral's flag at the fore.

By this time the *Emma* was well within range. They had long since exchanged signals, and now the *Emma* was coming under the *Boadicea*'s lee in her heavy wallowing fashion, while the frigate backed her foretopsail and lay to.

Jack took a last long look at the fleet, men-of-war and transports, and then lowered himself heavily down through the rigging, much as another man might have walked heavily down the stairs in his house, thinking not of the steps but of his own problems. He reached the deck and put on his coat as Pullings came up the side; and the contrast between the lieutenant's beaming face, white teeth flashing in the deep ruddy tan, and the Commodore's sombre look would have struck an eye far less observant than Stephen's. However, the mere force of Pullings' grin, his evident pleasure, brought an answering smile; and the smile grew a little more lively at the sight of a large bag hoisting up from the *Emma*'s boat, the much-loved familiar mail-sack.

'There is no one so welcome as the postman, Mr Pullings,' said Jack, inviting him into the cabin. 'Whence come ye, Tom?' he asked, once they were there.

'Straight from the Admiral, sir,' said Pullings, as though this were the best news that could ever be brought.

'From Mr Bertie?' asked Jack, whose protesting mind had faintly offered a hypothetical force bound for Java, perhaps, under a different vice-admiral, one with no responsibility for the Cape – an admiral who was merely passing by.

'That's right, sir,' said Pullings cheerfully. 'And he gave me this for you.' He took a dog-eared *Naval Chronicle* from his pocket and plucked an official letter from among its pages, marking the place with his thumb; but holding the letter aloft, not quite delivering it, he said, 'So no post, sir, since I last saw you?'

'Not a word, Tom,' said Jack. 'Not a word since the Cape; and that was out of order. Not a word for the best part of a year.'

'Then I am the first,' cried Pullings with infinite satisfaction. 'Let me wish you and Mrs Aubrey all the joy in the world.' He grasped Jack's limp, wondering hand, wrung it numb, and showed the printed page, reading aloud, 'At Ashgrove Cottage, Chilton Admiral, in Hants, the lady of Captain Aubrey, of the *Boadicea*, of a son and heir,' following the words with his finger.

'Give it here,' said Jack. He grasped the magazine, sloped the page to the light and pored over it intently. '"At Ashgrove Cottage, Chilton Admiral, in Hants, the lady of Captain Aubrey, of the *Boadicea*, of a son . . ." Well, I'll be damned. God bless me. Lord, Lord . . . upon my word and honour . . . I'll be damned to Hell and back again . . . strike me down. Killick, Killick, rouse out a bottle of champagne – pass the word for the Doctor – here, Killick, there's for you – God love us all – ha, ha, ha.'

Killick took the handful of money, put it slowly into his pocket with a look of extreme suspicion and walked out of the cabin, his lips pursed in disapproval. Jack leapt from his seat, took several turns fore and aft, chuckling from time to time, his mind filled with mingled love, happiness, fulfilment, and a most piercing nostalgia. 'I thank you, Pullings, I thank you with all my heart for your news,' he said.

'I thought you would be pleased, sir,' said Pullings. 'We always knew, Mrs P and I, how you wanted a boy. Girls are very well, in course, but they are not quite the same; you could not wish them about all the time. And then you never know what they will be at. But a boy! – Our nipper, sir, if ever I get a settled command of my own, shall come to sea the minute he is out of coats, and properly breeched.'

'I trust Mrs Pullings and young John are quite well?' said Jack; but before he could learn much of them, Stephen walked in, followed by the sack of mail. 'Stephen,' said Jack, 'Sophie is brought to bed of a boy.'

'Aye? I dare say,' said Stephen. 'Poor thing. But it must be a great relief to your mind.'

'Why,' said Jack, with a blush, 'I never had wind of it, you know.' Calculation had already established the fact that the distant nameless wonder was conceived the night of his leaving, and this made him bashful, even confused.

'Well, I give you joy of your son,' said Stephen. 'And I hope with all my heart that dear Sophie does well? At least,' he observed, as he watched Jack busy with the mail-sack, 'this will make a baronetcy more welcome: will give it more point.'

'Lord, what am I at?' cried Jack. 'Orders come first.' He dropped the sack, broke the seal of the Admiral's letter, found the expected words directing and requiring him to proceed with all possible dispatch to the flag at or off

Rodriguez immediately upon receipt of these orders. He laughed, and said, 'If there is any baronetcy in the wind, it don't come this way. I am superseded.'

He went on deck, gave one order for the signal that should set the squadron on its new course, away from Mauritius, and another to splice the mainbrace. To Seymour's astonished expression he replied, in a voice as offhand as he could make it, that he had just learnt of the birth of a son. He received the congratulations of the quarterdeck and many a kind look from the seamen nearby, invited Colonel Keating to take a glass in the cabin, and so returned. The bottle was soon out, the letters distributed; and Jack, giving Keating his packet, said, 'I hope, Colonel, that your news may be as pleasant as mine, to offset the rest; because you were too good a prophet by half, and I fear there may be a general waiting for you at Rodriguez, just as there is an admiral waiting for me.' With these words he retired with his letters to the quarter-gallery, his own private place of ease, leaving the soldier transfixed, pale and even trembling, with indignation.

A little before dinner he came out and found Stephen alone in the great cabin. Pullings had now, for the first time, learnt of the squadron's destination; and realizing that a little tactful delay on his part would have allowed the Commodore to carry out his plans and to reap honour and glory, had withdrawn to the taffrail, where he stood by the ensign-staff, cursing his untimely zeal. 'I wish you too may have had very good news, Stephen?' said Jack, nodding at the pile of open letters at Stephen's side.

'Tolerably so in parts, I thank you; but nothing that causes me a joy comparable with yours. You are still in a glow, brother, a roseate glow. Pray tell me of Sophie's condition.'

'She says she has never felt better in her life – swears it passed off as easy as a letter in the post - finds the little chap a great comfort, and excellent company. Now I know you are about as partial to children as old Herod, Stephen, but –'

'No, no. I am not doggedly, mechanically set against them, though I freely admit I find most babies superfluous, and unnecessary.'

'Without there were babies, we should have no next generation.'

'So much the better, when you consider the state to which we have reduced the world they must live in, the bloody-minded wolfish stock from which they spring, and the wicked, inhuman society that will form them. Yet I do admit of exceptions: the replication of such a creature as Sophie, and even I may say of yourself, can be seen as a good. But I am afraid I interrupt you.'

'I was only going to say, that you might like to hear Sophie's description of him. It appears that he is a most unusual, exceptional child.'

Stephen listened with a decent show of complaisance: the smell of roasting meat drifted aft, and that of fried onions; he heard the drum beat 'Heart of Oak' for the gun-room's dinner; his stomach called out for his own; and still the tale ran on.

'You cannot conceive, Stephen, how it extends a man's future, having a son,' said Jack. 'Now it is worth while planting a walnut-tree! Why, I may even lay down a whole plantation of oaks.'

'The girls would have gathered your walnuts. The girls would have sported under the oaks; and their grandchildren would have felled them.'

'No, no. It is not the same thing at all. Now, thank God, they have portions; and so eventually they will marry some greasy fellow called Snooks – you must admit, Stephen, that it is not the same thing at all.'

Just before five bells Jack was cut short by the arrival of Pullings, still sadly reduced, and of the Colonel, still trembling with rage; and at five bells itself Killick announced, 'Wittles is up,' with a courtly jerk of his thumb, and they moved into the dining-cabin.

Pullings ate his mutton silently, with little appetite; Colonel Keating, though allowed by convention to speak freely at the Commodore's table, remained almost equally mute, not wishing to spoil a happy occasion by giving vent to the words he longed to utter; Stephen was lost in reflection, though from time to time he did respond to pauses in Jack's cheerful flow. When the long meal was over, when the King, Mrs Aubrey and young Stupor Mundi had been drunk in bumpers of luke-warm port, and when the guests had moved into the open air to dissipate the fumes of their wine, he said to Jack, 'I scarcely know which I most admire, the strength of your philoprogenitive instinct, or your magnanimity in the face of this disappointment. Not many years ago you would have clapped your telescope to your blind eye; you would have evaded these orders; and you would have taken the Mauritius before Mr Bertie knew what you were at.'

'Well, I *am* disappointed,' said Jack, 'I must confess; and when first I smoked the Admiral's intentions I had a month's mind to steer due west for a while. But it would not do, you know. Orders is orders, bar one case in a million; and this is not one of those cases. The Mauritius must fall in the next week or so, whoever is in command, or whoever takes the glory.'

'Keating does not take it so philosophically.'

'Keating has not just heard he has a son. Ha, ha, ha: there's for you, Stephen.'

'Keating already has five, and a sad expense they are to him, as well as a grave disappointment. The news of a sixth boy would not have mollified his indignation, unless indeed it had been a daughter, the one thing he longs for. Strange, strange: it is a passion to which I cannot find the least echo, when I peer into my bosom.'

Colonel Keating's indignation was shared throughout the *Boadicea* and her companions. It was universally held that the Commodore had been done out of his rights, cheated of his due, and wiped in the eye if not stabbed in the back: and there was not a man in the squadron who did not know that two captured Indiamen lay in Port-Louis, together with a large number of only slightly less magnificent prizes, and

that the appearance – the totally unnecessary appearance –
of a seventy-four, eight frigates, four sloops, and maybe a
dozen regiments of lobsters, would reduce the share of all
who had done the real work to half a pint of small beer, if
that.

The indignation increased with brooding, and as the two
bodies slowly converged, meeting at Rodriguez, it grew to
such a pitch that when the *Boadicea*'s salute to the flag roared
out, the gunner said, 'And I wish they was loaded with grape,
you old –' without a word of reproach from the officers near
at hand. When the last gun had been fired, and before the
flagship began her reply, Jack said, 'Strike the pennant.
Hoist out my barge.' Then, a mere post-captain again, he
stepped into the cabin and called for his breeches, cocked
hat and number one coat to go aboard the Admiral. It had
been a hard moment, the striking of his pennant – for a
pennant could not fly in the presence of a flag without the
unusual compliment of a direct invitation – but little comfort
did he meet with below. Killick's sense of injustice had been
inflamed by the extra ration of grog served out to all hands.
It now overflowed on to the principal victim, and in his old
shrewish voice he said, 'You ain't got no number one coat,
sir. All bloody and mucked up, with figuring away aboard
the *Vénus*, when two minutes would of changed it. The
scraper will pass with a shove' – spitting on the lace of the
cocked hat and rubbing it with his sleeve – 'but you'll have
to wear it athwartships, on account of the rats. As for coats
and breeches, this is the best I can do – I've shipped the
old epaulettes – and if any jumped-up new-come son of a
Gosport fart don't like it, he may –'

'Bear a hand, bear a hand,' cried Jack. 'Give me my stockings and that packet, and don't stand muttering there all
day.'

The same sullen resentment was obvious in the bargemen
who pulled Captain Aubrey across to the *Illustrious*; it was
evident in his coxswain's rigour, in the vicious stab of the
boathook that clamped on to the two-decker's chains, removing a good hand's-breadth of paint, and in the expressionless

reserve that met the friendly advances of the seamen peering out of her lower-deck ports.

Admiral Bertie expected it; he knew very well what he was doing, and he was fully armoured against all reaction except cheerfulness. From the outset he adopted an attitude of jovial bonhomie, with a good deal of laughter: he spoke as though it were the most natural thing in the world to find a ready and willing compliance, no trace of ill-feeling or resentment; and to his astonishment he did find it. The Naval Instructions clearly laid down that he must find it, and that anything less than total abnegation, total perfection of conduct, would render a subordinate liable to punishment; but his whole service life had proved that there was a world of difference between the Navy in print and the Navy in practice, and that although in theory a senior post-captain must be as submissive to an admiral as a newly-joined midshipman, in fact an oppressed commodore, growing froward under ill-usage, might make things extremely awkward for his oppressor and still keep the right side of the law: he had himself used obstruction in all its refinements often enough to know what it could accomplish. He had been prepared to meet the cunningest ploys or the most violent expressions of dissent (his secretary was there to note down any choleric word): none appeared: he was taken aback, rendered uneasy. He probed a little deeper, asking whether Aubrey was not surprised to see so many ships coming to queer his pitch? And when Jack, with equal joviality, replied that he was not, that the greater the number the less the bloodshed (so repugnant to him, as to all right-feeling men), and that the more the merrier was his motto, the Admiral glanced at his secretary, to see whether Mr Shepherd shared his suspicion that Captain Aubrey was somewhat disguised, cheerfully disguised, in wine.

The suspicion could not be maintained. As soon as the captains of the fleet were assembled aboard the flagship, at the Admiral's request Jack Aubrey delivered to them a singularly lucid, cogent account of the situation, with all the facts, all the figures at instant command. To the anxious words about the notorious difficulty of the reefs surrounding Mauritius, the wicked surf that beat upon them, and the paucity of harbours, he replied with a chart, a little master-piece of hydrography, showing Flat Island and the Grande Baie, exactly surveyed by himself, with triple-sextant-bearings and doubled-checked soundings showing plenty of room and clean anchorage for seventy ships, as well as shel-tered beaches for a very great number of men. He ended his exposition by observing that in view of the lateness of the season he would respectfully suggest an immediate descent.

The Admiral was by no means so sure of that: long before Captain Aubrey was born the Admiral's old nurse had told him, 'The more hurry, the less speed.' He would take the matter under consideration – urgent consideration – and advise with General Abercrombie and the gentlemen of his staff.

When the meeting broke up he kept Jack for a while, by way of plumbing his mind: for Aubrey was either a nonpareil of docility (and that was not his reputation at all), or he had something up his sleeve. It made the Admiral uneasy. It seemed to him that beneath all his proper deference Jack regarded him with a certain detachment and something not far from a secret amused contempt; and since the Admiral was not altogether a scrub he found this extremely disagree-able. Then again, Mr Bertie had invariably met with hostility from those he had over-reached, a hostility that gave him a retrospective justification; and here there was none – con-tinuing cheerfulness, even benignity. It made him feel ner-vous, and on parting with Jack he said, 'By the way, Aubrey, it was quite right to strike your pennant, of course; but you must hoist it again the moment you set foot aboard the *Boadicea*.'

Admiral Bertie was more uneasy still by the time he reached his cot. In the interval, as the fleet lay at anchor in the road of Rodriguez and the visiting boats passed to and fro, Mr Peter had called upon his near relation Mr Shepherd. Mr Peter had seen a good deal of Dr Maturin, a simpler, more penetrable man than he had been led to suppose, particularly since this last flood of letters and information from home: and from Maturin's casual remarks, some of them really far from discreet, Peter had formed the conviction that General Aubrey, the Commodore's father and a member of parliament, was probably playing a very deep game, that he might be about to change sides, that he was secretly very well with the ministry, and that it was by no means impossible that he might shortly appear in an office connected with honours and patronage, if not on the Board of Admiralty itself. Stephen had poisoned too many sources of intelligence to derive much satisfaction from this elementary exercise; but in fact the sneaking underhand little tale was admirably suited to the ears that received it a few minutes after Peter's departure. It explained Aubrey's disconcerting nonchalance: a man with such allies must be handled with care.

In the morning a council, attended by the captains and the senior army officers, considered the plan of attack worked out by Jack and Colonel Keating. General Abercombie's plea for delay, strongly supported by his staff, was brushed aside with even greater strength by the Admiral himself. The General looked surprised and even injured: he was a stout old gentleman, and he stared across the table at nothing in particular, with a look of hostile stupidity in his protuberant eyes, as though he did not quite understand what had happened. But having repeated himself for the space of about three-quarters of an hour he yielded to the Admiral's insistence; and the plan, scarcely mangled in any important respect, was agreed to, though with very little grace. Half an hour later the flagship stood out to sea, with a fine topgallant breeze to send her north about Mauritius for Flat Island and the beaches up the coast from Port-Louis.

The conquest of Mauritius ran its leisurely course, with the regiments marching and countermarching in a scientific manner that pleased the generals on either side. The infantrymen sweated, but few of them bled. They had been landed smoothly, without opposition, and they presented

General Decaen with an insuperable problem. His numerous militia was no use to him at all: most of its members had read Stephen's broadsheets, many of them had already seen copies of Governor Farquhar's proposed proclamation, all of them were more concerned with the revival of their strangled trade than with the welfare of Buonaparte's empire. His Irish troops were clearly disaffected; his French regulars were outnumbered by well over five to one; and his navy was blockaded by an overwhelming force of ships. His only concern was to delay General Abercrombie's advance until his surrender should meet certain arcane military requirements, so that he should be able to justify his conduct at home and obtain honourable terms at Port-Louis for himself and his men.

He succeeded to admiration, and Abercrombie particularly praised his orderly retreat on the night of Thursday, when his flanking battalions fell back from Terre Rouge and the Long Mountain, changing face at the double in the most professional way. 'That is real soldiering,' said the General.

While these rural gestures were being made the emissaries passed to and fro, and although Port-Louis was still nominally French, Stephen Maturin walked up to the military hospital without his usual detour; and there he found McAdam on the verandah. 'How is our patient this morning?' he asked.

'Och, the night was good enough, with your draught,' said McAdam, though with no great satisfaction. 'And the eye shows some wee improvement. It is the neck that keeps me so anxious — slough, slough and slough again, and this morning it looked as ugly as ever. He will pluck at the dressing in his sleep. Dr Martin suggests sewing flaps of healthy skin across the whole morbid area.'

'Martin is a fool,' said Stephen. 'What we are concerned with is the artery-wall itself, not the gross exfoliation. Rest is the answer, clean dressings, lenitives and peace of mind: there is physical strength in galore. How is the agitation?'

'Fair enough this morning; and he has been sleeping since my early rounds.'

'Very good, very good. Then we must certainly not disturb him; there is nothing like sleep for repair. I shall come back about noon, bringing the Commodore. He has a letter from Lady Clonfert at the Cape; he wishes to deliver it himself, and to tell Clonfert how the fleet praises his noble defence of the *Néréide*.' McAdam whistled and screwed up his face. 'Do you think it imprudent?' asked Stephen.

McAdam scratched himself: he could not say – Clonfert had been very strange these days – did not talk to him – no longer opened his mind – remained silent, listening for gunfire hour after hour. 'Maybe it would be best if you was to come a few minutes ahead. We can sound him out, and if we judge the excitement would not be too much, the Commodore can see him. It might do him a world of good. He liked seeing you,' said McAdam with a burst of generosity that he instantly balanced by asking in a sneering voice, 'I suppose your Big Buck Aubrey is prancing about on shore, the lord of creation? How are things going along down there, will you tell me?'

'Much as we had expected. Mr Farquhar has landed from the *Otter*, and I dare say the capitulation will be signed before dinner.'

They talked about other wounded Néréides: some were doing well, some were at death's door. Young Hobson, a master's mate emasculated late in the battle, had passed through it that night, thankful to go. Stephen nodded, and for a while he watched two geckoes on the wall, paying some attention to McAdam's account of the French surgeon's words about the impossibility of saving patients when the vital spring was gone. After a long pause he said, 'McAdam, you know more about this aspect of medicine than I do: what do you say to a patient with no physical injury, no tangible lesion, who loses all real concern with his life? Who takes a disgust to the world? A scholar, say, who has edited Livy, Livy his sole study and his delight: he stumbles on the lost books, carries them home, and finds he has not the courage, the spirit, to open even the first. He does not care about Livy's lost books, nor about his books that are known, nor about any books or authors at all. They do not interest him. He will not lift the cover; and he sees that very soon his own animal functions will not interest him either. Do you understand me? Have you seen cases of this sort in your practice?'

'Certainly I have. And they are not so rare, neither, even in men that are kept busy.'

'What is the prognosis? How do you see the nature of the malady?'

'I take it that here we are to leave grace to one side?'

'Just so.'

'As to the nature, why, I believe he perceives the void that has always surrounded him, and in doing so he falls straight into a pit. Sometimes his perception of the void is intermittent; but where it is not, then in my experience spiritual death ensues, preceding physical death sometimes by ten years and more. Occasionally he may be pulled out by his prick.'

'You mean he may remain capable of love?'

'As between men and women I use the term "lust": but call it what you like: desire, a burning desire for some slut may answer, if only he burns hard enough. In the early stages, however,' said McAdam, leering at the geckoes, 'he may tide himself over with opium, for a while.'

'Good day to you, now, Dr McAdam.'

On his way down through the growing heat Stephen overtook two crippled boys, the one with his leg taken off at the knee, the other with an empty sleeve pinned over his breast, midshipmen of the *Néréide*. 'Mr Lomax,' he cried, 'sit down at once. This is madness: your stitches will burst. Sit down at once on that stone: elevate your limb.'

Pale young wraithlike Lomax, propped by his crutch and his companion, hopped to the stone, the mounting-stone outside a rich-looking house, and sat upon it. 'It is only another hundred yards, sir,' he said. 'All the Néréides are there. You can see the ship from the corner; and we are to go aboard the minute her colours go up.'

'Nonsense,' said Stephen. But having considered for a

while he knocked at the door: a little later he came out with a chair, a cushion, and two stout anxious care-worn black men. He put Lomax into the chair, properly padded, and the black men carried it down to the turn in the road where the little group of mobile survivors looked down on their frigate, tight-packed among the Indiamen, the merchant ships and the men-of-war in Port-Louis harbour. Some of their eager life seeped into him. 'Mr Yeo,' he said to a lieutenant with a great bandage covering most of his face, 'you may do me an essential service, if you will be so kind. I was obliged to leave a valuable bolster in your ship, and I should be most grateful if you would order the strictest search when you go aboard. I have already mentioned it to the Admiral and the Commodore, but –' His words were cut off by cheering away to the right, a cheering that spread as the French colours came down on the citadel, and that redoubled when the union flag replaced them. The Néréides cheered too, thin and piping, a poor volume of sound that was lost in the salvoes of artillery and then in a deep rolling thunder from the guns of the fleet.

'I shall not forget, sir,' said Yeo, shaking Stephen by the hand. 'Pass it on, there: the Doctor's bolster to be preserved.'

Stephen walked on, now quite through the town, where the closed shutters gave an impression of death, and where the few white people in the streets looked oppressed, as though the plague were abroad; only the blacks, whose lot could scarcely change for the worse, showed any liveliness or curiosity. He attended to various points of business, and met Jack at their appointed place. 'The capitulation is signed, I collect?' he said.

'Yes,' said Jack. 'Uncommon handsome terms, too: they march out with colours flying, match burning, drum beating – all the honours of war – and they are not to be prisoners. Tell me, how did you find Clonfert? I have his wife's letter here in my pocket.'

'I did not see him this morning: he was asleep. McAdam seems to think his general state to be much the same. He should come through, I believe, barring accidents: but of course he will be horribly disfigured. That will have a bearing on his state of mind, and in these cases the patient's mind is of great importance. I propose leaving you under the trees near the gate, while I attend to his dressings with McAdam. He may be in no state to receive you.'

They made their way up the hill, talking of the ceremony. 'Farquhar was astonished you had not been invited,' said Jack. 'He checked the Admiral so hard we all looked away – said your work had saved innumerable lives and that the slight must be repaired: you should be given the place of honour at his official dinner. The Admiral looked concerned, and salaamed, and said he would instantly do everything in his power – would mention you with the greatest respect in his despatch; and then he ran off like a boy to start writing it – had been itching to do so since dawn. And a precious document it will be, I am sure, ha, ha, ha. Much the same as most of 'em, only more so; but it will certainly have a whole Gazette to itself.'

'Who is to carry it?'

'Oh, his nephew, I dare say, or one of his favourite captains: it is the greatest plum to carry these last five years and more – attendance at court, kind words and a tip from the King, dinner at Guildhall, freedom of this and that: promotion of course or a damned good billet. I shall give the lucky man my letters to Sophie – he will go like the wind, cracking on regardless, homeward bound with such welcome news, the dog.'

Jack's mind flew off to Hampshire, and it was still there when Stephen said in a louder tone, 'I repeat, what do you think is our next destination?'

'Eh? Oh, Java, no doubt, to have a crack at the Dutchmen.'

'Java: oh, indeed. Listen, now: here are your trees. There is a bench. I shall be with you directly.'

The hospital courtyard was in a strange state of disorder: not only the confusion of a defeat, with people making the most of a vacation of power to carry off everything portable, but something quite out of the common. Stephen walked faster when he heard McAdam's raucous northern voice

313

calling out, and he pushed through a knot of attendants staring up at the verandah. McAdam was drunk, but not so drunk that he could not stand, not so drunk that he did not recognize Stephen. 'Make a lane, there,' he cried. 'Make a lane for the great Dublin physician. Come and see your patient, Dr Maturin, you whore.'

In the low-ceilinged room the shutters drawn against the noonday sun made Clonfert's blood show almost black: no great pool, but all there was in his small, wasted body. He lay on his back, arms spread out and dangling, the unshattered side of his face looking beautiful and perfectly grave, even severe. The bandage had been torn from his neck.

Stephen bent to listen for any trace of a heart-beat, straightened, closed Clonfert's eyes, and pulled up the sheet. McAdam sat on the side of the bed, weeping now, his fury gone with his shouting; and between his sobs he said, 'It was the cheering that woke him. What are they cheering for? says he, and I said the French have surrendered. Aubrey will be here and you shall have your *Néréide* back. Never, by God, says he, not from Jack Aubrey: run out, McAdam, and see are they coming. And when I stepped out of the door so he did it, and so bloody Christ he did it.' A long silence, and he said, 'Your Jack Aubrey destroyed him. Jack Aubrey destroyed him.'

Stephen crossed the blazing courtyard again, and under the trees Jack stood up, expectant. His smile vanished when Stephen said, 'He is dead,' and they paced down in silence through the town. A town busier now, with the shops opening, men posting up the proclamation, large numbers of people walking about, companies of soldiers marching, parties of blue-jackets, queues forming outside the brothels, several French officers who saluted punctiliously, putting the best face they could on defeat. Stephen stopped to kneel as the Sacrament passed by to a deathbed, a single priest and a boy with a bell.

'I trust he went easy?' said Jack in a low voice, at last.

Stephen nodded, and he looked at Jack with his pale, expressionless eyes, looking objectively at his friend, tall, sanguine, almost beefy, full of health, rich, and under his kindly though moderate concern happy and even triumphant. He thought, 'You cannot blame the bull because the frog burst: the bull has no comprehension of the affair,' but even so he said, 'Listen, Jack: I do not much care for the taste of this victory. Nor any victory, if it comes to that. I shall see you at dinner.'

The dinner was nothing in comparison with those usually eaten at Government House under the rule of General Decaen: many of his cooks and all of his plate had vanished in the brief interregnum, and a stray mortar-bomb had destroyed part of the wall. But even so the creole dishes made a pleasant contrast with the hard fare of recent days, and above all the ceremony provided an ideal occasion for speeches.

Something, reflected Jack, something came over officers who reached flag-rank or the equivalent, something that made them love to get up on their hind legs and produce long measured periods with even longer pauses between them. Several gentlemen had already risen to utter low compliments to themselves, their fellows, and their nation, and now General Abercrombie was struggling to his feet, with a sheaf of notes in his hand. 'Your Excellency, my lords, Admiral Bertie, and gentlemen. We are met here together,' two bars of silence, 'on this happy, eh, *occasion*,' two more bars, 'to celebrate what I may perhaps be permitted to call, an unparalleled feat, of *combined* operations, of *combination*, valour, organization, and I may say, of indomitable will.' Pause. 'I take no credit to myself.' Cries of No, no; and cheers. 'No. It is all due,' pause, 'to a young lady in Madras.'

'Sir, sir,' hissed his aide-de-camp, 'you have turned over two pages. You have come to the joke.'

It took some time to get the General back to his eulogy of Abercrombie and all present, and in the interval Jack looked anxiously at his friend, one of the few black coats present, sitting on the Governor's right. Stephen loathed speeches, but though paler than usual he seemed to be bearing up, and Jack noticed with pleasure that as well as his own he was secretly drinking the wine poured into the abstinent Governor's glass.

The General boomed on, came to a close, a false close, rallied and began again, and at last sank into his chair, glared round in surly triumph and drank like a camel with a broad desert before it.

A broad desert threatened, to be sure, for here was Admiral Bertie, fresh and spry, game for a good half-hour: and his first words about his inability to match the gallant General's eloquence struck a chill to Jack's heart. His mind wandered during the Admiral's compliments to the various corps that made up the force, and he was in the act of building an observatory-dome of superior design on the top of Ashgrove Hill – he had of course purchased the hill and felled the trees on the summit – when he heard Mr Bertie's voice take on a new and unctuous tone.

'In the course of my long career,' said the Admiral, 'I have been compelled to give many orders, which, though always for the good of the service, have sometimes been repugnant to my finer feelings. For even an Admiral retains finer feelings, gentlemen.' Dutiful laughter, pretty thin. 'But now, with His Excellency's permission, I shall indulge myself by giving one that is more congenial to the spirit of a plain British sailor.' He paused and coughed in a suddenly hushed atmosphere of genuine suspense, and then in an even louder voice he went on, 'I hereby request and require Captain Aubrey to repair aboard the *Boadicea* as soon as he has finished his dinner, there to receive my despatches for the Lords Commissioners of the Admiralty and to convey them to Whitehall with all the diligence in his power. And to this, gentlemen' – raising his glass – 'I will append a toast: let us all fill up to the brim, gunwales under, and drink to England, home and beauty, and may Lucky Jack Aubrey reach 'em with fair winds and flowing sheets every mile of the way.'

P.S.

Ideas,
interviews
& features

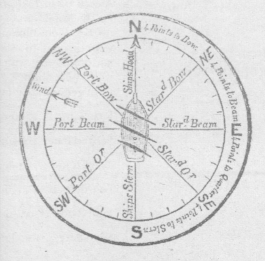

JACK AUBREY'S SHIPS
Brian Lavery

Patrick O'Brian, unlike other writers of naval fiction, often uses real ships as the basis for his plots. In the Hornblower stories of C. S. Forester, for example, the hero serves on only one real ship – the *Indefatigable*, which really was the ship commanded by Captain Pellew during the time when the hero served under him as midshipman.

Several of the Aubrey stories are based on real incidents and use real ships: in particular, *The Mauritius Command* is based on the real campaign in that area. The use of real ships which have a past adds to the effect of the story: the cutting out of the *Hermione* in the case of the *Surprise*, and the incident between the *Leopard* and USS *Chesapeake* in 1807, which led to difficulties after Jack Aubrey's capture by the Americans in *The Fortune of War*.

The Royal Navy of the Napoleonic Wars had nearly 1,000 ships at its peak in 1814. These were divided into six rates, according to size and gunpowder, with numerous smaller vessels which were unrated.

In general the rates were divided as follows:

First Rate	100 + guns	850 + men
Second Rate	90–98 guns	750 men
Third Rate	64–84 guns	500–720 men
Fourth Rate	50–60 guns	350–420 men
Fifth Rate	30–40 guns	215–294 men
Sixth Rate	20–28 guns	121–195 men

Unrated ships included sloops of 10–18 guns, brigs, bomb vessels, fire-ships, storeships, cutters, schooners, luggers, hospital ships, prison ships, and gun-boats.

After service as a midshipman and lieutenant, a successful naval officer would expect to take command of a sloop, with the rank of Commander. After promotion to Post Captain he would rise through ships of the different rates, perhaps reaching a third rate after seven to ten years in command of frigates. In the early stages, Jack Aubrey's career roughly conforms to this. As a commander he began in the tiny sloop *Sophie* and, after a period on the beach, he continued in the *Polychrest*. Following his promotion, Aubrey took temporary command of the 38-gun fifth rate, the *Lively*. This was rather a large ship for a newly promoted captain, but the command was temporary and the circumstances were exceptional. He then went to the *Surprise*, a sixth rate of 28 guns, a ship more appropriate to his seniority. His next ship was the *Boadicea*, a fifth rate of 38 guns. After that his career in frigates might have ended. With six or seven years of seniority he was offered the *Ajax*, a ship-of-the-line of 74 guns, but turned it down in order to go to sea more quickly in the *Leopard*, a 50-gun ship.

After this Aubrey's rise up the rates slows down considerably. Stephen Maturin's intelligence activities generally demand small ships, and Aubrey is certainly more at home in the single ship missions carried out by frigates, than service with the main fleet in a ship-of-the-line. His next command after the *Leopard* (apart from several ships as a virtual passenger) is the sloop *Ariel*. It is made quite clear that he is being given the ship because of 'a delicate, pressing piece of work that calls for a cool, experienced hand', and that it was 'fully understood that the command of the *Ariel* in no way represented the Board's estimate of Captain Aubrey's merits'; the ship was technically transformed from a sloop to a post ship by the mere fact of Aubrey taking command. [1]

In *The Ionian Mission* Aubrey's career briefly resumes a normal course, when he becomes captain of the *Worcester* of 74 guns. This, however, does not last for long and he soon returns to his old friend the *Surprise*. The association with this ship continues through the remaining books, even surviving his dismissal from the navy in *The Reverse of the Medal*.

Aubrey's first two ships, the *Sophie* and the *Polychrest*, were fictitious, and rather unusual vessels. The *Sophie* was described as 'almost the only quarterdeck brig in the service', and certainly such a deck, reaching from the stern to almost midships in a larger ship, was highly

1. Patrick O'Brian, *The Surgeon's Mate* (London: Collins, 1980), pp. 149 & 153.

unusual in one so small. Formerly known as the *Vencejo*, she had been captured from the Spanish. She was old-fashioned in construction and fitting, and was regarded as rather slow. She was about 150 tons in bur-then which would have made her about 70 ft long on the gundeck. Her main armament consisted of 14 guns, apparently very light ones firing 4-pound shot, but Aubrey successfully applied to have two 12-pounders fitted as 'bow chasers', firing directly forward. As a brig she would have been fitted with two masts, both carrying square sails.[2]

The *Polychrest* was even more unusual. She had been designed to carry a secret weapon, later abandoned. She was double-ended, in that head and stern were alike. She apparently had a very shallow draught, as she had no hold. This was compensated for by the use of sliding keels, rather like those used by modern dinghies (and in fact a few vessels were built with such sliding keels, mostly to the design of Captain Shanck). Her armament of twenty-four 32-pounder carronades was a very heavy one for a ship of her size, but would only have been effective at short range. She was three-masted, square-rigged, but was unusual in that she had two main topsail yards. She was 'the *Carpenter's Mistake*', 'a theorizing lands-man's vessel . . . built by a gang of rogues and jobbers'.[3]

The *Lively* is the first real ship we encounter, and she was a perfectly standard frigate of 38 guns. When Aubrey took up his acting command in the autumn of 1804 she was almost brand new, having been launched at Woolwich Dockyard in July. She was the first of a class of 15 ships, designed by Sir William Rule the Joint Surveyor of the Navy. She was of 1,076 tons, 154ft 1in. long on the gundeck, and 39ft 6in. broad. Like other ships of this type, she carried twenty-eight 18-pounder guns on the main deck, twelve 32-pounder carronades and two long 12-pounders on the quarterdeck, and two 32-pounder carronades and two long 9-pounders on the forecastle. Officially this type of ship carried a crew of 284 or 300 men, though in practice many were under-manned. By this time the 38 was the third most common type of frigate in the fleet. There were 45 of them on the list in 1805, compared with 53 frigates of 36-guns and 59 smaller vessels of 32-guns.

The *Surprise*, to which Aubrey was appointed after his temporary com-mand of the *Lively* had ended, was 'a trim, beautiful little eight and twen-ty, French built with a bluff bow and lovely lines, weatherly, stiff, a fine sea boat, fast when she was well-handled, roomy, dry'.[4] The real ship had dis-tinguished herself in 1799. Two years earlier the crew of the frigate *Hermione*, under the brutal Captain Pigot, had mutinied and butchered

2. Patrick O'Brian, *Master and Commander* (London: Collins,1970), pp. 13, 27, 44, 48 & 53.
3. Patrick O'Brian, *Post Captain* (London: Collins, 1972), pp. 157 & 175.
4. Patrick O'Brian, *H.M.S. Surprise* (London: Collins, 1973), pp. 77–78.

their officers. They had surrendered her to the Spanish, who were fitting her out for their fleet at Puerto Cabello, in what is now Venezuela. On the night of 21 October six boats from the *Surprise* went into the enemy harbour, stormed the *Hermione* and towed her out to sea.[5]

The *Surprise* had been the French frigate *Unite*, built at Le Havre in 1794, and rated as a 'corvette' in the French Navy. In April 1796 she was captured by the 38-gun frigate *Inconstant* in the Mediterranean. She was renamed *Surprise*, because there was already a *Unite* in the British fleet, and registered as a 28-gun ship, though she actually carried twenty-four 32-pounder carronades on her main deck, and eight 32-pounder carronades on her quarterdeck and forecastle, with two or four long 6-pounders on the quarterdeck and forecastle. It was a very powerful armament for a frigate, but with remarkably few long-range guns. There was some difficulty about how to rate her – 28-guns normally meant a sixth rate, but she was regarded as fifth rate from 1797 to 1798 and as sixth rate for the rest of her career. She was only of 579 tons, but carried the mainmast of a 36-gun ship (normally of about 950 tons), with the foremast and mizzen of a 28. According to one authority, 'thus rigged, the *Surprise* appears not to have been complained of as a sailor.'[6]

She sailed for Jamaica in July 1796 under Captain Edward Hamilton and stayed in the West Indies for several years. She was involved in the capture of several privateers before her exploits with the *Hermione*, but returned home after that. Here reality departs from fiction. The real *Surprise* was sold at Deptford in February 1802 and presumably broken up. The short-lived Peace of Amiens had begun and the government believed it had no immediate need for such ships.

The fictional *Surprise* was to continue for many years, appearing in several Jack Aubrey novels. It is worth describing her in some detail, both for herself and as a representative of ships of the period. In this we are helped by the fact that her plans, drawn by dockyard shipwrights some time after her capture, survive in the National Maritime Museum.

She was 126 ft long on the gundeck. This measurement did not give the full length of the ship, for it excluded the projecting gallery of the stern, and the figurehead and the knee of the head at the bows, not to mention the long projection of the bowsprit. But it was a useful way of measuring the ship, for it gave a real indication of the size of the hull, and the space that was available for fitting guns and accommodating men. At her widest point in midships she was 31ft 8in. broad, though under the planks she

5. Ibid., pp. 123–124; William James, *The Naval History of Great Britain from the Declaration of War by France*... (London: [n.pub.], 1822–24), II, 406–412; Dudley Pope, *The Black Ship* (London: Weidenfeld & Nicolson, 1963).
6. James, *The Naval History*, II, 406.

was only 31ft 2in. Using a standard formula, these figures could be used to calculate the tonnage of the ship, which was 578 73/94 tons. This gave no real indication of her weight or displacement, but was a useful comparison of her size with other warships.

The hull of a warship was a stout wooden structure. The straight keel formed the very lowest part and the backbone of the ship. At the forward end rose a curved piece, known as the stem. Aft rose a piece called the stern-post; this was made straight so that the rudder could be hinged to it. The three-dimensional shape of the ship was formed by the timbers, or ribs. Each of these was made up of several pieces of curved timber, called futtocks. In the midships, the ship had the characteristic 'tulip bulb' section, with a narrowing above the waterline known as 'tumblehome'. This was more pronounced on French ships than on British ones by this time, and is noticeable on the plans of the *Surprise*. At the bow and stern the structure was rather different. For most of the length of the ship the timbers ran across the keel, but at the bows they ran parallel to it – these were known as hawse pieces. Aft, horizontal timbers, called transoms, formed an essential part of the structure of the lower stern. Above the transoms, almost all ships of the time had a weak structure pierced with windows. Aggressive captains like Jack Aubrey dreamed of 'raking' an enemy by firing their broadside through these stern windows.

The timbers were covered with planks of varied thickness, both inside and outside. On the outside the thickest planks, known as wales, were fitted under the level of the decks. British ships of this period had single wales – those under the upper deck of a frigate would be about 7in. thick and 3ft 6in. deep. On a French ship like the *Surprise* the upper wales would be double, with two thick planks and thinner planks between them. The rest of the planking on a ship like the *Surprise* would be about 3in. thick. The underwater planks were covered by copper plates to protect the ship from weeds and shipworm.

In the hold the thicker planking, the thick stuff, was arranged to cover the places where the futtocks joined. Thick planks, called clamp, were also placed on the sides where they supported the decks. That between the gundecks was known as spirketting. The deck beams supporting the decks rested on the clamp. They were curved slightly upwards to give a camber which allowed water to drain to the scuppers in the sides of the ship. The beams were braced against the sides of the ship by L-shaped timbers known as knees. If fitted vertically, they were hanging knees; if horizontal, they were lodging knees. Between the deck beams were lighter timbers called carlines and ledges, and the plank of the deck was about two inches thick.

Like all frigates of the period, the *Surprise* had two complete decks running the full length of her hull. The lower deck was completely unarmed for it was just below the waterline – though perversely it was, for historical reasons, sometimes called the gundeck. It was used entirely for accommodation, with the men living forward of the mainmast and the officers aft, in an area known – equally perversely – as the gunroom. The *Surprise* was slightly unusual, in that this deck was not continuous. About halfway between the mainmast and the mizzen it dropped by about a foot, thus increasing the headroom for the officers. Natural light and fresh air on the lower deck were minimal, coming in through gratings in the hatchways of the upper decks.

Above the lower deck was the upper or main deck. Each side of the ship was pierced with 1 2 gunports for firing the main armament so the upper deck had to be strong enough to support these guns which with carriage and fittings weighed about two tons each. The central part of the upper deck – known as the waist – was largely open and was therefore useless for accommodation. Forward, the upper deck was covered with a short deck known as the forecastle. Under that, on the fore part of the upper deck, was an iron stove used to prepare all the crew's provisions, and stout pieces of timber – known as the main bitts – used to fasten the cables when the ship was at anchor.

The after part of the upper deck, as far forward as the mainmast, was covered by the quarterdeck. Situated under that, right in the stern, was the captain's cabin. It had a row of windows aft to give good light. A quarter galley projected from each side, one of which was used as toilet accommodation for the captain. Forward of the captain's cabin was an open but covered area, used as shelter for the crew on watch. It also included the lower part of the main capstan used for raising the anchor, lifting guns and other heavy duties. The heads of the ship's pumps were situated abreast of the mainmast. They reached down into the hold, and their most important duty was to empty the water from the lower part of the ship.

Both the quarterdeck and the forecastle carried guns; for reasons of stability, these were of lighter calibre than those on the upper deck. The quarterdeck of the *Surprise* appears to have had six guns and carronades per side, and the forecastle had two per side. The quarterdeck was fitted with the steering wheel and the binnacle containing the compass. It also had the upper part of the capstan. This was operated by putting a dozen bars into the holes in the 'drumhead'. Up to six men could push at each bar and the pressure of these men was used to haul at a rope wound round the drum. The quarterdeck was the main recreation area of the officers, but the crew had plenty of reasons to go there in the course of duty – for steering, operating the capstan, hauling on numerous rigging lines, or for working the guns.

The forecastle also served as the base for some rigging lines, mostly those associated with the foremast. It had a copper chimney for the galley stove on the upper deck, and it served as a station for much of the work to be done in raising the anchor.

The area under the lower deck was almost entirely devoted to storage. Right aft below the gunroom, the structure of the ship tended to rise and create an area slightly clearer of bilge water. This was the breadroom which was used to store the ship's biscuits. Just forward of that, still under the gunroom, was the magazine used to store powder in barrels and cartridges made up from paper or canvas. There was another small room forward of that, probably used for either alcoholic spirits or fish which were isolated from the rest of the provisions for reasons of security or smell.

The greatest past of the space under the lower deck made up the hold of the ship. Here the necessities of life – beef, pork, cheese, butter, peas, water and beer – were stored in wooden casks on top of iron or shingle ballast. In a sixth rate like the *Surprise*, the anchor cables, made of thick rope, were stored on planks placed on top of these casks.

Forward of the hold, three decks under the forecastle, were the warrant officer's stores where the bosun, the carpenter and the gunner kept supplies of timber, tar, blocks, rope, gun-carriage parts, tools, and hundreds of other items that were needed to keep the ship afloat and independent of the shore for months if necessary.

The *Surprise*, like all true 'ships', had three masts. The largest one – the main mast – was situated near the centre of the keel to give a balanced rig. The foremast was slightly smaller, and was placed just aft of the end of the keel. The mizzen mast was considerably smaller than the other two and was further from the stern than the foremast was from the bows, so that the gap between the fore and the main was very large. Each of the masts was made up of three sections. The lower part – the mast proper – passed through the decks to have its 'heel' fixed securely above the keel of the ship. As it passed through each deck it was secured by pieces of timber known as partners.

Above the mast were the topmast and the topgallant mast. Each overlapped slightly with the one below and was held close to it. At the head of the lower mast was a platform known as a top; at the head of the topmast were the 'cross trees'. Like the top, this too could serve as a base for the seamen working aloft and as posts for lookouts.

Forward of the hull, projecting at an angle of about 1 2 degrees from the horizontal, was a spar known as the bowsprit. It was extended by the jibboom and the flying jibboom in the same way that the masts were extended by topmasts and topgallants. The bowsprit could carry sails but its main function was to provide an anchorage for the rigging which supported the foremast from ahead.

Attached to the masts were the yards which spread the sails. In general, there was one yard for each mast and this took its name from the mast –

thus, for example, the mainmast had the main yard and the fore topmast had the fore topsail yard. The exception was the mizzen yard, which was for a fore and aft rather than a square sail. The foot of the mizzen topsail above needed a special yard – the crossjack – to extend it.

A ship like the *Surprise* needed about 30 miles of rope to support and control its sails and, apart from manning the guns in action, the operation and maintenance of it was the main task of the crew. The standing rigging supported the masts. It was thicker and stronger than the running rigging which controlled the sails and it was virtually fixed in position, except for maintenance purposes. It consisted of several types of rope. The stays supported the masts from ahead. The shrouds supported them from behind; the lower ones were fixed in 'channels' which projected from the ship's sides. Backstays went from the head of a topmast or topgallant to the channels, while the 'futtock shrouds' supported the lower end of the backstays of the upper masts. Certain specialised ropes, such as gammoning and bobstays, kept the bowsprit in place against the upwards pull of the fore stays.

Even a relatively small ship carried more than an acre of sails. They came in two basic types. Square sails were the dominant ones on a ship and were so called because in their neutral position they hung square to the line of progress of the ship. Fore and aft sails, on the other hand, were fitted fore and aft when not in use. Square sails were ideal with the wind behind; fore and aft were best when trying to make way into the wind. The square sails were lashed to the yards, while the fore and aft sails, with the important exception of the mizzen course, were attached to the stays. All sails were made of strips of canvas sewn together, the rope sewed round them for strength. Reef-points were lines of rope fitted to certain sails, so that they could be reduced in area in a strong wind.

The running rigging was used to control the sails and it too consisted of many different types of rope: the braces controlled the angle of the yards with the wind; sheets controlled the lower corners of the sails; buntlines and clewlines were used to furl the sails; and bowlines were needed to hold the leading edge forward when sailing close to the wind.

The basic art of ship handling was to deploy the sails most effectively. Too much sail in a given wind would be dangerous and inefficient, so some sails would be furled; others reefed. In very light winds, light studding sails were used to extend the normal sails. The sails also had to be braced to the correct angle, at about 15 degrees to the apparent wind. No square-rigged ship could sail closer than six points, or 67 degrees to the wind, so a ship could only go directly to windward by zigzagging or 'beating to windward'.

Two basic manoeuvres were 'tacking' and 'wearing'. In the former, the ship was turned to bring the wind on her other side by turning her bows through the wind. The helm was put down to begin the turn and the sails on the main and mizzen mast were braced round to the opposite side. The foremast was kept in its original position to help the bows through the wind and then braced round too. Wearing was the opposite manoeuvre – the stern was turned to the wind. It was easier than tacking and the ship did not need as much speed to carry it out, but it took up more time and space. Another manoeuvre was 'heaving to' when the sails were adjusted to cancel each other out so that the ship was held almost stationary in the water without the use of anchors.

A ship of this period carried about four large anchors. Two of these anchors – the bowers – were in more or less permanent readiness in the bows. The other two – the sheet and the spare – were for emergency use. The anchors on the *Surprise* would have weighed about one and a half tons each.[7] She also had two much smaller anchors, the stream and the kedge, either of which could be slung under a boat, rowed forward, dropped and used to haul the ship forward when there was no wind. The cable of each anchor was of thick rope. It was hauled up by means of the ship's capstans. When not in use, the bower anchors were 'catted', that is they were hung from the catheads in the bows. They were also 'fished', in that their crowns, or pointed ends, were raised up to make the stock horizontal.

A 28-gun ship was allocated four boats. All could be rowed or sailed, but some were more suitable for one than for the other. The 10-oared 28ft long barge was mainly for rowing the captain ashore or to other ships. The 28ft launch was the heaviest boat of the ship and was used for carrying stores. There were also two cutters – 24ft and 18ft long (the latter was often known as the jolly boat). These boats were usually clinker-built, with overlapping planks. They were particularly good for sailing and were general purpose boats.[8]

A ship of this size would normally carry a crew of about 240 men, though on one occasion at least she is recorded as having 197 men. [9] She would have about 18 officers, including a captain, two lieutenants and the key warrant officers – the master, the surgeon, the purser, the gunner, the bosun and the carpenter – and four midshipmen. The rest of the men were the crew, or the 'lower deck'. They slept in hammocks and ate their simple meals at tables, sitting on wooden benches. Some were marines (about thirty in the case of the *Surprise*) while, in a strong crew, the bulk of the rest were experienced seamen rated 'able' or 'ordinary'. In a weaker crew there would be a large proportion of 'landsmen', adults who were unused to the sea.

7. William Falconer, *An Universal Dictionary of the Marine*, ed. by W. Burney, rev. edn (London: [n. pub.], 1815) p. 14.
8. Brian Lavery, *The Arming and Fitting of the English Ship of War* (London: Conway Maritime, 1987), p. 299.
9. James, *The Naval History*, II, 405.

This large group of men had to be divided into teams for all the various manoeuvres that the ship might carry out. There were two or three watches, so that the ship could be sailed and all except the most major evolutions carried out while part of the crew rested. Some men, such as servants and craftsmen, were known as 'idlers', and worked mainly in the daytime. Each watch was divided into six or so parts. The fore topmen, main topmen and mizzen topmen worked up the masts and along the yards and included fit and skilled seamen. The forecastlemen, afterguard and waisters worked mainly on deck and were less skilled. The waisters, in particular, were the least skilled group of all. The marines might also be included in this organisation. A few were needed as sentries and wore full uniform, but most wore working clothing and helped the seamen about the decks. The organisation of the crew was the duty of the First Lieutenant, but Aubrey is professional enough to take a keen interest in the matter.

Aubrey is proud of the sailing qualities of the *Surprise*, and works hard to improve them. Catharpins, for example, are fitted to tighten the shrouds and allow the sails to be braced round further to catch the wind. He also has her restored to her original rig, with the mainmast of a 36-gun ship.[10] Apart from his own skills, Aubrey attributes the sailing qualities of the *Surprise* to her French build. In this he reflects the prejudices of sea officers of his time. Modern research tends to suggest that British ships, though slower than French ones in fair weather, were more robust and sailed better in storms and gales.

Aubrey's other ships can be dealt with more briefly. The *Boadicea* which features in *The Mauritius Command* was a real 38-gun frigate, built by Adams of Bucklers Hard in 1797. She was not broken up until 1858. The *Leopard*, the 'horrible old Leopard' of *Desolation Island* was a 50-gun ship launched, after long delays during her building, at Sheerness in 1790. Unlike the *Surprise* and other frigates, she had two complete decks of guns with an unarmed orlop deck below the water-line, a quarterdeck and forecastle. She was one of an obsolete type, too small to stand with larger ships in the line of battle and too slow to be an effective frigate. The *Java* and the *Shannon* of *The Fortune of War* were also real ships and their encounters with American vessels are accurately described. *La Fleche*, on the other hand, is fictitious.

The *Ariel* sloop of *The Surgeon's Mate* was evidently a real vessel, armed with sixteen 32-pounder carronades and two 9-pounders.[11] She was built in 1806 and survived ten years before being broken up at Deptford. This type of ship was essentially a scaled down frigate without, in this case, a quarterdeck and forecastle.

The *Worcester* of *The Ionian Mission* is a 74-gun ship of two decks – a true

10. James, *The Naval History*, II, 405.
11. Patrick O'Brian, *The Surgeon's Mate*, p. 156.

ship-of-the-line. The actual name was not used for a 74-gun ship of that period but the class to which she was said to belong, known to sea officers as 'the forty thieves', really did exist. There is, however, some deviation from the real facts. The first ship of the class was completed in 1809 but the fortieth was not launched until 1822; the nickname does not seem to have been used before then. They were despised by the sea officers, perhaps unfairly. Their design and building, though uninspired, was generally competent.[12]

After his transfer out of the *Worcester*, Aubrey returned to the *Surprise*, and that ship is dominant in the remaining books of the series. In his depiction of the ships of the Napoleonic era, Patrick O'Brian shows he has a firm grasp of the complexities of naval architecture as he does of a host of other skills and specialisms, a grasp which enables him to write of that period in a uniquely authoritative and entertaining way.

This essay is taken from *Patrick O'Brian,
Critical Appreciations and a Bibliography*,
edited by A. E. Cunningham,
and is reprinted here by kind permission of
the British Library.

12. Brian Lavery, *The Ship of the Line* (London: Conway Maritime, 1983), I, 134–139 & 188–189.

CREWING CORRECTLY

All nineteenth-century ships carried boats which, depending upon their size, could transport any number of men. These had various designations: the main ship's boat was called a launch, whereas secondary boats were referred to as cutters, pinnaces, yawls and jolly boats. Although there were regulations as to which class of ship carried which type of boat, substitutions were often made and in practice the launch of a brig might be of the same size and type as the yawl of a frigate.

In the strictly regulated life of the Royal Navy, the same degree of discipline applied to boats as it did to ships – there was a right way and a wrong way to do everything, and the wrong way could often prove fatal. If the crew did not pull together in heavy surf, they ran every chance of dashing themselves against the rocks that often presented themselves as obstacles to landing.

The illustrations and instructions below demonstrate the correct method of crewing a landing boat in response to the coxswain's shouted orders.

'Up oars!'   The crew toss up their oars, placing the looms on the
              bottom boards between their feet.

'Shove off!' The bowmen shove the bow of the boat off.

'Down'   The crew lift their oars about a foot, then let them fall quietly
         into the rowlocks. All oars are to be horizontal and blades
         feathered. This is the position of 'laying on oars'.

'Give way together!'
'One!'   The crew lean aft, straighten their arms and turn their knuckles
         down as the blade goes forward, bringing the blade square just
         clear of the water.

'Two!'   The crew drop the blade into the water and pull the loom towards their bodies, dropping the elbows and wrist as they arrive at the end of the stroke. The oar is then lifted out of the water to the position of 'laying on oars'.

Illustrations of 'Instructions for Boats' Crews by Numbers'
from *The Boy's Manual of Seamanship and Gunnery*,
by Commander C. Burney, London, 1871,
reproduced by kind permission of Paul Benyon

JACK AND STEPHEN,
THEIR TRAVELS

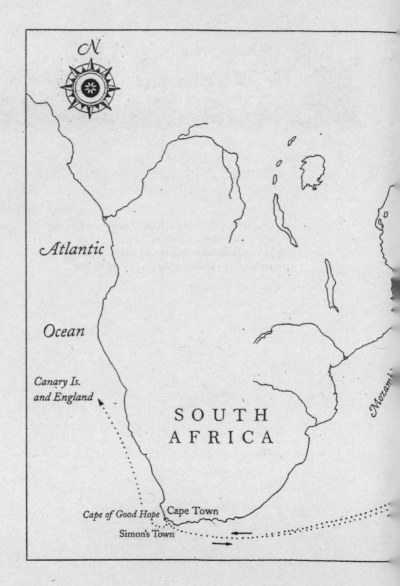

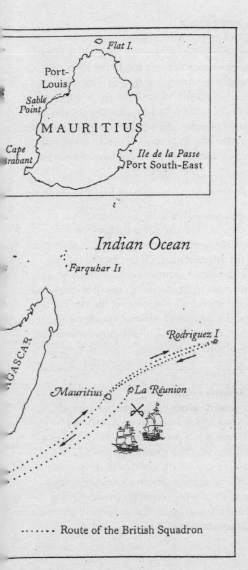

Flat I.

Port-
Louis

Sable
Point

MAURITIUS

Cape
Brabant

Ile de la Passe
Port South-East

Indian Ocean

Farquhar Is

MADAGASCAR

Rodriguez I

Mauritius

La Réunion

.... Route of the British Squadron

HAVE YOU READ?
The next three books in the Aubrey-Maturin series

READ ON

Desolation Island
Jack and Stephen are dispatched to restore order after popular unrest unseats New South Wales governor William Bligh, the ill-fated captain of the mutinous *Bounty*. Through doldrums and mighty storms, the gallant *Leopard* sails south to the treacherous waters of the Antarctic. Battle- and weather-worn, Jack must navigate a vast and empty ocean in desperate search of anchorage if he and his crew are to survive.

The Fortune of War
The year is 1812 and America has just declared war on England. But before they can take on this new foe Jack and Stephen must battle the elements after they are shipwrecked off the coast of Brazil. Adrift in waters prowled by the mighty USS *Constitution*, the two friends will be drawn into an historic conflict with disastrous results: illness, imprisonment and the perils of unrequited love . . .

The Surgeon's Mate
A successful career in espionage has made Stephen a wanted man. With American privateers in hot pursuit and Jack and Diana in tow, he must flee headlong through the eerie seascape off the coast of Nova Scotia. And if that weren't adventure enough, any hope of a quiet life is quickly banished by a delicate mission to the Baltic that will test even his powers of persuasion.

FIND OUT MORE

The Historical Maritime Society
(www.hms.org.uk) is a UK-based historical
research and re-enactment group, focusing
on the Royal Navy. The society concentrates
on the late eighteenth and early nineteenth
centuries, around the time Britain was
threatened by Napoleon Bonaparte and the
Royal Navy played a vital role in preventing
an invasion from across the Channel. The
aim of the HMS is to educate and inform
about shipboard life in the time of Nelson.

Patrick O'Brian

The Patrick O'Brian Compendium fansite
(www.patrickobrian.com) is regularly updated
and includes copious information about the
Aubrey-Maturin series, including timelines of
Jack and Stephen's adventures, a 'map room'
and a dictionary of naval slang. More for the
devotee than the casual reader, but nonethe-
less a fascinating and useful resource.